#1 *New York Times* Bestselling Author

MIKE EVANS

P.O. Box 30000, Phoenix, AZ 85046

The Volunteers

P. O. Box 30000
Phoenix, AZ 85046

Design: Peter Gloege | LOOK Design Studio
Cover Photo: Associated Press – ISRAEL BLOOD BROTHERS: Stanley Medicks, kneeling in front of a Star of David formed with rifles, poses with British volunteers in Israel in October, 1948. Medicks, commander of a platoon of soldiers who fought in Israel's 1948 War of Independence, was one of more than 3,500 foreign volunteers fighting for a Jewish state.

Hardcover: 978-1-62961-056-6
Paperback: 978-1-62961-055-9
Canada: 978-1-62961-057-3

This book is dedicated to

Chalmers Hubert Goodlin,

an American pilot who volunteered to serve
with the Israeli Air Force in 1948. As a Machal pilot,
he fought in the 1948 Arab-Israeli War and
was involved in the downing of three British Spitfires.
Following the war, he became the head test pilot for the IAF.
Later, as a civilian, he flew humanitarian missions,
transporting Jewish refugees to Israel..

PRINCIPAL CHARACTERS

Palmer Collins: attorney with Fortas, Brown & Hoffman who becomes involved in the effort to rescue post-World War II Jewish refugees

Olivia Collins: wife of Palmer Collins

Peter Thornton: pastor at the church attended by Palmer and Olivia Collins

Morris Ginsberg: Jewish businessman who lives and works in New York City

David Ben-Gurion: chairman of the Jewish Agency for Palestine, the de facto representative of Jews living in Palestine; later becomes Israel's first prime minister

Golda Meir: holds various key positions with the Jewish Agency for Palestine; later becomes Israel's fourth prime minister

Danny Schind: Haganah member who comes to New York to assist with boatlift to rescue post-World War II Jewish refugees from Europe and with arms acquisition for Israel's War of Independence

Joe Buxenbaum: active member of the Jewish Agency for Palestine in New York

Edward Robinson: MI6 agent sent to the U.S. to follow Danny Schind

Paul Shulman: former US naval officer, assists with training crews for ships used in the refugee rescue effort

Dewey Stone: Jewish businessman from Boston; assists in acquiring ships for use in effort to rescue Jewish refugees from post-World War II Europe

Hugh Clark: works in the engine and boiler room of the *Beauharnois*

Al Schwimmer: veteran US Army pilot, acquires aircraft in the U.S. and smuggles them into Palestine for use in Israel's War of Independence

Haganah: paramilitary group formed by the Jewish Agency for Palestine to protect Jewish farming settlements in Palestine; after independence it becomes the Israel Defense Forces (IDF)

Beauharnois: a Canadian corvette warship purchased along with sister ship the *Norsyd* from the Royal Canadian Navy as the first ships used in the effort to rescue Jewish refugees from Europe

CHAPTER 1

THE VOLUNTEERS

For the third time that morning, Palmer Collins repositioned his lanky, angular frame and re-crossed his legs. With a flick of his hand he straightened the leg of his gray trousers, then crossed his arms in his lap. A moment later, his foot bounced impatiently with a rhythm that shook the pew. To his right, Olivia, his wife, cut her eyes at him with a disapproving scowl.

Dressed in a navy blue suit with a fitted jacket, she sat with her back straight and poised, her legs discreetly crossed at the ankles. Her brunette hair was curled in back and held in place behind her head with a tortoise-shell clip. A round short-brimmed hat was perched atop her head, and she wore burgundy high-heeled pumps.

As Collins continued to bounce his foot, the vibration gently rocked the pew and with each rhythmic beat the scowl on Olivia's face deepened until for the third time that morning she gave him a quick jab in the side with her elbow. He responded, as always, with a tight-lipped smile, then shifted positions once more, this time with both feet firmly on the floor, and did his best to keep his mind focused on the sermon, but it was a futile effort. The week had been far too long and the weekend much too short. Already his thoughts raced ahead to the work that awaited him the following morning.

It was February 1946, and with the war over most of the soldiers were home from Europe and the Pacific. Everyone was eager to get on with their lives and Manhattan was more alive than ever, which meant business was good. Transactions, incorporations, and mergers—the kind of business upon which law firms relied—were at an all-time high and Fortas, Brown & Hoffman, the firm where Collins worked, was right in the middle of it. Collins' desk was stacked with files waiting for his attention.

The sermon that day was about being our brother's keeper, a predictable theme with oft-repeated words and phrases that rolled down from the pulpit with little meaning for Collins until Rev. Thornton mentioned the recent liberation of Jews from German concentration camps. Most of the lawyers at Fortas, Brown & Hoffman were Jewish and almost all of them had lost a friend or family member in the Nazi death camps. "Now," Thornton continued, "the Jews face another hour of liberation and, I fear, yet another war for survival." Only this time, he argued, the trouble was in Palestine as Jews attempted to return to their historic homeland and were met with opposition, hostility, and global apathy.

Slowly, Collins'thoughts turned away from the work that awaited him at the office but instead of focusing on the sermon, he was transported in his mind to a time before the war when he, newly married and fresh from Fordham Law School, practiced from an office in Queens. Beginning with only a single client, he built the practice into a lucrative business that afforded a comfortable, but by no means lavish, lifestyle. By the time America joined the war, Collins was older than most men who were drafted for military service and watched with growing frustration as friends and colleagues headed off to defend the country while he was left out.

Finally, when he could stand it no longer, he closed his law practice and enlisted in the army. After basic training, he was assigned to an infantry unit and months later deployed to North Africa. Three days after arriving there he was wounded by sniper fire and, much to his dismay, was sent home and discharged.

His father-in-law offered Collins a position in the family business, but Palmer was determined to contribute to the war effort and took a job with the government's War Production Board, which, among other things, regulated the conversion of manufacturing plants from domestic consumer items to the production of wartime materiel. Collins was assigned to an enforcement office in Manhattan where he worked to prohibit the manufacture of unauthorized goods. After three years with the board he was ready for something else and took a job with Fortas, Brown & Hoffman, a large Manhattan law firm with a diverse corporate client base. Two years later he made partner—junior partner, but partner nonetheless.

Still, a nagging sense of guilt lingered. Others had fought the war from beginning to end and returned home as heroes. Many more lay silent in graves on foreign fields, never to return home. He, on the other hand, spent the war in Manhattan enjoying a lifestyle that was luxurious by comparison. And though it was not so much a problem for him as before, that Sunday as he fidgeted and squirmed on the pew, the words he heard from the pulpit unexpectedly dredged up a dark and bitter pain that he'd worked hard to keep inside.

As the sermon wore on, Collins forced himself to concentrate on the moment at hand and soon became aware that Rev. Thornton was looking in his direction. And not merely looking but several times staring intently, letting his eyes bore in as though the words of the sermon were meant for Collins and no other. "We *are* our brother's keeper," Thornton's voice rose toward the conclusion. "If we claim the name of Christ as our own, we are no longer the people we used to be, living only for ourselves and taking all we can get only for self-indulgent pleasure. We are a people with holy obligations. The righteous among the living. And it's long past time we acted that way."

The last time Rev. Thornton looked and spoke like that, he'd had a message for Collins after the service concluded. A note from one of Thornton's old friends who worked with the British government—a sympathizer to the cause of the Jews in Palestine who knew things he wanted to safely pass along to *someone* but hadn't a clue to whom he could give them without creating unnecessary trouble. Thornton, equally sympathetic to the Jewish cause, was eager to help but could think of only one person—Collins—with access to people who might have influential contacts in the region. And so it had become an unlikely arrangement—a Methodist pastor, receiving confidential information from a government agent, and handing it to an attorney at a predominantly Jewish law firm. Unlikely, unpredictable, and yet, to Collins' utter delight, strangely mysterious and exciting.

When the service concluded, Collins stepped into the aisle and slipped on his overcoat while he waited for Olivia and their two children to join him. Once they were ready, he followed them up the aisle toward the vestibule and the church's front entrance. Already he could feel the rush of cold air from the street and he glanced ahead to see the doors flung wide and the brilliant winter sunlight filling the street outside.

Moments later, Collins and his family reached the entrance and approached the doorway. Rev. Thornton stepped forward to greet them, and Olivia offered him her hand. Then Thornton turned to Collins and grasped his hand in a firm handshake. As their palms met, Collins felt a slender, flat object pressed against his hand and at once recognized it as a small envelope. Before he could speak, Thornton moved even closer, rested a hand on Collins' shoulder, and said in a low voice, "I'm sure this one is as important as the last."

"Yes," Collins nodded. "No doubt it will be." He drew back his hand and deftly slid the envelope into the pocket of his jacket.

Olivia, standing a few steps away, noticed what transpired between them and as Collins came down the steps from the church to the sidewalk she joined him at his side. "What was that all about?"

"Nothing, really. Just some business we're working on."

"You lawyers." Olivia grinned and slipped her arm in his. "Always with your secrets."

"Yeah," he sighed. "Me and my secrets. Where are we going for lunch?"

"Surprise me," she said playfully. "I like surprises."

"No, you don't."

"Well, I like this kind of surprise," she grinned.

Collins walked with Olivia and the children to the corner, then hailed a taxi and rode over to P.J. Clarke's, a restaurant on Third Avenue. As they ate lunch, Collins took the envelope from his pocket and glanced at the note inside. Olivia leaned near. "What is it?"

"It's nothing." He returned the note to the envelope and stuffed it back inside his pocket. "But I have to go to the office for a while this evening."

"Again?"

"Can't be avoided."

"Can we at least finish lunch?"

"Sure. There's always time for Sunday lunch."

Across the table his son, Greg, piped up, "You promised to throw the football with me in the park."

"And we will," Collins replied.

Olivia raised an eyebrow. "Isn't it a little cold today for throwing the ball?"

Collins shot a look in Greg's direction. "Never too cold for football, is it?"

"No, sir," the boy beamed. "The Cleveland Rams played the Washington Redskins for the NFL championship last year and it was eight below zero."

"We're not in Cleveland," Olivia demurred.

"We'll be fine," Collins assured. "It's not *that* cold outside."

True to his word, Collins braved the cold wintry blast that swept through the city and spent the afternoon in the park throwing the football with his son. They returned home to the apartment in time for dinner and as everyone else prepared for a relaxing evening at home, Collins changed clothes and slipped downstairs to the lobby.

From the building's front entrance, the doorman hailed a taxi and Collins rode down to Fraunces Tavern on Pearl Street. With the practiced ease of a regular customer, he took a seat at a table in the corner and waited. A moment later, Stephanie, a barmaid, recognized him and came to the table. "Having your usual tonight?"

The question caught Collins by surprise but he managed to ask in a causal way, "And what is my usual?"

"Strawberry daiquiri."

"Yeah," Collins grinned, surprised that she remembered. "A strawberry daiquiri." The truth was, he'd never tasted a daiquiri—strawberry or otherwise—but he saw it once in a movie and, being the only drink he could remember, he ordered it when he needed the appearance.

In a few minutes, the barmaid returned with the drink and set it on the table before him. He lifted the glass to his lips as if taking a sip, then set it aside. When she was out of sight, he rose from the table and moved quickly through a service door that led to a narrow hallway in back.

At the far end of the hallway he came to an exterior door. He pushed it open and entered an alley in back. As Collins stepped away from the door, Sheldon Glaser moved out of the shadows to the right.

A large, burly man, Glaser was not much older than Collins but he'd seen far more of life and in a much harder way. With deep lines that creased his face and prematurely gray hair, he had the appearance of being much older. That evening, buried beneath a felt hat and heavy woolen overcoat, he seemed almost twice his age.

"Thought you weren't coming," Glaser said with a British accent.

"Got held up," Collins replied. It wasn't exactly true. He'd been caught up in tossing the ball with his son and forgot about the meeting, but he wasn't going to explain that to Glaser.

They walked up the alley a little way from the door, then Glaser turned to face him and said in a hushed tone, "As you know, the Anglo-American Committee of Inquiry has been meeting the past few weeks in Washington."

"I read about it in the *Times*."

"Our delegation to those talks has been instructed to reject Truman's suggestion that a hundred thousand Jews be allowed to immigrate to Palestine each year."

Collins looked at him with surprise. "Your prime minster rejected the suggestion?"

"Yes."

"Why would he do that?"

"Our Foreign Office insisted that your government help implement the proposal by providing troops to assist in policing the region. Truman made no offer of such help and signaled he didn't want to flatly refuse, but would if pressed."

"You have the mandate," Collins said. "It's your responsibility to police it."

"Yes, but our prime minister won't implement this latest suggestion on his own."

"Why not?"

"Because he likes being prime minister, and he doesn't think he can retain his office while supporting the Jewish cause without US help."

"So, he wants US involvement to give him political cover."

"Something like that." Glaser nodded. "Right now, as he sees it, the key to his political future lies in pleasing the Foreign Office more than in pleasing the Americans." He glanced at Collins with a wary look. "As you know, Ernest Bevin and much of the staff at the Foreign Office don't like Jews."

"I'm becoming more and more aware of that," Collins noted. "But I thought Bevin was favorable to the Jewish cause. He courted Jewish support during your most recent election."

"Only as a means of getting Attlee elected as prime minister."

"So now that Attlee's in office, they're both showing their true colors."

"Yes," Glaser nodded.

"Have they announced their decision yet?"

"No. They won't do that for another two or three days."

"Why the delay?"

"Bevin thinks responding now would be too soon and might be seen as an affront to your president. They're concerned that responding too quickly might make it seem as though they already had their minds made up before Truman ever offered his proposal."

Collins looked over at him. "Did they?"

"Yes."

"Why?" Collins asked with a hint of frustration.

Glaser glanced around and lowered his voice further. "They knew what Truman would say almost from the moment he decided it."

Collins looked concerned. "They have an informant in the White House?"

"Yes."

"Who is it?"

"I don't know," Glaser shrugged, "but I'm working on it."

"Think it could be Steelman?"

"No." Glaser shook his head. "Not Steelman. He's solid. Listen, here's the part I really wanted you to know. When they announce their plan, they're going to say that they are limiting Jewish immigration to Palestine to only fifteen hundred per month."

"That's only eighteen thousand per year," Collins protested.

"Yes," Glaser agreed.

"They already have a list of applicants twice that long."

"Three times," Glaser corrected. "The current waiting list is three times that amount."

"So, their decision means no Jewish refugees from Europe will be accepted."

"It would seem so," Glaser conceded.

Collins shook his head in dismay. "The British aristocracy always goes back on its word," he muttered. Then just as quickly he turned to Glaser with a conciliatory gesture. "No offense intended."

"None taken. But I would say," Glaser reminded, "this is consistent with the white paper we issued earlier."

"But," Collins countered, "it's not consistent with the Balfour letter. And it's the same thing they did to the Arabs during the Great War—made a deal with Hussein for an Arab Middle East and all the while Sykes and Picot were making a secret deal to divide the Middle East between France and England."

"Yes, well, you must consider," Glaser reminded him once more, "that we are your closest ally."

"And the Jews ought to be your ally as well," Collins rejoined.

"Yes, but they hate us."

"Only for the way they've been treated," Collins quipped.

"Small consolation."

Collins sighed. "It's 1946. We've fought two worldwide wars already this century. You'd think we'd be in a better place by now."

"Well," Glaser replied, "we're dealing with centuries-old problems. And we're not going to solve any of it standing here in the cold tonight. You'll pass the word?"

"Yes, of course. You'll find out the name of that informant in the White House?"

"I'll do my best."

"We'll meet again?" Collins asked expectantly.

"I'll contact you," Glaser replied. "Same way as usual."

"Be careful."

"Ah," Glaser smiled. "Careful is for the weak. I prefer adventure."

Collins watched as Glaser moved past him and made his way to the street at the opposite end of the alley. A car came to a stop in front of him. Glaser opened the rear door, ducked inside, and the car drove away.

As Glaser disappeared from sight, Collins returned to the bar, where he found the daiquiri still sitting on the table where he left it. The barmaid was gone so he stepped to the bar and offered to pay the bartender. "You didn't touch it. Something wrong with it?"

"Nah," Collins said with a wave of his hand. "Not in the mood for it anymore. What do I owe you?"

The bartender held up his hand. "Keep it. I got plenty more where that one came from."

Collins gave him a nod. "Thanks. I appreciate it."

As he started toward the door to leave, Collins noticed a man seated at a table to the left. Their eyes met and for a moment Collins was certain the man had been watching him since he came in from the alley. He pushed the thought aside, opened the front door, and stepped out to the street.

In the middle of the block Collins moved from the sidewalk to the street and raised his hand to hail a cab. Moments later, a taxi came to a stop just a few feet away. Collins opened the rear door and crawled inside. From his seat in back, he glanced to the left to see the man from the bar standing at a pay phone not far away. A shiver ran up Collins' spine and he scrunched lower in the seat, doing his best to stay out of sight.

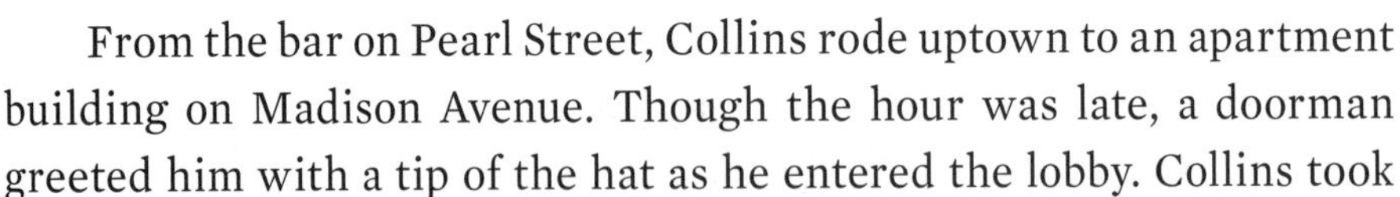

From the bar on Pearl Street, Collins rode uptown to an apartment building on Madison Avenue. Though the hour was late, a doorman greeted him with a tip of the hat as he entered the lobby. Collins took the elevator to the fifteenth floor and made his way to an apartment on the north side of the building. There he rapped on the door with his knuckle and waited.

In a moment, the door opened and William, the butler, appeared. "Mr. Collins," he said with a note of surprise.

"I need to see Mr. Ginsberg."

"It's rather late," William said with a hint of condescension.

"I know it's late," Collins said with a hint of frustration. "See if he can give me a moment. It's important."

"Well, if you insist. Wait here while I check." Then he pushed the door closed.

As the owner of American Foreign Steamship Corporation, Morris Ginsberg was quite wealthy and a longtime client of Fortas, Brown & Hoffman. Collins had been assigned to his files since joining the firm. The two men got along rather well, and as their relationship grew,

Collins took on more and more responsibility for Ginsberg's business with the firm. When Collins made partner, he took control of it all.

A moment later, the door opened and Ginsberg appeared. From the butler's remark, Collins expected to find him in a robe and pajamas but instead he wore a white shirt with the top button undone and brown tweed pants held in place by suspenders. His round spectacles were perched on the bridge of his nose, and he held the business section of *The New York Times*. Though in his late seventies, he had intelligent eyes and a regal air about him that instantly commanded respect.

"What's the matter?" he asked with a troubled look.

"We need to talk."

"It can't wait until tomorrow?"

"I had another meeting with Glaser."

Ginsberg's eyes opened wide in a look of surprise. Without hesitation he stepped aside and gestured for Collins to enter, then took him by the elbow, guided him down the hall and into the study. When they were alone he asked, "What did Glaser say?"

"As you know, British and American negotiators have been meeting in Washington in an effort to work out an arrangement for Palestine that they can both support."

"Yes," Ginsberg nodded. "I was just reading about it in the newspaper. What about it?"

"Truman proposed allowing Jews to immigrate at the rate of one hundred thousand per year."

"That is a number Ben-Gurion will accept."

Collins shook his head. "It isn't going to happen."

"Why not?"

"Glaser says the British have decided to reject the American suggestion and propose instead a rate of fifteen hundred per month."

"That's only . . . eighteen thousand per year."

"I know," Collins nodded. "I told him the same thing."

"Why would they set it so low?"

"I don't know how they arrived at that number, but in order to agree to the hundred thousand, they wanted the United States to commit troops to help police the mandate area."

"They never intended to agree to the hundred thousand," Ginsberg scoffed. "They made its acceptance conditional on the help of American troops merely to cover their senseless position. The Americans were never going to agree to participate at that level. When will they make their announcement?"

"Glaser said in two or three days."

"You're certain this information is reliable?"

"Reverend Thornton vouches for him, and the things he told us before all turned out to be exactly as he said."

"Yes," Ginsberg said thoughtfully. "Then we must inform Tel Aviv at once. I'll get dressed and send a telegram tonight."

"Just write it out and I'll take it," Collins offered.

"You'll do that? Don't you need to get home to your family?"

Collins checked his watch. "They're all in bed by now. It'll be okay. There's a telegraph office on my way."

"Well, okay," Ginsberg conceded. "Give me a minute to compose a message." A desk sat near the window opposite the door. He made his way to it and took a seat. Collins scanned the books on a shelf while he waited.

"Okay," Ginsberg said a few minutes later. He rose from the chair and came around to the front of the desk. "This should do it." He handed the note to Collins and gave him a pat on the back. "Thanks for doing this."

"It's my pleasure," Collins replied.

"Ask them to send that message immediately to David Ben-Gurion. You know the address?"

"Yes," Collins then turned toward the door and was gone.

It was late when Collins arrived back at the apartment building and as he rode up from the lobby he thought of all that had transpired that day. The note from Rev. Thornton, meeting Glaser in the alley, relaying the news to Ginsberg, stopping at the telegraph office to send a message all the way to Palestine. A smile broke over his face. To the infamous David Ben-Gurion, no less. It felt good. Like he was part of something. Something big. Something important. Not like the importance of the business he handled for his clients. That was personal business. Transactions and negotiations that largely affected only the client. But this . . . this was something different. This was something bigger than himself. Bigger than the practice of law. Larger than the ebb and flow of daily existence. And far more rewarding than anything he'd done since . . . since putting on that army uniform and heading off to fight the Germans in North Africa. This was putting action to the sermons he heard on Sunday. Doing what others only talked about. Helping the Jews find a homeland in Palestine. That was something bigger than life itself.

Olivia was waiting as he came through the apartment door and met him in the hallway with an angry scowl. "Where have you been?" she demanded in a coarse and caustic whisper. "Do you know what time it is?" She was dressed in a gown and robe scrunched tightly against her body by her arms, which were crossed in front. Her brunette hair was down and fell limply to her shoulders but her eyes sparkled with anger.

"I was taking care of something for a client," Collins gently pushed the door closed behind him. "And yes," he continued, "I am well aware of the time."

"What could you possibly do for a client at this hour of the night?" Before he could respond, Olivia's face lit up with a look of realization. "You've been drinking." She sniffed the air and jabbed at him with her index finger. "I smell alcohol on your breath."

"I haven't been drinking," he defended.

"I smell it," she argued.

"I put the glass to my lips to make it look like I was supposed to be there, okay? But I never took a sip."

"To look like you were supposed to be there?" She trailed after him as he moved past her toward the bedroom. "Why were you in a bar, looking like you were *supposed* to be there?"

"I was just trying to look the part," he sighed. The sense of elation he'd felt earlier was now totally evaporated. "I was just trying to look the part."

"The part?" she railed as they reached the bedroom and closed the door. "What part?" She followed him toward the bathroom. "The part of an unfaithful husband meeting a woman at a bar while his wife's at home taking care of the kids?"

He turned to face her. "No," he answered more sharply than he intended. "I didn't meet a woman. I didn't meet anyone in the bar. I just wanted to look like a guy who comes to a bar for a drink."

"Why?" she asked, her voice rising in pitch.

"So maybe no one would notice me," he explained.

A frown wrinkled her forehead. "What are you talking about? Why were you there?"

He slipped off his jacket and hung it over the suit rack in the corner. "I was there to meet someone."

"Ah-ha," she chortled. "You did meet someone. I knew it."

"I met someone, but I didn't meet him in the bar."

"Then where?"

"In the alley behind the bar."

"The alley?" Olivia had a look of horror. "You met a *man* in an *alley* at *night* behind a bar?"

"Stop it," Collins complained. "He had some information. My client needed it. I met him in the alley to hear what he had to say."

"What kind of information?"

"I can't tell you."

"Why not?"

"Because it's the client's business, not mine. I can't talk about it."

Olivia threw up her hands in frustration. "I can't believe you expect me to swallow this." She turned away, shaking her head as she moved toward the bed. "You leave us here alone all evening. Then come slinking back at . . . " She paused to glance at the clock on the nightstand. "Two in the morning. Won't tell me why you were out. Or who you were with. Or why you had to meet in an alley." She reached her side of the bed, threw back the cover, and looked up in his direction. "What am I supposed to think?"

"That I was doing what I said. Taking care of something for a client." He dropped his shirt in the dirty clothes basket. "It's late. We need to get to bed."

"You need a shower first."

"I know," he sighed as he turned toward the bathroom. "I know."

CHAPTER 2

THE VOLUNTEERS

While Collins slept in New York, the hourly transmission arrived at the Telex office in Tel Aviv. The operator, a slender man of twenty-three from Kingston Upon Thames, a small town southwest of London, took the message from the machine and checked it to make certain it was not garbled or fragmented. Satisfied it was accurately received, he turned to the counter that sat opposite the door.

The telegram was addressed to David Ben-Gurion at the Jewish Agency for Palestine and although the message was written in plain text the operator had no idea what it meant. But, as he often did with similar messages, he took a note pad from beneath the counter and jotted down a handwritten copy, which he stuffed in his pocket. Note made, he folded the message neatly, placed it inside a thin yellow envelope, and wrote the address on the outside. When it was ready, he rang the bell for a courier. Ten minutes later, the message was on its way.

After the courier departed, the operator placed a sign in the window indicating he would return shortly. Then he stepped outside, locked the door, and hurried across the street to the British High Commission's Tel Aviv district office. He found Stuart Gordon, a lieutenant in the British Army, seated at a desk in the back room. Of medium height and slender build, he had dark hair and a well-groomed mustache. Even in unsettled Palestine he remained the quintessential English male—at once precise, articulate, direct, aloof—and though assigned to a unit and wearing the military uniform, Gordon was actually employed as a field agent with MI6, the British Secret Intelligence Service.

The operator took a seat across from Gordon and laid the handwritten copy of the telegram on the tabletop. "This came in just now for Ben-Gurion."

Gordon unfolded the paper and quickly scanned the message, then looked over at the operator. "Has this been delivered yet?"

"It's out for delivery now."

"You read it?"

"Of course. How else would I know to bring it to you?"

"This is astounding." Gordon pointed to the note. "How do they know this already?"

"Know what?"

"How do they know what our people are deciding in London or Washington before they publicly announce it?" He shook his head slowly. "Of all people in Palestine, you'd think that we, the ones who are charged with maintaining peace and order throughout the entire region, would hear news of this magnitude before the Jews." He gave the operator a frustrated frown. "How did they get this information?"

"I don't know." The operator stood. "But I need to get back to the office."

"Right," Gordon nodded. "You did well."

"Certainly, sir," the operator replied. "Just trying to do my part."

Across town, David Ben-Gurion was propped in bed reading when he heard a knock on the door downstairs. Paula, his wife, answered it and in a few minutes appeared in the bedroom with a yellow envelope in hand. "This came for you."

Ben-Gurion, at sixty, had spent a lifetime promoting the Jewish return to Palestine. First arriving there in 1916 as a young man of twenty, he was already politically active and quickly rose to a leadership position in what became Mapai, a faction of the Jewish Labor Movement. In 1935, he was made chairman of the Jewish Agency for Palestine, the official Jewish representative to the British occupation army.

A thoroughgoing Zionist committed to the establishment of a Jewish nation, Ben-Gurion expanded the role and authority of the Agency. Under his leadership, the Tel Aviv office became the dominant voice of Palestinian Jews not only in the West but to Jewish organizations around the world, making it a de facto government in waiting.

Paula retreated from the room as Ben-Gurion ripped open the envelope and quickly read the message. "Negotiators to refuse U.S. suggestion on limits. Announce in 3 days. Set quota at 1,500 per month. Ginsberg." Ben-Gurion grumbled as he threw aside the cover, sat on the edge of the bed, and slid his feet into slippers.

All of his life he had worked tirelessly for the Jewish cause, patching together alliances, winning friends, standing up to enemies, often holding tenuous and fragile Zionist coalitions together by little more than the force of his own personality. Now his once-full head of dark brown hair was bald on top, thin along the sides, and snow-white. Short in stature, his midriff showed the extra heft of middle age and he was tired now, even when he awakened. Yet he remained nimble afoot, agile of mind, and more than willing to address the challenges of a new day. But with the sense that time was running out and the opportunity for a Palestinian homeland—a once-in-a-generation opportunity—was at hand, he had even less patience than before with those who couldn't see his vision of the future.

"The British," he continued to mutter as he reached for a robe, "can't see past their noses. Think they're so prim and proper and knowledgeable. And all the while they're as racist and bigoted as the worst German." He started toward the bedroom door. "Their arrogance has ruined everything they've touched in the Middle East from Syria to the Indian border. If we don't get them out of here soon, they'll ruin things for us, too."

Downstairs, he made his way to the kitchen and took a seat at the table across from Paula. "Was that telegram good news or bad?" she asked.

"Bad in substance." He paused to take a sip of tea. "Though not totally unexpected. But good to receive it in advance."

They ate a light breakfast of tea and toast, then Ben-Gurion came from the house to his car and started up the street toward his office at the Jewish Agency headquarters not far from the beach. It was not quite six-thirty in the morning and the sun was just rising. To the west was the blue-green water of the Mediterranean and all around him lay the arid coastal plain. Dry and dusty in summer, it came alive in the fresh, cool weather of winter and as he made his way uptown, Ben-Gurion lowered the window of the car to let in the crisp morning air.

A few minutes later he reached the Agency building and as he came through the doorway he turned to an aide seated at a desk nearby. "Where is Golda today?"

"In her office," the aide replied.

"Her office here, or in Jerusalem?"

Golda Meir performed many functions for the Jewish Agency and as a matter of convenience kept an office in both cities. Ben-Gurion was impatient with the need to explain himself and his voice had an edgy tone.

"She is here," the aide responded, suddenly aware of Ben-Gurion's point. "In her office upstairs. Shall I go up and tell her you wish to see her?"

"No," Ben-Gurion replied. "That won't be necessary."

By then he was already at the staircase and moved quickly up to the second floor. He found Golda in her office, seated at her desk. A darkly mysterious young woman when she first arrived in Palestine, she was now almost fifty years old. Manual farm labor in those early years, followed by long days and sleepless nights as she worked with Agency leadership to keep the dream of a Jewish state alive, left her looking worn and tired. Yet still in her eyes there was the fierce determination to overcome all odds and see this venture through to the end. To establish once and for all the dream of a Jewish homeland, free of persecution and the threat of anti-Semitic hatred.

With three long strides Ben-Gurion reached the desk and thrust the telegram toward Golda. "Read this," he directed in an authoritative tone.

She took the message from him and scanned it quickly. "Well," she said when she'd finished, "what did we expect?"

"We wanted to believe they would abide by their promises," Ben-Gurion said as he backed toward a chair and took a seat across from her.

"It's the oil," Golda explained. "The British need it."

"I know, I know," he reluctantly agreed. "Arabs have it, the British don't. But the British will never be able to control this region long enough to exploit it. They're too arrogant. The Americans could . . . maybe . . . but not the British."

"Yes," Golda nodded. "The Americans could get along with the Arabs, and keep them away from us, but the Americans have no need of oil right now and don't care to be bothered with the trouble of a region halfway around the world from them. Not now. Not after the war in Europe and the Pacific."

Ben-Gurion cut his eyes at her. "We have to make the Americans *want* to be bothered."

Golda nodded slowly but the look in her eyes said she thought it a waste of time. "So," she said instead, "what do you think we should do about this?" She gestured to the telegram. "Is there anything we *can* do?"

"We can get ready," Ben-Gurion said flatly.

"Yes, but ready for what?"

"For war. War on the ground and war in the air. War with no one to help us but ourselves."

It was a familiar conversation, one they'd had on many occasions and each time it began this way. The bombastic, defiant Ben-Gurion railing against the mediocrity of waiting. Boldly casting a vision in grand and glorious terms. Then Golda talking through it until he'd gotten the anger and frustration out of his system and could turn once more to the practical task of each day's challenges.

"And how do you propose we do all that?" she asked calmly.

"I don't know," Ben-Gurion sighed. "But it's long past time we began."

"Yes," she said thoughtfully. "There is much yet to be done, but we must decide what to do next and the next thing before us is this telegram."

Ben-Gurion heaved a heavy sigh. "We need to meet tonight to discuss the situation. See what the others have to say about it."

"You want to tell them about the telegram?"

"We'll tell them the news we've received."

"Maybe just read the telegram to them?"

"Yes," he said. "But not how we received it."

"No," she said. "Not how we received it. But you'll tell me?"

He looked at her a moment. "One day," he said finally. "But not now. Not today." He stood and moved toward the door to leave. "Get everyone together. We need to talk about it and find out what they think. We can meet at my house tonight."

✡

That evening, Ben-Gurion gathered with a group that comprised the executive and advisory leadership of the Jewish Agency. Everyone was there. Shimon Peres. Jacob Dostrovsky—chief of staff of Haganah, the Jewish paramilitary group that defended the farming settlements—Ralph Shultz, a Tel Aviv businessman, and twenty more, all crowded into Ben-Gurion's first-floor living room and spilling into the hall.

They were the best and brightest. The young, starry-eyed idealists who came to Palestine in the 1920s who now were the middle-aged old guard, and the young starry-eyed idealists of the 1940s who'd only just arrived and had so much to learn. In the world of Zionism, however, they were the practical ones. Among the zealous advocates of a Jewish homeland, they were the ones willing to compromise and take *something*, rather than hold out for everything and risk attaining nothing at all.

As they took a seat that evening, Ben-Gurion rose from his chair and stood before them. "I want to read for you a telegram we received from New York early this morning." He adjusted his glasses and began. "It says this: 'Negotiators to refuse U.S. suggestion on limits. Announce in 3 days. Set quota at 1,500 per month.'" Ben-Gurion glanced around the room, expecting to hear an angry outcry against the narrow-minded, self-absorbed British. Instead, he was met with only silence and inside he felt a sense of frustration slowly rising from his soul.

"We received this message from a confidential source," he continued bravely, turning back to the paper in his hand, "and although it is written in a necessarily cryptic fashion, the intent is clear to those of us who have been working on the issues we all face. For those of you who may not be quite so familiar with the matter, I'll give you a brief summary." He removed his glasses and held them in his left hand, the telegram in his right. "As we are all well aware, the British government has maintained control of this region since the close of World War I under a mandate issued by the League of Nations and later ratified by the United Nations. Events over the past two decades have moved the world toward a day when that mandatory authority will end. Rather than submit to a process dictated by the United Nations to accomplish that end, British and American negotiators have been meeting in Washington in an attempt to come to terms with a Palestinian policy on which they both can agree. Apparently, the two powers feel they can dictate terms regarding the future of Palestine without anyone else's help or participation." Several in the room responded with a chuckle, but Ben-Gurion was deadly serious. "As part of those negotiations, President Truman suggested Palestine should be allowed to receive a hundred thousand persons per year. More to the point, a hundred thousand Jews from the Displaced Persons Camps of Europe. This note," he gestured with the telegram, "tells us that the British plan to reject that suggestion and impose a strict limit of fifteen hundred per month."

"That's not many," Peres noted.

"Eighteen thousand per year," Shultz added.

At last, Ben-Gurion thought, *someone is still awake enough to think.* "It's not many at all and not nearly enough," he responded loudly. "And the question I want us to address tonight is what we should do about it."

"Hundreds of thousands of Jews are languishing in Europe," a voice spoke from the back of the room. "Do the British not even care about that?"

Others from around the room added their comments. "Many of the Jews in Europe are forced to live in the same camps from which they were liberated."

"Some are forced to live there with the same people who held them captive."

"At least the Nazis aren't in charge."

"No. The Jews of Europe have new prison guards. This time they're British soldiers."

"They aren't exactly in prison," someone demurred.

"There's little difference. They can't come and go as they please. They're confined to the camp."

"A camp surrounded by wire fences and secured with armed guards watching them day and night."

"Well, when you put it like that . . . "

This was not the discussion Ben-Gurion had wanted and after a moment he spoke up, hoping to turn the conversation toward a more concrete treatment of the greater threat they faced. "For decades now, we've waited for the British to help us," he said, reaching for that sense of Zionist enthusiasm and passion that had served him so well in the past. "Now it seems obvious they have no intention of helping us or the millions of Jews still trapped in Europe. And no intention of protecting our own best interests. It's time we learned to solve our own problems."

"We will need our own army," Dostrovsky said, taking his cue from Ben-Gurion.

"And we need our own weapons," Peres offered. "Manufactured in our own facilities, right here in Eretz Israel."

Across the room someone piped up, "We have our own army, Jacob," the voice said sarcastically. "You command it."

Laughter ensued but before Dostrovsky could reply, another responded. "He means an army in the classic term. Trained, equipped, and organized like the armies of the world. With professional soldiers."

Ben-Gurion's sense of frustration ebbed a little and for a moment he held out hope that the meeting might yet be saved. Then a voice from the overflow in the hallway said, "The refugees are what bother me. We need to do something about *that* situation immediately."

"We should bring them here ourselves," another added bravely. "Who cares what the British say?"

"A flotilla," someone added. "Overwhelm the British with refugees."

Ben-Gurion's forehead wrinkled in frustration as the meeting now veered out of control, bouncing wildly from one idea to another as a voice near the door picked up the latest comment. "The British don't have that many people working the waterfront and shoreline. If we swarm the docks they'll have to draw in all their personnel to handle the rush. Some of the beaches would be unprotected. We could land the bulk of refugees there."

Ben-Gurion could take no more. "I'm against using refugees like that," he interjected forcefully, his voice the loudest in the room and the loudest it had been all night. "We shouldn't force the immigration issue. The British can be ruthless. We'd be playing with civilian lives for political gains!"

"I agree," Peres added. "It's much too risky. They've already been through enough."

Finally Golda spoke up, her calm, even voice a stark contrast to the emotion bubbling around her. "What if we managed the risk?"

Ben-Gurion glared at her. She always took sides against him in private but never in public. Not in a meeting like this. "What do you mean?" he asked, forcing himself to remain calm and under control.

"What if we bring them over in ships—not tiny boats but actual ships—and have our own people onboard to manage the passengers. The British won't fire on the passengers if they aren't provoked. Our people could make certain the passengers understand how to behave. They could diffuse the trouble before it happens."

"They still won't get past the blockade," Dostrovsky argued. "No matter what size the ship."

"Maybe it doesn't matter if they get through," Golda countered.

Dostrovsky turned to face her. "What do you mean?"

"I mean, maybe it's more important that they try—that *we* try—rather than whether we succeed or not."

Ben-Gurion shook his head. "They'll just end up in a detention camp, Golda." The power was gone from his voice now, replaced by the twang of complaint, as if carping against a friend, which he was.

She smiled, "But at least they would be in Palestine."

"Then we could break them out," someone offered.

"I hear the local camps are almost filled to capacity," someone noted.

"But according to our sources," Dostrovsky added, "when the camps reach capacity the British intend to detain refugees at camps on Cyprus."

"Then we'll fill that camp, too," Golda replied, her voice slowly rising in intensity as she rose to her feet. "And the next camp. And the next. And in the meantime, we'll focus world attention on the problem and the calloused, uncaring attitude of the British. We'll show them for what they are and demonstrate to the world that their authorized agent for the administration of Palestine is corrupt, ineffective, and decisively anti-Semitic."

Ben-Gurion intervened in one last effort to turn the meeting toward the topic he wanted to discuss—arming the Jews for war—and the discussion between them quickly became a debate, as discussions between them often did. "You think it's right to use refugees as political pawns?"

"You think they aren't pawns already?" Golda challenged in return.

Having engaged the discussion from that angle, Ben-Gurion could not back down. "How will we get them over here? You sit here in this room, all of you," he glanced around at the group, "and spout off one idea after another without the slightest thought of the practical implications of what you say. We face real and present danger. Physical danger. The Arabs mean to kill us all and drive the ones they can't kill into the sea. If we don't address that threat first, solving the refugee crisis won't matter because there won't be any solution to offer them."

The room became quiet with Golda still standing and Ben-Gurion staring at her, awaiting her response. Then, in the calm, even tone she displayed earlier, she said, "I don't know how we should bring them over here, but I think the refugee crisis is the crisis we currently face. If we ignore the refugees and concentrate on equipping an army, we will spend all of our effort confronting the British—who will most certainly oppose our efforts in that regard—and we will portray ourselves to the world as nothing more than violent revolutionaries. If, instead, we concentrate on helping our fellow Jews in Europe, we will maintain the moral high ground, the British will be exposed as the aggressors, and the world will eventually come to our aid, if not to our defense."

"Do we have ships for such a venture?" Ben-Gurion challenged.

"No," Golda replied, "but we can find them."

"And who do you suppose will be willing to send their ships to Palestine, loaded with refugees, knowing that both cargo and vessel will be seized by the British?" He answered his own question. "No one will do that. Who would board such a ship, knowing they will never reach their supposed destination and will, instead, end up in just another camp? You'll have to lie to the ship owners to convince them to sail. Lie to the refugees to coax them onto the ships. Promise both owner and passenger things you can never deliver. Make the owners believe their ships are safe and make the passengers think they are destined for a land of opportunity, and all the while you'll be leading them both into grave danger."

Golda endured the cross-examination and refused to retreat. "We won't promise them anything," she said calmly. "We'll tell them up front exactly what they're getting into."

"The passengers and the owners?"

"Yes."

"It'll never work."

"It would if we owned the ships."

That suggestion struck a chord with others and Ben-Gurion knew it the moment she spoke. All around the room heads nodded in agreement and whispers flittered among them. She was right and it was obvious to everyone there that evening.

Then someone said aloud, "There are thousands of ships left over from the war. Maybe tens of thousands. We could probably get them cheap."

"But where?" Ben-Gurion demanded.

"England," someone suggested.

"England?" Ben-Gurion chided. "They'll never sell to us."

"We won't tell them who we are," someone responded.

"That's too risky," Ben-Gurion said with a dismissive gesture, but the fire was gone from his argument.

"Then we'll try France."

"They might be interested in us at some level," Ben-Gurion conceded grudgingly, "but the French are still set on avoiding a confrontation with the British. They need all the support they can get to rebuild their own country, and England is their nearest source for that. They won't do anything that might offend the British."

"Then," someone said flatly, "we'll go to the Americans."

"They're all the way across the Atlantic from the refugees," Peres countered sharply.

"But they have thousands of ships they no longer need or want. And they're begging people to purchase them."

"As is Canada," someone suggested.

Another asked in jest, "Canada has a navy?" And the room burst into laughter.

With the tension broken Dostrovsky rejoined the conversation, admitting the truth of what they'd just said. "Well," he began slowly, "in spite of my own misgivings, and in spite of the distance from America to Europe, if we were to purchase ships for such an undertaking it *would* be easier to buy them in the U.S. than anywhere else." His tacit support seemed to signal the end of any discussion that evening about military options. Ben-Gurion, sensing defeat, took a seat near the corner of the room and listened as Dostrovsky continued. "Americans sell government surplus to businesses all the time. The Port of New York is the busiest in the world and I'm sure people there regularly buy and sell ships. No one would pay us much attention."

"Lots of experienced navy people over there, too," another added. "Some of them might be interested in sailing one more time."

"And," another spoke up, "we already have organizations in America who can help."

"Yes," someone noted, "we have many friends there, but we would have to keep this quiet. The British have agents everywhere, even in the United States, and they are always looking to protect British interests."

Golda spoke up again. "We should see if the ships are available first, and what it would take to get them into service. After that, we can worry about a crew."

"Yes," someone commented. "And we should wait until we have both ships and crews before we start worrying about passengers. After the ships are in place and we're ready, then we can inform the refugees."

From his seat on the chair Ben-Gurion shook his head. "I still don't think it'll work."

Golda turned to him. "Is that your decision on the matter?"

All eyes were fixed on him and as he looked around the room a sense of benevolence came over him. Not the kind that tends toward sympathy for the misinformed but the kind that tends toward pride. The oldest of the younger crowd were barely half his age and all of them had been trained and tutored under his direction and leadership. And that night, they stood their ground against the old man. Not in arrogant defiance or rebellion, but in their own examination of the facts and circumstances. They had done what he had done many times before when faced with seemingly insurmountable issues and decisions, they had talked it through, argued it through, and in the end they won the room. Even Dostrovsky now took their side.

But Ben-Gurion could not bear to end the meeting on a note of resignation, and so, instead, he turned to the role that so readily lent itself to the moment. The parental role. With all eyes fixed on him, eagerly awaiting a response, he lowered his head and resolutely said, "Let me think about it." The discussion continued awhile longer but as the hour drew to an end the meeting came to a close.

By ones and twos those in attendance slowly slipped from the room and disappeared into the night. After they had gone, only Golda remained. "We have to do this, David," she said quietly.

From his seat in the corner Ben-Gurion looked over at her. "It's not right to promise them more than we could give them. Even if they came right now, freely, we couldn't give them all they hope for."

"I know. We will never be able to do that. Not now. Not ten years from now. Their expectation will always be greater than our ability. But if we wait on the British or the Americans to solve our problems, we'll be waiting while the Arabs seize control of the entire region and kill us all."

A smile flickered across his face. "That's what I wanted to talk about tonight. I wanted to talk about arming ourselves and preparing to fight."

"You think we can defeat the British?"

"No. But we don't have to. The British are going to leave. Maybe not tonight. Or tomorrow. But sooner or later, they'll be gone. Our fight is not with them, but against the Arabs."

"But we aren't there yet, and right now a move toward arming ourselves would be a move toward armed opposition to the British. Confrontation with the Arabs is two steps away from where we are today." Golda gestured to the empty chairs haphazardly scattered around them. "We aren't there yet historically. And our people aren't there yet personally. They don't see what you see. They can't see the looming threat of Arab hordes descending on us. They *can* see the refugee problem and they're willing to do something about it. And when they've done that, then they will be able to move on with you to other issues." She smiled at him. "They have to learn from us, just as we had to learn from those who came before. They just aren't up with you yet."

Ben-Gurion looked away. "I don't like it. Using refugees like that." He shook his head slowly. "I just don't like it."

"I know."

He stared at his shoes a moment, then asked, "How many do they want to bring over?"

"As many as they can."

He looked at her once more. "It would take ships, not the fishing boats we've been using."

Golda nodded in agreement. "People who were here tonight seemed to think the U.S. is the best place to get them."

"And you?"

"I think so," she nodded. "We already have extensive contacts there and of all the major nations in the world, the U.S. is most sympathetic to our cause."

"Sympathetic, but not very helpful."

"Yes, but Americans have a habit of saying one thing in public and doing the right thing when confronted by practical realities. We could give them a chance to see the practical reality of dealing with the refugee problem, and I think they would do the right thing."

"We'd have to send someone over there to get it organized."

"Yes," Golda agreed. "Absolutely."

"They'd have to be discreet."

"Right."

"And we couldn't tell the refugees what we're doing until after we find out if this will work."

"Right."

Ben-Gurion looked directly at her now. "What's the smallest number of people we could bring over and still make a statement?"

"I don't know." Her face had a puzzled expression. "Why the smallest?"

"If we do this," he explained, "I want to put the least number of people at risk while still making a statement."

"You see this as a political gesture?"

"I know you think of it as solving the refugee problem, and it is on a practical level. But in the wider sense, it's politics. We can't solve the refugee problem at once. We don't have the resources for that. There are at least a hundred thousand Jews in the Displaced Persons Camps and millions more who would like to come here. We can't accomplish that with merely our own efforts. But we can help some and in helping them we can make a political statement. So, my question again: What's the minimum number we would have to bring over to make a credible statement?"

"I think once we start, we'll be flooded with volunteers and when that happens we'll be hard-pressed to turn anyone away. Better to sit in a detention camp in Palestine or even on Cyprus than to wait in a camp in Europe."

"Well, perhaps so," Ben-Gurion sighed. "All right, then. Send someone to the United States to find out if this is possible. But I don't think we can accommodate more than . . . ten thousand a month, either in the transport or in resettling them here—should they actually make it through."

"Ten thousand would be a good start," Golda agreed. "Whom shall we send?"

"For a mission like this, it should be Danny Schind."

"He is with Haganah," Golda noted. "You think we should involve Haganah in a humanitarian mission?"

"You mentioned having our own people onboard to control the passengers. Do you think anyone else besides Haganah could do that?"

"No. I suppose not."

"And this may look like a humanitarian effort, Golda, and it may be fraught with political purpose, but at its heart—in practical terms—this will be a military operation. British intelligence will be watching. And when they see something suspicious, they will follow and harass our people mercilessly. Only a trained operative could keep calm under those circumstances. If we succeed in acquiring ships and loading them with refugees, when those ships get within three miles of the Palestinian coast, they'll be confronted by British warships. They'll be boarded by armed British marines. We must have trained people onboard who not only can sail the ship, but who can respond in the most extreme situations."

"Okay," Golda conceded. "But if it's going to be a Haganah operation, shouldn't we send Dostrovsky? He's the best they have at organizing and as I understand it, he's not directly involved in operations right now."

"Impossible," Ben-Gurion replied. "We can't possibly spare him. Schind will do just fine."

"Should we tell the office in New York that he's coming?"

"Let me talk to Schind first."

"Okay." Golda stood. "You want me to find him?"

"Tell Peres. He'll find him. Tell Peres to send Schind to see me. Don't tell anyone else about this until after I've talked to him."

In spite of the late hour, Golda left Ben-Gurion's house for her car and drove across town to the apartment where Shimon Peres lived. As part of his executive function, Peres held the Jewish Agency's security portfolio. Haganah and other similar but much smaller paramilitary groups were his responsibility. As such, he had a close working relationship with Jacob Dostrovsky and key Haganah personnel.

When Golda arrived, Peres led her to the kitchen, where they sat around the table and sipped a cup of hot tea. "You stayed to talk to him?" Peres asked.

"Yes."

"Any hint of when he might decide or what that decision might be?"

"He's already decided."

"And?"

"You seemed to take his view of things tonight."

"I can see his point," Peres nodded. "I was trying to help him make it. That's all."

"Well, he's decided to go forward with the effort to rescue the refugees."

"Good." Peres' face brightened. "He placed you in charge?"

"No." She shook her head. "He wants this to be a Haganah operation."

"Haganah?"

"They are the closest thing we have to an army. He thinks they stand the best chance of controlling the passengers when they ultimately confront the British navy."

Peres nodded resolutely. "That will happen, you know."

"Yes," Golda sighed. "I know. I don't understand why it has to be this way, but I know the British will never stand by and watch while Jews peacefully immigrate to Palestine. I mean, I understand their need for oil, I just don't understand why that need has to pit us against them and the Arabs."

Peres seemed uninterested in the bigger questions right then. "How many do you think we can rescue?"

"He wants to bring ten thousand a month."

Peres looked surprised. "Really?"

"Yes."

"That'll require a lot of planning and coordination."

"He wants Danny Schind to take control of the operation."

Peres leaned back from the table. "Schind is already involved in key Haganah operations here. They can't just pick up a phone and call him. Have you cleared this with Dostrovsky?"

"No."

"We'll have to talk to him first."

"*You* talk to Dostrovsky; he won't listen to me on this."

"Why not?"

"Because I'm Golda and not Shimon."

"He will listen to you."

"Well, regardless, we're not waiting on Dostrovsky to come around. If Ben-Gurion wants to talk to Dostrovsky, he can do it. I'm not. Find Schind. Take him to see Ben-Gurion. And do it quickly, before Ben-Gurion changes his mind."

"Okay," Peres chuckled.

"And before word of what we're planning leaks out," Golda continued, seemingly without noticing his response, "we need to get Danny on a plane for New York as soon as possible."

"New York?"

"Yes."

"Why?"

"We're going to buy the ships from North America."

"I agree we should help the refugees, and I heard the discussion earlier this evening, but do you really think America is the best place to do this? The ships would have to sail all the way across the Atlantic."

"I think we can get the best ships for the cheapest price there," Golda explained, "and we have people there who could fund the operation."

"I suppose you're right," Peres nodded.

"So, find Schind and send him to Ben-Gurion."

"May take a while."

Golda set her teacup aside. "Find him and get him to Ben-Gurion by noon tomorrow."

"That's impossible."

"No. It's not." She looked Peres in the eye. "I saw him two days ago at a café down the street. He can't be that far away."

Peres had a sheepish grin. "Well, I said he was involved in operations. I never said he was out in the desert."

"Find him," Golda repeated. "And take him to Ben-Gurion's office."

"You want me to meet with them, too?"

"Ben-Gurion will let you know about that. But you'll have to bring Schind up to speed on the kind of operation we want. And don't change the numbers. Ten thousand is the least we can bring over and still make a statement that the British and the world will hear. And make certain Schind knows to keep this quiet."

Peres bristled at the comment. "I won't have to tell him that," he said with a frown.

CHAPTER 3

THE VOLUNTEERS

True enough, Danny Schind had been in Tel Aviv two days earlier, but while Golda and Peres talked, Schind was on his way north, driving through the night toward Ein HaHoresh, a farming collective located a few hours outside of Tel Aviv. Just a month earlier, British officials had become suspicious that the farm was being used to house illegal immigrants—European refugees secretly deposited on the Palestinian coast and whisked to the interior. Troops had been dispatched to surround the farm's main compound, which they eventually occupied for weeks in a confrontation that revealed glaring deficiencies in the facility's ability to defend itself. Schind, one of Haganah's best logisticians, was on his way to survey the grounds and determine what could be done to improve defensive capabilities. He hoped to arrive there by sunup, finish his work by midafternoon, and return home that evening.

A wiry, lean man of medium height, had strong shoulders, thinning hair, and eyes that seemed always to be looking past the obvious, Schind was born in Russia but immigrated at a young age with his parents to Palestine. During the Great War he served in the Jewish Legion of the British Army. Afterward, he attended college in France, then returned to Palestine and joined Haganah. Very quickly, he became known as a naturally gifted leader. One who valued work over talk, action over contemplation, and deplored wasting time in pointless meetings.

Sometime before sunup, Schind reached his destination and, rather than taking time to rest, went straight to work, surveying conditions at the farming compound. Though only about fifteen years old, the site had blossomed into a sprawling complex with modern concrete administrative buildings, and rows and rows of greenhouses, and storage bins for fresh crops. The central campus was bounded by tall cedar trees but the miles and miles of irrigated fields that surrounded it were flat, treeless, and some of the most productive in all of Palestine.

About noon that day, as the warm winter sun shone down on him, Schind was busy making sketches of the farm's layout when a car turned from the road, rolled slowly up the driveway, and came to a halt near the dining hall. Moments later, the driver's door opened and Shimon Peres stepped out. As the Jewish agency's liaison with Haganah, Schind and Peres knew each other well and at his unexpected appearance that day, Schind put aside his sketch pad and walked over to greet him.

After a polite handshake, Peres got right to the point: Schind was needed in Tel Aviv for a meeting with Ben-Gurion. Delay was not an option. He must leave at once and report directly to the Agency's headquarters. Reluctantly, Schind collected his belongings, stowed them in his car, and followed Peres from the compound, but he was not happy with the interruption or the delay it caused. *Now,* he thought as he headed south, *I'll have to return, which means spending two days on a task that could have been completed in one.*

When they arrived in Tel Aviv, Schind parked near Peres and followed him inside the Agency's building. Scruffy and unkempt from the trip, he ducked into a shower facility in back where he cleaned up, shaved, and changed clothes. Half an hour later, he emerged more presentable in appearance but still disgruntled over the interruption in his schedule.

Schind dutifully made his way upstairs and found Ben-Gurion seated at his desk. Golda and Peres were there, too, seated opposite him in straight-back chairs. Despite being summoned by the Jewish Agency's most powerful executive, Schind did little to hide his sense of contempt. "If you don't mind," he spoke brusquely, "I'd like to get this over with quickly and get back to the field. We were in the midst of something important."

Ben-Gurion seemed unfazed by Schind's gruff demeanor and responded with a smile. "Have a seat, Danny. This won't take long."

Schind dropped onto a chair to the right of Ben-Gurion's desk. "Does Dostrovsky know you brought me here?"

"We cleared it with Jacob," Ben-Gurion assured.

Schind glanced around the room, saw Peres' eyes boring in on him with a disapproving look, and realized he'd not shown enough deference to Ben-Gurion's senior position. "I'm sorry," Schind said, turning his attention in that direction. "I just don't like spending an afternoon in a meeting and I don't like interruptions to the schedule."

"Well then," Ben-Gurion said, "I'll cut the discussion to a minimum. We've decided to increase our efforts to rescue refugees from Europe and bring them to Palestine."

About time, Schind thought, but he kept it to himself. Instead, he said as politely as possible, "As I've reported on numerous occasions, we are already doing as much as we can with the few small boats at our disposal. If you want to do more, you'll have to give us more boats. But we'll also need a better way to reach the refugees. Right now we're taking them from the coast about as fast as they arrive for pickup. We're keeping up with the volume. Sometimes our boats arrive at the pickup point and no one is there. So, we have some serious logistical flaws to address up and down the line."

Ben-Gurion rested his hands in his lap and laced his fingers together. "We were thinking of something a little larger than fishing boats."

"Like what?" Schind asked, curious now at what they intended.

Ben-Gurion glanced over at Golda with an expectant look. She turned to Schind. "We want to buy ships in the United States. Large ships. Sail them to Europe, load them with refugees, and bring them here."

This would be a dramatic improvement, Schind thought, but as before, he kept his thoughts to himself and said, "America would be a good place to buy ships. The British, however, would do everything in their power to prevent it. All of the ships you send over will be caught by the British as soon as they come near the coast. We have crews out there every day. We see them. We know what they're capable of. So far, we have been successful because we are using fishing boats that are small and more difficult to detect. But a ship the size you're discussing would be something the British navy could locate quite easily."

"We understand they will capture the ships," Golda agreed with a nod. "And when they do, we will bring more. And they will capture those. And still we will bring more. We intend to create a constant flow of ships from America to Europe. And with them a continual flow of refugees from Europe to Palestine."

"I'm in favor of bringing as many of our people here as possible," Schind replied. "But doing it with that kind of operation will cause a lot of trouble. The British will put the refugees in camps. Do you think they will still want to participate knowing what awaits them?"

"They're in camps now," Golda reminded him. "I don't think further interment will be much of an obstacle."

"They'll be miserable," Schind continued.

"They're miserable now."

Schind liked Golda—her intellect, her bravery, her willingness to try new things even when others thought they would fail. If he agreed to a project of this size now it would be only because of Golda and he looked at her a moment, thinking how blessed they were to have her. "You have a point," he said finally. Then he turned to Ben-Gurion with a curious look. "So, why did you send for me?"

Peres answered. "We want you go to New York and take charge of this operation."

"I'm in the middle of something right now," Schind reminded him, but his heart leaped at the opportunity. New York, a huge operation, an opportunity to change the lives of thousands and influence the politics of Palestine, even the world. This was what they'd been working for—what *he'd* been working for. How could he possibly say no? But he had to play the part a little longer. "I'm not sure I can get away just yet."

"I know," Peres nodded. "We'll hand your duties off to someone else."

"Look," Golda said, apparently concerned he might balk. "This operation is tenuous at best." Her voice was firm but not demanding. "Many of our own people are skeptical of it. Others are certain it won't work. If we send someone else, they'll go to New York, make a few phone calls, see that they face a huge challenge, and the whole thing will fall apart. We need someone who will take charge and make it happen. That's why we chose you." She gently jabbed the air with her finger to emphasize the point. "That's why you're sitting in that chair right now."

Finally, Ben-Gurion spoke up. "Danny, as you readily noted, this operation involves considerable risk. To lead it, to make it work, we need someone who is not afraid of risk, but also someone who is trained to keep calm in tense situations and minimize that risk. Not only in New York but on the trips when they sail over."

And, Schind thought, *you need someone willing to leave family and home long enough to bring it all together. And that's me.* But Ben-Gurion's last sentence raised a question in Schind's mind and he was sure it showed on his face. "You want me to accompany the ships?"

"No, no, no." Ben-Gurion shook his head. "Not in the least. But we do want people from Haganah on each of those trips. To control the passengers. You know the right people for that job."

Golda spoke up. "We need someone to put this together and make it happen. You're that person."

"Do I have a choice?" Schind asked it in a way that noted his acquiescence. He wasn't about to let anyone else take the job.

"Not really," Peres said with a grin.

"When do you want me to go?"

"As soon as possible," Ben-Gurion answered.

"I'll book you on the first flight out," Golda added. "The next one leaves three days from today."

Ben-Gurion leaned forward and rested his elbows on the desktop. "We'll notify New York you're coming. In the meantime, keep this as secret as possible. I know I don't have to tell you that, but this will involve a growing number of people and we have to start from the beginning by emphasizing the need for secrecy."

"So, I can bring in some of my own guys?" Schind asked.

"Yes," Peres nodded. "This will be a Haganah operation."

"And," Ben-Gurion added, "you'll be in charge of doing it all. You'll have to raise money, purchase ships, recruit crews."

"Use the best people you can find," Golda cautioned.

Schind had a wry smile. "We'll do our best to keep it quiet, but there's no way to keep an operation this big completely secret."

"You have to keep it more than quiet," Ben-Gurion warned. "The British will be listening with a thousand ears."

"Someone always talks," Schind sighed. "We won't be able to keep it completely secret."

"Which is why you'll have to keep it segmented," Ben-Gurion instructed. "Each person must know only what he needs to know to accomplish his task. You'll be the only person who knows what everyone else is doing. No one else can know more than he has to know."

"Right."

At last, Ben-Gurion stood. "Golda will get your ticket to New York. Pack your bags and get ready." He reached out to shake Schind's hand. "Was the meeting short enough for you?"

Schind clasped his hand. "Sorry for my attitude earlier."

"No need to apologize." Ben-Gurion smiled and nodded toward the others. "They're used to that from me."

Later that day, Ben-Gurion sent a courier to locate Schind and summoned him to a private meeting. Others could ignore the Arab threat, but he had no intention of following their lead. War was coming. Jews in Palestine had to be ready and they had to start taking steps to do that. With a man of Schind's ability in New York, Ben-Gurion was determined to take every advantage of it.

Schind was at Haganah headquarters when the courier found him.

He responded at once and arrived at Ben-Gurion's home a little before sunset. They sat at the kitchen table, just the two of them—talking over cups of hot tea.

"I wanted to discuss our work in New York a little more," Ben-Gurion began as he spooned sugar into his tea and gave it a stir. "As you know, for some time I've argued that we must begin now to establish an armed force of our own. A formal army like every other nation."

"Yes," Schind nodded. "You've argued for that on several occasions, although I'm not sure how many of our people agree with you."

"Not as many as I would like," Ben-Gurion smiled. "But in order for Haganah to become an actual army, we need genuine military equipment. Modern weapons and ammunition."

"Accumulating that now will be difficult with the British watching us and most of the rest of the world worried about open war in the region."

"Yes, but we have no choice," Ben-Gurion continued. "We must prepare to defend ourselves. War is rapidly approaching."

"I agree. And as soon as the British leave—and I think we both know they will be gone sooner rather than later—things will get much worse."

"Exactly," Ben-Gurion concurred. "As it stands right now, we can't compete with the Arab armies, especially since they have the support of the British. Our men are good and brave, but in terms of equipment we are grossly overmatched. We need American arms and American warplanes."

Schind found a smile irrepressible. "Are you asking me to find that in America?"

"Yes."

"In addition to the ships?"

"Yes."

"And you want me to raise the money to pay for all of it?"

"At least for now," Ben-Gurion said with a nod. "You'll have to cover it all." He leaned closer and lowered his voice. "The Americans have huge stockpiles of surplus from the war. We need it. There's no other way to get it and I don't think we have much time in which to do it."

"What sort of equipment am I looking for?"

Ben-Gurion leaned back. "Everything."

"Everything?"

"Automatic firearms, ammunition, cannons, tanks, artillery if you can find it," Ben-Gurion explained. "But most importantly, aircraft."

"Aircraft," Schind repeated with a skeptical smile. "You really want aircraft?" He did little to hide the skepticism in his voice.

"I know it sounds farfetched," Ben-Gurion admitted, "but we need everything. We have a long way to go to create a modern army. If we don't get started now trying to find the equipment we need, time will run out on us." Ben-Gurion leaned forward once more and propped his elbows on the table. "We may stumble around trying to figure this out. We may seem to some like we don't know what we're doing. But if we are going to form an active, living, vibrant state, we must pick ourselves up and get moving toward that goal. You're a man of action. You can do this. And we need you to take charge of it and make it happen. Not just the ships, which we talked about earlier today, but arms and armaments. Ammunition. Anything with which we may defend ourselves. We need everything."

"Well," Schind said slowly, "I don't know about artillery pieces and tanks—those are items with more obvious military application and little transference to other uses, so acquiring them may be a problem—but obtaining airplanes will be relatively easy. I understand the US government has thousands they want to sell. So, buying them might be a simple matter. Getting them back here will probably be more difficult."

"That's why I wanted to talk to you." Ben-Gurion leaned back and folded his arms across his chest. "I need you to figure this out."

Schind's demeanor changed as he moved on from reluctant participant to the problem-solving leader he was known to be. "Do we have anyone already over there who could help?"

"Henry Nadelson can help with fund-raising. He and I are old friends." Ben-Gurion rose from his chair and crossed the room to the counter. He opened a drawer and took out a piece of paper. "I'll give you his name and telephone number. Henry will know who to recruit to help with the money."

"I don't know him. Is it safe to tell him what we're doing?"

"Yes. You can talk to him." Ben-Gurion glanced over his shoulder, his demeanor tense and fiery. "But don't talk to Weizmann or his staff in the New York office. Not about the money or the arms. Weizmann won't like it. You can ask him about someone to help with the ships. And it would be a good idea if you *did* ask him. That way, he'll think he's part of the operation and won't press you for details about anything else you're doing. But don't tell him about the arms or planes or any of that. And don't tell him about the people you contact to help with the money, either." Ben-Gurion paused a moment and looked away as if in thought. Then his face lit up in a look of realization and he turned again to scribble something on the paper. "You can use Rudolph Sonneborn for fund-raising for the equipment and the airplanes. I'm adding his name to this list."

Schind had a questioning frown. "So, I won't run this operation through Weizmann's office in New York?"

"No." Ben-Gurion turned to face him and stood with his back leaning against the counter. "Let them know about the ships and refugees. Not the other. Set that up as a separate operation. Zionists in America are eager to help the refugees, but not so much the cause of war. They've always been afraid of that topic and if you tell Weizmann about what I've asked you to do—acquire military arms and ammunition—he will only try to stop you. So make sure he doesn't learn about it." Ben-Gurion paused again as if thinking, "For help with the airplanes, contact Al Schwimmer." He turned back to the paper on the counter to add Schwimmer's name and information. He continued to talk while he wrote. "Schwimmer is living in Los Angeles. He was a pilot during the war. Not sure what he's doing now. Last I heard, he was working for Lockheed Corporation. Tell him I sent you. He will handle the logistics, especially if you tell him I asked. He and Sonneborn are some of the few people we have who will respond without question.

Nadelson will respond, too, but he'll have more questions than the others. It's okay to talk to him—and to Schwimmer—about what we want," Ben-Gurion assured. "Schwimmer will be in California, away from Weizmann, and he'll know how important it is to keep quiet around the others." Ben-Gurion turned to face Schind and handed him the paper. "You can trust him."

"This will become a rather large enterprise."

"We have no choice. We must rescue the refugees and we must acquire arms with which to defend ourselves. Haganah *must* become a professional military—an army capable of executing a planned offensive on the ground with an air force capable of effectively exerting power over long distances."

"But with such a wide-ranging effort, the American government is bound to notice what we are doing."

"They might notice but they won't care when they find out it's us."

"What about the British? I'm certain they have MI6 agents active in the country."

"I'm sure they'll follow you, so be careful. The British alone can't stop us over there without American help. We don't want to give the Americans any opportunity to do that."

"We could always acquire weapons now and stockpile them elsewhere."

"That might work. You can discuss it with Schwimmer when you see him. You'll need to recruit good people to help, so very early you should contact Reuven Shiloah. He can help you check out the people you pick up along the way. Do you know how to reach him?"

"Yes. I know how to get in touch with him. What about communication back here?"

"What about it?"

"Telex and telephone security has bothered me. Too many people in the system have access to the messages and calls. Anyone along the line can read a telegram or listen to a call."

"You have a better idea?"

"Shortwave radio. We use it to communicate in the field."

Ben-Gurion was curious but not particularly interested. "Well, if you can work that in with the other things, perhaps we could give it a try. I don't want to widen this circle any larger than necessary, though. The fewer people who know the scope of the operation, the better."

"I don't think one more person would make that much difference at this point. We already have radio operators here who regularly communicate with people around the world."

"You can look into that when you get there." Ben-Gurion moved toward the door signaling the conversation was over. Schind rose from his place at the table to follow. "This is a rather large undertaking," he noted, "and we are beginning it from scratch. It will take time to pull everything together."

"Do it quickly," Ben-Gurion said with a grave tone. "The Jews of Palestine are counting on you."

CHAPTER 4

THE VOLUNTEERS

Early in the evening, the Telex operator in the Tel Aviv telegraph office set aside the paperback novel he'd been reading, propped his feet on the office trash can, and leaned back in his chair for a nap. He'd been there since long before sunrise and would be there throughout the night, too. Since the previous operator left for Paris, they were down to just two qualified men for the position, which meant both of them worked twelve-hour days, only now the other guy was sick, so he was on for an even longer stretch.

Just as the operator dozed off, the door opened and Golda Meir entered. The clerk on duty made her way to the counter but before she got there, Golda took a note pad from a tray to the left and began writing a message. She revised it once, then changed it again and handed it to the clerk. The clerk calculated the transmission fee and after paying, Golda turned toward the door and was gone.

A moment later, the clerk came to the operator's side and nudged him with her elbow. "Wake up. Send this to New York."

The operator opened his eyes, moved his feet from the trash can to the floor, and sat up straight. The clerk handed him the handwritten message and retreated to her desk. He rubbed his eyes a moment, then swung his chair around to face the Telex machine. As he typed out the information, he noted that the message was for Chaim Weizmann in New York. When the message was on its way, the operator stuffed the original handwritten note in his pocket and reached for the paperback novel he'd been reading.

In a little while, the door to the office opened again and Stuart Gordon, the British Army officer and MI6 agent from across the street, strolled through. He paused at the counter to flirt with the clerk, then continued to a back room. The Telex operator laid aside his paperback novel, rose from his chair, and started in that direction.

As the operator came into the room, Gordon was standing with a potholder in his hand, about to lift a kettle from a hot plate that sat on a table near the window. "You want some help with that?" the operator asked.

"Certainly. Didn't mean to intrude on your supplies, but you have tea and sugar. We don't."

"I don't mind," the operator replied as he took the potholder from Gordon, grasped the kettle by the handle, and gently poured hot water in the cup.

"Anything new?"

The operator shoved his hand in his pocket, took out the handwritten version of Golda's message, and handed it to him. "This came in a while ago."

Gordon glanced at it, then stuffed the message into his pocket. "Thanks," he said as he reached for the sugar bowl to sweeten his tea.

When he finished drinking tea at the telegraph office, Gordon walked down the street to British Army headquarters and made his way to the office of Henry Alston, a senior field officer with MI6. Alston was seated at his desk as Gordon arrived.

Not quite six feet tall, Alston was of a stocky build, with muscular arms and chest. His hair was trimmed shorter than most of his contemporaries and he was clean-shaven with not even a hint of mustache or sideburns. Always impeccably attired, he wore a khaki uniform with his shoes shined and brilliant, the button line of his shirt precisely in line with his trousers, and his name tag located exactly in the center of his pocket.

Gordon handed Alston the note. "This just came over from our contact in the telegraph office." He waited while Alston read. "They sent it to New York a little while ago."

"This mentions Schind," Alston said. "He's with Haganah. One of the leaders. Never really able to pin anything on him, but we are certain he was involved in that railroad bombing a few months ago."

Gordon, now seated across from the desk, leaned back in his chair and looked away. "Can't really blame them for defending their farms."

"Perhaps," Alston admitted. "But Haganah is much more involved than simply defending farms and farmers."

"You want me to look into it?"

"No. You keep tabs on the Telex office. I'll check into this and see what I can find out."

The following morning, Alston came from his office at British Army headquarters and walked up the street to a clothing store. The owner, Ralph Shultz, an older man of slender build, came from the far side of the room as Alston wandered toward a rack in the opposite corner. "We need to talk," Alston said as Shultz drew near.

"I told you last time," Shultz whispered, "I've got nothing more to say." His voice was an odd mixture of fear and frustration.

"And I told you," Alston said with cold, detached resolve, "your son will remain in detention unless and until you cooperate."

"What is there to talk about?" Shultz threw up his hands in a desperate gesture. "Nothing has happened since the last time we talked. And I told you then I didn't know anything."

"I understand there was a meeting last night."

Shultz's eyes darted away. "A meeting? What meeting?"

"You know precisely the meeting of which I speak."

"I'm not sure I—"

"A meeting at Ben-Gurion's house," Alston interrupted. "I know you were there. And I know—"

Just then, the door opened and a customer entered. Shultz said, "I can't talk about it now."

"Tonight," Alston said quickly. "Usual place." Then he turned away and started toward the door.

For the remainder of the day, Shultz alternated between defiance and fear. Angry that he had cowered to Alston and the threat of continued incarceration for his son. Fear that his son might never be released. The British were like that, he knew. Manipulative, deceitful, spiteful. The worst of them would let his son die a thousand deaths and never lift a finger to intervene—blaming him all the while for every evil history had to offer. The death of Christ. The Great War. The World War. And all the pestilence in between. And for what? Merely because he'd been born to Jewish parents. That's all. Nothing more than the coincidence of history.

But I should do it, he thought. *I should meet him. And I should come with a pistol. As soon as we are alone, I should pull it from my pocket and shoot him. Not even take time to aim. We'll be close enough. I'll just pull the trigger and watch while blood spurts from his body. And in a matter of seconds he'll be dead.*

Then what would happen to Eli? Tears filled Shultz's eyes as he thought of his son in a British detention camp. He'd be left in there for sure. "And I would join him," Shultz whispered to himself. "And then Eli would be forced to watch while they hanged me."

But the day passed and Shultz did none of that. No pistol. No plot to kill Alston. Just tended to the business and waited for time to tick slowly by. Finally, at sundown Shultz locked the door to the store and turned out the lights. He made his way slowly past the racks to the office in back for a cup of tea, which he sipped in the dark while he waited.

About ten that evening, Shultz slipped out the back door and crept through the darkness to an alley two blocks to the west. Halfway up from the street, he found a place in the shadows to hide. Twenty minutes later, a car turned toward him and the headlights switched off.

The car rolled toward him in the darkness and came to a stop just a few feet away. Shultz opened the front door and took a seat inside.

Alston turned to him with a thin, uncaring smile. "Now, as I was saying earlier today, I understand there was a meeting at Ben-Gurion's house last night."

"Maybe," Shultz said slowly.

"Our sources tell us you were there."

"No one can talk about these things," Shultz replied.

"Why is Danny Schind going to New York?"

"I don't know anyone named Danny Schind."

Alston turned in the seat to face Shultz. "If you don't cooperate, your son is going to be in that detention camp until he dies. And his sister might just join him."

Shultz clinched his teeth in anger. "You wouldn't dare."

"Oh, yes I would," Alston smiled. "Now, tell me about that meeting. I know you were there."

"You harm him or her, and you'll get nothing but trouble from me."

"Trouble?" Alston laughed. "What kind of trouble could a pitiful shopkeeper cause for me?"

"I know about the woman from the café," Shultz said as he straightened his shirt.

"What woman?" The mention of her had caught him by surprise and he let slip the importance of the matter in the tone of his voice.

"The brunette. The one they found by the road near the beach."

"What about her?"

"I want to see my son."

"Impossible."

"I want to see him or you can get your information from someone else."

"I'll see what I can arrange."

Shultz grasped the door handle. "Then call me when you've arranged it."

"Where are you going?" Alston snapped.

Shultz opened the car door. "I want to see my son. And I want your assurance that nothing will happen to my daughter."

"Okay," Alston said with disgust. "Nothing will happen to her. I wasn't going to do anything anyway."

"I want to see my son tomorrow."

"That can't—"

"Yes, it can. You go up to that camp every day."

"Okay." Alston banged his fist against the steering wheel. "We'll go up there in the morning. You can see him. Just tell me what happened in the meeting."

Shultz slid back on the seat and shut the door. "Ben-Gurion learned in advance that the British are going to turn down the US proposal to increase immigration to one hundred thousand refugees per year. He called the meeting to talk about it."

"Is that all you talked about?"

"Ben-Gurion tried to get us to talk about preparing for war."

"He wants to fight us?"

"No. Not at all. But he says your soldiers are leaving soon and we'll have to fend for ourselves against the Arabs. He thinks when the British are gone, the Arabs will attack us. The surrounding countries might even join them. Only way we can be free and secure is if we fight, and to do that we must be prepared."

"What did the others say?"

"They were more concerned about helping the Jewish refugees who are trapped in Europe. They want to bring them here."

"They'll never make it. Our navy will intercept them."

"Most seem to know that and don't seem to care."

"They think they can overwhelm us?"

"They think they can force you to react like Brits and that you will show the world who you really are."

Alston chuckled. "Showing the world who we really are will show the world how reasonable and tolerant we've been. Zionists think the rest of the world owes them something." He looked across at Shultz. "Do you Jews really think we're *all* that stupid?"

"I don't know." Shultz opened the car door. "But take me to see my son in the morning and on the way home I'll tell you why Schind is going to New York." Without waiting for a response, Shultz stepped from the car and disappeared.

A few days later, Edward Robinson, a field officer with MI6, was summoned to the office of Arthur Peel, MI6 assistant director for North American operations. Robinson, a slender young man with a bespectacled, bookish appearance, thought by many to be on the rise in the organization, was tense and nervous as he made his way up the stairs toward Peel's office. He'd never met anyone at the assistant director level—never met any supervisor other than his own. *I must have done something wrong,* he thought. *I must have done something terribly wrong. But what could it have been?*

After college Robinson had been recruited by MI6 as an analyst and shortly after liberation was posted to Paris, where he served without complaint. More recently, he'd been recalled to London and assigned to field work with an MI5 joint operation, tracking down remnants of a Soviet spy ring. That had gone well—exemplary, in fact—and he'd been awarded a citation with the director's own seal affixed, though it was promptly scurried away as soon as the presentation was finished. "Top secret," they said.

When he reached the office door, Robinson paused a moment, straightened his tie, and rapped lightly with his knuckle. A voice from inside commanded him to enter, and he pushed open the door.

Arthur Peel, easily sixty years old and at the top of his career, was seated at his desk. "Ah yes," he said with a broad smile. "Robinson. Do come in."

By then Robinson was in front of the desk, shoulders square, chin up, looking more like a first-year soldier than a ten-year veteran of the intelligence service.

"Relax, Robinson," Peel said with a wave of his hand. "Have a seat. Care for some tea?"

Robinson glanced around awkwardly, located a chair just behind him, and eased down into it. "No, thank you, sir. I'm fine."

"Well then," Peel propped his elbows on the armrest of his chair and laced his fingers together near his chest. "I suppose you're wondering why you've been called to this office."

"Yes, sir. I was wondering about that."

The door to the hallway was open and Peel rose from his desk, reached over, and gave it a shove. It banged closed and Robinson felt an awful dread sweep over him. He'd violated the first rule. Close the door behind you when you enter a room.

Peel seemed not to notice the gaff and as he settled back into his seat and continued to talk. "Our office in Tel Aviv thinks there's a threat brewing with Jewish immigration." A file lay before him, which Robinson noticed now for the first time. Peel took from it two documents, glanced at them briefly, and handed them to Robinson. "That first one is a copy of a telegram Ben-Gurion received a few days ago. The other is a copy of one Golda Meir sent to New York." He paused again and took yet another document from the file. "This is a report prepared by Henry Alston, our chief in Tel Aviv. It gives a summary of the discussion held during a recent meeting at Ben-Gurion's house.

Robinson skimmed over them. "I know Alston. He does good work."

"You've dealt with him in the past?"

"He was with us in Paris briefly."

"I see," Peel said with a nod. "Well, his report of the meeting and those two telegrams seem to indicate the Jews are plotting to increase the number of refugees they are surreptitiously bringing into the country."

"I've read some of the other reports from the area," Robinson had a satisfied smile. "At first they smuggled them through Europe into Turkey and then down to the coast. Picked them up in small fishing boats and brought them to remote locations on the Palestinian coast. They were successful at first, but I understand we're catching them now." Robinson heard the words as they slipped across his lips and they sounded good to him. Inside, he could feel his confidence growing and with it the force of the conversation shifting in his direction. This was his meeting now; he knew it in his heart and he felt good about it.

"You seem to know a lot about this area," Peel commented.

The look on Peel's face and the tone of his voice only served to reinforce the sense of control rising in Robinson. "The Jews have a long-standing relationship with the government in France," he explained. "Many of them were educated there. Those in leadership in the Jewish Agency are well acquainted with many of the most powerful French politicians."

"Well, our Middle East section thinks they may be planning an even bigger assault this time. Something much larger than fishing boats. They seem to think the Jews intend to switch to ships with far greater capacity."

"An attempt to overwhelm our facilities in Palestine with a new wave of illegal immigrants? Make a chaotic situation even more so?"

"Yes," Peel replied. "Our people seem to think so. And it would, too. A large increase in illegal immigrants would quickly overwhelm our capability and seriously erode our military strength."

"Then the army will have no choice but to transport the illegal immigrants to Cyprus, or return them to Europe." Robinson was comfortable now. He spoke with an officious, self-satisfied tone and, enraptured by the beauty and wonder of his own words, never noticed he'd made the rankest of amateur mistakes—telling a royal how *they* should act.

"Yes, well," Peel said with a condescending tone only an aristocrat could give, "I think the Foreign Office would object to returning them to Europe." He looked Robinson in the eye. "We would look rather like the Nazis, don't you think?"

But Robinson was too far gone now to retreat, so he pressed on. "Then, as I said, they'll have to send them to Cyprus. And I'm not so sure the Foreign Office would mind at all returning them to Europe. Everyone's about had enough of these simpering Jews. They were treated badly, of course, but it was Hitler who did it. Not us."

"Yes. Perhaps so." Peel took an even more dismissive tone and sat up straight in his chair. "At any rate, that is for the army and the Foreign Office to determine." The pace of Peel's voice picked up. "Our task, and your assignment, is to learn as much about this potential new threat as possible. One of Haganah's operatives, Danny Schind, is set to travel to New York. We want you to go there, assemble a team, and follow him. Get to the bottom of the situation. Find out why he's there, what he's doing, and what the Jews are up to. Note where Schind stays, who he meets, every contact he makes. See if you can figure this out. If they're planning something, we need to know what it is before they do it."

Robinson knew when to concede defeat, drop the pretense, and get on with business. "I'll get right on it," he replied in a crisp, clipped tone much like the one he'd used when he first entered the office.

"Good." Peel seemed to regain his composure as well. "You'll need to leave immediately to stay ahead of him."

"I will."

"This comes from the top," Peel added. "Highest priority. Use whatever resources you need to get the job done."

"Right. I'll see to it. Our New York office knows I'm coming?"

"No." Peel's voice was suddenly solemn. "And don't bother them with this. Keep this to yourself. If you need assistance, contact Geoffrey Reid. He's one of ours but he works from the embassy in Washington."

Robinson frowned. "That'll be a bit cumbersome, don't you think?"

"How so?"

"If I'm in New York and he's at our embassy in Washington. We'll be several hours apart if we should need to meet."

"Make it work," Peel instructed. "I don't want New York to know about this. I want to see your reports myself, not through their eyes. If they get in the loop they'll want all your reports sent through them. I don't want a sanitized version of this. I want it raw. I want the real picture, as if I were there myself looking it over in person with my own eyes."

"Yes, sir. I see." Robinson shifted positions in his chair. "But if I am to assemble a crew in New York, how shall I do that without the New York office knowing about it?"

Peel turned his chair sideways and stared out the window. He was silent for a moment and then, with his eyes still fixed on some imaginary point in the distance, asked, "Are you familiar with the British Passport Control Office?"

"Can't say that I am. Something from the Foreign Office perhaps?"

"Hardly. Though that is precisely what we wanted people to think." Peel turned his chair to face the desk and looked at Robinson. "What I'm about to tell you must stay strictly between us. You understand?"

"Yes, sir."

"Only two or three people in this building know what Passport Control really does and less than a dozen worldwide even know of its existence. We want to keep it that way."

"Certainly." A sense of excitement welled up in Robinson and he did his best to tamp it down. He'd let emotion take control earlier and it had almost ruined the moment for him. Now there would be no mistake. He focused his attention on Peel and did his best to remember every word.

"The British Passport Control Office," Peel began, "was an operation established in the United States to manage and coordinate our efforts to counter Nazi espionage against our interests in the Americas, and to promote a pro-British attitude among Americans. Agents working from offices in Rockefeller Center were engaged in efforts to identify and interdict Nazi infiltrators attempting to gain access to both North and South America and they were engaged in extensive propaganda operations designed to ease the United States toward involvement in the war."

"Was the FBI aware of its existence?"

"Yes. They were aware of it and worked with us in that effort throughout the duration of the war."

"And now?"

"Officially," Peel noted, "the Passport Control Office was closed shortly after peace was achieved in Europe."

Robinson raised an eyebrow. "But unofficially?"

"Unofficially, we have continued to maintain an office in New York that, as before, is engaged in a wide range of activities designed to protect British interests. This time, however, we are doing it without the assistance of the FBI, without the involvement of the traditional MI6 apparatus, and without strict regard for US law."

"You mean," Robinson said in a matter-of-fact tone, "the agents at Rockefeller Center office are engaged in the clandestine service."

Peel gave a dismissive wave of his hand. "You needn't trouble yourself with details of their operations. However, when you arrive and are settled, you should appear at their offices and ask for Mr. White."

"Is there really a Mr. White?"

"Doesn't matter. Ask for him by name. Someone will take you to his office. Tell him I sent you. He'll know what you need."

"We don't trust the Americans to help us?"

"We trust the Americans to act like Americans. Which means they can be easily distracted, often ill informed, and will not always have our best interests at heart. Have you been to New York?"

"Yes, sir," Robinson replied. "Once or twice."

"Then you shall have no trouble locating their offices. You will get your first assistance from them but that office is rather small. If you need additional men, ask Reid in Washington for help. But you must make certain you tell no one about Passport Control. Not even Reid."

Robinson's eyes opened a little wider. "Reid doesn't know about the Passport Control Office?"

"No. And neither does anyone else at our embassy. So make certain you keep it that way."

"Yes, sir."

Peel placed both hands on the edge of the desk and pushed back his chair to stand. "Any other questions?"

Robinson spoke up quickly. "Where shall I stay?"

"Oh," Peel smiled. "Almost forgot. We have an apartment we lease through a broker here in London. He lists the lessee as Southampton

Marine. We keep it solely for executive use. You can stay there. I'll have someone give you the address and make the arrangements."

"Good, then."

Peel stood. "You should get going. Schind has a head start on you."

Robinson jumped to his feet. "Certainly, sir."

Peel guided him toward the door. "We expect Schind in New York this coming Thursday. Be at the airport when he arrives and don't lose track of him."

"Certainly, sir," Robinson repeated. "I shall get right to it."

"See that you do." Peel grasped the doorknob and turned to look Robinson in the eyes. "This is a step up for you. A chance to run a real operation. This sort of opportunity doesn't come around often. Be sure to make the most of it."

As instructed, Robinson departed for New York on the next available flight and arrived there the following day. He took a taxi to the apartment Peel described, which was located on East Twenty-Third Street, and obtained a key from the doorman. In spite of the long trip and late afternoon hour, he deposited his luggage in the bedroom, then left immediately for the Passport Control Office at Rockefeller Center.

Whether Mr. White actually existed Robinson never knew, but when he arrived at the office he asked for him by name. The receptionist rose from her desk immediately and escorted him down the hall to a corner suite where he found a tall, broad-shouldered man of middle age seated at a desk near the window. Robinson introduced himself and stated that Mr. Peel had sent him. At the mention of Peel's name, the receptionist stepped from the room and closed the door behind her.

When she was gone, the man at the desk produced a list of agents he deemed suitable for the work London indicated Robinson would be doing. There was no small talk. No polite questions about his trip or whether he'd settled into suitable accommodations. All business, no personal interaction.

Robinson scanned the list quickly and, seeing no one on it whom he recognized by name, said, "If you think they will do, I am satisfied."

"These are our best agents."

"I'll need to see their files," Robinson replied.

"Certainly." The opened a desk drawer, took out a stack of file folders, and handed them to Robinson. "We prepared dossiers for each. You may retain the files for your own consideration."

Robinson was immediately suspicious. If Passport Control prepared dossiers for the agents ahead of time and was willing for him to hold them without determining whether he had a secure facility in which to store them, the dossiers could not possibly contain accurate information. Or, more likely, they contained cover stories someone *wanted* to be leaked as a way of deepening the layers of legend surrounding the agents' true identities. Making the agents even more useful the next time.

In spite of his misgivings, Robinson had no choice but to go along with whatever the man behind the desk offered. At least it was a start and rather than raising questions he simply took the files, thanked the supposed Mr. White, and asked him to send the agents to his apartment later that evening. Then he departed.

For the remainder of the day, Robinson sat at the dining table in the apartment and read the story on each of his new agents. There were six men in total. Among them were Richard Oldfield and Ian Dukes, both Cambridge men who, according to their files, eschewed the gentlemen's life for service to their country during the war, then stayed on afterward, apparently for the thrill of clandestine operations. Their work was noted as exemplary but their attitudes and motivations were seen as less than stellar.

Others on the team came from more typical backgrounds—Victor Loring and Ian Mitchell from the army, Jeremy Pike from the navy, and Eaton Ward who'd come from a restive attempt at journalism with the BBC.

When the team arrived at the apartment that evening, Robinson spent the first thirty minutes describing their overall mission—follow and investigate Danny Schind, track and log his activities, obtain information about his affairs. “Reports from Palestine,” he explained, “indicate the Jews may be planning some sort of operation. No one seems to know precisely what it means but there are indications they intend to expand the recent effort to bring refugees from Europe. One of our primary objectives is to determine whether Schind’s trip is part of that emerging effort, and if so, the exact nature of his involvement.”

Oldfield asked, “London thinks a Jewish plot to expand illegal immigration in Palestine has some connection to the United States?”

Something about Oldfield’s voice seemed out of place but Robinson dismissed the thought. “Yes, ships. We think it has to do with acquiring ships.”

“Sounds a little extreme, even for the Jews,” Pike added with a smile and his eyes darted around to the others.

“Perhaps,” Robinson noted, “but that’s our best information. The Jewish Agency for Palestine maintains an office here. We suspect that office is involved, or very shortly will be involved, in whatever this operation might be. They also have an extensive network of associated Jewish organizations capable of mustering volunteers and raising substantial financial support.”

“And Haganah,” Loring added. “They also have Haganah and its worldwide network.”

There was a lilt in Loring’s voice and now Robinson was suspicious. Still, he pressed on. “Yes, and on that note . . . ” He paused as he reached for a leather satchel that sat nearby, opened it, and drew out a file. From the file he removed a number of pages and began passing them around the room. “This is a report on Danny Schind. It contains information gleaned from a number of sources. Some of them protected, some of them public. As you can see, Schind is one of Haganah’s most respected leaders. The fact that he’s been removed from the field and sent here seems to indicate the seriousness of their present undertaking.” While the men glanced over the report, Robinson continued. “As I said before, it is our responsibility to determine precisely why he has come to New York and whether he is part of an operation that affects our interests in Palestine.”

"And by *our interests*," Dukes asked, "you mean the Crown?"

The tone of Dukes' voice had a hint of superiority and Robinson didn't like it. He hadn't attended Cambridge but he had a good education and his uncle was a professor at Oxford, for crying out loud. He knew things. He was a commoner, true enough, but he wasn't an ill-informed, inbred commoner like those in the rural townships. "Yes," he said coldly after a moment, anger beginning to boil just beneath the surface. "Of course I mean the *Crown*. We are all in service of His Majesty." The men grinned at Robinson's response and he glared at them. "Did I say something funny?"

"We aren't quite that formal over here," Oldfield explained.

"Formal?"

"This is the United States," Loring added. "You'll find that things are a bit more cobbled together. Less rigid than back in London. Not quite so stratified over here."

Ah, Robinson thought. Now he understood. Their earlier comments had been in jest. They'd been going along, playing along, not taking him seriously. Well, this might be his first command of field operations but he had no intention of allowing it to be his last. They were not going to ruin the experience for him.

"You mean you might actually consent to taking tea with me on occasion, what with us so far from the homeland?"

Loring had a sheepish expression. "I didn't mean—"

"Certainly you meant it," Robinson snapped. "You all meant it. I'm certain you've been thoroughly briefed on what we are expected to accomplish and I'm positive you know far more about me than I do about you." He tossed their files on the floor. "But we are going to do this job and do it well, or each of you will be reassigned from your cushy Rockefeller appointment by morning."

"Look," Dukes said. "All we're trying to tell you is that if you want to be conspicuously obvious—the Brit standing on the corner keenly observing someone and obvious to all—then fine. Act as you would in London and you'll stand out like a red flag. But if you want to go unnoticed over here, you have to blend in. You have to look and act like an

American. And they are quite an unassimilated bunch. That's all we're saying."

"Well," Robinson paused to straighten his jacket. "We'll see about that, I suppose."

When he'd gone over the mission in general, he turned to the immediate task of locating Schind upon his arrival at the airport. "Schind will arrive at LaGuardia tomorrow at two in the afternoon. We will be there to locate him and follow him. But nothing more." He turned again to the satchel and produced another handful of papers, which he once more passed around the room. "Each of you has an assignment which includes your cover occupation for this sortie, the nature of your clothing, and your suggested deportment. Make sure you are familiar with the details of your particular role." Robinson glanced in Dukes' direction. "We want to look and act as if we are supposed to be there."

Oldfield chuckled. "I'm supposed to be an airport employee. Dressed like a sweeper. Can I get one of those rolling carts with the bin and the dust broom?"

"They'll have one for you in the change room," Robinson answered. He still wasn't convinced they were taking him seriously but he resolved not to make a further issue of it.

"Good." Oldfield seemed to take delight in playing along with what the others obviously saw as Robinson's excess enthusiasm and over-planning. "I always wondered what that was like. How other people looked from that side of things." He glanced at Dukes. "How about you?"

"Airline employee. I think I should be a captain with flight wings and the whole thing." He grinned at Robinson. "Will you be there?"

"Yes. I'll be dressed as one of the passengers."

"Ah," Dukes quipped. "Come as you are." The others laughed. Robinson seemed not to catch the humor.

Ward spoke up in a more serious tone. "Have you informed the FBI?"

"No."

"Good," Ward said with a sly smile. "They don't know about us and anyway, Americans are much too sympathetic with the Jews. They believe everything they've read about the German camps."

Mitchell joined in. "The Jews have done a good job of using the worst of it to their advantage."

"That's not our problem," Robinson cut off the discussion before it went further. "Our assignment is to follow Schind, collect information, send reports to London, and do our best to determine what precisely he is up to. I want him followed every day, all day. And night. And don't get preoccupied with trying to straighten out American attitudes toward the Jews or anything else. That's not our job. We have one assignment and one assignment only. Anyone here have a problem with that?"

They all shook their heads in response. "Good." Then Robinson took one last item from the leather satchel, an envelope filled with pictures, which he poured out on a low table. "These are pictures of every known Jewish Agency operative and member working from the New York office. Study them. Memorize the face with the name on the back. And let's get ourselves ready so we can be in position at the airport by eleven tomorrow morning."

CHAPTER 5

THE VOLUNTEERS

Meanwhile, across town, Chaim Weizmann, director of the Jewish Agency's office in New York, met with his secretary, Fanny Barnett, to review the day's work and prepare for what lay ahead later in the week. The hour was late but Weizmann had been out of the office all day and there were matters that needed his attention.

Weizmann had begun his career in science, obtaining a PhD in chemistry from the University of Fribourg. While serving as a lecturer at the University of Manchester he became involved with British Zionist groups and quickly ascended to a leadership role. He worked tirelessly promoting the return of Jews to Palestine and the acceptance by world leaders of a Jewish state but advocated that position primarily from outside of Palestine where his education and cosmopolitan orientation were well suited. Now a dignified man of seventy, his short-cropped hair, neatly trimmed goatee and mustache, and deep-set eyes gave him a polished, academic appearance.

Fanny Barnett, his secretary, was the wife of a real estate developer who became involved with the Zionist effort in New York as a volunteer. Her organizational expertise kept the office operating in a timely and efficient manner. Her knowledge of the city and her extensive social connections made her indispensable.

After running through the next day's schedule with Fanny and addressing other routine matters Weizmann said, "There is one more thing. Danny Schind is coming from Tel Aviv. He'll arrive tomorrow.

His airplane gets in to LaGuardia at two. We need to send someone to the airport to meet him."

"Who is he?"

"Haganah," Weizmann said with a wary look.

"Do you know him?"

"I've met him a few times. He's a good guy. He's just . . . Haganah."

"I see." Fanny grimaced the way she always did when they thought Ben-Gurion was attempting to tell them what to do. "Why is he coming?"

"I'm not sure." Weizmann opened the top drawer of his desk, took out a telegram, and handed it to her. "This is all I know. It came a few days ago."

Fanny took the message from him and quickly read it. "I didn't see this."

"You were out."

"You should have shown it to me earlier."

"Why?" he asked with an amused grin. "What difference would it make?"

"I would have had longer to worry," she huffed as she handed the message back to him. "Who sent it?"

Weizmann held up the page and pointed with his index finger. "See the initials at the end?"

Fanny squinted. "G. M." She looked over at him. "Golda Meir?"

"Yes."

"She sent this personally?"

"Yes."

"She actually walked across the street to the telegraph office and sent it?"

Weizmann arched an eyebrow. "I think so."

"They usually don't come with initials or anything that identifies the sender."

"Right."

Fanny adjusted her position in the chair. "Well, I suppose that means it's important."

Weizmann opened the desk drawer again, dropped the telegram inside, and pushed it closed. "I'm sure it means something, I'm just not sure what."

"Are we supposed to take care of him?"

"Yes," Weizmann nodded. "If Golda took the time to send the message herself, I think it means he's coming in an official capacity and that it's a top priority with Ben-Gurion."

"Where will we put him?"

"Call Joe Buxenbaum. See if Schind can stay with him for a few days, until we figure out why he's here. Maybe Joe can go to the airport to meet him, too. It would be good for the two of them to meet. I think they might get along well together and maybe Joe can figure out why he's here faster than we can."

"I'll call him now and tell him." Fanny stood and turned toward the door as Weizmann called after her. "Make sure Joe knows to keep this quiet, at least until we find out what this is all about."

Fanny turned to face him. "I'm sure that won't be a problem."

"Just the same, make sure you tell him."

"Certainly."

Joe Buxenbaum was a rather burly man. Taller than most of his friends, he had broad shoulders and a muscular physique. His red hair always seemed unkempt and, with dimples in both cheeks and a twinkle in his eye, he seemed always to be "up to something." He was born in the Borough Park section of Brooklyn to parents who were Orthodox Jews. As a teenager, however, Buxenbaum broke with family tradition, moved to Baltimore, and lived with a distant relative. While there, he got into trouble and was arrested. The judge who handled his case gave him the option of joining the military or serving time in prison. Buxenbaum chose the US Navy. He was stationed at Pearl Harbor when the Japanese attacked. Later, he was injured during the Battle of Midway, honorably discharged, and sent home to New York City.

After returning from the war, he settled in the Bedford–Stuyvesant section of Brooklyn where he recovered and took a job on the docks. A hard worker, he gradually rose through the ranks of the Longshoremen's Association and was elected shop steward for one of the locals. As news of the war filtered home from Europe, Buxenbaum became aware of conditions faced by Jews living in Germany. Through correspondence received from relatives and friends, the details of those conditions became painfully obvious. As a consequence, he found a renewed urge to return to the faith he'd known as a child and began regularly attending Sabbath services at a synagogue near his apartment.

Contacts and information available through the synagogue told him about Jews who escaped persecution in Germany and wanted to return to Palestine. Buxenbaum made a concerted effort to learn more about the various Zionist groups in the United States who were working to help with the European problem. Not long after that, he began volunteering with the Jewish Agency for Palestine at the office in Manhattan.

At the Agency, his natural ability with people and his penchant for solving problems readily gave him a place in the organization. When something needed to be done quickly or when a hopelessly entangled situation needed to be untangled, the answer was usually "Send Buxenbaum."

As Buxenbaum gained experience at the Agency he learned the real movers and shakers in the United States were all members of Haganah. At the same time, men who already were members of the organization noticed him, too, and brought him into one of their underground groups working from Long Island.

On Thursday, as instructed, Buxenbaum left his apartment in the Greenwich Village section of Manhattan and drove out to LaGuardia. He parked the car near the terminal, walked inside, and checked the overhead board that showed arriving flights. When he found the listing for Schind's flight he noted the gate number and headed in that direction. He had never seen Schind before, but he was pretty sure he could pick him out.

As Buxenbaum made his way along the corridor, he noticed a janitor standing in the corner of the waiting area and another near one of the gates. The men were dressed correctly—with gray work clothes, a name tag above the right pocket, and a cap on his head—but it was Thursday already and their shirts and pants were clean and unstained. No one put on fresh work clothes that late in the week. And their shoes had a spotless shine. Two janitors, both with clean, crisp work clothes and both with spit-shined shoes. *Impossible,* he thought. *Something's not right.*

At the next gate, an airline attendant stood at a kiosk. He wore an Eastern Airlines uniform but while others around him were busy checking and rechecking passenger lists, answering passenger questions, and scurrying back and forth with last-minute details, this one did nothing but watch those who passed by in the corridor twenty feet from his station. "That doesn't add up," Buxenbaum mumbled to himself. Three people on the same corridor. All three out of place. Something was wrong.

Shortly before two that afternoon, Schind's plane arrived. Buxenbaum positioned himself near the doorway that lead from the gate and watched as passengers entered the building. A few were greeted immediately by family and friends. Two more entered the building, moved past him, and turned toward the corridor without pausing. The next, however, came through the doorway and stopped as if searching for someone. Buxenbaum stepped forward and thrust out his hand. "Danny?"

"Yes."

"Danny Schind?"

"You're from the Agency?"

"Yes," Buxenbaum replied. The two men shook hands, then Buxenbaum gestured to the right. "We go this way to get your luggage."

As they started toward the baggage claim area, Buxenbaum glanced suspiciously over his shoulder. Schind noticed and asked, "What's wrong?"

"Some of these people are out of place."

"Who?" Schind asked with a worried frown. "What are you talking about?"

Buxenbaum lowered his voice. "See the guy in the corner? To our left."

Schind glanced in that direction. "Yeah. What about him?"

"He's dressed like a janitor but his uniform is spotless."

"Right."

"It's too late in the week for that. His uniform should be wrinkled at least."

"Well," Schind offered, "maybe he spilled something on it. Or maybe they follow a different routine here."

"Not a different routine. They get fresh work clothes on Monday and they're expected to last the week."

"You know this for a fact?"

"Got a friend who works out here."

"Oh," Schind said with an amused nod.

"There's an airline employee over there standing near the gate," Buxenbaum continued. "Everyone around him is busy, but he's just standing there staring at people as they walk past."

"Okay," Schind said slowly.

"Three guys right here on this end of the corridor. Out of place. Not following a routine common to their occupation." Buxenbaum nodded to one of the janitors. "That guy over there hasn't moved from that spot since I got here twenty minutes ago."

"Yes," Schind said. "I see your point."

A man appeared up ahead, walking toward them. Buxenbaum nodded in his direction. "This guy coming here," he said in a soft voice. "This guy's wearing a pilot's uniform but he's got the insignia in the wrong place. And that guy over there with the hat. The one sitting near the lady with the two kids. He looks like a businessman but he just doesn't seem to fit. No briefcase. No newspaper. No magazine."

"So," Schind said, apparently convinced Buxenbaum's suspicions were well-grounded. "What are you thinking?"

"I'm thinking they aren't FBI."

"Why not?"

"Those guys all wear dark suits and don't care who notices."

A broad grin spread over Schind's face. "Isn't that more like something they do in the movies?"

Buxenbaum shook his head. "No, I've seen plenty of them and I know. They don't care who notices. Sometimes I think they want everyone to notice them." He gave a tip of his head to the left. "These guys watching us today are different. They're trying to blend in. And they're doing a poor job of it."

"Probably British," Schind said.

"They aren't American, that's for sure."

"Relax," Schind soothed. He was growing tired of the professional agent routine. "We'll be okay. Happens like this all the time back home. They can't touch us here unless the FBI gets involved. So," he said, repeating what he'd heard from Ben-Gurion, "let's not give them an opportunity to ask for help."

From the airport, Buxenbaum and Schind rode back to the apartment in lower Manhattan and Buxenbaum showed him where to put his things. The place wasn't much—a small living room with a tiny kitchen, and the two men shared a bathroom—but they both had a bedroom of their own and plenty of closet space.

When Schind was unpacked and ready, they walked up the street to a café and had a late lunch. On the way, Buxenbaum noticed one of the men they'd seen earlier at the airport and pointed him out to Schind.

"I know," Schind replied. "There's another one behind us."

Buxenbaum glanced in the reflection of a store window to check. "Should we say hello, or invite them to join us?"

"Let them have their fun for now," Schind smiled. "I'm hungry."

The next morning, Schind went on the subway with Buxenbaum and rode uptown to the Jewish Agency's office on Madison Avenue. Buxenbaum introduced him to Fanny, but Schind seemed not really to notice her. Nevertheless, she made a valiant effort to engage him in polite conversation.

In a few minutes, Weizmann came out to greet them and while Buxenbaum waited, Schind met with Weizmann in his office, alone. "We were delighted to meet you at the airport," Weizmann began as he took a seat at his desk, "but curious to know why you came."

At least he didn't waste time with small talk, Schind thought as he took a seat near the desk. "As you know," he began slowly, taking his time to settle into place, "many of our people are trapped in Europe, still living in the camps from which they were supposedly liberated at the end of the war."

"Yes," Weizmann nodded. "And we have been doing our best to find sponsors here in the United States for as many as possible."

"Sponsors?"

"Immigrants to the United States must be sponsored by someone who is already a citizen," Weizmann explained. "Someone to help them find their way and, if necessary, to help them financially. Locating people who would do that is difficult. Dealing with the European situation is a slow process."

"Ben-Gurion and the leadership in Tel Aviv have decided to speed up that process."

"Oh? How do they propose to accomplish that?"

"They want to obtain ships here in America, sail them to Europe, collect as many refugees as will possibly fit on each ship, and take them to Palestine."

"Nice idea," Weizmann said with a smile. "But they'll get caught. Every one of them."

"We know," Schind nodded.

"And the ships will be seized, too," Weizmann emphasized.

"We know that."

"The British won't return either of them—vessels or passengers."

"We know, too."

Weizmann frowned. "And still Ben-Gurion thinks this is a good idea?"

"Yes," Schind replied in a resolute tone.

Weizmann looked away. "I suspected he would try something like this," he sighed. He was silent a moment, then looked over at Schind. "How many refugees does he think he can transport?"

Without flinching, Schind said, "We want to send ten thousand a month."

Weizmann's eyes opened wide. "That's ambitious." He turned toward his desk, leaned forward, and propped his elbows on the desktop. "In fact, it's impossible."

"Not exactly," Schind countered, unwilling to let go of his assigned task.

"In the first place," Weizmann continued, "ship owners will never agree to make a trip like that."

"Which is why we're going to own the ships," Schind said with a wry smile.

"Oh." Weizmann paused and leaned back in his chair. "When you said 'obtain them' I thought you meant hire or lease them in the usual manner."

"We want to buy them," Schind reiterated.

"That's very ambitious."

"But it will work."

"Yes," Weizmann conceded. "It could work."

"Know anyone who can help us with that?"

"Maybe." Weizmann pursed his lips in a thoughtful pose. "I can make some calls and find out."

"Good." Schind moved forward in the chair to stand. "When can I expect to hear from you?"

"Give me the day to work on it..Come back in the morning. I should have an answer by then."

The meeting ended rather abruptly and Schind doubted he would hear further from Weizmann again on the matter. Perhaps there were others who could help. Maybe Buxenbaum knew someone. And if not, he could always call Al Schwimmer and get started on acquiring airplanes, but he knew how much the others were set on buying ships and rescuing the refugees. He also remembered what Golda had said about others coming over, quickly admitting defeat, and returning. "If this fails," he said to himself, "she will think I sabotaged the idea on purpose."

The night passed with Schind tossing and turning in his bed, but around midmorning the next day Weizmann phoned to say he had some ideas. Schind took a taxi to the Agency and arrived within the hour to find Morris Ginsberg waiting in Weizmann's office. Weizmann introduced them, noting for Schind that Ginsberg was president of American Foreign Steamship Company, a shipping company founded by Ginsberg's father. Schind seemed impressed and the three men quickly got down to business.

"I understand you are looking to purchase ships to collect refugees from Europe and transport them to Palestine," Ginsberg said, not waiting for Schind to broach the subject.

"Yes," Schind replied, aware now that Ginsberg and Weizmann had been talking before he arrived. "Are you able to help?"

Before Ginsberg could answer, Weizmann asked him, "Perhaps the first question is, will it work?"

"Oh yes," Ginsberg replied enthusiastically. "In fact, it's a brilliant idea. One that can't fail. If the British detain the refugees and place them in detention camps, the world will castigate them as the new Nazis. If they don't detain them, we'll be adding ten thousand people per month to the Jewish population in Palestine. Either way, we will be putting ourselves in a superior position relative to the general Arab population. And regardless, our cause will advance dramatically."

Weizmann seemed perturbed by Ginsberg's obvious excitement. "What about the risk to the passengers? Shouldn't we consider the potential for injury to the refugees in all this?"

Ginsberg turned to Schind. "How rough do you think the British will get?"

"I can't say for certain," Schind replied, "but the feeling is that they will only meet whatever resistance the passengers offer them. So, if we don't fight, they won't fight back."

"But you'll have to keep them under control."

"Right," Schind nodded.

Weizmann spoke up. "How do you plan to accomplish that?"

Schind could see Ben-Gurion was right in his caution about talking to Weizmann. Since they talked the day before, he'd done nothing but oppose the plan for the ships. If he knew about the airplanes, he'd be over the top. "We'll have our people on board the ships, too," Schind explained.

Weizmann had a disapproving look. "Your people?"

"We'll take care it. That won't be a problem. The big issue is how to obtain the ships and the crews necessary to sail them." Schind turned to Ginsberg once more. "I assume that's why you're here."

"Obtaining ships will be the least of our problems," Ginsberg replied. "Ships are cheap right now, very cheap. Lots of surplus from the war and most of it is being sold for scrap."

"How expensive will they be?"

"I can't say for certain about an exact dollar amount, but I'm sure we can get them for scrap or less."

Schind was unfamiliar with shipping industry terms. "Scrap?"

"A discounted price based on the value of the underlying steel," Ginsberg explained. "A commodity price. We just need money to make the purchases and someone to act as middleman."

Schind smiled playfully. "Know anyone who can help?"

"Yes," Ginsberg replied. "I know a man in Boston who does this sort of thing routinely." He glanced in Weizmann's direction. "Dewey Stone."

"Yes. Dewey Stone," Weizmann nodded. "Good choice."

"Stone lives right outside Boston," Ginsberg said for Schind's benefit. "He provides ships for a number of companies—arranges investor syndicates to purchase them, leases the ships to freight companies, fruit companies, that sort of thing. I'll set up a meeting."

CHAPTER 6

THE VOLUNTEERS

A few days later, Ginsberg phoned to tell Schind the meeting with Dewey Stone was set. Schind had misgivings—Weizmann brought in Ginsberg, now Ginsberg was bringing in Stone, and Schind didn't really know either one of them—he had no choice but to go along with it, at least for now, so he arranged for Ginsberg to pick him up in front of the apartment building the following morning. Schind was waiting when Ginsberg arrived and they left immediately for LaGuardia.

As they approached the corner just past the apartment building, Schind glanced out the window and saw two men seated in a car that was parked at the curb. Dressed in dark suits with white shirts and muted ties, they looked like any other New York businessmen, but their eyes were fixed on him and he was sure they recognized him. Schind was equally certain both men had been at the airport the day he arrived.

Ginsberg turned the steering wheel to make the corner. Schind kept his eyes focused on the side mirror. As he watched, the car behind them moved away from the curb and started in their direction. When it reached the corner, it slowly made the turn and trailed after them. Schind watched a moment longer, then looked over to Ginsberg. "Cut down this next street," he directed, pointing to the right.

"That's not the way," Ginsberg replied. "It's quicker to go—"

"Do it," Schind insisted, pointing out the window.

By then they were at the intersection. Ginsberg snatched the steering wheel hard to the right and the car veered in that direction. He swerved one lane over to avoid a man in the crosswalk and gave Schind a startled look. "What's the matter?"

Schind checked the side mirror again. "I keep seeing the same guys." His eyes were focused on the mirror but he gestured with his thumb over his shoulder. "Two of them are in that car behind us now."

Ginsberg glanced in the rearview mirror. "You mean like someone is following you?"

"Yeah."

"Who do you think it is?"

"Don't know for sure," Schind replied. "Joe thinks they're British."

"British? Why does Joe think that?"

"We saw them at the airport the day I arrived and later outside a café where we ate that afternoon."

"Joe picked you up at the airport?"

"Yes."

"Well," Ginsberg said with a wary glance in the mirror, "there's nobody back there now."

Schind looked over his shoulder and saw the car was gone. "But if there's one we can see, there are probably more we can't."

Ginsberg grinned. "Sounds like the voice of experience."

"Yeah," Schind said, still checking the side mirror. "We get a lot of experience with them in Palestine."

At the airport, they boarded a Northeast Airlines flight to Boston and took a seat near the front. Schind watched as the other passengers took their seats, checking to make certain none of them looked like the men he'd seen following them. When the plane was in the air, he at last turned his attention to the meeting with Stone. He leaned over to Ginsberg, "Tell me about this man we're going to see. I know he's in the shipping business, but what else do you know about him?"

"He's a businessman. He lives in Brockton, just south of Boston, and he's into far more than just shipping."

Schind found the answer evasive but he held that thought a moment and let the conversation unfold more slowly. "Think he'll help us?"

"Oh," Ginsberg nodded confidently, "I'm sure of it."

Schind waited for him to say more, but instead Ginsberg turned to look out the window. He waited a few minutes longer and when Ginsberg failed to return to the conversation he asked again, "So, what kind of business is he in?"

"Actually, he's involved in several. He has the ship syndication that I told you about—lining up investors to buy ships, which he then leases to other companies. He has a company that handles general freight by rail and truck. And, along with several family members, he owns a shoe company."

Schind found that amusing. "Bet that was an interesting transition."

"Quite lucrative from what I understand. He's the kind of man who sees opportunity before anyone else. Confident. Not afraid to take a risk. Gets in early, before anyone sees the potential. Sells out at the top, when others think it's the hot new investment. Very shrewd. He can buy the ships for us without anyone noticing."

Schind liked the sound of that. Especially the part about "buy the ships for us." He was rather certain he could locate ships. And probably find crews for them. But raising the money to pay for it . . . that was an entirely different proposition and one that left him more than a little uncomfortable. If Stone was prepared to handle the money part, they would be sailing for Europe within a matter of months. *This might be easier than anyone first thought.*

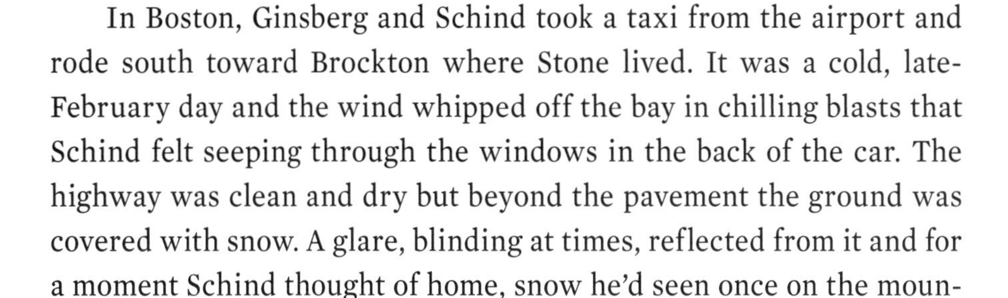

In Boston, Ginsberg and Schind took a taxi from the airport and rode south toward Brockton where Stone lived. It was a cold, late-February day and the wind whipped off the bay in chilling blasts that Schind felt seeping through the windows in the back of the car. The highway was clean and dry but beyond the pavement the ground was covered with snow. A glare, blinding at times, reflected from it and for a moment Schind thought of home, snow he'd seen once on the mountains near the Golan Heights, and how rare a sight that was.

Forty-five minutes later, the taxi came to a stop in front of a modest wood frame house on a quiet street in a residential neighborhood. Schind waited while Ginsberg paid the fare, then followed him from the car up a narrow sidewalk toward the front door of the house.

Before they reached the steps, the door opened and Stone stepped out. He wore a dark gray suit with white shirt and red tie. Not as tall as Schind, he was neat, slim, and had a full head of hair that was combed back from his forehead in a way that made his friendly smile seem all the more open, eager, and pleasant. With a wave of his hand he urged them inside, then closed the door quickly and helped them from their overcoats.

Ginsberg introduced Schind and they chatted briefly in the living room, then Stone led the way to a den in back where they warmed themselves with hot coffee and pastries. They continued to talk, Ginsberg and Stone discussing the shipping business and Schind adding an occasional comment.

Finally, as they moved to a second cup of coffee, the conversation turned to the point of their visit, and Ginsberg outlined the plan—acquire ships here, sail them to Europe, fill them with refugees, take them to Palestine. Schind described his role in the process—facilitate acquisition of the ships, recruit the crews, coordinate the logistics, get the ships on their way to Europe.

Stone looked over at Schind with a big smile. "I think this is a great idea. We should have done this a long time ago. I'm tired of waiting on British and American politicians to solve the situation our people in Europe face. And I'm sure our people in Europe are tired of waiting on them, too."

Schind, still wary of involving someone about whom he knew so little, listened closely and was pleased with Stone's reaction. But the question of secrecy was utmost on his mind. "One thing we need to make clear from the beginning. And this comes from David Ben-Gurion himself."

Stone had a questioning look. "What's that?"

"We have to keep this quiet," Schind said with emphasis. "The

British are already watching us. We don't want them to know the details of what we're doing."

"Sure," Stone nodded, apparently expecting to hear something different from Schind. "We can keep it quiet. I mean, we'll have to tell a few people in order to get them involved. Just like you told me about it to bring me in. But otherwise, we'll keep it from being a topic of general conversation."

"And I think we need a cover for this," Schind continued.

"A cover?"

"A story," Schind explained. "A front."

"Oh!" Stone exclaimed. "That part's easy." He threw his arms wide apart in a grand gesture toward himself. "I'm your cover."

That was an obvious answer, but using Stone as the cover story meant trusting him for the success of the mission and that was the crux of the problem for Schind—whether Stone was a man he could trust. He seemed all right so far, but he was also . . . brash which, in Schind's way of thinking, made him unpredictable but he couldn't say that without offending both Stone and Ginsberg. A comment like that would end the conversation right then, which wouldn't be good. Schind needed the kind of help these men could give, so instead of confronting the question of trust he simply raised an eyebrow and said, "*You* are our cover?"

"Yeah," Stone grinned. "Me."

"I was thinking of something more along the lines of a business cover. Perhaps even something we could make money at while moving the ships across the Atlantic."

Ginsberg looked intrigued. "What did you have in mind?"

"Well," Schind began, "since we must take the ships to Europe anyway to pick up passengers, I thought we could load them with tobacco products here and sell the cargo in Europe."

Ginsberg's countenance dropped. "That's not really as good as it sounds."

"Why not?"

"For one thing, we'd have to find a European . . . distributor." Ginsberg glanced at Stone with a knowing look. "That would make it really . . . cumbersome."

"If that's a problem, we could always sell it on the black market," Schind suggested.

Stone spoke up. "What Morris is trying to say is, it would be against the law. We can't touch it. Importing tobacco to Europe is illegal. What you're talking about, just buying ships here and sailing them over there, there's nothing wrong with that. It's perfectly legal. If we start trying to unload tobacco, we'll get caught and that would be very bad." He leaned back in his chair. "I'm not interested in being involved in that."

Schind didn't want to lose Stone's support, but his concern about trusting Stone wouldn't go away. "Well," he insisted, "we need some kind of cover story."

"Like I told you," Stone grinned playfully. "I'm your cover."

"How so?"

"This is what I do every day. This sort of thing you're trying to do is how I make my living." Stone leaned forward again and rested his elbows on his knees. "The FBI agents know me. Half the people in Washington know me. If I buy a ship and someone reports it to a government agency, the feds will say, 'That's just Dewey Stone doing what Dewey does,' and they won't think any more about it." He gestured with his hands. "You can't create a fake cover better than that. Nothing you could dream up would be anywhere near as good as the truth. You don't want the British to find out. That's understandable and I agree, but they aren't going to be a problem over here."

"Why not?"

"Because this is the United States," Stone replied. "They'd have to get the FBI involved to help them and as long as we don't give the FBI a reason, they won't be able to touch us."

"They won't try to stop us?"

"In America, this kind of thing—buying ships, selling ships, sailing them to Europe—that kind of thing happens every day." Stone gestured between himself and Ginsberg. “If we’re involved, no one will pay any attention to us.”

“But the British will pay attention,” Schind argued, “and anything that’s done publicly will be noticed by them. When they see what we’re doing, they’ll figure out our real goal—bringing large numbers of people to Palestine. And once they know that’s our objective, they’ll do everything in their power to frustrate and oppose us.”

“Then we conduct our business in a way that won’t be quite so obvious,” Stone grinned.

“How do we do that?”

“We buy ships through separate corporations,” Stone explained. “We register the ships in a foreign country for convenience, sail under a foreign flag. We can own the ships outright and we can sail them without anyone ever really finding out exactly who did what.”

Schind looked skeptical. “I have heard of this, but are you sure it will actually work? We are talking about human lives. Not a theoretical exercise. We want to actually do this, but we don’t want anyone to readily connect this activity with Haganah in Palestine.” As the words rolled off his tongue he realized it was the first time he’d ever admitted, tacitly or otherwise, that this operation had some connection to Haganah.

“They won’t connect it,” Stone assured. “They’ll connect the companies to the names we list on the formation documents and that is as far as the trail will take them. You can’t hide the information completely, no matter how many cover stories you invent. But we can make it difficult for them to figure out exactly what we’re doing with the individual ships. We can keep them at least a step behind us.”

“So how does this work?” Schind wanted to pin them down to specifics. “In terms of details, how would we set this up? What country would we use for the ships?”

“Here’s what we do.” Stone seemed to relish delving into the details. “We’ll form a corporation here, in the United States. Strictly legal. Strictly in compliance with the law. That corporation will, in turn, form a Panamanian corporation for each ship. Also absolutely legal.”

"Panama?"

"Easiest country to deal with," Ginsberg offered. "Very few regulations for ships using their ports."

Stone continued. "The individual Panamanian corporations will own the ships. The ships will be listed on the Panamanian registry with the Panamanian corporation as owner. And they'll fly a Panamanian flag. Each of those separate corporations will have its own officers. They'll be nothing more than names on the papers, but the British will have a hard time figuring that out." Stone pointed at Schind for emphasis. "You'll control the ships through the parent corporation."

"And you can do all of this legally?"

"Do it all the time to limit the financial risk of ship ownership. And if it makes you feel better," Stone added, "we can create signed leases for the ships leasing them to Corocito Fruit Company in New Orleans."

All those words seemed to buzz around Schind's head like flies and he struggled to make sense of it. "You're sure we can do that?"

"Yeah, sure," Stone said confidently. "I know Samuel Zemurray. He's president of the company. I lease ships to him all the time. He'll be glad to help out with the leases."

"No," Schind corrected. "I mean about the corporations. We can form them that easily?"

"Just need a lawyer and some money," Ginsberg suggested.

"And all of it will be completely aboveboard," Stone added. "Nothing to lie about. Nothing illegal."

"We have to be aboveboard," Ginsberg noted. "That's the only way to do this. We can dodge the British, but if we violate US law, the FBI will shut us down."

"Even though it's legal," Schind reiterated, "we still have to keep it quiet."

"We *will* keep it quiet," Stone said, apparently exasperated with the continual emphasis on secrecy. He looked over at Ginsberg. "Do you know a lawyer in New York we can use?"

"Yes," Ginsberg replied with a nod. "He's already helping us on other things."

"But can we trust him to keep quiet?" Schind asked.

Stone gave a frustrated sigh but before he could say more, Ginsberg spoke up. "Communication with an attorney is a confidential matter," he calmly explained. "And we don't have to tell him everything. We can just tell him we're shipping cargo across the Atlantic to Western Europe and Mediterranean ports. Or leasing the ships to a company in New Orleans. Whichever we decide. He doesn't have to know the details of our business. But discretion will not be a problem for this man."

Schind continued, "We have to keep it quiet among ourselves and avoid discussing this with our wives, girlfriends, family members, people like that."

Stone had a tight, thin smile. "I'm not talking."

"Me either," Ginsberg chuckled.

Stone pointed to Schind. "So, if you don't talk, no one will know." Schind didn't like the tone of that comment or the look in Stone's eyes, but before he could say anything Stone reached over and patted him on the shoulder. "Don't worry. We'll keep it quiet and we'll keep it legitimate. This will work out great. You'll see. It's going to be great."

"Well then," Schind said, resigned to moving forward, "where do we get the ships?"

"Surplus ships are everywhere," Stone explained. "Every port on the East Coast is full of them. All along the Gulf as far as Corpus Christi, too. Several government departments are offering them for sale. We need to find a list and see exactly what they have."

"I read an article the other day," Ginsberg said, "about Canada reducing the size of its navy."

Stone's eyes brightened. "That's right," he said, snapping his fingers. "I have a contact in Canada who tells me they are unloading over half their fleet and selling the ships even cheaper than the U.S."

Schind found the mention of Canada troubling. "Canada," he reminded them, "is part of the United Kingdom."

"But they have fewer regulations," Ginsberg replied.

"Okay," Stone said to Ginsberg in a tone that noted a shift from talk to action. "You get the lawyer started on creating the corporations. I'll take the lead on finding the ships."

Ginsberg nodded. "Do you want to be president of the company?"

"Fine with me," Stone agreed. "Just be careful and make sure everything is legitimate."

"The part about leasing the ships to a fruit company wouldn't be," Schind noted.

Stone grinned. "Yeah, that's right, but we'll fudge a little on that part if we have to."

They talked awhile longer and then, as they prepared to leave, Ginsberg asked Stone about a taxi. Stone crossed the room to a telephone to make the call. While they took care of that, Schind moved to the front window and scanned the street to the left and right, checking to see if anyone was out there who might be watching them. A moment later, Stone appeared at his side. "See anything interesting?"

Schind, concerned about how he might be perceived if he told Stone what he was really thinking, kept his concern to himself and said simply, "Just looking at the neighborhood."

Ginsberg joined them at the window. "He's worried that we were being followed."

Stone looked over at Schind. "Here? To the house?"

"Yeah," Schind sighed. "They were at the airport when I arrived the other day. They followed us from the hotel this morning."

Stone turned to look out the window. "See anyone now?"

Schind nodded to the left toward a car parked up the street. "Is that one supposed to be there?"

"I don't know," Stone shrugged. "Never seen it before. But that reminds me." He looked past Schind to Ginsberg. "I'm pretty sure someone has a tap on my phone. It doesn't bother me for normal business, but for this we should probably communicate through my sister."

Schind felt relieved—at least he wasn't the only one worried about being watched—but he was also worried about communicating through yet one more person he didn't know. He glanced over at Stone. "Through your sister?"

"Yeah," Stone replied. "It's okay. She lives a few blocks behind us." He gestured over his shoulder. "We go back and forth by an alley and a side street. No one can see us." He gave Schind a reassuring smile. "It's okay. She wouldn't rat me out. I wouldn't rat on her." He held up his right hand with two fingers crossed. "We're close like that." Then he looked back at Ginsberg. "So if you call me, use her number. Here," he said, turning away from the window. "I'll write it down for you." He stepped over to an end table where he found a little notebook and scribbled down the phone number. Then he ripped out the page and gave it to Ginsberg. "Just call her at this number. Tell her you need to talk to me. She'll send someone over. I'll call you back from her house. We do it all the time."

In a few minutes the taxi arrived. Ginsberg and Schind said goodbye in the living room and walked out to the car. When they were seated, Schind leaned over and said to the driver, "Turn around and take us in the opposite direction."

The driver looked at Schind like he was crazy. "They said you wanted to go to the airport."

"We do."

The driver pointed toward the windshield. "The airport is this way."

"Just do what I'm saying," Schind instructed. "Turn around and go the opposite direction."

Ginsberg spoke up. "Do what he says. I'll give you an extra five. Just make the block behind us."

"Okay." The driver gestured in frustration with both hands. "You pay, I drive." He put the car in gear and turned it hard right from the curb. "But the airport is that way," he pointed over his shoulder.

Schind glanced out the rear window and saw the car behind them move from the curb to follow. As the taxi made the next corner, the other car did, too. "They're coming," he said.

The driver pressed the gas pedal and the car accelerated. At the next street he turned right again and still the car was behind them. Ginsberg glanced out the rear window to check, then said to the driver, "Pull over and wait."

"Here?"

"Yes," Ginsberg insisted. "Pull over here."

The driver brought the car to a stop at the curb and caught Ginsberg's eye in the mirror. "You want out here?"

Ginsberg did not respond but watched out the window as the car that had been behind them now drove past their position. When it was gone, he leaned back in the seat and said, "Now take us to the airport."

"I'm trying," the driver protested as he moved his foot from the brake. "But you guys keep telling me what to do."

Ginsberg ignored the driver's comment and glanced over at Schind. "You were right."

"About what?"

"The car this morning. They were following us. And so were those guys just now."

Schind nodded. "We have to be very careful."

Half an hour later, they reached the airport and boarded the return flight to New York without further incident. Schind wanted to talk but Ginsberg seemed remote and uninterested. He slept most of the way back, leaving Schind alone with his thoughts.

It was late when they landed at LaGuardia. Ginsberg roused from sleep as the plane unloaded, then they walked together through the airport and out to the car. As they drove toward Manhattan, Schind finally asked, "What do we do about crews?"

Ginsberg moved one hand from the steering wheel, ran it into the pocket of his jacket, and brought out a business card, handing it to Schind. "Here, see this man. He might be able to help." The card was for William Ash and listed his address as 24 Water Street. "The office is in lower Manhattan." Ginsberg looked over at Schind. "You're staying with Joe, but do they have someone showing you around?"

"Joe's taking care of me," Schind said with a smile. "Buxenbaum."

"Joe is a good man," Ginsberg continued. "You need to get to know him. He'll be very useful for what we're trying to do. Show that card to him. He knows how to get you to Ash. And," Ginsberg added, "you're going to need an office. Ask Joe about that, too."

"An office?" Schind looked perplexed. "Can't we just use the apartment?"

Ginsberg shook his head. "You can't do business like this out of an apartment in the Village."

"Why not?"

"Talk to Weizmann. You need an office."

Schind turned away and glanced out the window. "I'll think about it."

"No. You don't understand." The expression on Ginsberg's face left little doubt how serious he was. "In order to buy ships without someone knowing the identity of the person who's really behind it, we'll need to set up those corporations we were talking about with Dewey today. To do that we need an address. Not Joe Buxenbaum's apartment address. They find that address and connect it to you, it takes them straight to Weizmann and the Agency. You need an office. It'll be necessary when you start raising the money to pay for this, too."

Schind was taken aback. *Raising the money? I thought Stone was taking care of it.* This time he said what he was thinking. "I thought Stone said he was buying the ships."

"He'll buy them," Ginsberg explained, "but he's not paying for them."

"I don't understand the difference."

"He'll handle the money as our agent, but we'll have to provide the money."

"It sounded simpler when we talked about it before. This sounds complicated."

"That's the point. Create multiple layers of corporations so it'll be difficult for anyone to figure out who really owns the ships and what we're really doing with them. Raise the money to cover the expenses from multiple sources and deposit it in the company's bank account. Keep all of it totally separate from Weizmann and the Agency. That way, any trail ends with you. No further. By the time anyone figures it all out, we'll be on to the next one. It's not illegal, just complex. And it involves a lot of paper. You have to keep all that paper straight and to do that, you need an office. See Weizmann."

"You sound aggravated. And your mood changed while we were at the house. What happened?"

Ginsberg sighed. "I didn't like the way you kept carping about secrecy."

"We have to keep this as quiet as possible."

"I know. But when you talk about it all the time, it sounds like you don't trust us."

"Well . . . that's a problem for me."

"To trust me? To trust Dewey?"

"To trust anyone."

"Well, you'll have to trust someone. You can't do this on your own."

"I know. And it's not so much about you or Stone as it is about me and the way we do things back home. We talk about secrecy a lot there, too, but we do it more as a reminder and not as an accusation. I don't doubt your integrity." But inside he still had doubts about how this would all work out.

CHAPTER 7

THE VOLUNTEERS

When Schind and Ginsberg left the apartment building for the airport that morning, Dukes and Mitchell, both MI6 agents, were in the car following them. They allowed Ginsberg and Schind to break away when they made the sharp turn just a few blocks from the hotel, then Dukes guessed the airport was their destination and took an alternate route. He and Mitchell arrived at LaGuardia as Schind and Ginsberg came from the car and entered the terminal.

Determining which flight Schind and Ginsberg took required only simple observation and they called Robinson from a pay phone near the gate as the two men boarded. By then it was too late to purchase tickets and board the same airplane. And besides, doing that posed a serious risk that Schind would recognize them—already he'd seemed to notice their presence. Robinson ordered Dukes and Mitchell to take the next flight to Boston and told them to call him when they arrived.

While they were en route, Robinson turned to the issue of why Ginsberg and Schind were traveling to Boston and how he could find an answer. It was a weekday. Ginsberg's office was surely open for business. He operated a far-flung enterprise with ships sailing every day to and from any number of ports. Surely, he wouldn't leave the city without providing his office with a phone number where he could be reached. "Someone has a phone number for him," Robinson said aloud.

A check of his files told him the name of Ginsberg's company—American Foreign Steamship. The phone book in the apartment gave him the telephone number. Armed with that information he placed a call to Ginsberg's office and asked for him by name. After a concerted effort, a secretary relented and gave him a telephone number where Ginsberg could be reached. "But," she cautioned, "he won't be at the number for at least another hour." Robinson thanked her profusely and then dialed the operator. Moments later, he had a name and address to match the number—Dewey Stone, Arlington Street, Brockton, Massachusetts.

About an hour later, the telephone in the apartment rang. Robinson answered it and heard Dukes say, "We're here. What next?"

"They're going to the home of Dewey Stone," Robinson replied. "He lives on Arlington Street in the town of Brockton. It's south of where you are. Get a map. Find the location. Catch up with them before they leave. I want to know who joins them at that address."

With Dukes and Mitchell in Boston following Schind and Ginsberg, Robinson sent Loring and Pike in search of Joe Buxenbaum. "Find him and figure out why he didn't go to Boston with Schind and Ginsberg."

When they were gone, Robinson took Ward and Oldfield to the library. "I want to know as much as possible about Dewey Stone and his business," Robinson explained, "but you only have a few hours to collect it. So work fast, but be thorough." And while they did that, he would search for information about Ginsberg.

Later that afternoon, Robinson returned to the apartment on East Twenty-Third Street and when Dukes and Mitchell came back from Boston, he gathered all six agents there to discuss the day's events and what they knew.

"Okay," Robinson began, "let's recap what we have so far. Schind arrived at the airport from Palestine. He was met there by Joe Buxenbaum and he's been staying at Buxenbaum's apartment since then. Not long after arriving, we followed him to the offices of the Jewish Agency for Palestine, where he met with Weizmann and later with Morris Ginsberg. Now, today, Schind traveled with Ginsberg to Boston. So," he turned to Dukes, "what happened in Boston?"

"We located Schind and Ginsberg at the home of Dewey Stone. He lives on Arlington Street in Brockton, just like you said."

"Anyone else present with them?"

"Only Stone's wife."

"They weren't joined by anyone else?"

"No."

Mitchell spoke up. "They spotted us as they were leaving the house. Tried to give us the slip again. We let them think they did."

"Which one was driving?"

"They called a taxi," Mitchell said. "We figured they were going to the airport so we headed in that direction. Caught up with them in traffic. They never knew we were there. Dukes jumped out at the terminal and got in their cab as it was leaving." Mitchell looked over at Dukes. "You didn't find anything, did you?"

"No," Dukes replied, shaking his head. "It was clean."

"Okay," Robinson said, "while you two were up there, Ward and Oldfield spent the day at the library searching for information about Stone." He turned in Oldfield's direction. "What did you find out?"

"Stone has a hand in a number of businesses," Oldfield began. "Logansport Rubber Company is the largest and most lucrative. It began as a raincoat manufacturer, but after Stone took over the company, it developed and introduced a line of rubber-soled basketball shoes. Nathan Moats works with them."

Robinson looked puzzled. "Nathan Moats? Who is he?"

"An American basketball legend," Oldfield answered.

"But never really played for anyone," Ward added. "At least, not professionally. Made most of his reputation conducting basketball clinics and selling basketball shoes."

Oldfield continued. "Stone and his family control Logansport and

several other businesses. Among those businesses are a couple of syndicates that own ships. Those ships are then leased to various companies that use them in the international shipping business. Their biggest customer is Corocito Fruit in New Orleans. Corocito leases several ships from him, and Stone's name is mentioned numerous times in association with that company. The ship ownership aspect seems to be an investment vehicle. A way to use profits from Logansport."

"Any siblings?"

"He has a brother, Harry."

"What does he do?"

"He's a judge."

"What kind of judge?"

"Probate," Oldfield responded. "Mostly administers estates and hears real estate disputes."

"Oh," Robinson said in a tone that reflected a lesser opinion of the position.

"Not as weak as it might seem," Ward offered. "Especially in a city the size of Boston. I'm sure he knows everyone. And in addition to being a judge, he held seats on a number of corporate boards before taking the bench."

"Yeah," Oldfield agreed. "Between them, the Stone brothers seem to have considerable influence, and not merely in Boston but across the country and even beyond."

"Okay," Robinson said. "Let's review what we've seen so far. We have Schind, an officer with Haganah. Comes to the United States. He's being shown around town by Joe Buxenbaum, a man who served in the United States Navy during the war. He was honorably discharged with the rank of petty officer. Joined the Longshoremen's Association and now serves as a shop steward for one of the locals." Robinson glanced around the room to make sure everyone was listening. "After that, Schind met with Morris Ginsberg, the president of American Foreign Steamship. That gives us a Haganah officer, a longshoreman, and a shipping company executive. And today they went to see Dewey Stone, an influential—" He paused to glance around the room again. "Can we say influential?"

"Yes," Oldfield nodded. "And wealthy."

"Okay." Robinson picked up a note pad and jotted down what he'd said so far, then continued. "Today they met with Dewey Stone, a wealthy and influential Boston businessman who, among other things, manages several syndicates that invest in ocean-going ships."

"Haganah, shipping, ships, longshoreman," Dukes said, counting off the points with his fingertips.

Robinson nodded in agreement. "That confirms what London suspects."

"Which is?"

"That Schind is here to work toward significantly increasing the flow of illegal immigrants to Palestine."

Loring spoke up. "The Jews think they can just sail a ship to Palestine and unload it, unopposed?"

Robinson shook his head. "They aren't that ignorant. Especially not Schind. He knows what our navy is capable of. He's been in the midst of the smuggling effort. He's seen our navy in operation."

"If that's what they're doing," Loring suggested, "I think it would be a good idea to expand our effort and follow all four of these men. Stone in Boston. Ginsberg and Buxenbaum here. Along with Schind, whom we already have under surveillance. We need to find out where these men go, who they see, what they do with their day."

"I don't know how much we'd get from Buxenbaum," Ward said. "But it would be good to follow Stone. Find out what he does, who he sees. Look for a pattern that fits with Schind and Ginsberg's activity. He really is an influential guy. Used in the right way, he could accomplish what you say London thinks they mean to do. He could buy a ship and sail it anywhere he wants it to go."

"I don't know," Oldfield said with a skeptical tone. "From what I read, Stone is a smooth operator. I doubt we'd get much simply from observing his routine."

"And he's in Boston," Robinson added, though he liked the way his men seemed to be embracing the mission, finally. "That's a long way from our work here in New York."

"What about Ginsberg?" Dukes asked. "Could we at least add Ginsberg?"

"And Buxenbaum," another suggested. "They're all equally involved right now."

Robinson thought for a moment, then said, "We don't have enough men for three. Maybe we could cover two of them. That would mean two of you on the target twenty-four hours a day, with two of you floating between the teams to provide relief. But trying to follow all three—or four if we added Stone—with just the six of you would stretch us much too thin."

"Seven," Dukes said with a mischievous smile.

Robinson frowned. "Seven?"

"Six of us, plus you."

"Oh," Robinson said, as if that was the first time he realized he could participate with work in the field. "That's right. But I think we still would be better off limiting ourselves to just two. That would let us rotate in and out with the seven of us and no one would have to work longer than twelve hours without rest."

Loring spoke up. "So how do we divide them up?"

"Stick with the current schedule one more day," Robinson said. "I'll come up with a new plan and we'll get ourselves organized tomorrow night."

Ward objected. "Why not do it now?"

"I have someplace to go tomorrow," Robinson replied.

The men were right and Robinson knew it. To figure out what was really happening with Schind, they needed to cover at least the key players in New York. But following three—and perhaps more—would press their crew too far. They could do it, but there would be little room for error. And Robinson, even with his limited supervisory experience, knew that errors always happened. In order for this mission to succeed, he needed additional agents and to get those he had only one source. Geoffrey Reid, the MI6 supervisor who worked from the British Embassy in Washington, D.C.

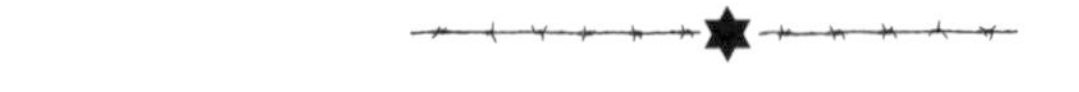

That evening, Robinson phoned Reid in Washington and arranged to meet him the following day. He took an early train from Penn Station the next morning and arrived in Washington just as the city was coming to life.

Reid, about ten years older than Robinson, was six feet tall but still with the lean athletic build of a soccer player, which he'd been during college. His light brown hair was almost blond and he wore it full on the sides but combed with a flip above his forehead in a boyish manner. Combined with hazel eyes that sometimes seemed blue, high cheekbones, and a square jaw, he was a strikingly handsome man.

From a slow beginning at the MI6 Portugal station at the beginning of the war, he rose steadily through the service's ranks. With subsequent postings to Turkey, Iran, Iraq, and Saudi Arabia, he spent most of the war in the Middle East. Intelligence generated by his section was instrumental in blunting German attempts to control the region, and for his help he was awarded an appointment to a supervisory role in London. He held that position only briefly when an opportunity developed at the British Embassy in Washington.

When Robinson arrived, he was ushered into Reid's office where, after a brief introduction, they sat at Reid's desk and talked. "I understand Peel assigned you to Danny Schind," Reid began.

"Yes," Robinson replied.

Reid cast his gaze to the desktop. "Interesting."

"Oh? How so?"

"He could have chosen any one of a dozen more experienced agents for the task, yet he chose you."

Robinson bristled at the comment but did his best to keep the reaction to himself. "I've been with the agency awhile, you know." There was a little more edge to his voice than he'd hoped but he felt compelled to defend himself. "I'm not a college kid fresh from a cloistered campus."

"I know," Reid nodded. "I've read your file. Splendid work in France."

"Thank you."

"I didn't mean you had *no* experience," Reid said somewhat apologetically. "I just noticed you have limited *supervisory* experience and this is an important case."

Robinson had thought of that issue the day Peel gave him the assignment, but he kept his questions to himself for fear that Peel, if he considered the matter further, might give the mission to someone else.

Robinson needed the opportunity. His career needed it. Otherwise, there was the very real possibility he'd be cast as one of *those* agents. The kind who rose quickly in the field but never went further. He thought of that as he considered what to say to Reid and in the end said the obvious. "There's always the possibility I was chosen for that very reason."

"Because of your . . . record?" Reid asked.

"Because if this thing falls apart, for whatever reason, Peel and everyone else has someone to blame. Someone with few personal ties to the agency and almost no tie to the monarchy."

Reid arched an eyebrow. "Keen observation."

"I try always to be aware of my place in life," Robinson added. "Though I try equally hard not to let that perception limit me."

"So," Reid said, changing the subject, "what brings you down here?"

"Peel said that if I needed assistance I should see you. We need more men."

"Sure," Reid agreed without even a single question. "Glad to supply them."

"All of them trained MI6 agents."

Reid looked at him with a knowing smile. "Got your first agents from the club?"

"The club?" A frown wrinkled Robinson's forehead. "What's the club?"

"That office Peel and his friends keep at Rockefeller Center. They call it the British Passport Control Office. We call it the club . . . those of us who know about it."

"Yes, well, they gave me the first men. Peel told me to see you for more."

"Right." Reid moved closer to the desk and rested his elbows on the desktop. "I don't mind helping you, but you should know—your perception of how this was laid out is spot on. Peel and his fellows in London are concerned about the Jews in Palestine, but they're even more worried about how the Americans react to our decision on Palestinian immigration. They fear that if we are seen as browbeating the Jews, the United States and the rest of the world will turn against us."

"From what I've seen," Robinson responded, "most of the people in the field think browbeating is just what the Jews need."

"That may be so," Reid acknowledged, "but Peel and his friends are worried about perception, not substance, and that cuts both ways. They want to keep tabs on what the Jews are up to, though they already have a pretty good idea of what that is, but if the wind of public opinion should change they want to be able to change with it. Even to denying whatever they've done on the matter previously. To give themselves that option, they needed to send someone to follow Schind and find out what the Jews really are doing, but they needed to use someone expendable."

"So I was right," Robinson said with a twisted smile. "I'm their expendable agent."

"Yes," Reid said slowly. "I'm sorry to say, but you are."

"They tied me to Passport Control so they could deny they knew anything about the operation?"

"So they could deny the mission and the office even existed. And they have all that arranged in a way that makes it very easy for them to do."

"Flush everyone at Rockefeller Center in the process?"

"That was the whole point of continuing that office after it was officially disbanded. So they would have an apparatus for clandestine service which they could eliminate if needed and leave no paper trail it ever existed." Reid's eyes darted away. "At least, that's their thinking on the matter." He looked over at Robinson and flashed a smile. "But cheer up. It could be worse."

"How so?"

"The office could be here in Washington," Reid quipped, "and then it would be *my* headache."

Robinson failed to see the humor in the situation. "You'll send the additional men?"

"How many do you need?"

"Eight."

"They'll be in New York tomorrow morning. You're staying in that apartment on East Twenty-Third Street?"

"Yes," Robinson said, consigned to the obvious—that Reid knew everything there was to know about him, his life, and his present situation. *Probably even knows my shoe size.*

When Robinson was gone, Reid phoned an assistant and asked her to locate Alec McKenna. An hour or so later, McKenna arrived at the office. Behind closed doors, Reid told him about Robinson's work in New York and how he'd been sent by Peel in London to follow Danny Schind. "They're now expanding that mission. He didn't tell me specifics, but I'm sure he wants to include Buxenbaum and Ginsberg in his surveillance program."

McKenna, an older field operative who never aspired to supervisory duty, had a wizened look. "We had a report about two of his men working up in Boston. They were sighted at the airport. Couple of men up there checked into it. Turns out they were following Dewey Stone."

"All the more reason for our concern."

"Think Robinson wants to cover Stone, too?"

"I'm not sure. I tried not to ask questions. I want him to think he has my confidence. If he's comfortable with me, perhaps he will disclose more information voluntarily. Much easier to keep tabs on him that way than by launching our own operation."

"Good idea," McKenna nodded. "Would be rather . . . cumbersome for us to have agents in New York watching him while he's watching Schind."

"So," Reid continued, moving the conversation forward, "he has asked for extra men and I have agreed to send them. Eight men will go up to New York and report to him in the morning. I want you to be one of those men."

"Okay," McKenna nodded. "Will I be there long?"

"You should plan on being there for the duration."

"I assume I can use the usual facility."

"Yes. Certainly."

"Any chance you could add Selwyn Butler to that list, too?"

"You enjoy working with Butler?"

"He's a good man. Experienced. Knows how to handle himself."

"Okay," Reid agreed. "I'll send Butler, too. When you get there, I want you to work for Robinson. Do whatever he tells you. Do a good job. Don't cause trouble. I'm not sending you up there to make this operation fail. I'm sending you to see that it succeeds."

"Right," McKenna nodded. "I understand."

"That said, this operation is working with some well-connected people. Robinson may not know that yet, but it's true nonetheless. Ginsberg has important ties all over the world. Stone, also. And both men are quite wealthy. So work for Robinson but make certain you report to me on his activities."

"Does Robinson know what he's doing?"

"He's never been in charge of anything quite like this before, but he's doing the right things. From what I can tell, he's following the evidence where it leads. As long as he follows that method and sticks to his task, everything will work out fine. But if it should fall apart, there could be serious consequences. Both for us personally and for the Crown. I want to know if that will happen before it happens."

McKenna nodded once more. "Will you tell Butler this same thing? That way, I won't have to keep what I'm doing for you a secret from him. Make it easier for both of us to do our job."

"Certainly," Reid agreed. "I'll tell Butler. The two of you can compare notes. Report to me separately or together, if you like. I don't have a preference. But make certain you keep me informed."

CHAPTER 8

THE VOLUNTEERS

The next day, Schind met with Weizmann and told him about Ginsberg's suggestion that they needed separate offices. He had no intention of telling Weizmann everything he was doing or of working the plan to acquire airplanes through Weizmann regardless of where he was located. But he thought he should pursue the matter in a friendly and cooperative manner, so he extended the courtesy of giving Weizmann an opportunity to be involved. Thankfully, Weizmann readily agreed.

"Ginsberg is right. You do need a separate office. And a separate bank account, too. If secrecy is a priority, you don't want any obvious association with the Jewish Agency. And to do that, you'll need to form your own organization."

Schind forced a weary sigh. "Okay," he said, feigning reluctance. "How do we find an office?"

"I'll get Fanny to help."

Schind knew he should recognize the name but he couldn't recall why and so he gave Weizmann a puzzled look. "Fanny?" he asked lamely.

"My secretary. You met her earlier. On your first day."

"Oh." Schind nodded. "Right." Fanny was the name of the woman seated just outside Weizmann's door. He hadn't paid attention to her that day, even when Buxenbaum introduced her, and had very little contact with her since.

"Her husband owns several buildings and is knowledgeable of New York real estate," Weizmann explained.

"Good," Schind said. "But how will we pay for it?"

"I'll find some donors who'll get you enough cash to get you started, but you'll need to get started raising money, too."

The dreaded subject, Schind thought. He was fast losing hope of putting it off any longer. "I'll need some help with that," Schind confessed with uncharacteristic candor. "I don't know who to contact or how to ask."

"You can begin with the Jewish Society of America. Rabbi Silver is the man to see. I'll introduce you." Schind didn't know Silver and was planning to see Henry Nadelson, as Ben-Gurion suggested, but he kept quiet about all that and let Weizmann talk. At the same time, he wondered why Weizmann and Ben-Gurion recommended different people from within the same organization. "Ginsberg will set you up with a lawyer to create whatever organization you need," Weizmann said. "He knows the lawyers much better than I. You call Ginsberg and talk to him about that. I'll call Rabbi Silver and get you started with the Society."

Schind talked to Ginsberg about finding a lawyer and he agreed to make the first contact. Then Schind asked Buxenbaum about William Ash. "He's a good guy," Buxenbaum replied. "He's a ship's captain but he works mostly for ship owners supplying crews. Why do you ask?"

"Ginsberg suggested I might need to talk to him."

"You looking to take a job as a sailor?"

"Hardly."

"Well, if you're looking for sailors, he's the man to see. I can take you there and introduce you."

"Good," Schind replied. "Can we go today?"

Buxenbaum checked his watch and smiled. "Yeah, Bill ought to be at his office now."

Ginsberg had phoned several days earlier to tell Ash that Schind might drop by for a visit, so he wasn't surprised when Schind and Buxenbaum arrived without an appointment. They gathered around his desk and after introductions were complete Buxenbaum excused himself and went to the outer office to wait while the two men talked alone.

Ash, a longtime sailor and sea captain, was older with thick gray hair and a craggy face accented by deep lines and a weathered look. He had a gruff voice and brusque demeanor but his eyes were kind and his smile assuring. Schind liked him immediately yet remained cautious about expanding the operation's inner circle.

"I understand from Morris that you are interested in acquiring ships and the crews to sail them," Ash began.

"Yes, that's the plan. Buy ships and locate a crew."

Ash nodded politely. "Is this a Haganah operation?"

Hearing that name caught Schind off guard. It seemed so out of place in America. He hadn't expected the name to be well-known. "You know about Haganah?"

"Yes," Ash replied. "I know about it."

"How so?"

"You kidding?" Ash grinned. "Everybody knows about Haganah. Reuven Shiloah's been here for months already. I saw him last week. And we read articles about Haganah in the newspapers almost every morning. Most of us have friends who are either in Palestine or on their way." He looked over at Schind and asked again, "So, is this a Haganah operation?"

In the adjustment to life in America, finding Ginsberg, and the arrangement with Stone, Schind had forgotten about Reuven Shiloah. As head of Shai, the intelligence arm of Haganah, Shiloah would be the perfect person to know if Ash was playing this straight or not. Far more reliable regarding who he could trust than the word of Ginsberg or Stone. But still, Schind could only give Ash a pleasant smile. "How do you know Reuven?"

"We met several years ago when he was trying to run guns out of Italy. After the Great War—before the most recent one that came after the one that was supposed to have ended it all."

"A vicious cycle, isn't it?"

"My wife tells me all the time I talk in circles."

"War's not easy to talk about."

Ash talked past the comment. "Reuven had a bunch of rifles he'd picked up from the French. Got them as far as Naples but couldn't find anyone willing to take them to Haifa. Everybody was afraid of the British. So, I told him I'd give it a try. We loaded those rifles beneath pallets of sardines. Inspectors didn't dig very deep into the hold. He and I've been friends ever since."

Schind felt ashamed for doubting Ash's integrity. He'd heard that same story from Reuven many times but he'd forgotten it until just then. He chuckled and said, "Here's what we want to do." Then he outlined the plan for acquiring ships in the United States, sailing them to Europe, and rescuing Jewish refugees who were trapped in the displaced persons camps.

"What do you need from me?" Ash asked, apparently ready to join the effort.

"Captains and crews," Schind responded.

"Crews?" Ash seemed surprised. "You have more than one ship in mind?"

"We hope to send a steady stream of them."

"But you don't have any right now."

"Not yet. But we're getting them."

"Isn't this illegal?"

"Owning the ships?"

"No, taking refugees to Palestine."

"There's no law against taking them."

"But the British won't let them in."

"The British have ridiculously low quotas for Jews entering Palestine," Schind elaborated.

"So, when they get there, the ships will be stopped."

"Probably."

"And the cargo seized."

"Yes."

"And the ships will be seized, too."

"Yes."

"What about the crews?"

"What about them?" Schind countered.

"Do you plan to let them stay in the detention camps, too?"

"We'll have a way to get the crews off the ships."

Ash looked skeptical. "Really? And what is that plan?"

"Are you in or not?"

"Yeah," Ash sighed. "I'm in. What are you paying?"

"We might arrange some walking-around money." Schind said it with a straight face.

"Walking-around money?" Ash howled with laughter. "You want to sail these ships with volunteer crews?"

"Yes."

Ash slowly shook his head at the irony of the idea. "Does Buxenbaum know about this?"

"No. I haven't told him yet. Why?"

"Because we Jewish sailors are few and far between and he knows at least as many as I do."

"We don't care if the crews are Jewish or not."

"I can appreciate that," Ash acknowledged, "but you're looking for a crew that won't mind getting arrested, won't mind spending weeks or months or longer in a detention facility, won't mind being roughed up by the British, and won't mind doing it for free."

"We don't plan on getting roughed up."

Ash chuckled. "It'll get rough whether you intend for it to or not and you have to tell the crews that, upfront, when they sign on."

Schind had other ideas about that topic. "You think it's wise to tell them upfront?"

"I think it's the only way." Ash's face turned suddenly serious. "You have to play this straight with the men. I won't help if you don't tell them."

Schind thought that was a bad idea but he needed Ash's help, so he said, "Okay. We'll tell them upfront. But how many crewmen are going to sign on when they learn the real conditions?"

"Not very many," Ash supposed. "I know some guys who would do it just for the adventure, but I don't know enough to fill a complete crew. That's why I think you should make a major effort to find as many Jewish sailors as possible. They would be the most likely to say yes. And Joe Buxenbaum is the man you need to recruit them. Especially the young ones. I can get you captains and other key men. He can get you the rest. What are you doing about training?"

Again, Schind was caught off guard. He assumed experienced sailors would know what to do and hadn't thought of the need for training. "I'm not sure about that. What do you think?"

"Well, we can't send them off to sea without training."

"Any ideas on who could take charge of that?"

"Maybe," Ash replied. "I know a guy. Naval Academy graduate. Served during the war. Not sure how much command experience he has but he's very well trained."

"What's his name?"

"Paul Shulman."

"Is he a good man?" Once again Schind thought of Reuven Shiloah. If he'd remembered Reuven was in the United States, and if he'd contacted him first, he wouldn't have to worry about background investigations and security checks. Reuven would take care of that. But he hadn't and he didn't, so he had to go with his own impression and was confident now that Ash was on their side, so he added quickly, "I mean, do you trust him?"

"Yes," Ash nodded. "I trust him. And if you're asking does he support David Ben-Gurion's idea of a Jewish state, I think so. He says his mother and Ben-Gurion's wife are friends. But if that's important for you guys, you'd have to ask Shulman himself."

"Okay, give me his information and I'll contact him."

"Let me contact him," Ash suggested. "I'll set up a meeting here and we can talk to him together." And Schind didn't mind that at all.

From Ash's office, Schind and Buxenbaum took a taxi back to the Jewish Agency's office. Schind wanted to follow up with Weizmann about locating office space. When he arrived, Weizmann was out but Fanny Barnett was there and told him she had located a place that might work as an office.

"Great," Schind said. "Where is it?"

"It's on East Sixtieth Street. My husband owns the building. I think you'll like it."

They took a taxi to the address and as the car came to a stop at the curb, Schind was the first one out. He glanced up at the building and saw the name along the end of the canopy at the front door. "Hotel Fourteen," he said aloud.

"It's the address," Fanny explained as she stepped out of the cab. "Fourteen East Sixtieth Street."

"It's an apartment building?"

"An apartment hotel," she corrected. "It caters mostly to wealthy widows and a few celebrities."

A nightclub called the Copacabana was located next door. Schind didn't like it and as he leaned back for a look to the top of the building, he realized the club was part of it. "I'm not sure about that nightclub."

"Why not?"

"What kind of people does it attract?"

"All kinds. The place is packed almost every night."

"That's what I mean. What kind of people go there and how much noise do they make? I don't want the police coming around all the time, asking a lot of questions."

Fanny rolled her eyes and said in a defensive tone, “It’s not that kind of place.”

“I think it’s perfect,” Buxenbaum offered in an upbeat voice. “Lots of people in and out of here at all times of the day and night. Many of them big-name celebrities.” While they talked, Frank Sinatra came from the hotel and tipped his hat to Fanny as he passed by. “See,” Buxenbaum grinned and pointed. “That’s what I’m talking about. People will be watching them, not us. We can come and go as we please and no one will ever notice us.”

“Yeah, I see what you mean.” Schind smiled at Fanny. “Let’s have a look.”

Fanny led the way to the elevator and they rode upstairs. When the doors opened, she guided them down the hall and into the room, which wasn’t really a room at all but a suite with a bedroom, bathroom, sitting area, and kitchenette. “You could work from here and live here,” she suggested. “That would get you out of Joe’s apartment and give you plenty of space.”

Schind was pleasantly surprised and liked the room immensely, but money was a big concern. “How much will this cost?”

“You’ll have to pay for what you eat,” Fanny said, “but the room is free if you want it.”

Schind’s eyes opened wide. “Free?”

“My husband owns the building,” she explained with a playful shrug. “I told him it was for a good cause.”

CHAPTER 9

THE VOLUNTEERS

A little before noon the next day, Palmer Collins was in his office at the Chrysler Building when an assistant handed him a note. "This was left for you up front with the receptionist." He thanked her, glanced at the message, and saw it was from Rev. Thornton. "Bergman's in an hour," it read.

Collins checked his watch. Time had passed since the message arrived. He had half an hour to get there and two more things to finish on his desk before he could leave. He stuffed the note in his pocket and got busy.

Twenty minutes later, Collins left the office and walked up the street to Bergman's, a restaurant two blocks away. Rev. Thornton was already seated at a booth when he arrived.

Thornton, a heavyset man of sixty, had curly gray hair, brooding eyes, and thick jowls. Intellectually curious yet deeply committed to the gospel, he would have long since been elected bishop but for his insistence on maintaining a strong evangelistic emphasis at each of the churches he served. That effort, seen by many as far too zealous for the modern professional minister, turned the upper echelons of the denomination against him. More recently, his attempts to push the congregation at St. Mark's Church toward the wider social implications of the New Testament message—care for the poor, civil rights advocacy, and support for justice among Jews in Palestine—got him branded as a liberal by many of the congregation's traditional denominationalists who wanted only the gospel and nothing more. Still, Thornton seemed not to mind that he was vilified by church members from both extremes and took it as the cost of his calling, a cost he gladly bore.

Collins took a seat across from him but before he could speak Thornton said, "I talked with Sheldon Glaser today, after morning prayers." He gave Collins a disapproving look. "You weren't there, by the way."

"Yeah, I know. I've been . . . busy."

"Never too busy to pray, I hope."

Collins ignored the comment. "What did Glaser have to say?"

"He said things have changed for him now. I'm not sure what that means. His usual schedule seems to have been realigned. Haven't seen him at church quite so much as before." Thornton took an envelope from the pocket of his jacket and slid it across the table toward Collins. "He left this for you."

Collins glanced at the envelope, then at Thornton. "What is it?"

"I have no idea. I didn't read it."

Collins looked once more at the envelope. "The flap isn't sealed."

"I know. I could have read it, but I prefer not to know too much. I'm sure the people you deal with will know what it means." Thornton's eyes darted to a menu that lay nearby. "Let's order lunch. I'm hungry."

Collins took the envelope from the table, tucked it inside his pocket, and picked up a menu for himself.

An hour later, back at his office and alone at his desk, Collins took the envelope from his pocket and glanced again at the back. Unlike Thornton, Collins preferred to know as much as possible about the matters he handled. With the envelope delivered unsealed, he had had little hesitancy in opening it and quickly reached inside for the contents.

The envelope, he found, held a three-page memo that was written by an analyst at the British foreign ministry and addressed to Herbert Butler, the deputy foreign secretary. The document outlined a proposed timetable for withdrawal of all British forces from Palestine. While the document stressed that no decision had yet been made to implement a withdrawal, it gave a proposed schedule that might be used should the government decide to terminate its obligations under the UN mandate.

The memo included potential dates and times for each stage of the operation.

Collins was startled, not that the memo included a proposed incremental removal with specific dates, places, times, and units, but that officials within the upper levels of the British government were now discussing among themselves the very real possibility that England would unilaterally end its participation in the UN mandatory administration of Palestine—a decision that would plunge the region into chaos.

After reading the memo once more, Collins reached for the phone and called Ginsberg's office, only to learn that Ginsberg was out for the day. A check with the butler at the apartment told him Ginsberg would return that evening. Collins thought about trying one more location, a club on Fifty-Third Street where Ginsberg sometimes met privately with clients, but doing that would require a trip from the office, and a check of his watch told him there wasn't time for that before his next appointment. Locating Ginsberg would have to wait until that evening. Olivia wouldn't like it—he'd be late getting home again—but there was no other choice.

Shortly after five, Collins left the office and rode to Ginsberg's apartment. Ginsberg had just returned and was caught off guard by Collins' sudden, unscheduled appearance but nevertheless met with him in the study. When they were alone and the door was closed, Collins took out the envelope he'd received from Rev. Thornton. "This came to me at lunch," he said as he handed it to Ginsberg. "I tried to find you earlier, but you were away from the office."

Ginsberg opened the envelope and quickly scanned the memo. The contents didn't seem to surprise him. "I'd been wondering when the British might do this," he commented as he glanced over the document again.

"Looks like the foreign ministry is serious about withdrawal," Collins opined.

"Yes." Ginsberg pointed to the names in the heading of the

document's first page. "This was sent from an analyst to an undersecretary. From a staff member to an executive. This isn't the sort of thing an analyst would create on his own and offer unsolicited to his superior—especially not with the way the British run their government. Someone requested a specific timetable." He pointed again to the document. "My guess is, the request came from either the undersecretary to whom this is addressed or the foreign secretary himself."

"Well," Collins noted, "it doesn't seem as though they've actually set a schedule yet. Merely discussed the possibility of setting one."

"But someone asked for this information," Ginsberg stressed, gesturing with the document in hand. "Which means they're already discussing it in detail at the deputy level. And if they're talking about it at that level, the discussion probably goes all the way to Bevin himself."

Collins pointed to the document. "You know what to do with that?"

"Of course." Ginsberg returned the memo to the envelope and placed it in a leather satchel that sat on the floor near his desk. "Same as I've done with the other information you've sent me. I'll see that it gets to the right people." He snapped the satchel closed and looked over at Collins. "I meant to call you today to talk to you about something else. Do you have time to discuss it now?"

"Certainly."

"It's late," Ginsberg insisted. "Are you sure you have time for it tonight?"

"Yes." Collins took a seat near Ginsberg's desk. "What did you want?"

"I want to form a new corporation."

"If this has something to do with your existing company, American Foreign, we might need to schedule a time at the office when we can include Mr. Fortas. He has a much longer history with your business than I do, and we should also think about your entire estate plan, to make sure—"

"This has nothing to do with any of that," Ginsberg said, cutting him off. "This is something completely different. A new venture."

Collins was surprised by the sense of urgency. "Okay, what is it you're trying to do?"

Ginsberg took a seat back behind the desk and lowered his voice. "What I am about to tell you must be held in the strictest of confidence."

Collins had a wary look. "What are you talking about?"

"As you are aware, Jews in Europe face a serious problem."

"You mean, the ones being kept in the refugee camps?"

"Yes," Ginsberg nodded. "They are living in miserable conditions and a few of us have decided to do something about that."

Collins looked concerned. "What are you going to do?"

"We are going to buy surplus ships and sail them across the Atlantic where we intend to load the ships with European refugees and take them to Palestine."

A smile broke over Collins' face. "You're not kidding, are you?"

Ginsberg had a solemn expression. "I have never been more serious in my life."

They sat in silence for a moment, each one smiling at the other with a satisfied look, then Collins said, "How may I help you?"

"We plan to register the ships in Panama and sail them under the Panamanian flag, but we want to create a certain level of . . . obscurity about the matter."

"Are you suggesting this might be illegal? Because I don't think it is," Collins added quickly. "At least not in the U.S."

"No." Ginsberg shook his head. "We're not concerned about the legality of it. But British intelligence services are constantly on the lookout for activities that might touch their interests. Some of us who are involved in this effort are quite well-known to them and if they see our names on public documents, they might begin to look more closely at what we are doing. We don't want that. We want to be perfectly legal, but we don't want to flaunt it."

"I understand," Collins acknowledged with a nod. "So you want a separate corporation for each ship."

"Yes. We want separate *Panamanian* corporations for each ship, but we want to control those corporations through a US parent company."

"Then we should form a US corporation," Collins outlined, "and have that corporation act as the incorporator of the others."

"If that's what it takes."

"That's the way to do it," Collins advised. "Otherwise, you'll have multiple individual corporations that are all independent of each other."

"The first way you described it is the way we discussed it."

"A single US company forming and controlling multiple Panamanian companies."

"Yes."

Ginsberg reached into the satchel and handed Collins a list. "These are the officers and directors of the US corporation. Dewey Stone will be president."

Collins scanned the list and asked, "Do you have a name?"

Ginsberg looked puzzled. "A name?"

"For the company."

Ginsberg chuckled. "In all the talking about this, no one thought to give the company a name." A novel lay on the corner of the desk and on the spine he saw the author's name was Michael Weston. Ginsberg smiled and said, "Let's call it Weston Trading Company." Collins reached for a pin from the desk and scribbled the name on the paper he held while Ginsberg reached for two more lists. "These are the officers and directors for each of the first two Panamanian corporations."

"First two," Collins noted. "How many more do you think you'll want?"

"We are reasonably certain we know where we can get two ships right away. The others will take a little more time. We'll eventually need a corporation for each of those, too, but I'll get you the information later."

"We need an incorporator for the US company," Collins said. "A name to include on the documents as the person who is causing the corporation to be formed." He gestured to the lists. "I assume since your name is not on any of these lists, you don't want your name on the documents we file to form the company."

"No." Ginsberg shook his head. "Keep my name out of it." He pointed to Collins. "You can put your name on the documents. You're the one drafting them. The incorporator only files the papers, right?"

"Yes."

"How soon can you have the papers ready?"

"We can be ready to file for the domestic company by tomorrow afternoon," Collins replied. "The Panamanian companies will take a little longer."

"Okay," Ginsberg nodded. "But work quickly. We don't have a lot of time."

After Collins was gone, Ginsberg located Schind at Buxenbaum's apartment and drove down there that night. Schind was waiting when he arrived.

"I thought you were going to find your own office space," Ginsberg said as he glanced around the cramped front room.

"I have. I'm just not in it yet. What's so important that we had to meet now? Has something happened?"

A dusty table stood nearby. Ginsberg rested the satchel atop it, flipped open the latches, and took out the memo. "This came to me today." He handed the document to Schind.

Schind read it quickly and handed it back to Ginsberg. "Ben-Gurion was right."

"About what?" Ginsberg asked as he returned the memo to the satchel.

"He has said all along that the British will be leaving Palestine. Lately he's been saying that they will leave sooner rather than later. He thinks we should be arming ourselves and preparing for war. When the British are gone, he's certain they will be forced to fight the Arabs."

"I know what Ben-Gurion would like to do about that issue but that is not something I or any of the others care to get involved in," Ginsberg said. "We are glad to assist with the acquisition of ships but we will not get in the arms business."

"Well . . . " Schind hedged.

Ginsberg gave Schind a look that conveyed the seriousness of his position on the matter. "The purchase of large stockpiles of munitions here in the United States would not go unnoticed. Especially if *we* were the ones doing it."

"You mean," Schind said in a snide tone, "if *Jews* are the ones purchasing the weapons."

"Exactly," Ginsberg responded. "The FBI would want to know why we were buying it. And while they might otherwise turn a blind eye to ships and refugees, if they discovered we were in the arms business, I think they would be forced to prevent us from doing anything at all. No ships. No refugees. It would all come to an end."

Schind folded his arms across his chest and his voice took a contemplative tone. "Someone told me the other day that he had a rifle he took from a German officer at Ambléve. He asked me if the people I knew in Palestine could use it."

Ginsberg looked concerned. "What did you say?"

"I said we could use it and thousands more just like it, but that I didn't know what to do about it. He wanted to give it to me right then."

Ginsberg's concern turned to worry, which was evident in his voice. "Did you take the rifle?"

"No, but I think if someone approached me about the topic, without being asked, there must be hundreds more who would be willing to give theirs, too, if we *did* ask."

"Steer clear of it," Ginsberg cautioned. "The last thing we need is the FBI after us. Treasury, British intelligence, even the US military we can dodge." He jabbed the air with his finger for emphasis. "But if the FBI gets interested, they will shut us down."

Schind thought for a moment, then nodded toward the memo. "What do we do with that document?" he asked, changing subjects. "We need to let someone in Tel Aviv know about it."

"It's too long for a telegram," Ginsberg observed. "I was thinking of sending a courier to deliver it by hand."

Schind's eyes were wide. "You mean, send a person to travel all the way to Palestine to deliver that document?"

"Yes."

"Wouldn't that be expensive?"

Ginsberg shook his head. "Not if we're talking about human lives."

CHAPTER 10

THE VOLUNTEERS

Three days later, a courier arrived in Tel Aviv carrying the memo from Ginsberg. He found a taxi at the airport and rode immediately to the Jewish Agency office. A young female clerk sat at a desk near the door and as the courier entered, the clerk greeted him. The courier ignored her greeting and asked to see Ben-Gurion.

"And what is the nature of your business?" the clerk asked.

"I was sent to deliver a document to him."

"I can give it to him," she held out her hand as if expecting to receive it.

The courier was unfazed. "I'm afraid that's impossible."

"Well, unless you tell me the nature of your business," she said, "you'll have to leave."

"I was sent by Morris Ginsberg."

"Perhaps you were, but that name means nothing to me."

The courier opened his leather satchel and showed the clerk the corner of an envelope with American Foreign Steamship's logo and address. "Tell Mr. Ben-Gurion I am here and that Morris Ginsberg sent me. I think he will see me."

The clerk disappeared upstairs only to return moments later. She gestured for the courier to follow and led the way to the second floor. Partway down the hall she came to a stop and pointed toward an open doorway. The courier stepped through it into an office, where David Ben-Gurion was seated at a desk. "What's this all about?" Ben-Gurion asked with a perplexed expression.

"I was sent by Morris Ginsberg to deliver this to you." The courier opened the pouch, took out the envelope, and handed it to Ben-Gurion. Without hesitation, Ben-Gurion took it from him and read the memo. As his eyes scanned the last page, he looked up at the clerk, who still was standing in the doorway, "Ask Golda to come here, please." The clerk disappeared and Ben-Gurion turned to the courier. "You brought this document all the way from New York?"

"Yes, sir."

Ben-Gurion smiled. "Very good. When do you go back?"

"My return flight leaves in four days."

"Well, then, you'll get to see some of our country and how we're forced to live."

"Yes, sir."

Ben-Gurion laid aside the document. "You can wait downstairs. I'll have someone take you over to the hotel. We'll put you up there until your flight leaves. And I'll get someone to drive you around so you can see the sights."

"Thanks you, sir."

In a few minutes, Golda Meir appeared in Ben-Gurion's office. He showed her the memo and waited quietly while she read it. As she turned to the final page he said, "I told you they were leaving."

"They haven't decided yet," she remarked.

"No, but they're thinking about it. And you know how government machinery works. Once they raise the issue to this level," Ben-Gurion said, pointing to the memo, "and a position on an issue forms as this one has, it gathers its own momentum. We should be arming ourselves now."

Golda still was studying the memo and she glanced at him from the corner of her eye. "Wouldn't that merely provoke British ire against us?"

"Their ire is already provoked against us," Ben-Gurion roared. "They're provoking us, too! They're provoking the world and the world doesn't even know it. Free people around the globe—all of the allies who fought for the liberation of Europe—should be outraged at British conduct and policy toward us. The world should be sending arms and men to join us in opposing the king's army. Instead, their leaders sit by and watch."

Golda laid the memo on the desk. "Someone in New York is doing more than sitting by and watching."

A frown wrinkled Ben-Gurion's forehead. "What do you mean?"

Golda pointed to the memo. "This information came from Ginsberg, right?"

"Yes." Ben-Gurion dismissed her point with the wave of a hand. "Morris is one of us."

"But he gets his information from someone else. A lawyer, as I recall. Someone with connections."

Ben-Gurion demurred. "I don't think we should talk about that."

"But my point is," Golda continued, "people are helping. Not everyone, but some of them. We need to give them every reason to continue helping and no reason at all to stop."

"So, what are you saying?"

"We should keep moving forward with the work at hand, and hope those who already are with us will join us in a greater way when the time comes, rather than giving them a reason to abandon us now."

Ben-Gurion leaned over the desk and lowered his voice. "When the time comes we must be ready, and the only way we can be ready *then* is to get ready *now*."

"So, what do you want to do?"

Ben-Gurion looked away. "I've decided to go to Paris," he announced in a quick, clipped pace.

"For what?" Golda insisted.

"We have contacts in Paris that are at least as good as those we have in New York. Maybe our friends there will help."

"We have contacts in Paris, but those contacts don't have the resources our friends in New York have," she argued.

"But the French government holds tons of Allied war surplus,"

Ben-Gurion countered, "and I hear they would like nothing more than to get rid of it. I intend to give them that opportunity."

"You think you can convince them to do that, even in the face of British opposition?"

"The French hate the British almost as much as we do. I think they'll be delighted to aggravate them one more time. And if not the French, then someone else." He looked at Golda, his eyes ablaze. "We will not stop. We will not give up. If we stop, we die. If we give up, we end up back in the camps like before. That cannot happen again."

CHAPTER 11

THE VOLUNTEERS

Meanwhile, in New York, William Ash took the city bus from his home in Queens to a stop near Colfax Café, a longshoremen's favorite on the waterfront in Brooklyn. As he entered, he caught sight of Hugh Clark at a table in the corner.

Clark, like Ash, had spent most of his life at sea. Crusty, gruff, and plainspoken, he had curly snow-white hair that stuck out beneath the tam he wore for a cap. His skin, unusually fair for a sailor, was ashy and dry from years of neglect. He had thick, muscular shoulders, visible even beneath the heavy sweater that he wore, and hands that were short but wide and powerful. Though he wasn't particularly tall, he made up for it with the force of his personality and had a way of dominating the room with the power of nothing but his voice.

Ash made his way to the back of the café and took a seat across the table from Clark. "What have you been doing lately?"

"Working a little, here and there," Clark replied. He paused to take a drink from a bottle and glanced away as he swallowed. "Mostly just taking it easy. I spent the last five years sailing for the navy. Now I'm picking up a little work here and there. Filling in on the dock when they're short. Going to school on the GI Bill. Spending time with my wife." He looked over at Ash. "Want any more detail?"

Ash grinned at Clark's wry sense of humor. "Think you'd like to sail again?"

Clark shrugged. "I don't know, maybe. My wife likes having me around. Not sure why, though." He tipped up the bottle and took another drink, then looked over at Ash. "What are you up to? You never used to talk this much before."

"Before the war you used to tell everybody how Hitler was going to kill the Jews. You were saying that long before anyone else realized what was happening."

"Yeah," Clark said. "And he did, too."

"Yeah," Ash replied.

"We shoulda never let that happen."

"You still feel that way?"

"Yes," Clark had a questioning look. "Why are you asking me all this?"

"It seems to me not much has changed, really." Ash was moving slowly, testing Clark to see how interested he was in the topic of helping the Jews, before he went further into specifics about the voyage. "Now, instead of the Nazis holding the Jews, it's the Allies who are holding them. Most of the Jews in Europe—the ones who survived, the ones our boys liberated—are still in the same camps where the Germans held them. Some of them living in buildings with their former guards. All of them being held there together. By us. Against their will."

"I know." Clark nodded his head. "Makes it look like we think about as much of the Jews as the Nazis. As if somehow the Jews brought all the misery on themselves." He looked over at Ash again. "But you still haven't told me why we're talking about this."

Ash leaned closer and lowered his voice. "There's a thing going on you might be interested in."

Clark had an amused expression. "A thing?"

"Yeah."

"What kind of . . . *thing*?"

When Ash talked to Schind he'd insisted they had to be honest with potential recruits and tell them about all the risks inherent in the voyage, right from the beginning. Ash intended to do just that and give everyone, including Hugh Clark, the option of backing out with grace. But just then, sitting in the café, face-to-face with Clark, he realized Schind had been right, at least in part. Not many would agree to sail with them if they were confronted with all the risk at once. So he fudged and said, "Some guys are getting up a shipload of supplies to take to Palestine."

Clark frowned. "Supplies for the Jews?"

"Yeah. They need a crew to sail the stuff over there. You interested?"

"Who is it that's doing this?"

Ash was coy. "A private outfit."

"Private," Hugh grunted in a derisive tone. "Am I ever going to know who this *private* outfit is?"

"Probably."

"How much would it pay?"

Before he could stifle it, a grin broke over Ash's face and he said with a chuckle, "Nothing."

"Ha," Clark laughed out loud. "You want me to crew a ship all the way to Palestine for nothing?"

"You aren't getting paid now. What difference does it make?"

"Good point," Clark said with a nod. "When do they want to sail?"

"In a month or two."

"I don't know what I'll be doing in a month or two."

"I'm pretty sure you'll be sitting right here, as long as your money holds out."

Clark laughed again. "You're probably right about that."

"So, are you in?"

"I'm interested. But after being away all this time with the war, I'll have to talk it over with my wife."

Ash knew there was no arguing with that. "All right. Think you can get others to join us?"

"Maybe. You want me to find Jewish sailors?"

"No, I want you to find sailors."

"Okay."

"And listen, we need to keep this quiet," Ash cautioned. "Don't spread this around too much. Talk to people, but be selective."

A skeptical frown wrinkled Clark's brow. "Is this illegal?"

"Not in the United States."

"But the British won't like it."

"No." Ash shook his head. "The British won't like it much at all."

"Good. I never cared for the British, and anything that makes them mad makes me happy."

"Okay." Ash pushed back from the table. "But be careful who you talk to. We don't want just anyone and we don't want word to get around to the wrong people."

"I'll find out who's interested," Clark assured.

For all the friendly talk, Clark left the café unsure whether Ash was telling all he knew about the proposed voyage. He was confident the trip had something to do with Jews—that much seemed obvious—but the rest was much less forthright than it seemed. For one thing, even though Ash said they were sending a shipload of supplies to Jews in Palestine, all he talked about was the condition and plight of Jews trapped in Europe. And he never once talked about the conditions in Palestine or why the supplies were needed there. That left Clark wondering if there wasn't more to the story than Ash was willing to say.

But even with reservations, Clark was intrigued by their discussion and didn't want to press the matter too hard. Even from the scant information offered by Ash, Clark knew he wanted to make the trip. Convincing his wife he should do it would be much easier if he told her about taking supplies to Palestine. A trip like that might be something she'd see as a low-risk venture—a quick trip over and back to help someone. Solving the European refugee problem would be considerably riskier. He was sure his wife would be against his involvement in something like that.

After dinner that evening, Clark helped his wife wash and dry the dishes, and as they stood together at the kitchen sink he said, "I talked to William Ash today."

"What's he know?" she asked without looking up.

"Not too much."

She cut her eyes in his direction. "You mean he's looking for a crew?"

Clark had a sheepish grin. "Yeah, something like that."

"Where's the ship going this time?"

"Palestine."

Her eyes opened wide and she turned to him with a startled expression. "Palestine?"

"Nothing's happened yet." He gestured defensively with one hand while the other gripped a plate. "I haven't said I'd do it. We're just talking about it right now."

"Who would you be sailing for?"

"I don't know who's doing it."

She turned back to the sink. "He didn't say?"

"We haven't gotten that far into the discussion."

"So why'd he come to you?"

"Thought I might be interested, I guess."

"He knows how you feel about the Jews."

"Yeah."

She turned toward the stove to retrieve a pot and dunked it in the soapy water. "So . . . what did you tell him?"

"I told him I had to talk to you first."

She ran the washcloth around the inside of the pot. "I thought we were going to settle down now. Work short trips. Maybe the inland routes." Her voice softened. "Have a family."

"We are," he insisted. "It's just . . . "

"You want to do this first."

"I'm interested. Yeah."

"And after this there'll be another."

"No," he insisted. "It's not like that."

"Why isn't it like that?" Her voice took a sharp edge. "When you came home you said that was it. You weren't leaving again. But all you've done since then is sit down there in that bar and dream of going back to sea."

"Now, that's not fair. I've been taking classes."

"Yeah," she said tersely. "Classes toward getting a captain's license."

He looked surprised. "Yeah."

She arched an eyebrow. "You didn't think I knew what you were really doing, did you?"

"I wasn't trying to—"

She cut him off before he finished. "But you weren't trying to be straight with me, either."

"It's just a math class," he said lamely. "That's all. It doesn't commit me to anything."

"But to get the GI money you had to give them a reason for taking it, and you told them you were studying to be a ship's captain."

"I had to fill out the form."

"And that's what you said."

"Yeah. That's what I told them."

They worked at the sink in silence awhile, neither one saying a word to the other. When they finished with the dishes, Clark moved away from the sink and took a seat at the kitchen table. "There's a little coffee left," she said. "Do you want a cup?"

"Is there enough for us both?"

"Yeah." She filled two cups, then brought them to the table. "So," she began as she took a seat across from him. "What are they taking to Palestine?"

"Supplies," he replied.

"What kind of *supplies*?"

"Ash didn't say."

"So, you don't know who you'd be sailing for, don't know what you'd be carrying." She paused to take a sip of coffee. "Do you know who the captain would be?"

"No," Clark said, shaking his head.

"Or how long you'd be gone." He shook his head once more. "Well, did he tell you what they were paying?"

"I know that," Clark said with a smile.

"Well, at least we have that much," she sighed. "What are they paying?"

"Nothing."

She set her cup on the tabletop and looked him in the eye. "You want to set off on a voyage to Palestine, taking a cargo of who-knows-what on a ship owned by some unknown person, be gone for months, and do it for free?"

"We just talked about it. That's all." He took a sip from his cup. "It's just talk."

Tears filled her eyes. "You just got back," she whispered.

He reached across the table and grasped her hand. "I know. I know."

In spite of his wife's reaction, Clark made the rounds among his friends and contacts on the docks, talking to those he felt might be interested while taking care to avoid those he knew would be against the idea altogether. He spoke to each one individually and by the end of the week he'd contacted a sizeable group, many of whom expressed agreement with the idea as Ash first pitched it to him—sail a ship to Palestine to bring relief to the Jews.

Clark reported their responses to Ash and two days later, Ash and Clark gathered everyone in the basement of a church in Brooklyn to give them a more detailed version of what the trip involved.

"All of you have talked to either me or Hugh," Ash began, "and you've expressed interest in working a trip to Palestine. I want to come clean with you, however. You were told this was a trip to take relief supplies to Jews in Palestine. We *are* bringing relief, we *are* going to Palestine, but we're not taking relief supplies to Palestine."

"Ash," a voice spoke from the back of the room, "you're not making much sense."

"I know," Ash said. "Let me explain. The people sponsoring this trip are in the process now of purchasing a ship. They intend to bring that ship here to New York for its initial fitting, then sail it to Europe where we will collect as many Jewish refugees as the ship will safely hold. Then we are going to take those refugees to Palestine."

"Why all the secrecy?" someone asked. "Seems rather straightforward."

"Because the British won't let them enter Palestine," another answered.

Ash added,. "British regulations currently restrict Jewish immigration into Palestine to only fifteen hundred per month. That quota is already booked for the next ten years. Meanwhile, tens of thousands of Jews are being held against their will in camps all across Europe. The same camps from which they were supposedly liberated."

"I hear some of them are forced to live with their former prison guards. Is that true?"

"That's correct," Ash said. "And most of those being held in Europe want to resettle in Palestine. The people who are sponsoring this trip want to help them get there."

"Why won't the government do it?"

"The US government doesn't want a fight with England over the issue." Ash waited a moment and when no one else commented he continued. "Because of British opposition to Jewish immigration, and because we will likely encounter the British on this trip, you'll have to travel under an assumed name."

"Why?" someone asked.

"For any number of reasons. One of which is, we don't want the crew to appear to be obviously American."

"They won't pick us out in a crowd?"

"They might. But if we can give them a reason to think otherwise, it might help avoid an international incident. We don't want the U.S. to be forced to choose sides."

"Why not?"

"Because we want all of you to return home. Now, I know many of you are married and you'll need to talk to your wives about this. When you do, all you can tell them is what I told you. That we're taking a shipload of supplies to Palestine for the Jews. That's it. You can't give them any other information about it. We'll sail sometime in the next month or two, but you won't know the exact date, and when we leave you'll depart without the usual dockside good-bye. Some of you won't have time to tell anyone you're leaving."

No one seemed to react to those conditions at first, then a hand went up and Ash braced for a question. To his relief, it had nothing to do with how they told their wives. "You said we'd be traveling under a different name. Will someone give us identity papers?"

"Yes," Ash said, eagerly moving on with the discussion. "All of you will need a US passport to get back in the country when you return. This is not a government authorized mission. It won't be like when you deployed for service during the war. So if you don't have a passport, apply for one now. You'll bring your passport with you when we leave, but you'll surrender it to someone on board the ship after it clears US waters. The passports will be returned when you reach Palestine."

"If we reach Palestine," someone said in a sarcastic tone.

"I thought you said we wouldn't be allowed to enter Palestine?"

"Our passengers will very likely be detained by the British," Ash explained. "But the plan right now is to slip the crew away as you disembark."

"They have people in Palestine who can do that?"

"Yes. But I must stress," Ash said in a serious tone, "there is no guarantee of what will happen when we get there."

"Will the Europeans let us in and out of their ports?"

"We will sail to a port that does," Ash assured them.

"And still no pay for us for this?"

"We might be able to arrange a hundred dollars for each of you. Just so you have cigarette money in your pocket, but basically, you'd be doing this for free. And for the pleasure of rescuing people from a desperate situation." A note pad lay on a table near him, and Ash picked it up. "I have a pad here. If you want to commit to the trip, or if you think you might want to commit to it, I need your full name and correct address."

Someone asked, "Where's that list going?"

"We have to check your backgrounds."

"Are you reporting what you find to anyone?"

"No," Ash chuckled. "We're just using it for our own purposes."

Someone stepped forward. "I'll sign up." He took a pen from Ash, leaned over the note pad, and began writing his name and contact information. "You can check me all you want," he said as he finished. "But you might not like what you find."

Ash grinned. "What we find like that might make you more suitable than you think."

When the meeting with Ash was concluded, Clark went home to his wife. They sat together on the sofa in the front room of their apartment and, contrary to Ash's warning, he told her all he knew about what they were planning to do on the trip they'd discussed earlier—sail to Europe, load the ship with Jewish refugees, and take them to Palestine.

"Why didn't Bill tell you that before?"

"Because British regulations won't allow the Jews to immigrate to Palestine, and he wants to keep this as confidential as possible."

"They don't want the Jews returning to Palestine?"

"No."

"Why not?"

"I'm sure they have their reasons. I read somewhere that it's really about the British need for oil. Probably has more to do with their . . . dislike of the Jews."

She snuggled next to him. "I don't like the idea of you being gone. And I sure don't want you to get into trouble. Is this illegal?"

"It's not here."

"What will the British do when you get there?"

"They'll seize the ship."

Her head jerked up and she looked at him with wide eyes. "And what about the people on board?"

"They'll seize them, too."

"Will they let you out?"

"Ash says they'll have a way to slip us out of there before we're detained."

"How are they going to do that?"

"He didn't say."

"Right," she said with a skeptical tone. "That just means they *hope* they can get you out." She pressed herself closer against him. "I hope this is the right thing to do."

"I just keep thinking about the way things turned out for the Jews and I've been wondering what would have happened if we'd taken them in here—in America—before Hitler killed them. They were looking for a place to go. He was looking for a place to send them. What if we'd been that place?"

"That many people arriving all of a sudden would have been tough to handle."

"But they were only six million," Clark said with a plaintive tone. "The ones who died. They were only six million. Isn't that what they're saying?"

"Yeah."

"We have so much space in this country, we could have made room."

"I suppose we could have." She looked up at him. "You really want to do this?"

"Only if you're okay with it."

She looked at him grimly. "I don't think you have any choice."

"Me either."

"How long will you be gone?"

"A couple of months."

"You'll write to me?"

"When I can. But I don't know if they'll let me."

"Let you? Who's putting this trip together?"

"No one's really saying up front but I'm pretty sure it's the Haganah."

"What is that?"

"Kind of like the military, I guess. From what I've read. They protect Jewish farming communities in Palestine. Sort of like the army."

"And they won't let you write?"

"No one has said, but I doubt it. They're all being so secretive."

"That'll be a long couple of months."

"Yes. And without any income from me." He looked over at her. "Think you can manage?"

She poked his side playfully. "I managed things for the entire war. A few more months won't hurt."

CHAPTER 12

THE VOLUNTEERS

In spite of their efforts to keep the trip to Palestine a secret, news of Ash and Clark's recruitment efforts drifted through the waterfront community. Longshoremen talked about it among themselves and soon almost everyone knew what the two men were doing. At least, they knew a version of what they were doing. As rumors often do, this one developed into multiple accounts. No one knew for certain which one was the truth, or if any of them were. They only knew that something was up.

One of those who heard the rumors was a man named Winston Grey. English by birth, he served in the Royal Navy during the war and had been assigned to assist the Canadians in protecting the eastern coast of North America. When the war ended, he was discharged in place and given the option of returning to London or remaining in Montreal where he'd last been stationed. Single and without other obligations requiring him to return home, he chose to stay.

A year later, he drifted down to New York, took a job on the Brooklyn waterfront unloading ships, and settled down. He was legally present in the U.S., and he intended never to return to England, but he also could never be anything other than an Englishman. His loyalties, both politically and culturally, remained at home in Basingstoke—the town outside London where he'd been born.

When Grey learned of the rumors about Ash and Clark, he asked around and discovered most of the rumors had two common factors—Jews and ships bound for Palestine. Knowing the British government's policies on Palestine and its position regarding expansion of Jewish settlements there, he became concerned. He also felt conflicted.

America was his chosen place of residence and Americans, in general, were tolerant of most people. Owing to its large Jewish population, New Yorkers were particularly attuned to Jewish issues, and Grey was not without sympathy for what had happened to the Jews of Europe under Hitler. But he was also British. Not merely a citizen of the United Kingdom, but a Brit. A native-born son of the land of Anglos and Saxons, and of the ancient Brits. The rumors he'd heard suggested nothing short of an attempt to violate British policy and, though he enjoyed living in America, he felt honor-bound to report what he'd heard. After all, he'd been a member of the Royal Navy and had pledged himself to the Crown.

After a few days to consider the matter, Grey decided to contact Peter Wright, a man who also served in the Royal Navy and settled in the United States after the war. Unlike Grey, Wright had maintained formal ties to the British government. Ties he spoke of only in circumspect terms. Grey, however, couldn't help but notice that Wright never seemed to lift a finger in manual labor, yet never seemed to lack, either.

Late one afternoon, Grey placed a phone call to Wright. "Don't you know people who are connected to the government?" Grey asked when he had Wright on the line.

"The American government?"

"No, *our* government. London."

"Yes, of course," Wright replied. "Why do you ask?"

"I've heard something on the docks that our boys might be interested in."

"What is it?"

"I don't want to say on the phone."

"The war is over, you know," Wright chided. "You don't have to be so hush-hush now."

"I do about this. Can you put me in touch with someone?"

"I'll see what I can arrange."

A few days later, Wright phoned Grey at home. "Smitty's Bar," Wright said. "Be there in one hour. The man's name is Oldfield."

An hour later, Grey entered Smitty's, a waterfront bar not far from Colfax Café. Richard Oldfield, one of Robinson's MI6 agents, was there seated at a table in the corner. With a short haircut, clean-shaven face, and tweed jacket, Grey had little trouble picking him out from the regular rough-and-tumble crowd. "Are you Oldfield?" he asked confidently as he took a seat at the table.

"You're Grey?" Oldfield asked.

"Yes."

"Let's step outside," Oldfield suggested.

"Not together." Grey glanced around warily. "Do you have a car?"

"Yes."

"I'll go out the front. Pick me up on the street outside. There's a door in back past the bathroom. You go out that way." Without waiting for a response, Grey rose from his chair, walked to the front door, and stepped outside. When he reached the sidewalk, Grey shoved his hands into the pockets of his coat and wandered casually up the street away from Smitty's.

Outside in the cool crisp air he wondered if he was doing the right thing. Ash, he hardly knew. But Hugh Clark was a nice guy. They knew each other well and often at the end of the day they'd meet for a drink at the Colfax, then walk home together. Their apartments were in buildings that stood across the street from each other. He'd hate to see—

A car came to a stop beside him and Grey bent down to see Oldfield seated at the steering wheel. He got inside and as they drove away, Oldfield asked, "What's this all about?"

"I've heard rumors," Grey began.

"What kind of rumors?"

"Rumors about people recruiting sailors to sail a ship to Palestine."

"And you think there's something wrong with that?"

"One version says they're taking supplies for the Jews in Palestine," Grey elaborated. "Another version says they're going over to Europe first to pick up refugees."

Oldfield glanced over at him. "Any idea who's involved?"

By then Grey had made up his mind. Ash could fend for himself, but he had no intention of implicating Hugh Clark. "All of the rumors point to one person as the organizer. A man named William Ash."

✡

That evening, Robinson gathered those of his men—less than half the total crew—who were not on duty conducting surveillance of Schind, Ginsberg, and Buxenbaum. Selwyn Butler was there. Alec McKenna was working.

They talked that evening about what they'd learned so far—about the obvious things—ships, sailors, and longshoremen—then Robinson said, "We received word recently of rumors on the docks about a ship being prepared to deliver supplies to Palestine. Actually, there are two versions of that rumor. One says the ship will be taking supplies, the other says they will be taking refugees. Richard talked to someone just this afternoon about this and I've asked him to brief us on what he learned."

"I was approached by an informant," Oldfield began, "who told me a friend of his wanted to talk. I arranged to meet that friend of a friend and he turned out to be someone named Winston Grey. According to Grey, a man named William Ash is organizing an effort to recruit people who are willing to sail a ship to Palestine. Grey says there are several versions of this rumor. One says the ship is taking supplies for the Jews and is sailing directly from New York to Palestine. Another version says the ship will travel to Europe first, load with refugees, and then go on to Palestine. And," Oldfield chuckled, "he's supposedly asking people to do this for free."

The others in the room laughed. "Can we believe any part of it?" Ward asked in derision.

"Not many people would be willing to do either of those trips for free," Loring offered.

"Well," Oldfield continued with a hint of irony in his voice, "that's the interesting part. Grey says they've lined up enough people who are interested in doing the trip to man two ships."

Robinson spoke up. "Does anyone know anything about this William Ash?"

"From what I've heard," Oldfield offered, "he's a former captain in the merchant marine. Doesn't sail anymore but spends most of his time doing just what these rumors suggest—recruiting crews for ships."

"Okay," Robinson said. "We know Schind met with Ash on at least one occasion. But we have no record of any meeting between Ginsberg and Ash. Do any of you have any information on whether Ginsberg and Ash know each other?"

"They're from quite different classes," Loring offered. "Not much possibility there would have been social interaction between them. One a wealthy ship owner. The other a Longshoreman and one-time ship's captain."

"Ginsberg's a Jew," Mitchell said. "What about Ash?"

"He's Jewish also," Oldfield said. "I did a little research on him after I talked to Grey. Not much out there but from what I could learn he was born in Poland. Came to the United States with his family."

"And," Loring added, "there was one meeting between Schind and Ash."

Ward had a skeptical frown. "Really?"

"Yeah," Loring said. "Buxenbaum took him. Several of us ended up down there together. Two on Schind. Two on Buxenbaum."

"That's right," someone offered. "I was there."

Robinson flipped through his notes. "I have a report on that meeting. But it doesn't indicate any topics that might have been discussed or anyone else who might have been present."

"Probably just another Jew," Ward groused.

"Any of these guys have any contact with *anyone* outside of their own religion?" someone asked.

"Ginsberg uses Palmer Collins," Mitchell offered. "The lawyer with Fortas, Brown & Hoffman. I'm pretty sure he's Protestant."

Loring's eyes opened wide with a look of realization. "That's right. He's Methodist."

"How do you know that?"

"I have no idea," Loring shrugged.

"Collins' firm handles mostly corporate clients," Mitchell added. "Mergers, acquisitions, transactions."

"Think Collins is part of whatever Schind and Ginsberg are doing?"

"No one seems to know."

"What else do we know about him?" Mitchell asked. "Anything?"

"About Collins?" Loring asked.

"Yes," Mitchell clarified. "Aside from the fact that you think he's Protestant, do we know anything else?"

Robinson spoke up. "The file on Collins says he had a law practice in Queens before the War. Served in the US Army almost from the beginning. Wounded early in the fighting. Sent home. Later recovered but was discharged. Took a job with the government at the War Production Board for a while, then went back to law practice at Fortas, Brown & Hoffman. Made partner rather quickly."

"So, he didn't bring Ginsberg to the firm, as a client?"

"No," Robinson said. "Ginsberg and his company, American Foreign Steamship, were clients of the firm long before Collins arrived. He was assigned to them by the firm's managing partner, Nathan Fortas."

Mitchell spoke up. "We need to find out more about this Collins fellow and what he's doing for Ginsberg."

"That will be difficult, I'm afraid," Butler noted.

"Oh? How so?" Mitchell wondered.

"He's an attorney," Butler said. "His records and files are confidential. Difficult to get them even with a court order."

"We can't get a court order."

"No," Butler said with a condescending tone. "I suppose not."

"But we need to find out what he's doing."

"Well," Loring said with a sly grin, "there's always the self-help method."

"Self-help?"

"Get inside his office after hours," Loring explained, "and help ourselves to whatever we can find."

They all laughed but Robinson took the proposal seriously. "Think we could pull it off?" he asked.

"Well . . . " The men glanced nervously at each other, like schoolboys who'd suggested a prank that someone actually wanted to pull. "I suppose," Loring said finally. "But there would be considerable risk. I mean, what if we get caught?"

"That's easy," Robinson replied. "Don't get caught."

That evening, Geoffrey Reid arrived home from a Washington reception a little before midnight. He'd had a long day and was eager to get to bed when the phone in the hall rang. He thought about letting the operator at the embassy take it—she would pick up on the fifth ring—but at the fourth he had a change of heart and snatched the receiver to his ear.

The call was from Selwyn Butler, who told Reid about the proposed operation to break into Collins' office. Reid was alarmed. "When do they plan to do it?"

"Tomorrow night."

"If this goes wrong," Reid said, "we'll all be in the dock."

"Then I guess we better make sure it doesn't go wrong."

"Anything I can do?"

"I don't know," Butler sighed. "Most of the men seem to know what they're doing." He paused for a moment. "Maybe if you could make certain the cleanup crews for that floor are out of the building when we get there. We don't need any surprises."

"I'll get someone to work on it."

"Do we still have contacts with the New York police department?"

"Yes, but we may want to save them for later. If any of you get arrested they might be more useful then."

When Reid finished with Butler, he phoned Alec McKenna and asked him about the proposed break-in at Collins' office. Having worked that evening on the surveillance detail, McKenna wasn't present at the meeting when the operation was discussed. However, he made no attempt to hide his opinion. "It's too risky, and a foolish thing to try. Sometimes I think Robinson is little more than an amateur. Do you want me to deliver your order to stand down?"

"I can't interfere," Reid sighed. "This is a London operation, you know."

"Right."

"Robinson is working directly for Peel. Strictly speaking, he's higher on the organizational chart than am I."

"So, what do we do?"

"Talk to the others who weren't at the meeting," Reid suggested. "Make sure they understand what's happening. Then be prepared to disappear, if necessary. Unless they send you into the building, you should be in the clear, but you ought to review your exit strategy just in case."

"How will we know something's gone wrong?" McKenna asked.

"Butler is inside," Reid explained. "If the police get involved, Butler will know what to do. I'll get a call from the watch commander before they book anyone. If I should hear from them, I'll phone you."

"Butler is going in with them?"

"Yes."

"Okay." The concern in McKenna's voice was evident. "I'll wait for your call."

Robinson and his men spent the next day studying floor plans, firm employee lists, and details about Fortas, Brown & Hoffman's known clients. That night, four men from Robinson's team, dressed as janitors, entered the Chrysler Building and rode a service elevator to the twenty-third floor where the law firm's offices were located. Butler stood watch near the entrance while the others moved down a hall toward the inner portion of the floor.

Collins' office door was unlocked and they quickly searched his desk and credenza. When they found nothing of interest there, they moved to the nearest secretary's desk and worked through the files and papers stacked on it.

"Here," Loring said at last, his voice a stage whisper. He pointed to files that lay at the corner of the desk. "There are several more with it."

Mitchell and Ward joined him, and Loring handed each of them a file. "Ginsberg's name is all over this one," Ward said. "Something called Weston Trading Company. Incorporated in New York." He pointed. "That guy Stone from Boston is part of it. His name's right here."

"This one is for a company with a Spanish name. Arias and Arias," Mitchell said, gesturing to the file in his hand. "Apparently incorporated in Panama." He glanced at the file beneath it. "This one does, too."

"We don't have time to read them all," Loring declared. "Lay the pages flat on that desk." He pointed with one hand to a desk nearby while he reached with the other into his pocket for a Minox miniature camera. "I'll take pictures of the documents. We can figure out what it means later."

Ward and Mitchell removed the documents from the files and placed them in order atop the desk, then Loring quickly photographed each page. As they were finishing, Butler appeared. "We need to get moving. Night watchman will be by in a few minutes. Someone downstairs will wonder why we're taking so long."

"We're done," Loring returned the files to the desk where he found them and started toward the door. "Let's go."

When they were safely clear of the building, Loring stopped at a pay phone and called Robinson. "It's done," he said.

"Meet me," Robinson replied and hung up the phone.

An hour later, Loring and the other three returned to the apartment on East Twenty-Third Street, where Robinson was waiting. As they entered the room, Loring handed Robinson the camera. "We found several files with Ginsberg's name on them. They were all recent corporations Ginsberg formed through Collins."

"Anything interesting about them?"

"One is an American domestic corporation," Ward offered. "The other two were formed in Panama."

Robinson looked puzzled. "Panama?"

"Ships," Butler said.

Robinson glanced over at him. "What do you mean?"

"Panama has some of the most lax regulations in the world. You could sail a tub from there if you could get it to float. If a ship is flagged in the United States, it's not only subject to stricter regulations, it's also subject to US trade restrictions. That would limit the ports on which you could call. Panama doesn't do that."

"Ships," Mitchell said. "Here we go with ships again."

"What about the American company?"

"Something called Weston Trading Company," Loring said. "Looks like that guy Stone from Boston is part of it. His name is on the documents. You'll see when you develop the film."

"So," Ward asked, "what do we do?"

"Get a good night's sleep, all of you," Robinson replied. "Then tomorrow two of you need to pick up surveillance on William Ash. His office is on Water Street." He copied the address from the file and handed it to Loring. "Choose who should take it, but two of you need to cover him."

"That's twelve hours each."

"I know, but after the report we heard from Oldfield about their activity on the waterfront, we need to cover him."

"What about Collins?"

"Don't worry about him," Robinson gestured with the camera. "Once I get this film developed, we'll know exactly what he's up to."

Ward shook his head. "And you want the two of us to cover Ash?"

"Yes."

"Our team's already covering Schind, Ginsberg, and Buxenbaum," Ward lamented.

"I'll rearrange some of the other guys as soon as I can work out the schedule," Robinson replied. "But don't wait on that. Decide which of you will handle Ash and get started first thing in the morning."

CHAPTER 13

THE VOLUNTEERS

Two days after his meeting with Ginsberg about the British memo, Schind moved into the apartment at Hotel Fourteen. When everything was in place, he called Buxenbaum over for a meeting. They sat together in the front room and talked.

Schind was sure that Buxenbaum had overheard enough to piece together the gist of the plan he was working to complete, but that day, for the first time, he told Buxenbaum details about what they were trying to do—purchase ships in the United States, refit them for carrying passengers, sail the ships to Europe, load them with refugees, and take the refugees to Palestine.

Buxenbaum sat with rapt attention, soaking up every word. "I knew it was something big," he said finally. "But I didn't think about it being that big. That's a lot of logistical problems to overcome."

"It won't be easy," Schind acknowledged, "either in buying the ships or sailing them across the Atlantic."

"What will the British think of it?"

"Not very highly. When the ships reach Palestine, we're rather certain they'll be stopped by the British naval blockade."

"What will happen to the passengers?"

"They will be taken to British detention camps."

"And the ships?"

"The ships will be seized."

"What about the crew?"

"Hopefully, crew members will be removed before the British can take them away, but that might not always prove possible. We have people in Palestine who will do their best to get them out of the ships before any of that happens, but there's no way to guarantee what will happen."

"So, it's a challenge," Buxenbaum observed.

"Yes," Schind agreed. "And there's one more thing."

"What's that?"

"Crew members won't be paid for the trip."

Buxenbaum's eyes opened wide. "You want to do this with volunteers?"

"Yes," Schind nodded. "We'll give them a hundred dollars each for pocket change, but that's all. And even that is in doubt."

Buxenbaum looked thoughtfully at the floor for a moment, then glanced up at Schind. "Are you asking me to join a crew as a sailor?"

"No," Schind said insistently, gesturing with both hands for emphasis. "We want you to recruit the crewmen."

That seemed to please Buxenbaum and he had a look of relief. "Okay," he said with a satisfied grin. "I'd be glad to do it."

"Ash is recruiting, too, but he thinks Jewish sailors would be more likely to agree to go and he says you know them all."

"I know many of them," Buxenbaum affirmed. "Ash can't reach them?"

"We need all the help we can get," Schind assured. "If this works out like we want it to, we'll be sending over a steady stream of ships. We'll need to maintain recruiting on a continual basis. It's not just about a single ship. We want to send many ships. Filling out the crew will be a task too big for one person."

"Okay. But if it's going to be that big of a project, we'll have to talk to anyone who'll listen."

"I know, but concentrate on Jewish sailors for now. We need these first sailors quickly. Our fellow Jews are the best bet for a quick response."

Buxenbaum placed his hands on the armrest of the chair as if to stand. "I know exactly where to start. Should I begin now?"

"Yes."

Buxenbaum started to push himself up but then hesitated. "I know you've stressed the need for secrecy when we've talked to others, but we'll have to tell recruits what we're doing if we want them to say yes. Which means more people are going to know. Word will get around."

"People always talk," Schind noted. "But we have no choice. We can't sail without a crew and we hope to buy the first ships in a few weeks."

On Friday evening, Buxenbaum did something he hadn't done in a long time. He attended a service at the synagogue down the street from his apartment. He sat on the back pew and listened as the cantor read from the Torah and then the rabbi gave his message. Around him people recited the prayers at the appointed time but Buxenbaum had long since forgotten what they meant.

To pass the time, he took a prayer book from the rack that was mounted on the pew in front of him and opened the book. It was written in Hebrew and he wondered if he could still read it. As he flipped through the pages, a leaflet fell out. He picked it up from his lap and saw it was an announcement about a training camp in New Jersey for those who wanted to learn how to farm in preparation for moving to Palestine.

Not for me, Buxenbaum thought as he tucked the paper back inside the book. He would help others get there, but he had no intention of going himself. Certainly not as a farmer.

When the service ended, Buxenbaum moved quickly outside and waited near the bottom of the steps as worshippers came from the building. He wasn't there that evening for the prayers or the readings, or the rabbi's message. He was there for one purpose. To see Leon Redner, a merchant marine, known to everyone up and down the wharf. A man he was certain would be crucial to recruiting Jewish sailors for Schind's refugee relief ships.

Before long Redner, a slender, wiry man about Buxenbaum's age, emerged from the building and Buxenbaum moved in his direction. "We need to talk," Buxenbaum said.

"I can't right now," Redner replied. "I have to get home."

"What about Sunday?"

"Okay. Where?"

"Come to my apartment," Buxenbaum suggested.

Two days later, Redner arrived at the apartment and they sat at the kitchen table while Buxenbaum pitched the idea to him—sail ships to Europe, load them with refugees, then transport the refugees to Palestine.

Redner was interested but hesitant about the money. "I have a wife and two kids," he explained. "I'm not sure we can make it for three months without an income."

"Do you know anyone who might be interested and in a position to go?"

"Maybe, but the lack of a salary will pose a problem. Most of our guys are workingmen. They have families, and sailing is the way they provide for them. But I can see. You want me to ask around?"

Buxenbaum answered, "Yeah, but we'll need to move promptly. The first ship will be ready to sail in a couple of weeks. And we'll need to be careful."

"Not sure how to ask around *and* be careful," Redner said with a chuckle.

"Talk to people you already know," Buxenbaum suggested. "Don't mention it to strangers."

"You mean, stick with Jewish men."

"Yes. They're the ones most likely to be interested."

"But I'll have to tell them what we're doing. These are our own people. They'll be sympathetic to the cause. But they'll never say yes without at least a little information on the trip."

"I know, but don't tell them everything. Tell them we're recruiting for a relief trip. Invite them to a meeting. Tell them you'll get back to them on a date and location. Assure them they'll be told more details at the meeting. Then give me a list of names of people who are interested in attending the meeting."

"You're going to check them out or something?"

"Yeah."

Redner looked over at him. "It's that serious?"

"Yes. It's that serious."

"They'll want to know who's doing this," Redner continued. "It'll work better if I can tell them that much."

"Okay." Buxenbaum paused a moment as he glanced around the room. On a table near the window he saw a copy of *The New York Times*. An article on the front page caught his eye. It was about the cost of real estate in the U.S. and how the labor market was flooded with soldiers returning home from work. Land and Labor. A smile spread slowly across Buxenbaum's face. "Tell them the trip is sponsored by an organization called Land and Labor for Palestine."

"Okay." Redner grinned. "You just made that up?"

Buxenbaum ignored the question. "Tell them it's an organization that acquires land in Palestine and recruits people who are interested in moving there as settlers."

A few days later, Redner phoned Buxenbaum and asked to talk. They met at Katz's Deli.

"I've found some men who are willing to make the trip," Redner said with excitement.

"You told them what it was about?"

"I told them we were taking a cargo to Palestine on a relief trip. That it was a little risky with the British keeping tight control of the ports, and they'd be doing it without pay."

"They were agreeable?"

"Yes. What kind of ship are we sailing?"

"We?" Buxenbaum asked with a note of surprise.

"I'm going, too," Redner said with a grin.

"Good." Buxenbaum was genuinely glad to have him for the trip. Recruiting was going slower than he'd planned and already he was wondering if they could find enough men to fill the crew.

"What kind of ship are we sailing?"

"I don't know yet."

"Well, whatever it is, we're gonna need a lot more people if we're sailing it all the way to Europe."

"Yeah." Buxenbaum looked over at him. "How many did you get?"

"Seven," Redner said sheepishly. "Maybe eight . . . depending."

Buxenbaum had expected more and he was unable to suppress the frown that wrinkled his forehead. "That's all you could find?"

Redner looked crestfallen. "You thought there'd be more?"

Buxenbaum forced a smile. "I hoped there would be. But, we'll take what we can get. I'm sure you had to work hard to get those."

"I talked to about three times that many," Redner explained. "I assumed you didn't want me to ask the goy."

"Right," Buxenbaum nodded.

"Some of them might be interested."

"I'll think about it. But it looks like we might have to fill out the crew with inexperienced people."

Redner seemed put off by that suggestion. "That'll be touchy."

"Yeah," Buxenbaum nodded. "But non-sailor volunteers might be easier to find than seasoned sailors willing to work for free."

"That'll be adventurous."

"I know," Buxenbaum said with a grin.

"We could do that for most of the slots," Redner conceded, "except for the engine room and boiler. We need people in there who know how to operate the equipment, otherwise we could have real trouble."

"Know anyone?"

"Not really. Most of my contacts work on the deck or above."

"Well, don't worry," Buxenbaum said confidently. "I'll find someone."

When Buxenbaum left Katz's Deli, he walked back toward his apartment. As he made his way in that direction, he was soon lost in thought about where he could find people to crew the ships they planned to send to Europe. Asking people to do it for free was a problem. He didn't want to admit it to Redner, but it was a real hindrance. And understandably so. As Redner had said, not many could afford to leave for three months—or longer—with no means of supporting their family. "But there has to be a way to do this," he mumbled. With millions of Jews living in the New York area, surely two dozen would come forward to help.

About halfway home, he remembered seeing the flyer in the pew at the synagogue near his home—something about a training camp for people who wanted to work on farms in Palestine. Most of the people who went to Palestine did so as volunteers and most of those were young people. Moreover, no one expected to be paid to emigrate from the United States. And no one expected to be paid much once they reached a farm in Palestine. But most exciting of all, those who made the trek to Palestine had to pay their own way. They had to buy their own ticket for the ship or airplane that carried them over. Buxenbaum grinned at the thought of it. Passage to Palestine was the one thing he and Schind could offer. The only thing the volunteers had to do in return was work onboard the ship while they traveled. "This," he said aloud, "is a group readymade for service on the ships."

Buxenbaum quickened his pace and a few minutes later arrived at the synagogue. He moved quickly up the steps, pulled open the door, and stepped inside the foyer.

From the front entrance, Buxenbaum intended to make his way straight to the sanctuary and the pew where he'd been sitting on Friday evening, hoping all the while that the notice was still tucked inside the prayer book, but as he crossed the foyer he caught sight of a bulletin board hanging on the wall to the far left. There, thumbtacked in place, was a copy of the notice about the training camps. As he made his way toward it, Rabbi Amram came from the sanctuary. "Are you interested in traveling to Palestine?" he asked.

"I'm interested in knowing more about this camp," Buxenbaum replied, pointing to the notice.

"There are several in the area. This one is located in New Jersey. It's operated by the Zionist youth organization known as Habonim. They train people—mostly young people—for life on a kibbutz in Palestine."

"Where is it in New Jersey?"

"A place called Cream Ridge, just outside Hightstown. A little east of Trenton."

"Any idea who's in charge?"

"Saul Newman."

"Friend of yours?"

"Sort of. You can use my name when you meet him, if you like. I don't mind."

"Thanks."

As Buxenbaum turned to leave, Amram added, "Your sister was here last weekend."

"Oh."

"How long since you spoke with her?"

"I . . . " Buxenbaum hesitated. "I don't remember."

"Don't you think it's about time you did? She's all you have left."

"You should ask her about that," Buxenbaum retorted as he pushed open the door. "She knows where I live."

Buxenbaum moved quickly down the steps to the street and started toward the apartment. As he did, tears filled his eyes and ran down his cheeks. He wanted to see his sister. Thought about it many times. But the things she said when their mother died. The things she blamed him for about their father. That was more than he deserved. As far as he was concerned, she owed him the first move.

Three days later, Buxenbaum drove across the river to New Jersey and located the Habonim farm off Etra Road outside Hightstown. He arrived there unannounced and asked for Saul Newman. Someone pointed him toward a barn and Buxenbaum made his way toward it.

Inside, he found two men attaching a plow to a tractor. One of them, a middle-aged man, dressed in overalls and blue work shirt with a red cap atop his head, worked with the practiced ease of experience as he slid the pieces in place. The other, a young man not more than twenty years old, did his best to assist but was obviously inexperienced.

Buxenbaum waited quietly to one side and when they were finished, the older man wiped his hands on a rag and turned to face him. "I'm Newman," he said. "You must be Buxenbaum."

"How did you know?"

"Rabbi Amram told me you might come to see me. Said you'd probably drop by unannounced."

"He knows me too well."

"What can I do for you?"

Buxenbaum glanced around and saw others working in the barn. "Is there someplace we can talk?"

"Sure." Newman led the way to an office in the farm's main building. He switched on a fan, closed the door, and moved behind a metal desk that sat in the corner near the wall. "Have a seat," he gestured to a dusty chair that sat nearby.

"Now," he said when they were comfortable. "What did you need to discuss?"

As briefly as he could, Buxenbaum described the basic plan. Taking a ship to Palestine. Need a crew.

Newman had a wary look. "What's the cargo?"

"Relief support," Buxenbaum hedged.

Newman smiled. "This is about rescuing the refugees from Europe and taking them to Palestine?"

"Why would you ask that?"

"I hear things, Mr. Buxenbaum. Things about you and Danny Schind and Morris Ginsberg." Newman cut his eyes at him. "I hear things."

"No one else will help them," Buxenbaum lamented. "The nations of the world who were so outraged at what the Nazis did to us before, now are doing the very same thing to those they liberated. We can't sit by and watch in comfort. Not now. Not again."

"So why did you come to me with this?" Newman gestured with a wave of his hand to their surroundings. "We train farmers."

"I need people who will help sail the ship," Buxenbaum explained. "And I need them for free. Young people are eager for a cause. I think they might be willing to do it. And if they help, they'll get free passage to Palestine."

"Interesting offer," Newman observed. "But we have not many sailors among our students."

"They don't have to be trained mariners. Fishermen, boaters, weekend sailors on the lake. I'll take whatever you have."

"Well . . . " Newman leaned back in his chair and assumed a thoughtful pose. "I have a few who might be familiar with recreational boating. Some have been fishing. But most of them have never sailed the sea, not even as a passenger. Some of them have never even been in a boat. And I'm not sure how they'll feel about volunteering their services for free. But passage to Palestine would appeal to them and I can ask them if they're interested in helping."

"Don't ask them," Buxenbaum responded. "Just select the ones you think might work out, gather them as a group, and I'll meet with them to give them more of the details."

Newman leaned forward. "Our students are scattered over the farm today. I'm not sure I can get them back very quickly."

"I don't have to see them today. Take a day or two. Select the ones you think would fit our project and let me know when you are ready." Buxenbaum took a business card from his pocket and handed it to Newman. "You can reach me at this number."

Newman glanced at the card. "Land and Labor for Palestine," he read aloud.

"Yes."

Newman pushed himself up from the chair and flashed a smile. "I'll see what we can work out. Give you a call in a day or two."

As promised, Newman called a few days later to say he had a group of students who were interested in hearing more about working on the ships. Buxenbaum arranged to meet with them the following day at the farm. They gathered in the farm's main building, just down the hall from where Newman kept his office.

Speaking as frankly as possible about the risk but as obscurely as possible about the actual purpose of the trip, Buxenbaum told the students the cover story—that he worked for an organization called Land and Labor for Palestine, that he was recruiting people to sail a cargo ship to Palestine on a relief mission. Newman was present when he spoke, and although Buxenbaum had tacitly admitted to him the real purpose of the trip, he kept quiet.

"We aren't paying anything for the trip," Buxenbaum said after he'd outlined the general plan, "but you can stay in Palestine once you arrive."

An eager student spoke up. "You mean we get to go to Palestine for free?"

Buxenbaum knew that would be incentive enough for some of them, but he didn't want anyone to think it was going to be a pleasure trip. "It's not exactly a free trip," he corrected. "You'll have to work on the ship as we go over. And that work might sometimes be difficult."

Another student, Marvin Liebman from Long Island, said, "My father is a fisherman. I've worked on the sea all my life. I think we can get a boat to Palestine without much trouble. It's not that difficult."

"It's a ship."

Liebman had a questioning expression. "Sir?" he asked.

"It's a ship, not a boat."

Stanley Ritzer asked, "What's the cargo?"

"This is a relief trip," Buxenbaum replied, dodging the crux of the question. "We're going over there to bring help." He glanced in Newman's direction, but Newman seemed not to notice.

They talked awhile longer with several more students asking questions. Then Buxenbaum asked for those who were interested to step forward and give him their name and contact information. Ten students expressed an interest in making the trip. All of them were residents at the farm.

✡

Instead of returning to his apartment in Manhattan that afternoon, Buxenbaum traveled out to Long Island to the town of Hauppauge and made his way to the home of Walter Blount, a retired sailor.

Walter grew up on a farm in Pennsylvania and seemed destined for a rural life, but when he turned sixteen he ran away to Philadelphia, lied about his age, and went to work on a ship, first as a deckhand, then later in the engine room before finding his place tending the boiler. He worked in the boiler room of the *Bay of Biscay*, a worn-out freighter when Buxenbaum boarded it for his first trip.

Young and inexperienced, Buxenbaum took the brunt of the bullying and hazing administered by older seamen. Walter knew from experience what that felt like and took Buxenbaum under his wing, showed him how to survive at sea, and looked after him while he learned. The two had been friends ever since.

It was almost four in the afternoon when Buxenbaum arrived at Walter's house. They sat on the back porch, sipped coffee, and talked about memories from days gone by. The older, gray-haired Blount had more to remember; the younger, energetic Buxenbaum was ever eager to listen.

Finally, as they reached their third cup of coffee and conversation lagged, Buxenbaum turned to the reason for his visit. "Walter," he began, "we're taking a ship to Europe to pick up Jewish refugees. Then we're sailing them to Palestine."

Walter shook his head. "The British won't like it."

"I know."

"When are you leaving?"

"Not sure yet. Still working out the details."

"You got something you need me to look after while you're gone?"

Buxenbaum shook his head and took a sip of coffee.

Walter looked over at him. "Then why'd you come to me?"

"Need a boiler man," Buxenbaum said. "You were the best."

"I'm retired." Walter looked away, his eyes focused on something in the distance. "I'm out of the game now."

"You've been out three years," Buxenbaum grinned. "That's all. You've got at least one more trip left in you."

"Maybe." Walter shifted positions in the chair and reached for his coffee cup. "Who's the captain?"

"Don't know yet."

"What's the name of the ship?"

"Don't know that, either."

"What's the pay?" Walter leaned forward and took a sip from the cup.

"There isn't any."

Walter choked on the coffee, coughed once or twice, and looked over at Buxenbaum. "You can get sailors to volunteer?"

Buxenbaum avoided his gaze. "I can get a crew."

Walter looked suspicious. "What kind of crew you gonna get for free?"

"A few veterans."

"And the rest?"

"Mostly young people."

"Young people?"

"Yeah."

"What kind of young people you gonna get who know how to sail a ship across the Atlantic?"

"Young, inexperienced but very enthusiastic farmers in training."

Blount howled with laughter. "Are you kidding?"

Buxenbaum shook his head. "I'm as serious as I can be."

"Sounds like a recipe for disaster."

"Or adventure," Buxenbaum countered.

"More like disaster."

"So, what do you say?" Buxenbaum grabbed Walter's wrist and gave it a friendly shake. "One last adventure to support the cause of a Jewish state?"

Walter grinned. "I'll have to think about it."

"Okay, but don't think too long. And don't talk to anyone."

Walter shot him a look. "I'll have to tell my wife."

"Don't tell her much."

"I'll have to tell her as much as she wants to know. That's how we've made it all these years."

"Okay," Buxenbaum smiled. "Tell her what you have to."

CHAPTER 14

THE VOLUNTEERS

With Ginsberg and Stone moving forward on the effort to acquire ships, and with Ash and Buxenbaum recruiting sailors, Schind was forced to address the one part of Ben-Gurion's plan that he dreaded the most—raising the money to pay for it.

When he met with Ben-Gurion before coming to New York, Ben-Gurion told him to contact Henry Nadelson. As head of the Jewish Society, Nadelson had access to Jewish organizations in every major city in the country. Not only that, he knew and was known by the Jewish leadership in each of those cities. With a single phone call he could reach almost anyone in the Jewish community. Schind needed the help of someone with that kind of ability. The success of their effort to rescue the refugees and bring them to Palestine depended on raising large sums of money. Doing that would require the participation of many people. Nadelson was the man who could put him in touch with those who could make that happen.

Having no other choice than to get on with the fund-raising, Schind telephoned Nadelson, briefly explained his situation—noting that Ben-Gurion had suggested the two of them should meet—and asked if they could talk. Nadelson readily agreed and invited Schind to lunch the following day at Nadelson's home in Queens.

As he made his way to Queens, Schind thought about how much of the plan he should disclose to Nadelson. Acquiring ships was his first priority and he needed Nadelson's help in paying for it, but Ben-Gurion's instructions also included the acquisition of warplanes—a matter Schind had yet to address. He needed to get moving on that aspect of the plan, and if Nadelson could reach people all across the country, he would know the right people to talk to about it.

At the same time, he knew nothing of Nadelson personally, only the scant details conveyed by his reputation, but to get Nadelson's help, Schind was certain he would need to explain the plan—either the part about the ships, the part about the airplanes, or both—and he would need to do so in detail. That meant taking the risk that Nadelson might talk. If he talked to the wrong people, they could encounter serious trouble. And so began a tug-of-war in Schind's mind. If he told Nadelson everything, Nadelson might talk. If he didn't tell him enough, Nadelson might not agree to help with any of it. If Nadelson didn't help, they had no other fund-raising option except to start from scratch, probably with Weizmann's help—and he already knew how Ben-Gurion would feel about that.

Trapped between competing arguments in his mind, and with no comfortable choice on either side, Schind decided to apply the lessons he'd learned in dealing with Ginsberg and Stone. Honest men could be trusted to act in an honest manner. Nadelson, he knew, was an honest man. That being so, he would tell Nadelson as plainly as he could—and in as much detail as Nadelson desired—the instructions Ben-Gurion had given him and he would talk about their efforts thus far to make that plan a reality. He would be as straightforward with Nadelson as he would be with Ginsberg or Stone about everything—but not about the airplanes. That much he would hold in reserve. Ben-Gurion already had warned him that there was a limit to how deeply American Zionists would follow them into their Palestinian experience and he would wait to see Nadelson's level of interest before broaching the subject of airplanes and war preparation.

Schind arrived at Nadelson's house to find Nadelson—a man of moderate stature with neatly trimmed hair, olive complexion, and dark eyes—standing at the door, waiting to greet him. They visited a moment, then Nadelson led the way to the dining room, where the table was set and the food already in serving dishes. Schind was certain someone had prepared it on Nadelson's behalf and wondered who else might be in the house, listening as they talked, but he chose not to make an issue of it and moved toward the nearest chair.

The two men sat across from each other and as they ate, Schind told Nadelson in detail the plan to acquire ships in America, use the ships to rescue refugees from Europe, and take them to Palestine.

"What progress have you made toward doing that?" Nadelson asked.

"We're making good headway. I've made a number of helpful contacts and we have people looking for ships to buy and for the sailors to sail them."

"Morris Ginsberg will locate the ships for you," Nadelson said in a matter-of-fact tone, "and I'm certain he'll negotiate a great price for them."

Schind was surprised by the mention of Ginsberg's name and wondered how Nadelson knew of his involvement. "You know Morris Ginsberg?" he asked as naturally as possible.

"Oh my, yes. I know all the major players." Nadelson looked over at him. "That *is* the person who's helping you, isn't it? Morris? You didn't bring in an amateur, did you?"

"No, we didn't bring someone else in. Morris is helping." Schind avoided the mention of Stone. There was no way of knowing how Nadelson felt about him, and Schind didn't want to derail the discussion.

"Good," Nadelson said and paused to take a drink.

"Our major concern right now," Schind continued, "is not with locating the ships. That seems to be a straightforward matter. Our bigger concern is with how to pay for them."

Nadelson set his glass aside and without looking up replied, "I assumed that's why you came to see me."

"Yes." Schind was amused by Nadelson's frank response. "I need help organizing the fund-raising."

"Ships I can help with." Nadelson put down his fork and focused on Schind. "All the major Zionist groups will be eager to help alleviate the suffering of Jewish refugees in Europe. But I know David Ben-Gurion is set on raising an army to defend against the Arabs, and he's right about the threat they pose, but you won't find support for that with the usual Zionist groups. At least not now. After the fighting starts, they'll probably come around to the idea, but right now it would be a waste of time to ask."

Schind decided to plunge ahead and so he asked, "If we were interested in support for purchasing weapons and ammunition, where would we find it?"

"Small groups." Nadelson picked up his fork and began to eat again. "The larger, wealthier Zionist organizations are dominated by people who came to America years ago, made it big, and live a comfortable life. War is risky. Even mere talk of planning for it poses a threat to their lifestyle. Or so it seems to them. To their way of thinking, if they write a check to help save a refugee, no one will mind. If they write a check to purchase munitions with which to kill people, someone in power might not like it and if those people in power don't like it, they might want to do something about it." He spoke with a cadence and tone that belied a well-rehearsed discourse. "Exporting arms without a license and without government approval is illegal in the United States. If you want money for ships, the groups with which I'm associated will help you. If you want money for the means of war, you'll need to see someone else."

"If I saw someone else about that," Schind pressed, "who should I see?"

"Rudolph Sonneborn," Nadelson said without missing a beat.

Schind made a mental note of the name and continued. "What about speaking to the groups you know?"

Nadelson looked up at him, his eyes alert and a troubled frown on his brow. "About acquiring weapons for war? I already told you, it'll be a waste of time and it might destroy their support for the entire project."

Obviously, Nadelson had misunderstood the question, but the intensity of his response left Schind suspicious that the real reason Nadelson was reluctant to raise money for weapons was because

Nadelson himself was opposed to the idea. "No," Schind replied, correcting the mistake. "About the ships. Do you think we could arrange for me to speak about the ships?"

"Oh." The expression on Nadelson's face softened and he glanced away as he dabbed the corners of his mouth with his napkin. "Scheduling a full slate of meetings will take time," he said after a moment, "but there's a meeting tonight of the American Friends of the Hebrew University." Nadelson smiled. "Our guest speaker had to back out at the last minute. I told them I would find someone." He pointed to Schind. "You can be the speaker."

The short notice bothered Schind. "Tonight?" he asked, unable to hide his concern.

"Yes," Nadelson nodded. "It's a good group and talking to them will give you a way of gauging the response you can expect from others."

Schind knew he had no choice but to accept. "Sounds like fun," he said with a smile. "What time?"

"Seven."

The meeting that evening was held in a ballroom at the Drake Hotel. Schind had never seen a hotel so palatial and he was nervous as his time to speak approached. But as Nadelson introduced him, something Nadelson said reminded Schind of home and he thought of the men with whom he'd served in Haganah. Those men back home faced the threat of constant danger—if not from the Arabs who wanted to kill them, then from the British who wanted to inter them in prison camps. *They* were his real cause. He was in New York to organize refugee relief because of them and when he spoke, he did not speak for himself but for them.

As he thought of that, a sense of peace swept over Schind, and when Nadelson concluded his introduction, Schind rose from his chair and strode toward the podium with the confidence and ease of the man he truly was—one who'd looked death in the eye and come away the victor. Nothing could intimidate him after that.

"I rise to greet you this evening," he began, "not as a spokesman for a cause, nor as a proponent of a position regarding an abstract policy issue. I stand before you this evening as a messenger on behalf of a beleaguered people."

From the corner of his eye he saw Nadelson suddenly tense and worried, as though he feared that Schind, in spite of his repeated warnings, was about to launch into Ben-Gurion's standard speech regarding Jews in Palestine, the need for independence, and the coming war with Arabs. He needn't have worried. Schind had other plans.

"For tonight I am a spokesman," he continued, "of my people. A messenger of your people. An advocate for our fellow Jews who are this hour suffering in the misery of displaced persons camps throughout Europe. Held there against their will by barbed-wire fences, at facilities patrolled by armed guards still marching the grounds, and overseen by armed guards still in the towers above. For many of them, the camp where they are being held now is the same camp from which the Allied army supposedly liberated them almost two years ago. The soldiers who man the fences and towers are no longer the soldiers of the Third Reich, but of the British Empire, the United States, and the Allied nations who claim to have liberated us from Nazi domination."

It was a speech Schind had always wanted to give and one he'd run over and over in his mind a thousand times, but until that evening it was a speech he'd been too afraid even to try. He'd stormed houses occupied by terrorists, hurled himself at onrushing soldiers in hand-to-hand combat with a fury no one could tame, and led men through the night on harrowing missions, but until that night the thought of standing before a crowd to deliver an address left him immobilized with fear. That evening, however, Schind threw aside the paralyzing anxiety that had plagued him in the past and for an hour spoke with candor and emotion about the desire of many in Palestine to once and for all liberate their fellow Jews from the European camps and bring them to a new home in Palestine.

"The homes they knew in Europe have been destroyed, and those that remain have been conveyed to others. Unraveling those conveyances would disrupt a European society already in shambles from the war and require an effort of a scale and magnitude no nation is now willing to undertake. Incremental attempts to alleviate their suffering have been largely ineffective, undermined primarily by the emergence of centuries-old hatred and prejudice that has once again come to the surface. But there is one place that could alleviate all their suffering. One place willing to take them all. One place that offers them a home. And it's the one place to which most of them want to go. That place is Palestine."

When the meeting ended the audience gave him a standing ovation and when they finally quieted and began to leave, a line formed near the front of the room as many in attendance waited to speak with Schind. One by one they grasped his hand to shake it, and Schind felt the press of a check, a business card, or a note against his palm.

And as they grasped his hand, many of them leaned close and said things like, "Morris Ginsberg is my friend. Tell him hello for me." Or, "I am associated with Dewey Stone. Let me know what I can do." Schind was glad to have their support, both financially and personally, but realized to his horror that word of what they were doing was getting out. Whether he liked it or not, people knew and soon there would be no point in maintaining even the pretense of secrecy. Yet for the first time since coming to New York he realized that might not be such a bad idea. After all, this was the United States of America. He could talk about anything he wanted to discuss. The British might make trouble—they might not—but the response that evening confirmed for him that they were on the right path and maybe, just maybe, this crazy project that Ben-Gurion, Golda, and Perez had given him wasn't so crazy after all.

As the group dwindled and Nadelson came to Schind's side, a tall, broad-shouldered man approached. He was dressed in a business suit with a white shirt and tie that any Wall Street broker would have been proud to wear, but the style of his haircut and the way he carried himself told Schind he was a man with military experience, probably an officer. Before Schind could ask, the man thrust out his hand and said, "I'm Mickey Marcus," and, like many others that evening, he handed Schind a business card.

Schind glanced at the card, then up to Marcus. "You're a lawyer."

"Yeah," Marcus acknowledged but quickly moved on. "That was an interesting presentation you gave tonight."

"Thanks," Schind replied.

"I appreciated what you had to say, but I was especially intrigued by what you *didn't* say."

Schind was puzzled. "The part I didn't say?"

Marcus nodded. "Yeah, the part you left out."

"Which part was that?"

"The part about the coming war in Palestine."

Schind glanced at the card again. The name—Mickey Marcus—looked familiar but he couldn't quite place it. "You think there'll be war in Palestine?"

"Yes," Marcus replied. "And so do you."

"Why do you think war is so certain?"

"Well," Marcus began, "from what I've read, Ben-Gurion is determined to form a Jewish state in Palestine. The political climate in the world favors it, but not to the extent of removing the Arabs. Which means you'll have to compromise. You won't be able to gain total control of the entire region. The best you can hope for is a divided Palestine. And since Jews aren't in the majority, you won't get a majority of the land."

"Ben-Gurion has already said he would agree to that," Schind noted, "provided the lines are drawn correctly."

"But," Marcus countered, "the Arabs are categorically opposed to compromise of any kind. They want total control of the entire region and they want all of the Jews out of there. And just as soon as the British withdraw, all of the neighboring Arab nations will join the Palestinian Arabs in fighting against a Jewish state."

"You seem to understand the situation well."

"Comes with the training."

"Army?"

Marcus answered, "Made a career of it. Got out not too long ago."

"Well," Schind said, "we could find a place for you on a ship." He was kidding. "But if you aren't interested in the army, you're probably not interested in that."

"Don't know much about ships," Marcus replied good-naturedly. "But I might be able to help in other ways."

Now Schind remembered why Marcus' name sounded familiar. He was on the legal staff that prosecuted German war criminals at Nuremburg.

"What was your rank when you left the army?"

"Colonel."

"You were at Nuremburg?"

"Yeah." Marcus had a satisfied look. "I tried some of the cases there. But my real expertise is in planning, logistics, organization. That sort of thing."

"We could use some help with organization."

"Well, keep me in mind."

As Marcus walked away, Nadelson spoke up. "He's an interesting guy. Army used him in several capacities and wanted him to reenlist. Even offered him a promotion to general but he turned them down."

"Why?"

"Said he'd had enough. And I think the army life was tough on his family. That's what he says when he talks about it."

"The army life can be tough for a family," Schind replied and for a moment he thought of home, his wife, and the long months of separation his service in Haganah had cost them. He stared after Marcus until he disappeared through the ballroom doorway, watching his gait, the movement of his arms, the tilt of his head, hoping to see in him a glimmer of hope that family and army wouldn't always require so much, but he saw nothing that told him otherwise.

After the meeting Nadelson drove Schind back to Hotel Fourteen. On the way, they talked about all that had transpired and how well it went. Schind, still feeling the rush of adrenaline from the experience, was eager to move forward with the fund-raising effort in other places. "We need to develop that full schedule of meetings we discussed."

"I was thinking the same thing tonight while you spoke," Nadelson agreed. "I'll get started right away. We should focus on the Midwest and begin with Cleveland."

Schind's mind, however, was already on California and the need to work on Ben-Gurion's desire for airplanes. "What about fund-raising in California?"

Nadelson looked doubtful. "The West Coast is not such a good place for us. And certainly not for this kind of thing. The Midwest will be much better."

"I need to visit California," Schind gently insisted.

Nadelson lifted an eyebrow with an expression that seemed to indicate he understood Schind had other purposes for going there, but he didn't ask. "Then . . . I will schedule meetings there for you as well," he conceded. "How soon would you like to go?"

"As soon as you can work it out."

"Okay. The Midwest will be easier to arrange and I think much more productive, so I'll get that together first. That will give you a sure source of money you can receive quickly and keep the underlying work—locating the ships and buying them—progressing on schedule. After we get the Midwest set up, we can take care of California and the West Coast. But it won't be easy."

Schind didn't care whether it was easy or difficult. Ben-Gurion was counting on him. The men of Haganah were counting on him. Jews in Europe and Palestine were relying on him to come through with ships and planes and any weapons he could find. For Schind, how difficult that might be wasn't even a consideration. He just wanted to get started.

CHAPTER 15

THE VOLUNTEERS

By the time Schind reached his room at Hotel Fourteen that evening, four hours had passed since he stepped from the podium and began shaking hands. Yet in spite of the late hour, he was wide awake and much too excited to sleep. So instead of tossing and turning in bed, he sat in a chair near the window, sipped from a cup of hot tea, and thought about what to do next. Nadelson had suggested he contact Rudolph Sonneborn for help raising money to buy weapons. Schind knew nothing of Sonneborn—not even his reputation—but his name was on the list Ben-Gurion gave him. If Ben-Gurion thought he was helpful, and if Nadelson mentioned him without prompting, perhaps he should give Sonneborn a call.

Sometime around midmorning the following day, Schind phoned Rudolph Sonneborn, an oil executive and businessman who lived in Manhattan not too far from Hotel Fourteen. Schind's introduction of himself, always an awkward moment for him, took surprisingly little effort. Sonneborn seemed to be expecting the call and quickly agreed to meet with Schind at Sonneborn's office later that day.

This time, unlike his experience with Ginsberg, Stone, or Nadelson, Schind felt little hesitation in discussing the details of his mission and plan. He told Sonneborn about Ben-Gurion's interest in forming an army, the need to prepare for war, and the desire to establish at least a rudimentary air force with which to leverage their much smaller ground force into an army capable of defeating the Arabs.

Sonneborn agreed. "We have to use every means possible to

maximize the men and women we have available for fighting. But we must get busy with preparations now. Before the fighting begins. If we don't prepare now to defend ourselves," he said, speaking as though he were one of the Palestinian Jews himself, "the refugees will have no homeland to come home to. And the Jews in Palestine will either be gone or dead."

With such a ringing endorsement, Schind dispensed with further detail and went straight to the point. "Can you help with fund-raising?"

"Yes," Sonneborn answered, "but this won't be as easy as it ought to be." Then he repeated some of what Nadelson told Schind the night before. "Not all Jews in the United States support the effort to address the situation in Palestine the way Ben-Gurion wants to address it. Many would help with the European refugee issues. They'll eagerly pay to purchase Palestinian farmland and they'll support Palestinian construction projects. They'll even lobby their congressmen for help in obtaining better treatment for Palestinian Jews from Great Britain, but supplying arms and munitions scares them." He paused as a smile spread across his face. "But then, I assume that's why you came to me."

"I was told you were interested in the military side of the issue."

"I am," Sonneborn assured. "I just wanted you to understand the task we face."

"I realize it won't be easy."

"It won't be easy," Sonneborn reiterated. "But it won't be impossible either."

"So, what do we do?" Schind was eager to get started and thought it important to keep Sonneborn moving. "What needs to happen next?"

"I suggest," Sonneborn said tentatively, "that we . . . begin with . . . a small group." He seemed to be thinking the matter through as he talked. "That may not be what you had in mind . . . but I think that's best."

"I'll do whatever you think we should do," Schind said eagerly.

"I know people—individuals of significant financial ability and people with significant relationships—who will support the acquisition of arms. Not many," Sonneborn added, qualifying his remarks, "but I know a few. I think they would respond well to a more . . . private discussion. One in which you could be more frank with them about the situation we face."

"That sounds good," Schind agreed. "When can we do it?"

"We could do it this Sunday," Sonneborn offered.

Having pushed for action, Schind was taken aback at the quick response. "You can arrange it that soon?"

"I can if we phone everyone." Sonneborn's pattern of speech became noticeably more rapid as his enthusiasm for the project took over. "We'll have the meeting at my apartment. Something small enough to pass for a Sunday luncheon. I'll come up with the menu and have it catered. But we'll keep it small. Not too many people. Not too elaborate. So it won't attract too much attention. And we can all sit around the living room, which will allow you to interact with the participants on a more informal basis. They can ask questions. See you face-to-face. That'll make them feel like they're being included in a clandestine operation."

Schind had an ironic smile. "They *are* being included in a clandestine operation."

"Yes," Sonneborn grinned. "And they'll like that." He leaned back in the chair and crossed his legs. "I'm not sure what the immediate outcome will be," Sonneborn cautioned, "but I think this is the way to start."

"Yes," Schind nodded. "I do, too."

The following Sunday, Schind arrived at Sonneborn's apartment to find a group of men eagerly awaiting him. He glanced down the hall toward the living room, then located Sonneborn in the kitchen overseeing the food preparation with the catering staff. "This looks like a good crowd," Schind said.

"It *is*," Sonneborn beamed. "As good as we could hope for."

"How many were invited?"

"Seventeen," Sonneborn replied proudly.

"And how many came?"

"Seventeen," Sonneborn announced. He was so pleased with the turnout he could barely contain himself. "All of them came."

"All of them local?"

"No." Sonneborn shook his head. "Only about half. The rest are from . . . everywhere, almost."

Using a format much like the one he used when briefing Haganah leaders, Schind spent much of the day explaining the situation Jews faced in Palestine. He outlined for the group the general scenario—the pending British withdrawal, restrictions on Jewish attempts to arm themselves, and the attacks expected to begin the moment the British were gone—but gave most of his attention to a detailed examination of the atrocities foisted upon Jewish residents by their Arab neighbors. Crops were burned or otherwise destroyed, livestock was mutilated, and buildings bombed in seemingly deliberate and well-planned attacks. On top of that, there were random shootings and stabbings. And all of it going on under the watchful eyes of British soldiers who stood by and did nothing until Haganah or one of the paramilitary organizations responded. Then there were house-to-house searches, always for the Jews. Never for the Arabs.

According to Schind, it was not uncommon to find dead bodies hanging from trees by the side of the road, or to learn that entire families—including women and children—had been slaughtered in the night while they slept.

When Schind concluded his presentation, the discussion turned to the task of what to do about the situation. With Sonneborn's help, the group identified three primary tasks with which they could assist. The first was fund-raising. "That is the primary means by which we can assist Haganah and the Jews in general," Sonneborn emphasized. "They need arms—weapons and ammunition—and we can supply the money with which to purchase them," one of the members stated.

In addition to funding, the group also decided to conduct local meetings for the purpose of recruiting additional participants and to develop contacts and information about weapons and materiel available for purchase in their areas. "We will create a network that stretches all the way across the country. Small, local organizations just like this one." He glanced around the room. "Each of us will form a meeting like this one in our own city. And then we will branch out from there."

"What will we call ourselves?"

"Do we have to call it anything?"

"A name is not necessary."

"What will we do with the money we raise?"

"Send it to me," Sonneborn said. "I will handle the money."

"Then maybe we should call ourselves the Sonneborn Institute," someone suggested.

Everyone laughed, but before they went home that night they decided to do just that. It would be an informal association. In reality, nothing more than a single bank account for handling donations, the idea that they could make a difference, and their mutual commitment to the ideals outlined that day.

The meeting lasted until almost dark. When it was over and the guests had departed, Schind took a seat on the sofa and said, "I think that went rather well."

"Yes," Sonneborn agreed as he collapsed onto a nearby chair. "I think that was the best Zionist meeting I've ever attended."

The following day, Schind received a call from Ash asking him to come to the office on Water Street and meet with Paul Shulman. Schind agreed to visit with Shulman that afternoon. "Provided you're there," he added. "You're the one who knows him."

"We'll be waiting for you," Ash assured.

When Schind arrived at Ash's office, he noticed the name Land and Labor for Palestine, Inc. had been added to the door. "That was Joe Buxenbaum's idea," Ash's secretary explained.

Schind was puzzled. "Joe's idea?"

"He's working from our office now. Land and Labor for Palestine is his organization."

"What does it do?"

"You'll have to ask him."

Schind glanced around. "Where is he?"

"He had to step out for a minute," she said. "He'll be back in a little while."

Just then a door opened and Ash emerged from his office. "Let's talk a minute," he guided Schind toward the extra office.

"Is Shulman here?" Schind asked.

"Yeah." Ash nudged Schind into Buxenbaum's office and closed the door. "He's here."

"Well, is there a problem with him? Why are we in here?"

"Lower your voice," Ash insisted. "There's no problem with him. I just thought we should talk a minute before we get in there."

"Why? There's not much for me to say. I don't know anything about the guy."

"Well, look, here's the thing," Ash began. "Somehow Weizmann found out Shulman was coming down here to meet with us and called to put in a good word for him."

"Oh," Schind sighed. "Weizmann knows him."

"Ben-Gurion, too."

"Ben-Gurion?"

"Yeah. Ben-Gurion and the guy's parents are good friends."

"Okay," Schind said, nodding slowly. "Then we might have to use him for something whether he works out or not. What can we do with him?"

"Like I said before, I really think he would make a good training officer. Not to actually train the crewmen, but to run the program. He's a graduate from the Naval Academy at Annapolis. He must have learned *something* in all that time."

"Maybe," Schind responded. "But I seem to remember you told me he had never commanded a ship."

"That's correct," Ash nodded. "I don't think he ever commanded anything."

"What rank was he when he got out?"

"Lieutenant."

"Lieutenant," Schind mused, thinking aloud. "That's like a captain in the army?"

"Yeah, but captains in the army actually command troops in the field. This guy doesn't have that kind of experience."

"Okay. So we'll talk to him and see what he has to say and if he doesn't fit we'll keep him around until we think of something."

Ash reached for the door. "Come on in. I'll introduce you." He led the way back to his office and held the door while Schind entered.

Shulman, a tall, slender young man was seated on the far side of the room and stood as they entered. He was dressed in dark gray slacks, light blue shirt, and navy blazer accented by a red tie and black wing-tip shoes. But for the shoes, he could have easily arrived straight from the yacht club.

Ash introduced him to Schind and they all took a seat facing each other. Shulman, they learned, was an engineer by training but he had been to sea numerous times. "During the course of the war," he explained, "I worked on board several ships. Destroyers, mostly. Chasing German submarines in the Atlantic."

"Ever have any command experience?" Schind knew the answer but wanted to hear what Shulman would say.

"I was in charge of the mechanical crew on two of the ships—boiler room, engine room, electricians. They all reported to me."

That was something, Schind told himself, but nothing like the experience even the newest Haganah recruits received. "Do you know what we're trying to do?"

"I understood through Mr. Weizmann that you are planning to acquire ships and use them to ferry refugees from Europe to Palestine."

Schind shot a look in Ash's direction. Ash glanced away. Both of them realized Weizmann was talking too much about the operation. "That's the basic idea," Schind said.

"Do you have crews for these ships?" Shulman asked.

"Not yet, but we're working on it."

Shulman looked perplexed by that response. "Not yet?"

Ash spoke up. "We're still recruiting men."

"There shouldn't be any difficulty in hiring a crew." Shulman spoke with a hint of condescension. "We have a glut of sailors here in New York."

"That's just it," Schind said. "We're asking people to do this job for free."

Shulman's eyes opened wide with a look of surprise. "For free?"

"Yes."

"You want them to sail all the way to Europe? For free?"

"And then on to Palestine," Ash added. "We have almost enough for a crew on the first ship."

"What do you want me to do?"

"We'd like for you to set up a program to train the crew," Ash said.

"You want me to train them? An all-volunteer crew?"

"No." Ash shook his head. "We don't want you to train them. We want you to set up the program to train them. Figure out the topics they'll need to know, establish an instructional regimen, recruit instructors, that sort of thing."

Shulman still appeared skeptical. "How many of these . . . volunteers will have sailing experience?"

Ash said, "Not many."

"Well, I'll have to see a list of those we've found so far."

Schind spoke up. "I'll see what I can do about that."

Shulman shook his head. "I really don't think you want to do this with novices."

"I think that's exactly what we'll do it with." By then Schind had had enough of Shulman's attitude.

"I assure you," Shulman continued, oblivious to Schind's mood. "That will be quite impossible. Perhaps you could—"

"That's why we contacted you," Ash interrupted, trying to beat Schind to a response. "We have a challenging job ahead of us and we need the best people we can get. You're one of the best."

"But," Shulman continued to lament, "you expect me to prepare a ship's crew, to sail a ship to Europe and then to Palestine, and do it with unpaid, inexperienced volunteers?"

Ash patted him on the shoulder. "I knew you'd like the challenge."

They talked a little longer, then Schind stood and thanked Shulman for his time. "We'll be in touch."

When Shulman was gone, Ash came to Schind's side. "Well," he said. "What do you think?"

"Send him home and never contact him again."

"He wasn't that bad."

"No. He was worse. The man hasn't any idea how to adapt and overcome. I've spent the last ten years leading men who can take down a platoon with a length of wire and a starter pistol. This guy Shulman . . . has nothing to offer."

"Except that he's friends with Weizmann and Ben-Gurion."

"Yeah," Schind said with a frustrated sigh. "And then there's that." He turned away a moment in thought, then said, "Set him up with the training program and we'll see how he does. But he doesn't have long to prove himself. If he isn't going to work out, we'll have to replace him in a hurry."

As Schind turned to leave, the door to the hallway opened and Buxenbaum entered. Schind took him aside to ask about the name on the door. "What's all this Land and Labor for Palestine about? I thought you were recruiting crewmen for the ships."

"I am," Buxenbaum replied. "I have a group lined up already."

"What's with the name on the door?"

"That's our cover. But look . . . about the crews. We can't find enough experienced Jewish sailors to man the ships. In fact, we can't find enough of any kind of sailor to do it."

"What's the problem?"

"Most of them are married now. They can't really leave home that long and especially without pay."

"So what do we do?" Schind asked.

"We started looking for the next best thing."

"Which is?"

"Weekend sailors, fishermen, that sort of thing," Buxenbaum suggested.

"Find any?"

"A few, but they're young."

Schind had a skeptical look. "Young?"

"Most of them are from an agricultural training facility over in New Jersey," Buxenbaum explained. "They were training to work on farms in Palestine. We lured them away."

"With what?"

"A free trip."

"Good idea," Schind replied.

"Yeah, but we need to broaden our search even further."

Schind thought for a moment. "This is the riskiest part," he said after a moment. "Trusting a wider array of people."

"Right now," Buxenbaum explained, "we're talking about it in terms of a relief trip, free passage to Palestine. Telling them they can remain there if they like. It works well with young people."

"Okay, but be careful. We need to be clever about recruitment, but we don't need a lot of people leaving when they learn what we're really doing. We don't have time for that. And make sure you find out as much as possible about them."

"Right." Buxenbaum picked up a stack of papers. "That's what this is."

"That's good." Schind nodded, then lowered his voice. "Listen, we were meeting just now with Paul Shulman. Do you know him?"

"Not well," Buxenbaum answered. "Just know he was in the navy. Went to Annapolis, I think. Is he helping us?"

"We've asked him to set up a training program for the crews."

"Did he say yes?"

"I think so. But look, I need you to keep an eye on him. Maybe help him out. Once this gets rolling, we'll be pressed for time and I'm not sure how much experience he has in . . . you know . . . improvising, making do, piecing things together."

"I understand," Buxenbaum said. "I'll keep him pointed in the right direction."

From Ash's office, Schind took a taxi uptown to see Ginsberg. He had checks in his pocket from the meeting with Nadelson and they needed to decide how to handle them.

Schind arrived at Ginsberg's office unannounced. "It's a good thing you came by," Ginsberg said as he ushered Schind to a chair near his desk. "I have a package of documents from the lawyer."

"The lawyer?"

Much had transpired since they last talked, and it took a moment for Ginsberg to get him caught up. "Our corporations have been formed," Ginsberg said.

"Oh." Schind nodded. "Our US corporation?"

"Yes. And the first two Panamanian corporations as well."

"Great timing," Schind said, then he reached inside his jacket and drew out an envelope, which he dropped onto the desktop. "We need to do something with these."

"What is it?" Ginsberg asked as he picked up the envelope.

"Checks," Schind said with a grin.

Ginsberg opened the envelope, glanced inside, and smiled. "Where did you get these?"

"Henry Nadelson set me up with a speaking engagement the other night."

"Who did you speak to?"

"Friends of the Hebrew University."

"Impressive group," Ginsberg said with an approving look. "Nadelson has agreed to help?"

"He's working on a schedule of meetings now." Schind pointed to the checks. "What do we do about those?"

"We need to open a bank account for the corporation."

"What does it take to open an account?"

"Well," Ginsberg began, "it would be less complicated if I took care of that. We can add you as a signatory on the account, but you aren't an American citizen and if people at the bank ask questions about that, they might hesitate about opening the account or call it to someone's attention."

Schind shook his head. "We don't need any more attention than we're already getting." He arched an eyebrow as he spoke and there was an unmistakable note of concern in his voice. "Word is getting around."

"I know," Ginsberg nodded. "Two people asked me about the ships this week."

"Which is what I meant when we met with Stone. Someone always talks." Schind looked worried. "Word always gets around."

"All the more reason you should let Dewey Stone and me take care of the legal and financial details. No one will ask questions if we do it."

Schind gestured to the checks once more. "Will this be enough to get us started?"

"It's a start. But we'll need much more before this is over."

"What do we do next?"

"You get back to raising money. I'll tell Stone to get moving on purchasing the ships."

"You have one identified already?"

"There are two in Canada we think will work." Ginsberg looked over at Schind. "Do we have enough crewmen for two?"

"If we have two ships," Schind said confidently, "we'll find the men to sail them." He wasn't about to slow them down.

"Good." Ginsberg stood and came from behind the desk. "Keep raising money," he said as he escorted Schind from the office. "You're off to a great start."

CHAPTER 16

THE VOLUNTEERS

With money in hand from Schind's initial speaking engagement, and with fund-raising plans taking shape through Nadelson, Ginsberg notified Stone to move forward with finding a ship. Stone's first attempt took him to Montreal, where he met with Alexander McDonald, a Canadian businessman with whom Stone had done business in the past. McDonald had contacts in the Canadian government. If there were deals to be had, McDonald would know how to get them. They sat in McDonald's office at the Sun Life Building in downtown Montreal.

"What brings you this far north?" McDonald asked as they sat across from each other at his desk.

"I'm involved with a couple of businesses that are in the market for ships. I've heard the Canadian government is selling off a large portion of its navy and wondered if they might have something we could use. Any idea who I should talk to about that?"

McDonald opened a desk drawer and took out a pamphlet. He held it for Stone to see. "This is a list of what they are offering *this* week. They've been issuing these publications for months. Selling war surplus as fast as they possibly can. Ships, machinery from factories, trucks, just about anything you can think of." He handed the pamphlet across the desk to Stone. "I'm not sure how current it is, but that's the latest public information I have."

Stone scanned the brochure as if seeing it for the first time. In reality, however, he'd been studying Canadian ship sales since the day he'd first met with Ginsberg and Schind. He knew every ship the Canadians wanted to sell, every one they'd already sold, and those they listed for sale but had no intention of parting with. After a moment, he pointed to a page. "What about these two? They're listed as Flower-class corvettes. *Beauharnois* and *Norsyd*. What are those?"

McDonald leaned forward, glanced at the page, then leaned back in his chair. "As you probably know, Flower-class corvettes are light, fast vessels. They were originally designed for open-sea escort—shepherding merchant vessels across the North Atlantic and that sort of thing. The Flower-class corvettes built here in Canada were different from those built in England. Ours proved to be lighter than most, which made them fast but not that great on the open sea. They were used primarily for coastal patrol. Minesweeping. That sort of thing. Their lighter weight and different hull gave them a shallow draft. Perfect for shoreline work."

"This says they were built by Morton."

"Yes," McDonald nodded.

"I didn't realize Morton got into the defense business."

"Oh my, yes. Especially in the second half of the war. Vastly expanded their business. Some say they became too large. Rumors have it they're in financial trouble, what with the war over and all."

"So, these ships weren't around from the beginning."

McDonald shook his head. "No, *Beauharnois* and *Norsyd* were constructed later in the war. They're newer versions of the Flower-class. Their design incorporated things learned from the navy's experience at sea with the earlier versions. They have newer engines, better gear, that sort of thing."

Stone laid the pamphlet on the desk and sat with his legs crossed. "You seem to know a lot about these ships."

"My cousin served aboard a corvette and I've assisted two others in purchasing vessels from that class. So, yes, I'm up on them, as they say."

"Your cousin came through the war okay?"

McDonald nodded. "He did well. Making a career of the navy now. When the war ended, everyone rushed for the exits. He stayed and with everyone else gone got a big promotion. So they're happily enjoying the naval life in Nova Scotia," he said with a roll of his eyes. "Great place to vacation. Not interested in living there."

"What kind of shape are these ships in?" Stone asked, returning to the matter at hand. "Are they seaworthy?"

"These two corvettes should be in quite good shape. I'm not sure if they'd suit your purposes but you might get a little more service out of them than some of the others. Some of the ships on these government lists have been in service quite a long time and as they aged, many of them were not maintained that well. But these two were only at sea for two or three years. If you have time to wait, there are two government ships in the yard that are under construction. You could pick up the contract on them for about half the original cost."

Stone had tried that before, and cost overruns almost bankrupted him. "I think we'll stick with these corvettes. How could I get a look at them?"

"War Assets Corporation has custody of them both, but I suspect they're moored at Morton's. I'm sure you could see them without any trouble at all. Would you like for me to make some calls for you?"

"Sure."

With McDonald running interference, representatives from the War Assets Corporation readily agreed to allow Stone a tour of the ships. The following day, McDonald picked him up at his hotel and they rode over to Morton Engineering and Dry Dock Company in Quebec. Shipyard officials escorted them aboard.

After an hour with the ships, Stone had seen enough to know both vessels could easily make the trip to Europe and on to Palestine. When he indicated he was ready to move forward with buying them, McDonald agreed to make arrangements with War Assets officials for proposal of a formal bid.

✡

The following afternoon, McDonald took Stone to see Arthur Tupper, a vice-president in the sales department at the War Assets

Corporation. Stone was familiar with almost everyone on the East Coast who was involved in the shipping industry, but Tupper was a man with whom he'd never dealt. Still, he knew Tupper's basic story—son of Canadian expats who lived in the United States, retained his Canadian citizenship, worked his way up through the ranks at Claxton Yard in Boston, and took a job with the Canadian government where he oversaw wartime construction for several classes of naval vessels.

But while Stone didn't know Tupper personally and had never dealt with him on any matter, Stone knew McDonald well and he knew McDonald and Tupper had a connection. He couldn't figure out what that connection was, but he knew there was something between them. Whatever that might be, he was hoping it would push this transaction forward.

"I understand you're interested in acquiring some of our ships," Tupper began.

"Two of them," Stone said. "The *Beauharnois* and the *Norsyd*."

"Are these for you, or for a client?"

"A client."

"I know a few people who have been involved in your ship syndicates," Tupper frowned. "Most of your ships carry fruit, don't they?"

"Yes," Stone replied.

"Why would you be interested in these corvettes?" Tupper asked. "They're both quite small compared to the ships you'd normally use. And they aren't configured for cargo."

"These ships would be used to deliver small-bundle cargo to shallow ports. The center portion of the ship can be reconfigured to accommodate that kind of freight without much difficulty. The ships suit our purpose perfectly. Small-bundle cargo. Shallow harbors. And they're faster than the typical freighter, which is important in making the costs work out." Stone made most of that up on the fly and felt rather proud of himself.

"Who will actually own the ships?"

"Weston Trading Company."

"An American corporation?"

"Yes."

Tupper looked across the desk at Stone a moment, then said, "Normally, we would request a written bid with a few boxes of supporting documents, and then we'd take weeks to review it, but since you're with McDonald and because the government is after us hot and heavy to dispose of these things quickly, I'll make you a deal." He paused to shoot a look in McDonald's direction, then said to Stone, "Both ships for one hundred fifty thousand dollars each. No discussion on the price. Take it or leave it."

That price was far lower than Stone had imagined possible, but he didn't want to appear too easy or show how pleased he really was. "I think the price will suit my client just fine," he nodded his head slowly.

"Good." Tupper rose from his chair and extended his hand toward Stone. The two men shook hands over the desk. "I'll hold the ships for ten days while we prepare a letter of intent. But I'll need your signature on the letter by close of business ten days from today."

"I'll look forward to receiving the initial agreement documents," Stone replied.

As they left the office, McDonald leaned close and said in a low voice, "That is a steal."

"Thanks for your help," Stone replied. "Whatever there is between the two of you, I owe you for it."

"Don't mention it," McDonald grinned. "It's always a pleasure doing business with you, Dewey."

Ginsberg was at home in his apartment in New York when a telegram from Stone reached him. "Deal set for two items. 300 total for both. Details later." Ginsberg picked up the phone and called Schind at Hotel Fourteen. "Looks like Stone is buying two ships."

"Two?" Schind was both surprised and excited. "He really did it?"

"Yes."

"I know we talked about the possibility but I thought we were starting slow and working into it."

"That would have been a good plan," Ginsberg agreed, "but he got an incredible deal and didn't want to let it get away."

"What kind of ships did he get?"

"I just received a telegram from him but it doesn't have any details about the ships other than that he bought two and got them for a total price of three hundred thousand dollars."

"That's a lot of money."

"Yes, but it's unbelievably cheap for ships. Whatever they are, this is a good deal."

"When do you think we'll have them in New York?"

"I don't know. Dewey is on his way back from Montreal now. I'll talk to him tomorrow or the next day and get the details. You better tell Buxenbaum as soon as you can. He needs to know we'll need sailors for two ships."

"He'll love that."

"Joe's a good guy," Ginsberg said. "He'll be excited by the challenge."

"Yeah, probably so. But I don't know if Shulman can train two crews at once."

"Everyone will have to make do with what they have. Including us. Which means you need to help Shulman be successful. We have to use the people who show up. We don't have the luxury of picking and choosing the ones we think are the best."

"I know, but some of them get on my nerves."

"I'm sure they do," Ginsberg chuckled. "Welcome to the world of business."

"I think it's like that in everything."

"Yes," Ginsberg agreed. "It is. We go through this in every organization I belong to. Even the synagogue. Same thing."

"All right," Schind said. "I'll phone Joe and we'll keep moving forward."

"You'll find the people," Ginsberg assured. "This mission to save the refugees has to be done. People will show up to help. Just make sure you're available to receive them."

CHAPTER 17

THE VOLUNTEERS

In Montreal the following day, Fred Kingsmill, an assistant in the War Assets Corporation's legal department, was busy at his desk when a clerk brought a message that Dean Jamison, one of the department's younger attorneys, wanted to see him. Kingsmill dutifully rose from behind his desk and made his way upstairs to Jamison's office.

"They sent us another transaction," Jamison said, hardly looking up from the clutter atop his desk. "I need you to handle the details."

"What are they giving away now?" Kingsmill asked sarcastically.

"Two corvettes." Jamison opened the file, glanced inside, then handed it to Kingsmill. "Looks like you aren't far off on your assessment."

Kingsmill took the file from him, opened it, and scanned the top sheet. His shoulders slumped when he read the price. "Why do they do this?"

"Someone at the top said to get rid of them. So they're getting rid of them."

"Yesterday it was trucks. Today it's ships. Tomorrow they might try to give *us* away."

"Well," Jamison quipped, "let's hope they get a better price for us than they're getting for this stuff."

"We need to keep this transaction on schedule so no one yells at us." Jamison's voice took on a businesslike tone as he shifted from office banter to the work at hand. "So prepare a letter of intent. Standard stuff. Use the letter from a previous transaction as a form. Snag the description of the ships from the documents in the file. Make sure the details in the letter conform to the terms of this particular deal."

Kingsmill looked through the pages in the file. "Do we have everyone's address?"

"Address of the purchaser is on the cover sheet. We don't need much detail, just the gist of the deal. Don't get lost in minutia. They'll be looking for the letter of intent by tomorrow."

"Anything else?"

"After you finish the letter, prepare the usual documents—contract, bill of sale, that sort of thing. Whatever else we've been doing with the other sales." Jamison gestured to the files on his desk. "I have to stay busy here with this. You take care of that and let me know if you hit a problem." The expression on his face changed and his voice became stern. "But don't come up here every five minutes to ask me a question. I need you to do this yourself."

"Very well," Kingsmill said. With the open file in his hands, he turned toward the door to leave, then stopped and glanced back at Jamison. "Where are the bid documents?"

"There weren't any."

"Why not?"

"Just create the letter of intent and get moving," Jamison snapped in an irritated tone. "The deal is done. Not our job to question why or how."

"Tupper signed off on it?"

"Yes. Read the file. And close the door on your way out."

Back at his desk, Kingsmill went to work preparing the letter of intent for sale of the two corvettes. Creating that document was a simple task and took little time. When he was finished, he set it aside for later review and went to work on the more complex documents—the contract, bill of sale, statement of condition, and terms of delivery. Doing that took him deeper into the file where he noticed the names associated with the transaction. Not only had Tupper approved the sale, but Alexander McDonald's name was attached to it as well. The annoyance Kingsmill felt when Jamison handed him the file turned to indignation and contempt.

This was the fourth transaction in the past month that came from Tupper's office. All of them done the same way. No bid documents. No independent valuation. No approval from business affairs. Each of them with mention of McDonald. Each of them approved by Tupper. As Kingsmill continued to work, his anger grew until he was furious.

"Jamison might not want to do something about it," he muttered to himself in disgust, "but I surely can. And I will."

For the remainder of the afternoon, Kingsmill followed the office's guidelines as he meticulously assembled the necessary information for the required documents, taking care to produce instruments that belied no predisposition on his part, but as he worked through the information in the file he jotted down the transaction details on a separate note pad. Names of the parties, description of the vessels, accepted price, location of the yard that built them, date of commission and launch, present location of both ships, and the proposed date of delivery—everything one would need to properly identify the transaction, the subject matter, and the people involved.

At the end of the day, Kingsmill tore the sheet from the note pad, folded it carefully, and placed it in the pocket of his jacket. Then he reached for the phone, called a friend, Julian Glenister, and invited him to meet for a drink after work.

On the way that evening, Kingsmill stopped by Dominion Square Tavern on Metcalfe Street. It was an old bar and his favorite. As he pushed open the door and made his way inside, he saw Julian Glenister already seated at the bar. From the empty glasses before him, and the one in his hand, Kingsmill surmised he was on his third drink.

Glenister, a tall, slender man of about thirty years, was an agent with MI6, part of the intelligence contingent sent over during the war to help look after British interests in North America. Kingsmill came to know him at a time when the Canadian government was busy constructing and acquiring ships for its navy. Glenister was assigned to an MI6 unit tasked with securing Quebec shipyards against the possibility of sabotage.

Now that the war was over, the government's attention turned to liquidating military inventory at a pace almost as furious as it had been assembled. Glenister was assigned to monitor transactions involving dual-use items—equipment and materiel with both an industrial and military application—in an attempt to keep sensitive technology from reaching the hands of Communists and others perceived as a threat to the British Crown.

Kingsmill threaded his way past the press of patrons and took a seat beside Glenister, then glanced up at the bartender and ordered a drink. "How's your day going?" he asked with a sideways glance.

"Not bad," Glenister replied. "From the tone of your voice when you called this afternoon, I'd say mine was better than yours."

"No doubt."

"Trouble?"

"It's these liquidation sales," Kingsmill groused. "Some of the transactions are all right. I mean everything's going cheap. But some of them are giveaways."

"Oh?"

"Yeah." The bartender set a glass of liquor on the bar in front of Kingsmill. He took a sip, then continued. "I mean, I don't mind a deep discount, but the prices on some of these transactions are half again below scrap. And for ships that are still seaworthy." He paused for another sip. "Better than seaworthy."

"What kind of ships?"

Kingsmill glanced over his shoulder, then lowered his voice. "We got this deal today. Came down from the top. They're selling two corvettes—neither of them even five years old—they're selling them for a hundred fifty thousand each."

"US?"

"Yeah," Kingsmill nodded. "US dollars."

"Who's buying them?"

"A company in New York named Weston Trading."

"Never heard of them."

"Me either, but I've heard the names of some of the individuals involved with this deal," Kingsmill said with more than a hint of sarcasm.

"Who is that?"

"Arthur Tupper, for one."

"He works for War Assets, doesn't he?"

"Yeah. He's a vice-president in the sales department. And there's a guy named Alexander McDonald. Owns several businesses here."

"Yeah," Glenister nodded. "I know of him." He took a sip from his glass. "You seem rather bothered by this."

Kingsmill shrugged. "I don't know. Maybe it's nothing. Maybe I should do like Jamison says and just do my work, mind my own business, and go home at the end of the day."

"Well, if your goal is to work until you retire and then spend your time fishing, I suppose that might be good advice."

"It's just that, this is about the fourth or fifth transaction like this to come through our office."

"Like what?"

"Ridiculously low price, no outside valuation on the items being sold, no formal bid documents. No financial disclosure forms from the purchaser. And all of it approved by Tupper and associated with McDonald." Kingsmill looked over at Glenister. "It just doesn't sound right."

"Maybe so," Glenister said. "Get me the details. We'll check into it."

Kingsmill took the transaction notes from his pocket and handed them to Glenister. "That's why I wanted to talk to you."

Glenister glanced at the papers, then smiled. "Good. We'll get into it." He tucked the notes into his pocket and turned to the bartender. "We'll have another." Then he pointed to the empty glasses in front of them and said, "These are on me."

At midmorning the next day, Glenister arrived at an office building in downtown Montreal, hung over and bleary-eyed. He'd stayed at the bar long after Kingsmill was gone and stumbled back to his apartment just before dawn. With considerable concentration just to put one foot in front of the other, he plodded across the building's lobby and rode the elevator up to an eleventh-floor office that housed the Canadian headquarters of MI6.

As he flopped into a chair at his desk, Jimmy, an office assistant, appeared at the door. "You don't look so good," Jimmy offered.

"Thanks," Glenister groaned. "You don't look so good, either."

"Rough night?"

"I don't remember." Glenister leaned back in his chair and closed his eyes, but waved Jimmy over from across the room. When Jimmy was at his side, Glenister handed him the transactions notes from Kingsmill and said, "Work this up for a report to London."

Jimmy glanced at the handwritten pages with a perplexed expression. "What is this?"

"The company listed in those notes is preparing to purchase two former warships from the Royal Canadian Navy." Glenister lifted his eyelids long enough to point to the page. "The names of the ships are right there. Find out the details and prepare a report."

"Do we know this company? This Weston Trading Company? Do we know them? Have they ever been on our list?"

"I don't recognize it," Glenister replied.

"Then why are we doing this? Why are we wasting our time looking into it? I have a thousand other things on my desk, all of which you said were top priority."

Suddenly Glenister rocked forward in his chair and abruptly stood. Without a word of explanation or direction, he grasped Jimmy by the elbow and guided him out the door and down the hall to an empty conference room. "You're new to this office," Glenister said when they were alone in the room. "So I'll explain how things work around here just this once. This is how we work. We notice things, we prepare reports about it, and we send those reports to London. Someone over there sorts it all out and decides what to do with it. Got it?"

"I know what we do," Jimmy retorted.

"No, you don't," Glenister snapped. "Because if you did, you wouldn't be arguing with me. We gather information. We send that information to London. That's our job."

"But why are we interested in this transaction? Is there something about it I should know?"

Glenister let go of Jimmy's arm and reached up to squeeze his fingers tight against the bridge of his nose, hoping somehow to relieve the throbbing in his head. "Look," he said after a moment, "I have a friend in the War Assets Corporation. They're in the process of liquidating excess inventory from the Canadian Navy. Right now the Canadian Navy is one of the largest navies in the world. When War Assets gets through with it, it'll be one of the smallest."

"They have a lot to sell."

"Yes," Glenister agreed. "My friend works over there in the sales section. When a major deal comes across his desk, he sends me a note about it. We use his information, track down the details, and send the information to London for their review. Whether the deal catches the eye of someone in London, or whether it catches our eye as suspicious is irrelevant."

"But don't you want to—"

"I would point out to you that this transaction involves two potentially lethally armed, rather fast warships of recent vintage. If possible, I think we'd like to know where they're going and what they're going to be used for, and we'd like to know that before the buyer takes delivery. Regardless of how the deal came to our attention." As the last sentence trailed from his lips, Glenister turned to the door, pulled it open, and pointed toward the hall. "Now, get back to your desk, get busy, and prepare that report. We need to transmit it as soon as possible. While the information still means something."

CHAPTER 18

THE VOLUNTEERS

A few days later, Collins left work as usual and rode home to his apartment. Olivia was in the living room, sitting on the sofa, when he arrived. He kissed her lightly on the lips and asked about dinner. "You have a meeting tonight," she recalled.

"A meeting?" Collins frowned. "What meeting?"

"Men's club," she said in a matter-of-fact tone. "At the church."

"Oh." He flopped onto the sofa. "I forgot all about it."

"You made a reservation."

"I know," he sighed. "But it's late."

"No, it isn't," she countered. "You have time to take a shower, get a cab, and still be there early."

He smiled at her playfully. "Are you throwing me out?"

"No, but the kids and I have plans."

"Plans?"

"Pizza. A movie. A night with . . . something different."

"That sounds like fun."

"Yeah," she grinned. "But we were planning it for us."

"Oh," he said with mock disappointment. "Okay."

"You need to go to the meeting," she said, her voice turning serious. "You don't go to Sunday school anymore and you—"

"I'm there on Sundays," he said, interrupting her. "*Every* Sunday."

"Yes, but you just drink coffee in the kitchen while we go to class."

"I can't take Delwyn's teaching."

"I know," she agreed. "It's not the best, but the meeting tonight will be different."

"Not really."

She pushed him to get off the sofa. "Get moving. Take a shower and change your clothes. They're serving steak tonight."

"I can get a steak at a dozen places."

"Lyman Pillans will be there. You like talking to him."

"Yeah. I do." He looked over at her. "You know for a fact that Lyman will be there?"

"I talked to his wife yesterday. She said he's planning to go." She nudged him once more. "Now get moving."

An hour later, Collins left the apartment, made his way to the lobby, and caught a cab for the ride to St. Mark's Church. He arrived in the fellowship hall to find a large crowd already there. A table with soft drinks stood to one side and he made his way there, found a bottle of Coke, and sipped it as he wandered across the room.

About halfway to the podium, which stood along the far wall, he spotted Charles Vickers and Lyman Pillans standing together. Pillans was a lawyer at Newman Aiken, a Wall Street firm that specialized in corporate mergers and acquisitions. Collins met him when a client sold an apartment building to the Ryder hotel chain. Ryder was a Newman Aiken client. He knew Vickers because their sons attended the same school and were in the same class. They'd been together on a couple of grade-school field trips.

Collins made his way toward Vickers and Pillans. "Lyman," he said by way of greeting as he approached. "How's it going?"

"That's what we were just discussing," Pillans said. "Are they keeping you busy at the office?"

"Pretty much all day." Collins glanced at his wristwatch. "I could be down there right now, as a matter of fact."

"Counting all that money," Vickers needled.

"Yeah," Collins didn't like the way Vickers said it, but he let the comment pass. "We're raking it in."

"Seriously," Pillans said, "is business good?"

"Yeah. It's really good."

"We've been slow lately."

"Maybe we should come over to work at your firm," Vickers quipped with a gesture to Collins. "Think they would hire a couple of Methodists like us?"

"I don't know," Collins replied, "but that would be fun, wouldn't it?"

"Fun for them. Not for me." Vickers turned aside. "I'm gonna get something else to drink. Either of you want anything?"

"No, thanks," they both said and Vickers moved away.

When he was gone, Collins looked over at Pillans. "What's up with him?"

"I don't know." The tone of Pillans' voice said he knew more than he wanted to say. "Come on." He gestured to the tables. "Let's find a place to sit. I'm hungry and they'll start serving before long."

Collins and Pillans moved across the room to a table with open seats near the front. Two other men already were seated there but seemed glad for the company. Collins knew neither of them but did his best to engage in polite conversation.

A few minutes later, Vickers joined them. Collins felt the back of his neck stiffen, but before anyone could speak, Rev. Thornton appeared at the podium to welcome everyone, then offered a prayer of invocation. When he was finished, waiters came from the kitchen and began serving.

Before long the din of conversation and the clatter of silverware filled the room as the men talked and ate. Much to Collins' surprise, the meal was delicious and he began to wonder if the evening might turn out better than he'd expected.

As he took another bite, Vickers spoke up. "Palmer, I don't know how you do it."

"How I do what?"

"How you work in that law firm."

Pillans sighed and wiped the corner of his mouth on a napkin. Collins swallowed a and said, "Are you implying we're unethical or something?"

"No," Vickers retorted. "I'm simply stating the obvious. You're the only white guy there."

"We're all white," Collins said with a resolute tone.

"You know what I mean."

"Yes," Collins said coldly. "I'm afraid I do."

"What kind of attitude is that?" Vickers groused.

Collins was astounded by his arrogance . . . and ignorance. "They're good men, Charles."

"Good or not, I'm not working with them. I'm not associating with them. I'm not saying hello to them." Vickers leaned forward and lowered his voice. "And I don't care how much Reverend Thornton preaches about them on Sunday morning. Jews aren't white and I don't want to have anything to do with them."

Collins was offended by Vickers' remarks and in most instances would have kept quiet, but since working at the firm and with Morris Ginsberg he'd come to see the lunacy of some Western prejudice—not just against Jews but against Blacks, Asians, and every other racial group—and he'd become less comfortable with remaining silent.

"I'm a partner," Collins replied. "Not an employee."

"Partner or not, if you work with a Jew, you work *for* them. They don't work for you."

"I'm sorry. I didn't realize you were so . . . prejudiced."

"It's not a prejudice," Vickers argued. "It's the way they are. Money. That's all they think about. Money and control."

"Control?"

"They're out to rule the world," Vickers continued, "and they've already got a good start on it here in New York."

"Charles," Pillans said, "we're in church. We ought to at least conduct ourselves with a sense of civility."

"You're right," Vickers countered. "This is church, and what we ought to be talking about is the truth. Just think about it for a moment. Jews already own most of the city. The newspapers. The radio stations. Everything we hear on the news is slanted in their favor. And everywhere they go, all they cause is trouble. Look at what they're doing in Palestine."

"What are you talking about?"

"I'm talking about the trouble they're causing. First they moved in and stole the land from the Arabs—who'd been living there since the beginning. Now they're terrorizing British troops."

"They didn't steal the land. They bought it. Every square inch of it."

"Says who?"

"Real estate records, history books, articles in the *New York Times*."

"You think they bought the land?"

"I know they bought it. And the Arabs haven't been living in Palestine since the beginning."

"That's why I wouldn't work down there," Vickers smirked. "You hang out with a bunch of Jews, you start to think like Jews."

"No," Collins countered. "If you read and searched for the truth, instead of reading that Charles Coughlin propaganda you like so much, you'd start believing the truth."

Muscles along Vickers' jaw flexed and his eyes flashed with anger. "What's wrong with Coughlin?"

"Nothing if you don't mind avoiding reality," Collins said calmly. Without waiting for a response, he glanced over at Pillans. "I need some coffee. Would you care for any?"

"I think they'll serve it with desert," Pillans said.

"I'd like some now," Collins replied. He pushed his chair back from the table and started across the room.

A moment later, Pillans caught up with him. "Sorry about that back there," he said.

"Has he always been that way?"

"As long as I've known him."

"I had no idea."

"A lot of these men feel the same way," Pillans added, referring to the men in the room. "They just won't say it."

"Why?"

"Why won't they say it?"

"No," Collins corrected. "Why do they feel that way?"

"It's the easier way to make sense of the world."

Collins frowned. "Easier way?"

"Look," Pillans explained in a conciliatory tone, "you understand Palestine far better than most people, but you came to that understanding through years of work and reading. And through what you picked up from the men in your firm who've experienced these things."

"What I know about the situation isn't much."

"What you know is far more than what most people know. Most of these guys don't have that kind of time, or the inclination, to learn much of anything except their job. And most of them don't associate with anyone who doesn't think like they think. So they go for the easy answer."

"But it's wrong," Collins retorted.

"I know."

"It's worse than wrong," Collins continued. "It's evil."

"I know that, too," Pillans agreed. "But this is the reality we face."

"Well, I don't have to face it tonight."

Pillans had a questioning look. "What do you mean?"

"I mean I'm not going back to that table and listen to Vickers' stupid comments the rest of the evening."

"What are you going to do?"

"I'm going down to the King Cole."

Pillans checked over his shoulder, then leaned close and said, "Want some company?"

"Sure," Collins replied, and they started toward the door.

CHAPTER 19

THE VOLUNTEERS

After agreeing to work with William Ash, Paul Shulman was given a small table to use as a desk at the office on Water Street. The table was crammed against the wall in a tiny space that until a few days earlier had been Ash's utility closet. He sat there as he had for the past three days, staring at notes he'd scribbled on the pages that lay before him. Words and phrases gleaned from years of training but which now made no sense to him at all. The assignment from Schind and Ash—train volunteer crewmen to sail a ship to Europe—seemed simple at first, but now, as he faced the task of actually doing it, of piecing together the practical steps of a training regimen designed to meet that goal—it all seemed overwhelming and beyond impossible.

As a graduate of the naval academy at Annapolis, Shulman knew the mechanical operation of a ship and how the US Navy's training programs operated—concise classroom instruction supplemented by rigorous hands-on exercises conducted in facilities tailor-made for the specific purpose of transforming raw, uninformed recruits into capable seamen—but he had none of that now. No time-honored curriculum. No dedicated facilities. No skilled and proficient instructors. The people around him were experts in only one thing: improvising, adapting, making do—skills that were foreign to Shulman and to the operational system he'd learned.

For three days he'd sat at the table, wondering what to do. Finally, late in the afternoon of the fourth day, Shulman had reached the end of trying. So with a sense of resignation and guilt, he rose from his makeshift desk in his makeshift office and went in search of someone who could help.

Shulman's first thought was to talk to Ash, but a quick check with the secretary told him Ash was out of the office and besides, Ash was the one who gave him the training job. Asking him for help didn't seem like a good idea. The only other person in the office that day was Joe Buxenbaum. *He's been sailing most of his life,* Shulman thought. *Maybe he could help.*

Buxenbaum glanced up as Shulman came near. "How's it going?" he asked.

"Not so good."

"What's wrong?"

"I need some direction."

"Okay."

Shulman took a seat next to Buxenbaum. "The program we learned at Annapolis," he began, "was thorough and good, but it depended on specially designed facilities with classrooms and books and a large support staff."

Buxenbaum shook his head. "You don't have that here and you'll never get it."

"I realize that now."

"You gotta make this up yourself," Buxenbaum added, "and make it work with the least amount of specialized people and equipment possible."

In frustration Shulman sliced the air with his hand. "But that's just it, how do I do that?"

"Well," Buxenbaum said in a slow, thoughtful tone, "I guess you begin by breaking it down."

Shulman's brow was furrowed in a puzzled frown. "By breaking it down?"

"Yeah. That's what I do when I have a big problem or a big job," Buxenbaum explained. "I break it down."

Shulman shook his head. "I'm not following you."

"Okay." Buxenbaum sat sideways in the chair and propped an

elbow on the desktop. “Think about the task. You gotta train a ship’s crew, right?”

“Yes.”

“So look over all those books you have and review all the experience you picked up from your time in the navy, then figure out the minimum number of people necessary to operate a ship safely.”

“Okay,” Shulman said with a nod. “But what kind of ship?”

“Any ship.”

“That’s just it,” Shulman objected. “They’re all different.”

“Yes, but they all have crewmen in common. Positions that are the same. Every ship has a captain.”

“Right.”

“And every ship has someone in charge of the engine room.”

“Yeah.”

“Keep going. What are the other positions? What are the individual positions in the engine room? And then figure out the least number of those positions you need.”

“The least number?”

“The ships we’ll be using will be smaller than most in the navy. Certainly smaller than the typical freighter. We’re not talking about training a crew for a battleship. More like a destroyer or smaller.”

“Okay.” Shulman nodded. “A smaller ship.”

“Right. And on top of that, we’re relying on volunteers, so the crews will be smaller in number anyway.”

“All right,” Shulman said in a cooperative manner. “But even so, we’ll need more than just one person for each position. They can’t work twenty-four hours a day, all the way over to Europe.”

“True enough,” Buxenbaum agreed. “But you aren’t building a crew for a ship yet. You’re designing a training exercise. You just need to know which positions to train.”

Shulman’s face brightened. “Oh. Yeah,” he said, a look of realization coming over him. “I need to think of this as a class. An instructional unit. Break the sailing of a ship into units.”

“Right,” Buxenbaum agreed. “You’re constructing a series of

classes. One for deckhands. One for firemen in the boiler room. And all the other sections. And then there are some basic skills everyone on the ship will need to know. So you'll have a few classes that everyone will take."

"What do I do for a training facility? We'll need a location."

"Well, I suppose we could find a few rooms in a building somewhere that you could use for classrooms, but I think you'd do better just using a ship."

Shulman frowned again. "A ship?"

"Yeah."

"I thought we didn't have a ship yet."

"We don't," Buxenbaum chuckled. "But there are plenty of them tied up at the docks around here."

"You mean just take over one of them for training?"

"No," Buxenbaum laughed. "I mean rent one."

"We can do that?"

"Yeah, but check with Schind first."

"What do I say when the ship owner asks me why I want it?"

"Tell him . . . tell him you're starting a school," Buxenbaum suggested.

"A school."

"Yeah. A maritime school. You're a former navy guy starting a school for merchant marines."

"A school," Shulman grinned. "I like that. But it'll need a name."

"Call it New York Maritime School," Buxenbaum suggested.

Shulman shook his head slowly. "No, New York Maritime *Academy*."

Buxenbaum smiled. "There you go."

"Know where I can find a ship we could use?"

"I'll find someone for you to ask about a ship. You talk to Schind about paying for the lease."

Two days later, Shulman asked Schind about locating a ship to use as a training facility. When Schind learned the details of what Shulman was planning, he agreed to help and asked Morris Ginsberg for assistance. "There's a freighter anchored up at Jones Point," Ginsberg said after making a few phone calls. "Near the navy's reserve fleet. Hasn't been there too long. Atlantic Fruit Company owns it but they've taken it out of service. Let me find out if we could get it."

With Ginsberg paving the way, Schind rented the ship and had it towed to a dock in Brooklyn. When it was tied up and the gangway secured, Buxenbaum took Shulman to see it. What they found was a ship that hadn't been to sea in over two years. Paint on the superstructure was peeling and in some places missing altogether, exposing large patches of rusted steel. Some railings were damaged or missing and the ship's main deck was in poor condition.

Inside, the ship was in much the same shape. Discarded beer bottles, brown paper sacks, and empty tin cans lay scattered about. Cobwebs filled the corners and the air was heavy with the acrid odor of urine.

"Someone was living in here," Shulman observed.

"More than one," Buxenbaum added.

Shulman walked over to a hatch and glanced down the steps that led to the lower levels. Below the second rung he saw only the eerie darkness of a long-abandoned hull. "Can we get shore power for it?"

"Yeah, I'm sure we can. Think you can make this work?"

Shulman looked back at him. "This ship is useless," he said with a look of disgust. "They should have scuttled it instead of letting it sit like this."

"It might be useless for the sea," Buxenbaum conceded, "but for what you need, it's perfect."

"Perfect?" Shulman looked perplexed. "It should be sitting on the bottom." He glanced around at the space where they stood. "It's old and dirty and outdated. I don't even know why they kept it this long. It'll never sail again."

"Sounds about like what we'll be using for the trips."

"But it's a mess," Shulman protested, his face contorted in a look of disdain.

"Isn't cleaning included somewhere in your training program?" Buxenbaum asked in a dry, humorless tone.

"Well," Shulman shrugged. "Every sailor needs to know how to do that. But I—"

"That could be the first class," Buxenbaum cut him off. "A class that all of your students could take, regardless of their ultimate position on the crew."

Shulman looked over at him. "Do I have a choice?"

"Not really. You gotta make this work. This is how we do things."

"Okay," Shulman replied with a sense of resignation, "got any recruits for me?"

"I'm working on it. But I have someone who might work as an instructor. I wanted to take him as a crewman because he's a good boiler man, but I'm not sure he wants to be away from home anymore."

For the first time that day, Shulman sounded interested. "Does he have any naval experience?"

"He was in the navy during the Great War, then served in the Merchant Marine in the last one. Been at sea a long time. He'd make a good instructor for you."

"Sounds like he might be helpful. What's his name?"

"Walter Blount."

"Blount." Shulman seemed to hesitate. "He's not . . . "

"No," Buxenbaum said before Shulman could finish. "He's not Jewish. But he's a good man."

"Will he talk to me?"

"He will if I call him first. I'll give you the address when we're back at the office. He lives farther out on Long Island from here. Maybe you can go see him tomorrow."

Early the next afternoon, Shulman drove out to the town of Hauppauge to see Walter Blount. Buxenbaum had called earlier. Blount was expecting the visit. They sat at the kitchen table and sipped coffee while they talked.

"It's like I was trying to tell Joe this morning when he called," Blount said, "I'd love to help take relief supplies to the families in Palestine, but I just can't now. I've been away from home too long already. I can't be gone anymore. I tried to tell him that but he insisted I talk to you first. Said you might have something for me."

Shulman realized Buxenbaum had never told Blount the full story of what they were doing nor had he explained the reason for the visit. "I know it's tough being away," he said, trying to string the conversation along until he could size up Blount and get to the point. "I just got out a few months ago myself."

"You were in the navy?"

"Yes, sir."

"Enlisted man?"

"Captain," Shulman replied.

"You must have gone to school somewhere."

"Yes, sir. Annapolis," Shulman said proudly.

"Then you know what it's like. I was gone the whole war and it was too much for me and my wife."

"Joe said you served in the Great War, too."

"I was in the navy back then. This last war, I was in the Merchant Marine."

"I'm sure your wife missed you."

"Yes," Blount nodded. "And I missed her."

"Well, what about this," Shulman said, shifting the tone of the conversation. If he was going to ask Blount to help, he might as well just do it and get it over with. "What if you helped us but didn't go to sea? What if you worked with us here to help train the crews?"

Blount's eyes opened wide with interest. "Here? In New York?"

"Yes, sir."

"That might be something I could do. What did you have in mind?"

For the next hour, Shulman outlined the training program, telling Blount the topics they wanted to cover, the positions they needed to fill, and the exercises he'd planned to get the crewmen ready. Then he asked for Blount's suggestions and listened for another hour as Blount, the older and experienced sailor, told him about the failures and successes he'd seen over a lifetime spent at sea.

As the afternoon turned to evening, Shulman prepared to leave. He pushed back from the table and stood, then turned to Blount one last time. "So, will you help us?"

"I'd be glad to."

"Great." The two men shook hands. "I'll get you a schedule as soon as it's ready," Shulman said.

"There's just one thing," Blount added.

"What's that?"

"Joe and me are good friends . . . " He glanced down at the floor. "And I've known him a long time and all . . . " There was a moment of awkward silence, then Blount looked up and said, "But I'm not Jewish."

"I know," Shulman said with a pat on the shoulder. "Joe told me. We're just glad to have you on our team."

CHAPTER 20

THE VOLUNTEERS

When Schind first arrived in New York, security of the operation was utmost on his mind. He'd tried to address that issue by demanding absolute secrecy. When that proved impossible to achieve he settled for discrete disclosure. Telling people about the ultimate goal of their operation—to sail ships to Europe, rescue refugees, and take them to Palestine—became a necessary risk and he grew to be more comfortable with a measured disclosure of information. One risk he was not comfortable with was the risk that seemed apparent in communicating with the Jewish Agency's office in Tel Aviv.

Most of the messages sent to Tel Aviv were transmitted over the telegraph system known as Telex, which routed messages by undersea cable to England, then along a circuitous route, part of which was broadcast over the airwaves, before reaching Tel Aviv. Messages transmitted that way were sent as plain text—translated to Morse code but open and obvious for anyone to read.

Messages not sent by telegraph were delivered simply by phoning the office. This was the simplest and most direct method of communicating, but in order to reach Tel Aviv the phone calls were routed through several open switchboards. Placing a call was also time-consuming, cumbersome, and expensive. A call generated on the New York end was simple enough—phone the operator, who contacted a US overseas operator, who then contacted the next switchboard down the line—usually someone in London—who then contacted the next operator, and so on until the switchboard in Tel Aviv came on the line. Often the process had to be repeated several times in order to schedule access to a line on the Tel Aviv end of the call. Telephone capacity in Palestine was quite low.

Rather than relying on those two methods, Schind wanted a third. He wanted a radio link between New York and Tel Aviv. A shortwave link directly from a radio operator in New York to an operator in Tel Aviv. No open switchboards with operators listening to the calls. No cumbersome scheduling a time to talk on the other end. Get on the air, raise the other party, send the message. Clean and simple. And when the transmission ended, there'd be no record of its occurrence except for the operators' notes on either end.

Schind invited Joe Buxenbaum to the apartment at Hotel Fourteen to discuss the matter. He was certain Buxenbaum would know someone who could help.

"When we communicate with Tel Aviv, we use the telegraph," Schind began. "I don't like it."

"Because of the cost?"

Schind replied. "No, because anyone on the Telex line could potentially read our messages. They aren't encoded."

"Telex is dangerous," Buxenbaum agreed. "In the past, we always assumed the British were listening, so we kept the messages simple and as cryptic as possible without raising any questions from the operator. We just relied on the people at both ends to fill in what was left out."

"We need a better way of communicating."

"I agree. Using the telegraph was Weizmann's idea. He thought it was good enough. I never liked it. Got any ideas?"

"Yes." Schind nodded. "I think we should use radio."

Buxenbaum seemed unconvinced. "You think that would work?"

"I know it will. Do you know where we can get one?"

"Sure. They have them for sale. War surplus. But you'll still have the same problem."

"What do you mean?"

"If you transmit in code—genuine code designed to keep anyone from reading the message—FCC agents will notice it and they'll want to know who's sending the message."

"FCC?"

"Federal Communications Commission," Buxenbaum explained. "I don't know much about radio, but the guys I know who do know something about it say the FCC patrols the airwaves and agents are listening all the time for suspicious communications."

"I think even transmitting in plain sentences would be better than the telegraph or the telephone," Schind insisted. "There are just too many people in that link. If we used a radio, we'd be just one more signal in the vast array of signals." He looked over at Buxenbaum. "You think we could get a radio transmitter powerful enough to reach Tel Aviv?"

"No doubt. I've been to several surplus auctions in the area and I've seen thousands of shortwave radio sets for sale."

"Are they expensive?"

"No. They're cheap, like everything else the government is selling."

"We have a couple of people with radios in Tel Aviv and Jerusalem. Do you know anyone here who would be able to operate one?"

"Yeah, I know several guys."

"See if one of them is interested in helping."

"We should use someone with a license," Buxenbaum added.

"Of course."

"Want me to find a radio, too?"

"No . . . not yet," Schind added. "Let's see if we can find an operator. He might be able to tell us the kind of radio we need to purchase."

A few days later, a clerk in the lobby of Hotel Fourteen rang Schind's room to tell him Isaac Bernstein was there to see him. Schind didn't know Bernstein and was reluctant to bring him up to the apartment. Instead, he went downstairs to meet him.

Schind rode the elevator to the first floor, then made his way up the corridor toward the front of the building. As he entered the lobby he saw a tall man with broad shoulders standing near the windows, staring out at the street. He stood with both hands in his pants pockets and from that angle Schind could see he was dressed in a business suit with a white shirt and black wing-tip shoes. Schind crossed the room toward him, and the man turned to face him.

After introducing themselves, they took a seat on the opposite side of the lobby, out of view from the window.

"Joe Buxenbaum suggested I come see you," Bernstein began. "I'm an attorney by training, but I'm also a licensed amateur shortwave radio operator. Joe said you were looking for some help with that."

"Perhaps," Schind said. He'd been intrigued by Bernstein's appearance and the way he simply showed up, but now that he was face-to-face with him the old worries about security returned with a vengeance. Something about Bernstein's mannerism put Schind on edge. Not that he was dishonest, just unpredictable. Schind had come to value predictability, discipline, and routine.

They talked a few minutes longer and Schind learned that Bernstein had an office in Manhattan but lived on Staten Island. He'd first obtained a license while a student in college but hadn't operated a radio in the past few years. That meant his proficiency with a telegrapher's key—the means by which messages were tapped out over a radio frequency in Morse code—would be rusty.

After a few minutes more with Bernstein, Schind cut the conversation short on the pretense of having an appointment. He escorted Bernstein to the front entrance and saw him off, then returned upstairs to the apartment. Whatever there was about Bernstein that made him suspicious he could only satisfy by learning more of his background. And that worried him, too. He had no one who could conduct a thorough vetting and didn't have time to do that himself while trying to run the operation. Buxenbaum was busy recruiting seamen and anyway, this wasn't the man for the job. "Not precise enough," Schind said to himself. Still, Buxenbaum no doubt knew more about Bernstein than he'd learned that day, and Schind decided to pay Joe a visit.

A little after seven that evening, Schind appeared unannounced at Buxenbaum's apartment. "Your friend Bernstein came to see me today."

"Oh, I didn't realize he was going to do that. I was going to call first." Buxenbaum sounded surprised.

"That would have been better."

"Yeah. I realize that. Sorry."

"What do you know about him?"

"He's a good man," Buxenbaum said. "Think we can use him?"

"I don't know. How do you know him?"

"I met him through . . . " Buxenbaum looked away. "My sister."

"Your sister?"

"Yeah."

"She and Bernstein were lovers?"

"No. It wasn't like that," Buxenbaum said, still not facing Schind. "It's complicated."

"You think he's okay?"

"Yeah."

"You checked him out?"

"No. I didn't check him out. I know the guy." Buxenbaum looked over at him finally. "You think there's a problem?"

"I don't know if there's a problem. And that's the problem. We got people everywhere and we don't know two things about any of them."

"Not sure we can do this without people to help. Sailing a ship is a big job. And if they're going to help, they're gonna want to know what it is we're trying to accomplish."

"But if we're going to sail a ship across the Atlantic," Schind lamented, "and fill it with refugees, we ought to know that the people working for us are really with us. That they're really one of us and not out to sabotage the whole operation."

"We've been doing the best we can."

"I understand, but I want to tighten up the security side of things a little."

"Fine with me. But are you still interested in using a radio?"

"Yes."

"Bernstein is the best operator I know. Did he tell you he's an attorney?"

"Yes." Schind took a seat. "So, how is it you met him through your sister?"

"I'd rather not say."

Schind was taken aback. "Well," he said with a hint of irritation in his voice, "I'd rather you did."

"I'm not talking about it," Buxenbaum snapped, then he moved from the front room to the kitchen and began cleaning the dishes.

Schind appeared at the doorway. "I need to know a little more about him. And your reluctance to discuss him is making me even more suspicious than before."

Buxenbaum threw the dish towel he'd been holding into the sink. He braced himself with both hands against the edge of the counter and lowered his head. "Look," he said after a moment. "It's got nothing to do with any of this." He looked over at Schind. "Nothing at all, okay? It's between me and my sister."

"Maybe so, but—"

"I'm not talking about it. Use him. Don't use him. Use me. Don't use me. I'm not talking about it."

Schind wanted to know more and the military training he'd received left him expecting Buxenbaum to tell him all he wanted to know, but he could see this conversation was going nowhere. After a moment he said quietly, "Go ahead and purchase one of those shortwave radios you mentioned."

"Did you ask him which kind was best?"

"No. We didn't get that far."

"Which kind do you want?"

"The kind that's the best for transmitting to Tel Aviv," Schind replied, then he pulled open the door, stepped outside, and started toward the street.

✡

As Schind walked back to Hotel Fourteen that evening he wondered what it was that Buxenbaum refused to tell him. He could only imagine but whatever it was, it must have been big, or deep, or painful. Of all the people he'd met since coming to New York, Buxenbaum had proved the most cooperative and the most eager to do whatever was required. Which made his refusal to disclose the issue with his sister and Bernstein all the more odd. But in a strange way it also reassured Schind that the matter was most likely personal and had nothing to do with their work. After all, Buxenbaum was perfectly willing to include Bernstein in their operation, but he'd never once suggested to Schind that he even *had* a sister, much less bother to introduce them. And telling Bernstein just to show up at Hotel Fourteen was totally unacceptable. "He didn't even tell me the guy was coming," Schind mumbled to himself.

Although he was confident of Buxenbaum's loyalty, the incident nevertheless confirmed for Schind the need for a formal security operation to check the background of all volunteers. Right now they were all doing what Schind had just done—evaluating recruits and volunteers on a personal basis, trusting each other that the people they brought into the organization were trustworthy and committed to the cause. Schind didn't mind so much trusting his own instincts and abilities in that regard—he'd been doing that for a long time—but creating a system in which others were given the same prerogative—particularly people further down in the ranks who were not from a Haganah background—left him very uneasy and he decided once and for all to contact Reuven Shiloah.

✡

When Schind returned to the apartment at Hotel Fourteen, he located a telephone number for Shiloah and arranged to meet him for breakfast the following morning. Having worked together in the past, getting reacquainted took no time at all and they enjoyed a leisurely meal.

Afterward, they went to Schind's apartment, where Schind brought Shiloah up to speed on what they were doing—not every operational detail, but he outlined the main pieces for him. He was sure Shiloah already knew about the refugee rescue operation anyway.

"Sounds like you've done a lot," Shiloah said when Schind was through.

"It doesn't feel like it. It feels like the more I do, the more there is to do."

"These things take time," Shiloah noted. "You're dealing with people, and a lot of them, which can be a huge logistical nightmare. And a huge headache from all the personalities involved."

"Well," Schind said slowly, "I was wondering if you could help with the personnel."

"Sure," Shiloah responded. "Is there a problem?"

"Not yet. But I'm worried about security."

"I could see how that would be a concern. You know, British agents are crawling all over New York."

"Yeah," Schind nodded. "They were at the airport when I arrived and they've been following some of us ever since."

"No way to stop that."

"I know," Schind conceded. "I've tried to remind everyone to be careful. Which brings me back to the point. We need to clear all of these volunteers with background checks and I don't have anyone who can do that."

"How many people do you have?"

"Less than a dozen right now, but we're about to begin training crewmen for the first ship. That'll add a couple of dozen to our organization. Can you handle the background checks?"

"Yeah," Shiloah nodded. "I can do it. But do you have the time for it?"

"We'll have to make it work. We can't just grab people off the street and sail with them to Europe. We need a dossier on each person we use."

"But you need it quickly," Shiloah added.

"We do. At least you could check the major sources and then maybe work into a thorough routine as we move forward."

"You'll need this on an ongoing basis?"

"Yes," Schind said with a hesitant smile. "Is that too much for your staff?"

Shiloah answered, "No, it's not too much. I just need to know what you expect. We'll find a way to get it done." He looked at Schind with a thin smile. "That's our job."

"Good." Schind reached for a file from the table behind him. "Here's the first person you need to check." He opened the file, took out a slip of paper with Bernstein's name and address, and handed it to Shiloah. "See what you can find on him. We're thinking about using him as a radio operator."

"What are you using a radio for?"

"I want to use it to communicate with Tel Aviv."

"Good idea. I've argued that for a long time but no one here in New York would agree with me. They think it'll attract too much attention from American officials."

"It's the only way I know to have a functional link with our people in Palestine and do it without the British reading every message. I mean, they might hear a message every now and then, but as it is now I'm pretty sure they're reading everything we send."

"At least." Shiloah stood. "Send me a list of the other names as you have them. We'll get to work on them, too."

As they started toward the door, Schind remembered the lawyer he met at the Hebrew University event he attended with Nadelson. "Well," he said sheepishly, "now that you mention it, there *is* one other person."

"Okay," Shiloah said with a wary smile. "You sure there's just one more?"

"For now." Schind walked over to the table in the corner and began rummaging through a stack of papers. "He's a lawyer, too, like that guy I just gave you. Has an office on Park Avenue. I met him at an event. Offered to help. Recently discharged from the army as a colonel. Mickey something-or-other. I have his card somewhere."

Shiloah spoke up. "You mean Mickey Marcus?"

Schind turned to face Shiloah. "That's his name. You know him?"

"Everybody knows Mickey. I'm surprised you don't. He was a lawyer in the army. Tried a number of cases at Nuremburg."

"Yeah," Schind said. "I knew that much, but I didn't know he was that widely known."

"Great guy. Born problem-solver. The Army tried to get him to stay in after the war. Offered him a general's star and an assignment as liaison at the embassy in Moscow."

"He mentioned something about that. Said he turned them down."

"I think he wanted to go back to practicing law."

"So, he's a good guy?"

"Yes. Very good. And if he offered to help, you should take him up on that offer."

Schind thought for a moment. "Work up a dossier on him anyway and give me a report. We can't be too careful."

"Okay," Shiloah laughed. "I'll check into him."

A few days later Shiloah gave Schind a clean report on Bernstein. "I'll use him if you don't want him," he added. "I like your radio idea and finally have some support for one of our own."

"Okay," Schind said. "I'll let you know if we use him. What about Mickey Marcus?"

Shiloah reached into a briefcase and took out a folder. "Actually, we've been tracking Marcus for quite a while."

"Oh," Schind said, surprised by the news. "You knew this when we talked before?"

"Well," Shiloah said with a sheepish grin. "Sort of."

"Why the interest?"

"His work at the Nuremburg trials caught Ben-Gurion's attention. He asked us to keep up with him. Thought he might be someone useful."

"So, Mickey Marcus is okay?"

"Yes," Shiloah chuckled. "Mickey Marcus is okay." He opened the file and talked while he flipped through its pages. "Some of this you already know about him. Graduated from West Point. Did a tour on active duty with the US Army before the war. Discharged and obtained a law degree from Brooklyn Law School. He was appointed as an assistant US attorney and led a team that prosecuted Lucky Luciano. Probably would still be doing that kind of work but Fiorello LaGuardia, the mayor of New York, appointed him commissioner of the New York City Department of Corrections. He was serving there when the United States entered World War II."

"Sounds good," Schind nodded. "Not sure what we'd do with him, but his record sounds good."

"There is only one negative about him," Shiloah cautioned.

"What's that?"

"He has no prior association with Zionism."

"Well," Schind mused, "that would be a problem in Palestine, but is it really an issue with our people here in the U.S.?"

"In this case, I don't think so," Shiloah said. "He has a proven record. Stellar performance. Someone who can actually perform above their level of credentialed expertise. As opposed to a lot of the guys we see who over-promise but always *under* perform."

"Yeah," Schind said with a roll of his eyes. "There's a lot of that going around these days, especially here."

"You should contact Marcus," Shiloah said as he returned the file to the briefcase. "Follow up with him. Make sure of his level of interest."

"I'll call him and see if we can have lunch or something."

"We could use his help and a dozen more just like him."

"Would be an odd fit, though, don't you think?"

"How so?"

"For one thing, he's an American. For another, he's a lawyer. Where would he fit in?"

"Organization and training."

"Maybe."

"Right now," Shiloah explained, "Haganah operates as a paramilitary unit. That worked in the past, and it'll work for the time being. I mean, in Palestine we're an illegal organization as far as the British are concerned. Being lightly armed and having a decentralized command structure suits us well. But once we become an official state, we'll need to reorganize into a more traditional military structure."

"Do we really?"

"If you're a renegade operation against an obviously bigger, oppressive colonial power, you can do just about anything. But once you claim the status of a nation, the other nations of the world will expect you to look and act like a nation. They all have organized armies with well-defined command structure. The reputable ones do."

A broad grin spread across Schind's face. "You sound like Ben-Gurion."

"Yeah. I get accused of that a lot." Shiloah stood to leave. "Marcus would be perfect for getting us organized. And he would be great at setting up training programs. He did some of that for the Americans during the war. You should get him while he's available."

"Think he'll come to Palestine?"

"I don't know." Shiloah turned toward the door. "But you should talk to him and find out."

Schind reached for the doorknob to open it. "Do you want to talk to him?"

"No, he made the contact with you. You should see it through. Just get him involved and seal the deal. We need him."

CHAPTER 21

THE VOLUNTEERS

A few days later, Schind called Mickey Marcus and arranged to meet him for lunch. They talked about Marcus' work during the war and the nature of his legal practice now. Then Schind told him the gist of the things Shiloah had mentioned—the need to reorganize Haganah into a more traditional military structure and the need for a formal training program.

"War is coming," Schind said. "Some of us are determined to get ready for it, whether others like it or not."

"Well," Marcus agreed, "I think you're right. War is coming. The Arab nations of the region have signaled that."

Schind decided to dispense with the sales talk and get to the heart of the matter. "We need help, Mickey."

"What can I do for you?"

"If we are to win the coming war—and there is no other alternative—we must win. But if we are to do that, we will need many more soldiers than currently on our rolls. Almost all of them will serve as volunteers and they'll come from every occupation imaginable."

"That's a tall order," Marcus offered. "You'll be fighting some well-trained armies. Jordan's best units are as fine as any the British have. They don't have nearly as many, but the ones they have are solid as a rock."

"We have a bit of structure in Haganah, but nothing like what we need and nothing that can absorb a large influx of volunteers. What we need is an organized training program and a structure designed to make the most of their varying abilities. That's what we'd like you to do. Design the training program and create the structure. Think you can help with that?"

"I agree that those are the keys for you. But I'm not sure how much help I can give you." Schind knew what was coming next. He'd heard it before as he tried to convince people to help them. "I've been away from my wife a long time," Marcus explained. "We have children and I've missed almost every major event in their lives. They're still young enough to live at home and while they are, I need to give them my attention."

"That's certainly understandable," Schind said. What could he say? He could see from the expression on Marcus' face how torn he was. "Could you help us find someone who could do it?"

"Yes," Marcus said hastily. "That I could do. And in fact, I have a couple of people in mind who might be just the kind of person you need. But before I call them, I need to know a little about Haganah's current force and the nature of its readiness. That way, when I talk to them I'll sound like I know what I'm talking about. Can you give me the rundown on what you have?"

"No," Schind said. "I've been over here too long to tell you where we are right now in force strength and readiness, but I know several people who can. Shall I arrange a meeting?"

"Yes. Absolutely. As soon as I have that information, I'll start calling around for someone to help."

Two days later, Schind and Marcus met again at Hotel Fourteen. This time, however, they were joined by Reuven Shiloah. Schind introduced them to each other, then excused himself to tend to other business, leaving them to talk alone.

Marcus rested a legal pad on his lap, took a pen from the pocket of his jacket, and glanced up at Shiloah. "So, let's start with the basics, and for me that begins with armaments. What kind of artillery do you have?"

"None, really."

Marcus looked surprised. "None?"

"Only a handful of short-range mortars, most of them handmade."

"Armored vehicles?"

"One or two converted buses."

Marcus frowned. "Converted buses?"

"More like large panel trucks. We welded plating on the sides for extra protection."

"No half-tracks?"

"No."

"No tanks?"

"No."

"No troop carriers?"

"None."

Marcus gave him a questioning look. "What do you fight with?"

"Most of our men carry rifles and handguns."

"What kind?"

"Primarily, older pieces from World War I. A few have some newer ones. Early-issue carbines, that sort of thing."

Marcus grimaced. "Anything bigger than that?"

"Half a dozen light machine guns. A couple of fifty calibers. That's about it."

Marcus arched an eyebrow as he scribbled a note on the legal pad. "And how many men do you have?"

"We have thousands of members. Not sure exactly how many. They're organized into a dozen brigades of two or three thousand each."

"That's good," Marcus nodded.

"Sort of," Shiloah said in a qualifying tone.

"What do you mean?"

"The organization really exists only on paper. Most operations are conducted at platoon strength or less and many of those units are assembled with an eye toward the skills we need for a particular operation."

Marcus made more notes. "What about training?"

"We have no organized training schedule. All of our members are volunteers. They all work full time at something else. So getting them together for extensive training sessions is . . . "

"Difficult?"

"Nearly impossible."

"All of your members are volunteers?"

"All but a few of the officers."

Marcus glanced at his notes. This was worse than he'd imagined. "I understand the ad hoc, mission-based approach," he said after a moment. "But you face some serious problems with structure and training."

"I know."

"The countries around you have highly regimented, well-trained, Western-style armies. Tightly organized structure and repetitive training allow them to fight in a disciplined manner, which increases their efficiency exponentially. You could get by without the structure but training is the key. Fighting is not a natural act. The only reason guys stand and fight instead of run and hide is because they've done it so many times in training they don't really think about what they're actually doing. They just repeat physical skills they've been practicing all the time."

"I know," Shiloah said. "We need help."

Marcus rubbed his brow and wondered if any of the officers he knew were actually up to the task. They needed someone with organizational *and* tactical expertise. That was a rare commodity, but they also needed a teacher. And they needed that person to assume the task without pay. A task that could only be completed by traveling to Palestine. "Well," he said finally. "It'll be a challenge to find someone who has the skills to pull this together and who'd be willing to go to Palestine for a year to do it."

"And do it for free."

"And then there's that," Marcus smiled. "Right now I'd say the low pay is the least of our worries."

The next day, Marcus phoned Arthur Bates, a retired general who lived in Seattle, and arranged to meet with him. Two days later, Marcus flew to Seattle and took a taxi to Bates' house. They sat on the back porch and talked.

After giving Bates a brief sketch of the situation in Palestine, Marcus made his pitch. Would Bates be willing to travel to Palestine and spend a year helping organize and train Haganah units?

"I'm interested," Bates replied, "but I'm concerned about whether I could lose my pension. Serving in, or even closely associating with, the military of a foreign nation is touchy business at the Pentagon. If you can solve that problem, I'd like to help. Otherwise, I'll have to pass. My pension, this house, and a lot of memories are about all I have left of a lifelong career."

The following day, Marcus flew to Washington, D.C., and visited friends who worked in the army personnel office at the Pentagon. Each of them gave roughly the same answer. "Bates is right. Association with the military of a foreign nation is a serious issue, but it's handled on a case-by-case basis. There are no clear guidelines. It might not be a problem, but no one can guarantee anything in advance."

Marcus phoned Bates to tell him what he'd learned and received the expected response. "Then I'm out," Bates said. "I think Haganah needs help. I'd love to help them. But I just can't jeopardize my retirement. My wife has tolerated a lot from me over the years. Probably a hundred moves, some of them to places no one should have to go. And there were a lot of things she saw others have that she had to do without. Now that she's in a position to live a more relaxed and comfortable life, I can't risk taking that away from her."

Marcus understood. He made a similar decision when he decided to leave the army, but he knew what Haganah faced and unless someone helped them, they wouldn't stand a chance against armies like the ones from Jordan or Egypt. So he continued to contact former army officers, visiting and cajoling them to take the position. Like Bates, most understood Haganah's need for help, but all of them turned him down. They'd all been away from home too long, put too much of their lives on hold fighting the last war, and now wanted to be at home with their families.

Finally, after two weeks of endless calls and the continual negative response from each person he contacted, Marcus came to the conclusion that finding someone to take the position with Haganah would be impossible. Resigned to the obvious, he phoned Shiloah and arranged to meet at Shiloah's apartment the following day to discuss the situation.

When Marcus arrived, he found Moshe Sharett, secretary of the Jewish Agency's political department, waiting to meet him. Shiloah introduced them, then the three men sat around the kitchen table and sipped coffee while they talked.

"What did you find out?" Shiloah asked. "Is anyone willing to help us?"

"The short answer is no," Marcus replied. "None of the prospects were willing. They all understood the situation. They all agreed you needed help. But none of them would agree to take the job."

"I am not surprised," Sharett replied. "They've just finished a long war. Many were already near the end of their careers when the Japanese attacked Pearl Harbor. Their wives and families have paid a huge price for their service and now they would like to give something back to the loved ones who made it possible."

Marcus looked over at Shiloah. "You've told him about what we're doing?"

"Haganah has kept an eye on your situation," Shiloah replied.

"On my effort to find someone to help?"

"No," Sharett said. "On you."

Marcus looked over at Shiloah. "I don't understand."

"In our opinion," Sharett explained, "none of the men you contacted were as qualified as you. And, to be honest, you're the man we really want. And we've wanted you from the beginning."

Marcus frowned. "How do you know anything about me?"

Shiloah spoke up. "It's our job to make sure Jewish Agency leadership has access to sound intelligence."

"We noticed you at Nuremburg," Sharett explained, "and we have been following you ever since. We want you to take the job. Ben-Gurion wants you to take the job. The Jews of Palestine need you to come to Palestine and help us."

"Gentlemen," Marcus replied, "I would agree with you that none of the men I attempted to recruit have the total skill package you need. But before we pursue this, you should know I've never been part of any Zionist organization."

"We know that," Sharett said with a kindly smile. "And you haven't been very diligent in attending shul, but we think your heart is with us. And Reuven thinks you really want to do this."

"I know it," Shiloah said. He looked over at Marcus. "You wanted it from the first time we discussed it."

"We think you're the only person who can do this," Sharett said. "We need you."

"I appreciate your vote of confidence," Marcus replied with grace. "But I'm in the same position those other guys were in. I have a wife at home who gave up a lot for my military career. I can't make a decision about this without involving her. And I'll have to find a way to do it that doesn't jeopardize her lifestyle."

"Can you do that?" Shiloah asked.

"I'm not sure. But I have some friends who would go farther out on the limb for me than they would for some of the others. So I'll ask and find out."

That evening, Marcus went home to his wife and as they ate dinner he talked about his recent trips, the role Haganah played in the lives of Palestinian Jews, and the threat that awaited them once the British were gone.

As they finished dinner and moved back to the kitchen to wash the dishes, he stood at the sink and told her about the proposition from Shiloah and Sharett.

"They want me to go to Palestine and help reorganize their current structure, converting it into a regular army. And then organize a training schedule to get them ready to fight."

She looked up at him with tears in her eyes. "And you want to do it."

"They don't have anyone else," he replied.

"But you just got home from the war," she lamented, the tears now streaming down her cheeks. "You've been gone a long time, Mickey."

"I know."

"And you promised me this kind of thing was all behind us."

"I know. But these folks are going to die if they don't get organized. They can't defend themselves with their military in disarray."

"Let someone else do it," she sobbed. "You've done your part." She dropped the plate she'd been holding into the water and turned to face him. "Every time someone asked for help, you've rushed to their side. Now it's someone else's turn."

Marcus put his arms around her shoulders and pulled her close. "I tried to find someone else. I called Arthur Bates in Seattle. That's why I went out there to talk to him. I talked to every person I know who could do the job."

She looked up at him. "And what did they say?"

"They were all interested but not interested enough to leave home. Bates was willing to do it but he had a question about whether it would put his pension at risk."

"At risk?" She had a deep frown across her forehead. "How would it risk his pension?"

"People in army personnel take a dim view of prior servicemen developing serious associations with a foreign military. They're particularly troubled when those associations involve high-ranking officers. If they disapprove strongly enough, they can penalize them by withdrawing or curtailing pension payments."

She looked worried. "You could face the same thing."

"Yes. I could," Marcus admitted. "Which is why I have an appointment at the Pentagon with Miles Chaffee tomorrow afternoon. I wouldn't take the position in Palestine if it put us at that kind of financial risk."

"So, your mind's already made up?"

"I think there's no other choice. If Chaffee tells me I'm good, I think I have to go."

She draped her arms around his neck and rested her head on his chest. "Why does it always have to be you? Why, Mickey? Why you?"

CHAPTER 22

THE VOLUNTEERS

Meanwhile, large shipping boxes containing what appeared to be a shortwave receiver and shortwave transmitter arrived at Hotel Fourteen. Too large and heavy to lug upstairs, Schind had them moved to one side of the lobby and called Isaac Bernstein to come by the apartment.

Bernstein arrived later that day and examined the contents of the boxes. "It looks like everything is here," he said. "An RCA receiver, a transmitter as big as a house, the message key, plugs for the power, and the antenna. And enough cable to cover the city of Brooklyn." A broad smile spread over his face. "We should be able to get it operational without any trouble."

"We need to decide about the way we're going to send messages," Schind said.

"I've been thinking about that and I think we should use a simple code. Normal words that have our own meanings—that way if someone hears the transmission, they won't know immediately that it's being sent in code. They'll just recognize it as a word."

Schind had a questioning frown. "Is it a problem for them to think it's an encoded message?"

"It will be if the FCC hears it. They have people listening all the time for coded transmissions and they're easy to spot. They don't miss many."

Schind realized this was the same thing Buxenbaum told him. "What's the difference?" "I mean between a plain code, where a word has a different meaning, and a more complex code where letters or numbers have different meanings?"

"Messages in plain codes are messages with real words. They won't make any sense in a sentence, but anyone listening would hear recognizable words. Coded transmissions are simply a series of letters that don't form words or anything intelligible. When you hear them in a transmission they sound like what they are—a series of letters or numbers. Anyone who's the least bit familiar with radio communication and Morse code would spot it as encoded right away."

Schind still didn't understand the problem. "And that's bad?"

"It is from an FCC standpoint. A casual listener without the translation key to our underlying code wouldn't know what it meant and would move on to another frequency. But the FCC would come looking for the transmitter."

"Looking for it?"

"Physically. They would figure out where the transmitter is sitting."

"Triangulate their way to it?"

"Yes. It might take them a while to pinpoint the site but they'd eventually locate it."

"Why don't they want people transmitting in code?"

"Russians," Bernstein replied.

"Russians?"

"The federal government is worried about Russian spies. Communists. That sort of thing. They're looking everywhere for them. It's ridiculous, but that's what post-war life is like right now. We don't want to give them a reason to come looking for us."

"Well," Schind sighed, tacitly conceding the point, "if we use a simple code, how would we get the code key information to Tel Aviv? How would we tell them what we're doing and what the words mean?"

"You could send it over with someone, I guess," Bernstein suggested.

"Not too many people traveling to Tel Aviv these days."

"Then, the simplest way of handling it is to tell them the code in the first sentence of the transmission."

"Tell them?"

"Say we're using plain words, for instance. Easy to use, easy to translate, no need to have a complicated key. We arrange our message so that every third word in the sentence is a code word. Then in the first sentence we say something like, 'This is the third time I've talked to you.' The operator on the other end will know from that hint that we're using every third word."

"Okay," Schind nodded slowly, thinking. But you still have to tell them what the words mean."

Bernstein's eyes clouded with a perplexed look. "I'm not sure I—"

"In our code, cabbage wouldn't mean literally cabbage. It would mean anything we wanted it to mean. So someone has to tell the guys on the other end what the code words mean."

"I suppose," Bernstein suggested, "we could simply broadcast in another language, tell them what we're doing, and let the British figure it out if they can."

"You mean, hope they didn't know what it meant or couldn't translate it fast enough?"

"Yeah."

"We could do that, I suppose. Or break our instructions into separate messages and translate the pieces in different transmissions at different times on different frequencies." Schind looked over at him. "Are you good enough at Hebrew to handle it?"

"My brother can help me. He's good with Hebrew. But it's a risk just hoping they won't figure out what we're doing."

"But it will get us going," Schind explained, "until someone goes over there with an actual code and we can set up a better method."

"Okay," Bernstein said. "Maybe. But I don't like it."

"Think of it this way. You'll begin at the beginning and educate the operator in Tel Aviv. Tell him a little bit each time, only bury it in the middle of a longer transmission about nothing much at all."

"I don't know," Bernstein shrugged. "Worth a try, I guess. I'll get the radio set up and we'll see what we can do."

"The person I want you to contact in Tel Aviv is Yehuda Lachmann." Schind turned to the table in the corner for a scrap of paper and wrote the name. "His call sign is ZC5AA."

"Write that down, too."

Schind added the call sign, then turned to Bernstein. "If you reach Yehuda, tell him, 'Uzi wants to know about Arthur Biram.'"

Bernstein frowned. "He'll understand what that means?"

"Yes."

"Okay, my brother Hank has a truck. I'll send him over here tomorrow to pick up the boxes."

"Good. I'll be waiting for him."

The next day, Hank Bernstein collected the boxes from Hotel Fourteen and drove them to Isaac's house on Staten Island. The house, a stately three-story Italian renaissance structure, sat atop Todt Hill, which afforded a great view of the bay and beyond it to the Atlantic Ocean. When he arrived, Isaac came out to the driveway to help him unload.

All day long, Isaac and Hank worked to snake the antenna cable from the first-floor room where the transmitter and receiver were located, up to the attic, and across the rafters to a vent at the eave. Then, with Hank on the roof and Isaac in a nearby tree, they strung the cable away from the house and across the yard, moving from tree to tree, until the antenna reached the far end of the property.

"That is the longest antenna I've ever seen," Hank said admiringly when they were finished.

"I think we can catch a signal from anywhere in the world anytime we decide to turn on the radio."

"Will it transmit to anywhere?"

Isaac grinned. "They sent us an RCA unit that will transmit to the moon."

"Think the neighbors will notice?"

"They might see the lights dim when we turn it on," Isaac joked.

The radio equipment was located in an unused first-floor bedroom near a table that had been shoved against the far corner. The transmitter, a single unit about four feet in height, stood to the right. The receiver sat on the table.

When the antenna was connected and the message key in place, Isaac took a seat in front of the receiver and turned it on. Hank flipped a switch on the transmitter.

Isaac plugged the headphones into a jack on the front of the receiver, adjusted them over his ears, and gave the key a click. "Key works," he reported with a thumbs-up gesture.

"See if it'll transmit."

"Gotta wait for the tubes to warm up." Isaac glanced at his watch. "Won't take long."

"You timing it?"

"No. Just checking," Isaac said. "Getting late."

"Yeah," Hank replied. "And I'm getting hungry."

In reality, Isaac was calculating the time difference between New York and Tel Aviv and wondering if there was still time to reach someone over there. He didn't want to tell Hank that because they hadn't yet talked about the real reason Isaac had the radio. He would need Hank's help if they decided to transmit messages in Hebrew, but until then he wanted to work the radio on his own, without having to explain to his brother what it was all about. Sometimes, Hank didn't understand things that clearly.

After a moment, Isaac leaned forward in his chair and looked through the vents on the back of the receiver. Inside he saw the tubes glowing brightly. "I think it's ready. Check the transmitter."

Hank knelt beside the transmitter, cupped his hands around his eyes to block out the light, and peered through the air vents on the side of the unit's metal case. "Looks good."

"Great," Isaac smiled. "Let's give it a test and then have dinner."

"Good," Hank replied. "I'm hungry."

"Hope I can remember all the code."

"I think it's like riding a bicycle."

Isaac adjusted the headphones and began tapping out a message in Morse code with the key. After a moment he looked over at Isaac with a grin and said, "The set works perfectly. I've got someone from Texas." He lifted the headphones from his ears and handed them to Hank. "Here, have a listen."

Hank slipped one side over an ear for a moment, then pointed to the radio. "It has a speaker. Unplug the headset."

"Oh. Right," Isaac laughed nervously. "Forgot about that." He unplugged the headset, and the sound of the signal played through a speaker mounted near the top of the receiver. Someone from Dallas was on the air and they listened to the signal, translating it together with each dot and dash.

Fifteen hours later, at about eight the following evening in Tel Aviv, Yehuda Lachmann crawled through a narrow passageway and into a secret room in the basement beneath his house. Measuring twelve feet by twelve feet, the room had walls made of clay bricks. The floor was made of earth tamped to the hardness of concrete and rubbed smooth with hours of physical labor.

In the far corner, resting against the back wall of the room, was a long table made of lumber salvaged from shipping crates spread across equally spaced orange crates that were stacked three high. On that makeshift table were a shortwave radio receiver and a transmitter, which were originally designed by General Electric for use by the US Army as a mobile communications center.

All day and most of the night, Lachmann sat in that room, sending and receiving messages for Haganah. Sometimes to units in the field and sometimes to operatives in places like Paris, London, and Prague. When he wasn't doing that, he was passively listening for signals of interest. Sometimes the British. Sometimes a transmission from one of the Arab nations in the region. And once in a while, a message from someone on the other side of the world who just wanted to say hello.

This was Lachmann's part in the war for a Jewish state. A war that he and many others saw as already begun, even though the British Army hadn't withdrawn and no one had declared their independence.

That evening, as he sat with the headphones clamped tightly to his head, Lachmann heard someone signaling with his call sign, "CQ, CQ, CQ from WL0W calling CQ for ZC5AA. WL0W standing by and tuning for ZC5AA."

WL0W was a call sign assigned to the United States. Lachmann was fluent in English but preferred to communicate in Hebrew, so he keyed an answer in Hebrew but after repeated attempts with no response he gave up and moved on to another frequency.

An hour later, he came back to the original frequency and heard again, "CQ, CQ, CQ from WL0W calling CQ for ZC5AA. WL0W standing by and tuning for ZC5AA."

This time Lachmann responded in English. "ZC5AA CQ for WL0W. Are you in the United States?"

A moment later came the response, "Uzi wants to know if you've heard from Arthur Biram."

For a moment, Lachmann sat motionless, staring ahead at the receiver, stunned by what he'd just heard. Slowly, he leaned back in his chair, slipped the headphone from his ears, and ran his fingers through his hair.

Uzi was the name of his childhood friend, Uzi Doran. They were classmates at the Reali School in Haifa when they were teenagers. Arthur Biram was the headmaster at the school. After graduation, Lachmann went to work at Neve Yam, a farming collective south of Haifa. Uzi Doran joined the Jewish Legion of the British Army and fought with the Allies during World War I. When the war ended, Uzi returned to Palestine, joined Haganah, and was killed in an operation south of Jerusalem. How would someone in the United States—if that's really where the operator was located—know about Uzi?

After a moment, Lachmann adjusted the headphones around his ears and returned to the conversation. "Not sure about Biram," he signaled. "Will check and respond tomorrow. Same time, same frequency."

With the shortwave conversation over, Lachmann switched off the radio, crawled back through the passageway, made his way upstairs, then hurried out the front door. A bicycle was propped against the front wall and he quickly climbed on, pushed off with one foot, and pedaled his way up the street.

Fifteen minutes later, he reached Haganah headquarters at the Red House located near the beach just north of the center of town. He parked the bicycle near the door and went inside. A clerk seated at a nearby desk acknowledged him with a nod but paid little attention as Lachmann made his way upstairs to the office of Jacob Dostrovsky.

Dostrovsky was Haganah's chief of staff and though he and Lachmann were by no means peers they often worked together in a manner that transcended their relative positions. Lachmann was one of the primary links between Haganah, its units in the field, and outlying farming settlements, almost all of which relied on radio communication rather than telephone.

Lachmann stepped into Dostrovsky's office and closed the door. Dostrovsky looked up with his eyes opened wide, apparently taken aback by the sudden intrusion. "I didn't realize we had a meeting today."

Lachmann ignored the comment, leaned over the desk, and in a hushed tone said, "Just a little while ago I received a signal from a radio operator who says he's in the United States. He chatted for a moment about nothing, then said, 'Uzi wants to know if you've heard from Arthur Biram.'"

"Don't recognize the name. Lots of people named Uzi. Do you know anyone named Biram?"

"Arthur Biram was headmaster at a school in Haifa. I attended that school when I was a kid. Uzi is Uzi Doran, one of my classmates.

But why would someone in the United States know about him? Or about Biram?"

"How many of your classmates *could* know?" Dostrovsky asked.

Lachmann thought for a moment, then his eyes opened wide. "Danny Schind," he said with a look of realization. "Schind is the only guy from our class who was in Haganah when Uzi died."

"The only one?"

"Yes," Lachmann replied. "Others joined later but he was the only one who was in when Uzi went out on that patrol. I'm sure of it." Lachmann backed away from the desk and took a seat on a straight-back chair. "I used to see Schind around once in a while, but I haven't seen him lately. Is he in the United States?"

Dostrovsky glanced away. "I'm afraid I can't comment on that."

"Okay." Lachmann stood. "I guess that's enough of an answer right there."

"You're certain this operator was in America?"

"He had the right call sign for it, but that doesn't mean a whole lot with some people. Some guys try to hide their real location by using call signs that are assigned to other countries. But he signaled me using my call sign, on a frequency I often monitor, and he knew about Biram and he knew about Uzi. It would be almost impossible for anyone but Schind to know all of that."

"Any way to verify the call sign of the radio operator?"

"Not really. But if Schind is over there, and you have a reliable way of reaching him, you could send him a Telex."

Dostrovsky thought for a moment, then asked, "What would we say?"

"Tell him . . ." Lachmann moved near the desk. "Tell him . . . 'Biram is fine, should we check on Rivka?'"

Dostrovsky frowned. "Rivka?"

"Yes."

"Schind will know what that means?"

"Yes."

"And if we knew where Schind was and we sent this message to him by a known method of communication, what would it accomplish?"

"If he responds with, 'I don't date married women,'" Lachmann said with a grin, "we'll know the operator is working with Schind."

Dostrovsky looked aggravated. "This sounds perfectly stupid," he scoffed. "We'll look like a bunch of children yammering in the schoolyard."

"We were teenagers when we were at that school together," Lachmann chuckled. "What can I say?" He turned toward the door. "Send that message and we'll find out if the guy on the other side of the radio is working for Schind." Lachmann reached for the doorknob and pulled open the door.

"I'll think about it and let you know," Dostrovsky called.

Early in the morning in New York, a delivery boy arrived at Hotel Fourteen with a telegram for Schind. A clerk at the lobby desk phoned the apartment. Schind came to the lobby to retrieve the message and glanced at the heading to see it was from Jacob Dostrovsky. "Biram is fine," the note said. "Should we check on Rivka?" Schind laughed out loud. He turned to the clerk. "Has the delivery boy left already?"

"Yes. I'm afraid so."

Schind stuffed the message into his pocket and started toward the street. The telegraph office was only a few blocks away. He could walk there and send a response. But when he reached the corner he paused a moment. There was no need to send a telegram. He knew what he needed to know. Bernstein had reached Lachmann. They had the right operator in Tel Aviv. Bernstein could take care of the response with the radio.

The next morning, in Tel Aviv, Lachmann tuned his radio to the frequency where he'd found the American the day before. He signaled for WLOW and in a few minutes received a response. "Uzi doesn't date married women." Lachmann's heart skipped a beat.

CHAPTER 23

THE VOLUNTEERS

As Robinson and the team from MI6 followed Schind, Ginsberg, and the others, they generated daily reports which Robinson dutifully forwarded to the office in London. As part of that regular process, a detailed account of the information gleaned from Collins' law office was added, including information about the formation of Weston Trading Company and the two Panamanian corporations that were to hold title to the *Beauharnois* and the *Norsyd*.

When those routine daily reports reached MI6 headquarters in London, they were reviewed and summarized according to the agency's standard procedure. Items of note were added to the daily analyst supervisors meeting for consideration of inclusion in the prime minister's daily brief, then cataloged and indexed for future reference.

While Robinson was reporting daily from New York, Julian Glenister was reporting from Canada. The tip he'd received from Fred Kingsmill led to a wealth of information regarding sale of the two Canadian corvettes to Weston Trading Company, which he included in his routine missives to London. Like all other reports, Glenister's were reviewed, cataloged, and indexed into the MI6 records system. In due course, his report regarding sale of the corvettes arrived on the desk of Morgan Sawyer, an indexing specialist who worked in the final stage of review—the tedious task of creating index cross-references.

When Sawyer turned to the entry for Weston Trading Company that was included in Glenister's report, he noticed the index contained a reference to that topic in Robinson's reports from New York regarding information taken from the office of Palmer Collins. Curious about the connection, Sawyer retrieved the files for the reports from Glenister and Robinson and compared the two. That led him rather quickly to details about Morris Ginsberg, Dewey Stone, Danny Schind, Chaim Weizmann, and the Jewish Agency office in New York. When a review of the agency's file on Danny Schind revealed he was a member of Haganah, Sawyer notified his supervisor, who ordered a full and complete report of the matter.

Several days later, as Robinson left his apartment building in New York, the doorman handed him an envelope. "A gentleman said to give this to you," the doorman said. Robinson took a five-dollar bill from his pocket and handed it to the doorman, then stuffed the envelope into his pocket and proceeded up the street. Half a block away, he lifted the flap on the envelope and found a note that read, "Drinks at noon."

At noon that day, Robinson entered Earl's, a bar located a few blocks from the apartment. He approached the bartender and asked, "Did someone leave a package for me?" Without a word in response, the bartender reached beneath the counter, took out a large manila envelope, and handed it to him.

Envelope in hand, Robinson returned to the apartment, where he opened it and found a memo reporting details of the sale of two Canadian corvettes—the *Beauharnois* and the *Norsyd*—to an entity known as Weston Trading Company. Dewey Stone from Boston handled the transaction. Palmer Collins prepared the documents necessary to form Weston, along with two Panamanian companies believed to be corporate vehicles for holding title to the corvettes. Stone was noted as the incorporator, but information from Collins' files indicated the companies were formed at the insistence of Morris Ginsberg. Details regarding the separate businesses of Ginsberg and Stone were added. The sale price for the ships was set at $150,000 each. The transaction was approved by Arthur Tupper, a vice-president in the sales department at the War Assets Corporation in Montreal. Alexander McDonald, a Canadian businessman, assisted. The report failed to note whether the transaction had closed.

Much of the information reported by Robinson regarding ongoing contact between Weizmann, Ginsberg, Schind, and Stone was included, as was his analysis from earlier reports of the meeting at Stone's residence in Boston. "I tried to tell them they were up to something," Robinson fumed. "I told them all of this except the names of the ships and the details from Canada. Why are they just now catching on?"

After reading the memo a second and third time, Robinson phoned Geoffrey Reid in Washington. "We need to talk," he said when Reid was on the line.

"Very well," Reid replied. "Come to my office tomorrow."

"We need to talk earlier than that," Robinson insisted. "We need to talk now."

"Okay," Reid said. "Then I'll see you as soon as you get here."

Robinson caught an afternoon flight from LaGuardia and arrived in Washington around three o'clock, then went straight to Reid's office. They met in a conference room down the hall.

"What was so urgent you had to see me today?" Reid asked as he pushed the door closed.

Robinson showed him the report from London. "Okay," Reid said as he glanced over the pages of the memo. "The Canadian Navy sold two corvettes to Weston Trading Company. Everyone's selling off unnecessary items from the war."

"Have the ships been delivered yet? The report doesn't say."

Reid pointed to the memo. "According to this, it's been several weeks since Stone's meetings in Canada. I suspect they have, but I can call and find out. If not, perhaps we can find someone to convince the Canadians to back down." He glanced at his watch. "It's after hours in London. There's always someone at the office in London, but I'm not sure how much they'll be able to tell us. I'll give them a ring and find out."

Reid left the room and was gone for almost twenty minutes. When he returned he said, "They're checking into it. Might be tomorrow before they have anything to report."

"How did this slip past them?"

"Who?"

"The office in London."

"Big office. Lots of information. All of it processed by hand. Just takes time to get to the details and see the relevance. Rather efficient of them to find it at all, I'd say."

"Weston is a company with ties to Danny Schind, Morris Ginsberg, and the Jewish Agency for Palestine." Robinson pointed to a paragraph in the report. "And I am certain it is nothing more than a front for Haganah."

"Schind is definitely a Haganah man," Reid noted.

"This is not good, Geoffrey."

"No, it's not." Reid continued to read through the report. "I see the documents used to form Weston were prepared by Palmer Collins, an attorney with the firm of Fortas, Brown & Hoffman." He tapped the page with his index finger for emphasis. "That's a rather large firm."

"Yes, it is."

"Perhaps I should see what we can do about that from our end. Whether there's some angle to work with them."

"An angle to work?"

"Several of our British companies have officers in New York. One of them might do business with the firm."

"You mean, as a way of pressuring them somehow?"

"Yes. You know. Get them to pull that business and go elsewhere."

"That might help on an ongoing basis, but it won't stop their receipt of the ships."

"Just thinking out loud," Reid said. "Depending on what we hear from London, that may be all we have."

"Pressure Fortas, Brown & Hoffman into cutting ties with Mr. Ginsberg?"

"Yes." Reid looked over at Robinson. "It's not much, but it would let them know that we know what they're doing. Perhaps disrupt whatever else they're trying to accomplish. Which brings up a good question. What do you think they're trying to do?"

"Schind and his Jews are recruiting crewmembers and talking about sailing to Palestine with relief for the Jews living there." Robinson accented the word *Jews* with disgust. "We interviewed a dockworker who told us about it. That information is not in the memo."

"I suppose that would be disruptive to our troops in Palestine."

"There are also rumors that what they're really preparing to do is sail to Europe, fill the ships with refugees, and bring them to Palestine."

"To force the immigration issue?"

"Yes," Robinson replied.

"Jews arriving unannounced in quantities far greater than the law allows. I *know* how London would feel about that. Not much doubt their reaction would be severe. Have you forwarded that information to London as well?"

"Yes. I filed it with all the other reports."

Reid leaned back in his chair, "Well, I suppose we should alert London to the complete details of the situation."

"I will," Robinson assured, "but that seems likely to generate nothing more than a protracted sort of bureaucratic paper response, rather than an immediate attempt to thwart their efforts to do whatever it is they're trying to do."

Reid looked over at him. "What did you have in mind?"

"I don't know, but it seems like we ought to be able to do something besides file one more memo or one more report. Or contact clients of the firm to pull their business. It all seems rather . . . weak for a superpower that just won the war."

"You know," Reid said, thinking aloud, "not all Jews in the United States care to be associated with events in Palestine. Some are perfectly content to live in comfort right here in America."

Robinson folded his arms across his chest. "Perhaps we should see what sort of Jews these Fortas, Brown & Hoffman lawyers turn out to be. Maybe they would help us from the inside."

"What about Collins himself? Do you have him under observation?"

"No," Robinson replied. "We don't have the manpower for it and we already know what he's doing. I mean, he's working for them as a lawyer but that's all. And other than breaking into his office again there isn't much we can do to learn the details from his files."

"Are you sure that's all he's doing?"

"I think so. Do you have an indication otherwise?"

Reid lowered his voice. "We have reports that someone in the Foreign Office is leaking information to an American contact. No one knows for certain who that might be, but our people seem to think the information trail leads to someone in Manhattan. Collins is in a prime position to be a link between that information and the Jews working through the Jewish Agency. If we put a team on Collins we'd know precisely what he's doing with his time." Reid had a devious smile. "Perhaps if you applied some *observation* in a more . . . *obvious* manner, you might convince him none of this is worth the risk. At least make him pay a price for his involvement. That would be *something*."

"He has a family," Robinson responded. "Wife. Children. We might be able to do something."

"Good, that gets us moving, at least, while still remaining within the confines of our original mandate—to follow and observe."

"You'll supply the men for it?"

"I'll send you a dozen more. You can decide how best to use them." Reid sat up straight in his chair and faced Robinson across the desk. "But pay attention to what they're doing. This operation is growing quite large. Think you can keep it all together?"

"Just send the men," Robinson replied. "We'll take care of the rest."

"Be sure that you do," Reid cautioned. "If an operation this size gets exposed, it wouldn't be good for any of us."

In London, Philip Cripps, director of MI6, reviewed the report on the sale of the Canadian corvettes to Weston Trading Company and sent a memo to Ernest Bevin, the foreign secretary, suggesting several courses of action to prevent the sale or, if necessary, to interdict delivery of the ships. Bevin responded with a terse message indicating the Foreign Office had reviewed the matter and determined no action was necessary. By then, almost a week had transpired since the report first surfaced.

Incensed by the Foreign Office's response, Cripps scheduled an appointment with Bevin to argue the matter further. They met in Bevin's office.

"I read your report," Bevin said as Cripps entered the room. He was seated at his desk and did not bother to stand. "And we conducted our own review."

"And all you can say is, 'No action is necessary'?" Cripps asked as he dropped onto a chair.

"I'm afraid that is the truth. There is nothing the Foreign Office can do about the matter."

Cripps had a troubled frown. "Nothing we can do?" he sighed in disgust.

"The ships have already sailed from Quebec." Cripps' shoulders sagged at the news. "But cheer up," Bevin continued. "I can't see what harm two ships will do. If the Jews want to sail around in worn-out naval vessels, let them. I don't think they'll get very far."

Cripps refused to cede the issue, "Sir, allow me to explain once more. Weston Trading was created at the direction of Morris Ginsberg—"

"As I said, Philip," Bevin interrupted. "I've read the report." There was a hint of impatience in his voice, but Cripps seemed not to notice.

"Ginsberg's name is not listed as an officer or director of the company," Cripps continued, "but we have information from their planning discussions that indicates Ginsberg was the one who contacted the lawyer who formed the business. As you are aware, Ginsberg is heavily involved with the Jewish Agency for Palestine through their New York office. He and Chaim Weizmann, the Jewish Agency's director, are good friends. Danny Schind, a known ranking member of Haganah, has been meeting with them also and was involved in the formation of this company."

Bevin seemed interested. "Schind is in the United States?"

"Yes," Cripps blurted in frustration. "That's what drew our attention to this matter in the first place. Our analysts are convinced this is part of a broad, covert Jewish operation, promoted and sponsored by Haganah, in a blatant attempt to bring illegal immigrants to Palestine."

Bevin leaned back in his chair. "Assuming you are correct, is there any serious threat to our troops from such an attempt? Surely the navy will intercept them before they reach shore."

"We don't know for certain what the threat level might be. But I would remind you," Cripps pontificated with an imperious arch of his brow, "corvettes are warships, not commercial vessels."

Bevin, put off by Cripps' melodrama, turned away and stared up at the ceiling. "Canada has sold quite a few of these corvettes in the past year or so," he observed in a casual manner. "All but these two were sold to individuals for conversion to private yachts. Rather large yachts," he noted with a smile in Cripps' direction, "but yachts nonetheless. No one has attempted to put them to military use."

"There's always a first time," Cripps said in a coldly disdainful tone.

"The armaments have been removed?" Bevin asked.

"Yes. Of course."

"Good." Bevin sat quietly a moment. "Well, Philip," he said finally, "I appreciate your concern." Bevin sat up straight and turned to face him. "But your suggestion that we should do more, and your recommendation of specific actions this office should undertake, reaches beyond your area of responsibility, doesn't it?"

Cripps took the comment as an affront. "I'm afraid I don't like the implication that I—"

"Your job is to gather information," Bevin continued, talking over him. "Policy—whether a thing should or should not be done—is for someone else to decide. Primarily, it is the province of this office to make those recommendations. As to the execution of a particular course of action, that is a matter reserved solely for the prime minister's decision."

"I fail to see how this is beyond the scope of—"

"What would you have us do?" Bevin asked sharply, cutting Cripps off yet again. "The ships are sailing—presumably with a non-Canadian crew—under the control of their new owner. Do you know their destination?"

"We believe they will bring them to New York. That's the best information we've had from sources in Canada at the time of the sale."

"And you would have us seize ships owned by a US company, while sailing in waters off the US coast?"

"Sir, I am not suggesting we confront the United States with military action," Cripps countered. "I am, however, suggesting that we should urge the prime minister to press the Americans to detain the ships at New York until we can determine precisely what the owners are doing. If we ask for US cooperation, I feel certain they would oblige."

"Well . . . " Bevin said hesitantly, as if only just then considering that possibility, "I'll take this to the prime minister, but I must say, I see little possibility the Americans will view this with the same seriousness as we."

"In my opinion, they should view it far more seriously than we. They have a much larger Jewish population."

"Yes, well . . . " Bevin glanced away. "Perhaps that's the reason they're unconcerned."

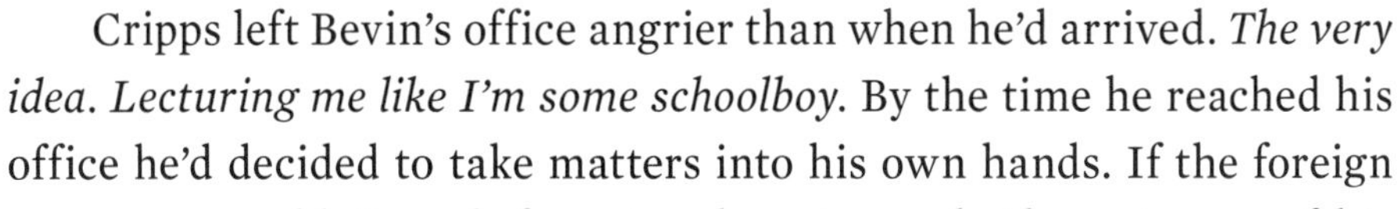

Cripps left Bevin's office angrier than when he'd arrived. *The very idea. Lecturing me like I'm some schoolboy.* By the time he reached his office he'd decided to take matters into his own hands. If the foreign secretary wouldn't push for a tougher stance, he'd create one of his own. "I am not without power to act," he muttered.

Within the hour Cripps cabled Reid in Washington with instructions to approach the Americans at the sub-minister level. "Feel them out regarding assistance in detaining *Beauharnois* and *Norsyd*. Avoid troubling the ambassador. No need to bring it to that level."

Reid received the message at his desk and read it quickly. He'd worked in intelligence for a long time and understood the language of agency-speak at least as well as anyone. In those terms, the cable was quite clear. London officials at the ministry level were less than enthusiastic about addressing the sale of the ships directly with their American counterparts. If the Jews were to be stopped, they must be stopped through use of government officials at the next lowest level—agents, operatives, undersecretaries who served in senior positions but who were not political appointees subject to the behest of the prime minister or confirmation by the US Senate.

A smile turned up the corners of Reid's mouth as he read the message a second time. He'd anticipated correctly the gravity of this situation within the agency during his conversation with Robinson. They were, indeed, to push forward with their own solution. Robinson was primed for action already. Now he needed to take it one step further. "And I know just the person to see," Reid said to himself.

The following morning, Reid drove across the Potomac River to the War Department's new Pentagon headquarters for a meeting with Tom McElroy, an officer with the US Army Intelligence Service. McElroy, he knew, was deeply anti-Semitic. *The perfect person to see if one wants to thwart a Jewish operation.*

Over coffee in McElroy's office, Reid outlined the transaction—the Canadian government, in a hurry to unload unwanted war surplus, sold two navy corvettes to a renegade group of Jews from Palestine. "We aren't sure of their intention, but there's little doubt these could be used against our forces currently on station in Palestine."

"This was a Haganah operation?" McElroy asked.

"Yes," Reid agreed. "That is a confirmed fact."

"What does the office in London think?"

"Our office thinks this is a travesty."

"I take it not everyone in the government shares your office's opinion."

"Other ministries have priorities that go beyond the safety and well-being of our troops," Reid replied, as he sensed McElroy taking the bait. "For them, soldiers in the field are . . . of secondary importance to . . . sane policy . . . and their careers, of course."

"Stupid Jews," McElroy seethed.

Yes, Reid thought as he suppressed a smile. *He's with us.* "They appear to be expanding their program. I think your president's recent call for increased immigration has emboldened them."

"They're getting rather bold over here, too." McElroy was clearly aggravated now. "You'd think they'd be grateful and humble after all they've been through and the millions of good men who died trying to save them. But no, they want even more. Taking positions and jobs that should go to regular citizens."

"I see you understand our problem."

"Yes," McElroy said, his eyes ablaze with anger. "And London doesn't want to do anything about it?"

"Well . . . " Reid answered slowly, trying to be coy. "They don't want to address the issue on a . . . ministerial level."

"I see," McElroy had a knowing look. "They want to respond without responding."

"These things always fall to men of determination and strength. Not the kind of people found at the top of our governments."

"No," McElroy agreed. "You won't find that kind of man at the top."

"We're putting together a response at our level from our side," Reid offered. "Perhaps your men could have a look around. See what you can find on the matter. You have far better resources than we on this side of the Atlantic. Maybe there's some compelling American interest that could be used as leverage to get the machinery of your government focused on this matter, as we try to leverage ours."

"Yes," McElroy readily agreed. "Perhaps we can." He shook his head in disgust. "The Jews can never leave well enough alone, can they? They're always up to something. Even here in America where they have it far better than anywhere else in the world, they still try to play the system."

Reid waited a moment as the thought settled in, then stood to leave, "Well, I see you understand what we're up against."

"Yes, I do," McElroy assured as he walked with him to the office door. "I'll . . . look into it."

"That would be greatly appreciated."

"You might also ask Bob Smith at Treasury. See if he'll . . . look into it as well. Do you know him?"

"No. I don't think so."

"He's over at the Treasury Building. Easy to find. Tell him I sent you." McElroy had a wry smile. "He shares our view of these issues."

"I'll look him up."

"They might have some means of getting involved through their enforcement operation. Taxes, contraband, that sort of thing." McElroy raised an eyebrow. "And even if they don't have some obvious reason, they might be willing to get involved anyway."

"I'll find him today," Reid said as he stepped into the corridor.

"There's a party at Ralph and Patty's this weekend. Will I see you there?"

"Wouldn't miss it," Reid called.

"Tell Smith to phone me about it if he needs to," McElroy added one last time.

Reid responded with a wave over his shoulder as he rounded the corner at the end of the hall.

CHAPTER 24

THE VOLUNTEERS

Before British officials could convince their American counterparts to intervene, the *Beauharnois* and the *Norsyd* arrived at a boatyard on City Island, off the east side of the Bronx in New York. Workmen there stripped the ships of all remaining armament and military insignias and prepared them for refitting. While the ships underwent that work, Schind, Buxenbaum, and Shulman came out to have a look.

"They're in rough shape," Shulman observed, "but they seem seaworthy. Who brought them down from Quebec?"

"We hired a Canadian crew," Schind replied.

"Are those men still here?"

"No. They've all gone back."

"Did they have any trouble on the way?"

"A little difficulty with the boiler on the *Beauharnois*," Schind explained, "but otherwise nothing else."

"We need to have someone look at the boiler," Shulman commented.

Schind looked over at Buxenbaum. "Think your boiler man could do it?"

"Walter Blount?" Buxenbaum replied. "I'm sure he can."

"We need to save as much money on this as we can and having him tell us what needs to be done would help." Neither man responded and after a moment, Schind turned to Shulman. "I need a list of all the volunteers you are using."

"It's the same list Joe gave me."

Schind had expected a more compliant answer. "I need a list from you, too," he said with an edge.

Buxenbaum looked over at him. "Worried about security?"

"Always worried about security."

Shulman spoke up. "I assure you these men are—"

"Just get me the list," Schind said curtly. "Okay? I don't want to discuss it." Then he turned away and started toward the car.

Meanwhile, at a berth across the way in Brooklyn, Shulman and Walter Blount continued training the first group of crewmen using the ship rented from the Atlantic Fruit Company. The days were long, hot, and often boring as the class learned to clean the ship and reviewed the basic skills of seamanship. Most of the men were young and inexperienced. After a few days, they chafed at being told to mop the deck or wash down the walls and griped about winding rope and stowing the ship's worn-out gear. Among the loudest complainers were Marvin Liebman and Stanley Ritzer, both from the farm in New Jersey.

Hugh Clark, the seasoned seaman Ash had recruited earlier, did his best to keep them in line but after a week of menial tasks even he began to complain. Finally he approached Shulman. "This general seamanship work is good but what are we actually going to do? What positions will we fill? We all need a specific job, even if we don't get to do it right away. These guys need to know they're working toward a goal."

Shulman's first thought was to react with the typical officer's response, ordering Clark to do his job or face the consequences. Then he remembered he was no longer a naval officer and Clark was a volunteer, so instead of a short response, he said, "What sort of experience do you have?"

"Since the war ended I've been working as a deckhand but during the war I was in the boiler and engine room."

Shulman's eyes opened wide in a look of surprise. Although he and Buxenbaum had succeeded in locating people to fill unskilled positions in the crew, they had been unable to find anyone with boiler or engine experience. "Well," Shulman responded, "I guess you'll be assigned to the boiler and engine room."

"Good," Clark grinned. "Think I could take a look at the boiler and engine on *this* ship?"

"I haven't been down there yet. Not sure what kind of shape it's in."

"Then why don't we have a look?"

With Clark leading the way, they followed an overhead string of single electrical bulbs down three levels to the bottom of the ship, then made their way toward the stern. The air was heavy and stale, and soon they were soaked with perspiration.

After a few minutes of threading their way over rusty steel grating and around shadowy corners, they reached the boiler room. They stepped into the boiler room first.

Clark glanced around admiringly. "This is a big room," he observed.

"It's a nasty, creepy room," Shulman replied, glancing around warily.

"Yeah." Clark looked around. "We could use some more light."

"Need to get it cleaned up, too."

"We'll need some help."

"I'll send you some men."

"Mind if I pick them myself?" Clark asked.

"Who'd you have in mind?"

"How about that Liebman kid."

"Marvin Liebman?"

"Yeah. And the other one that's always with him. Rizker or Rigler or something like that."

"Stanley Ritzer, from the farm in New Jersey?" Shulman asked.

"Yeah."

"Okay. I'll have them come down."

Forty-five minutes later, Liebman and Ritzer, eager young men who'd only recently been at the training farm in New Jersey, appeared in the boiler room. Clark announced that they'd been assigned to him permanently and began explaining how the boiler system worked.

"If you want to make one of these ships move, the first thing you need is water." He stepped to the right and pointed. "This is the freshwater feed tank. We fill it with fresh water every time we're in port."

"That'll hold enough water to get us all the way to Palestine?" Ritzer asked.

"No, but it'll hold enough to get us started while we make some more. At sea, we use seawater."

Ritzer had another question. "If the boilers can use seawater, why bother filling the tank with fresh?"

"We use seawater, but we don't use the salt," Clark replied. He turned to a piece of equipment that stood farther to the right. "This is an evaporator. It heats seawater and produces water vapor. The water vapor rises up through the top into these pipes," he continued, pointing to a maze of pipes behind the machine. "In the process, the salt that was in the water gets left behind in the evaporator. The steam goes through the pipes to that thing over there. That's a condenser that cools the vapor. As it cools, the vapor turns back into water that is salt free, which then passes into the feed take."

"What happens to the salt?" Liebman asked.

"It settles to the bottom of the evaporator." Clark reached behind him and patted the evaporator. "Ends up right there. Part of our job is to open this up and clean it. Otherwise, it'll fill up and salt will collect in the wrong places and the evaporator will stop working and we'll be dead in the water."

"That's a lot to remember," Ritzer sighed.

"Yeah," Clark said. "And we're just getting started." He turned to a boiler that stood to the left. "This is the boiler itself. One of them." He pointed to a machine next to it. "That's one, also."

"Two boilers?"

"This ship has four," Clark explained. "Look behind you and you'll see the other two."

Liebman and Ritzer turned to see. "Why so many?" Ritzer asked.

"Because these things are machines," Clark replied. "They break down. Things go wrong. When something happens to a boiler at sea, if you only have one, you're stuck. This way, there's always backup. And extra power." Clark continued. "The boiler heats water to produce steam. Actually, superheated steam. That steam goes into here." He pointed overhead to a large gray pipe. "Which takes it to the engine room."

"Where's the engine room?"

"Behind us."

"Which way is behind us?"

Clark pointed over his shoulder. "Down there."

"What happens to it in the engine room?"

"In the engine room," Clark explained patiently, "the steam drives the engine that turns the shaft that turns the propeller." He pointed to a valve on the side of the boiler. "Now, pay attention. This is a check valve. It keeps the boiler from building up too much steam. If it builds too much pressure, it'll crack the casing. Once we get this check valve set, don't touch it. Some people like to pinch it down. They close it a little to generate excess power. Don't do it. And above all, never open it all the way."

"Why not?"

"Like I said, pinch it too much and it'll build too much steam."

"And crack the boiler casing," Liebman offered.

"Right," Clark nodded. "But if you open it up all the way, it'll cause the pressure to suddenly drop. A sudden loss of pressure is more damaging than too much pressure."

"But some people do adjust it," Ritzer added.

"Yes, but you don't have the experience to know where to set it. So leave it alone. Got it?"

"Right," they both said with a nod.

"Get some tools and let's open this evaporator so you can see what we're talking about."

"I thought they said we were going to be cleaning up down here," Ritzer said.

Clark shot him a look. "You want to go back to the mop?"

"No," Ritzer said lamely.

"Then get some tools," Clark ordered, "and let's get busy."

A couple of weeks later, a temporary crew sailed the corvettes down to Brewer Dry Dock on Staten Island. The trouble with the *Beauharnois* boiler recurred even on that short trip and Shulman made arrangements at Brewer's to have it serviced while workmen refitted the ships for an Atlantic voyage.

When repairs and modifications to the ships neared completion, Shulman brought the trainees from the training ship in Brooklyn to the corvettes. Clark took Liebman and Ritzer to the boiler and engine room, where half a dozen more volunteers joined them to learn the boiler and engine room tasks in anticipation of creating a crew for each ship.

Not long after that, Schind came to the dock to check on Shulman's progress in preparing the ships and crew for sailing. After a tour of both vessels, he and Shulman paused on the deck of the *Beauharnois* to discuss the work yet to be done. While they talked, Schind noticed a black car parked just down the docks from the two ships.

"How long has that car been there?" he asked.

Shulman glanced in that direction and shrugged his shoulders. "I don't know, I never noticed it before."

"You gotta pay attention," Schind groused. "That's part of the job. Keep your eyes open for every detail. Didn't they tell you that in the navy?"

Shulman bristled at the remark. "I can't be below deck checking on the engine crew and up here standing watch."

"Post someone."

"If they're doing that, they won't be training."

"Use people from the less-essential positions. Rotate through them." Schind sounded frustrated and he turned to leave. "See if *they* can pay attention to detail."

CHAPTER 25

THE VOLUNTEERS

Not long after the *Norsyd* and *Beauharnois* reached Brewer Dry Dock, Ash telephoned Schind with news they'd both been waiting to hear. "I've located two men who can work as captains," Ash announced with excitement.

Schind was elated but did his best to keep his emotions in check. "Are they qualified?"

"I think so. Talk to them and see for yourself."

"Do they have licenses?"

"The Coast Guard won't let them off the dock if they don't have a license. So, yes, I made sure of that."

They arranged a meeting for later that afternoon at Ash's office. Ash was waiting by the secretary's desk when Schind arrived. "They are here?" Schind asked as he came through the doorway.

"Yes," Ash replied as he steered Schind aside. "They are waiting in my office."

"What are their names?"

"Javier Lopez and Gabino Molla." Ash held a file, which he now opened. "Both men are licensed Panamanian captains," he took the licenses from the folder. "We found them through our friend Stone in Boston."

"He thinks they're okay?"

"I assume he would not have sent them if they weren't. They normally sail from New Orleans for one of those companies Stone leases his ships to."

Schind glanced over the licenses then handed them back to Ash. "Well," he sighed, "let's talk to them and find out a little more."

Ash led the way over to his office and pushed open the door. Lopez and Molla stood as they entered. Lopez, the older of the two, was about Schind's height with dark hair, olive complexion, and a quick, friendly smile. Molla was a little taller with sharp, angular features and a reserved demeanor. Ash introduced them to Schind, then they all took a seat.

Schind looked over at Lopez. "Mr. Ash tells me you work from New Orleans."

"Yes," Lopez replied. "We have been sailing ships for Mr. Samuel Zemurray of Corocito Fruit in New Orleans."

Schind remembered Stone mentioning Zemurray when they met earlier. "Where did that work take you? What route were you sailing?"

"Normally from New Orleans to Honduras."

"Ever sail across the Atlantic?"

"I have," Lopez answered. "Gabino has not." He gestured to Molla, who was seated beside him.

Schind looked at Lopez with a puzzled frown. "Can he speak English?"

"Yes," Molla replied with a smile. "I speak English, but Javier likes to talk, so I let him talk for both of us."

"Mr. Zemurray assigned us to Captain Ash," Lopez continued. "He said you needed captains for a transatlantic voyage. We are both prepared for the trip. However, we were wondering about the nature of these voyages. What exactly will we carry and where would you like us to take it?"

Ash glanced over at Schind, then said haltingly, "I'm not sure . . . we're ready to . . . "

"No, it's okay," Schind spoke up. "I'll tell you plainly. You are sailing to Europe to pick up refugees. Jewish refugees. And then continue on to Palestine where you will be met and most likely detained by the British Navy. We have agents on the other end who will do their best to see that you are released as expeditiously as possible, but the nature of your voyage will be rather perilous and there are no guarantees about when you will return."

Lopez glanced at Molla. "We were informed of the basic danger of the trip."

Schind was surprised. "By whom?"

"A friend of Señor Zemurray. He did not tell us our destination but he told us there was considerable likelihood we would be detained. At least for a short time. He said you have obtained two corvettes from the Canadian Navy."

"Yes."

"You have crews for these ships?"

"Yes," Ash answered.

"We would very much like to meet them. At least get acquainted with them. Review the condition of the ships. These things are very important."

Schind glanced over at Ash, "We can look at them now, if you like."

"Good," Lopez said with a nod. "How soon would you like for us to sail?"

"How soon can you be ready?" Schind asked.

"We are ready to cast off tomorrow. Mr. Zemurray would like us to cross and get back in the minimum time. Not to rush things. It's just that the four of us are needed in our usual positions."

Schind and Ash exchanged questioning looks. "The four of you?" they asked.

"We brought our own navigators," Lopez replied.

"Oh," Schind said with a tone of surprise. In all of the planning and preparation, he had neglected to consider the need for navigation. "Good. Then tomorrow it will be."

"You can be ready that quickly?"

"We can have the ship provisioned overnight and be ready to cast off tomorrow afternoon, if that's what you want."

"What about our destination? I know you have told us we are sailing to Europe, but what port are we putting in at? We need to know specifically where we are going."

"You'll be given those instructions once you have cleared US territorial waters."

"We'll need maps."

"They're already on board."

"Good, then." Lopez stood. Molla joined him. "You seem to have thought of everything."

"We tried," Schind said.

"Then may we inspect the ships?" Lopez asked.

Ash rose from his chair to open the door. "Certainly."

From the office in lower Manhattan, Schind and Ash rode with Lopez and Molla to the docks on Staten Island. They found Shulman aboard the *Norsyd*. While Ash took Lopez and Molla below deck for a look around, Schind took Shulman aside to the stern. "How's the crew? Are they ready?"

"No, but with a few more months of training they might actually be able to survive an Atlantic crossing. They are not ready. Not now. Some of them still bump their heads when they pass through the bulkhead hatchways."

A broad grin appeared on Schind's face. "Well," he said with a dry sense of humor. "We'll have to make do with what we have, I suppose."

"They're better than I expected," Shulman continued, unaware of what Schind was hinting at. "But they are still months away from sailing. I thought maybe in two or three weeks we could take a shakedown trip out to the end of Long Island. Put them through the routine of getting under way. See how they do. But that would be strictly for evaluation."

"Your men will have to learn faster than that," Schind chuckled.

"What do you mean?"

"I mean we are delivering provisions to the ships tonight. Both ships are sailing tomorrow evening."

Shulman's mouth fell open and he stood there in stunned silence. "Tomorrow?" he asked finally.

"Yes."

"But they aren't prepared to sail. They *can't* sail. They've never sailed a ship of any kind."

"What they don't know, they can learn at sea."

"They will die!" Shulman said emphatically. "They will not survive."

Schind put his hands in his pockets and looked away for a moment, then turned back to Shulman. "Will the ship sink if they aren't properly trained?"

"No, but—"

"Then they'll make it." Schind turned aside and gestured for Shulman to follow. "Come on. I'll introduce you to the captains."

"Captains?" Shulman asked, trailing behind as they moved up the deck. "What do you mean *captains*?"

"Can't sail without a captain." Schind smiled playfully over his shoulder at Shulman. "Even the best-trained crew in the world needs a captain."

"I didn't know you were looking for captains," Shulman complained. "I expected to be included in the process."

"Ash took care of it. These are good men." Schind glanced back at Shulman with a serious look. "So be nice."

As they reached the forward superstructure, Ash emerged from a hatchway with Lopez and Molla following. He introduced Shulman, and the five of them talked briefly about the ships, then Lopez asked again to meet the crew.

"They are still in the midst of training," Shulman said with a glance in Schind's direction. "They're not really presentable to anyone. Let alone a captain ready to take their command."

"Captain Molla and I would like to decide that for ourselves," Lopez answered.

Schind looked over at Shulman. "Gather the men from below and send someone over to get the others from the *Beauharnois*."

A few minutes later, all the men were gathered on the deck of the *Norsyd*, standing in ranks along the starboard side. Schind, Ash, and

Shulman stood aside while Lopez and Molla looked them over. After a moment Lopez turned to Schind. "I have sailed with a crew that looked much worse than this." He glanced back at the men. "We will survive. Might not be pretty, but they will learn." Lopez moved slowly down the ranks once more and paused when he came to Walter Blount and Hugh Clark. "Are the old men coming, too?" he asked over his shoulder.

"Only Clark," Shulman replied. "The others are my training staff."

"Which one is Hugh Clark?"

"I am," Clark replied.

"Very well," Lopez said with a faint smile in Clark's direction. "I shall be honored to sail with a man of such experience."

"You know Hugh Clark?" Shulman asked.

"Indeed," Lopez nodded with a smile. "I know my Hugh Clarks, and all of them are among the finest men who ever put to sea."

After one more pass through the ranks, Lopez turned to Shulman. "You have done well with the men you were given. Will you divide them according to their ship and turn them over to us?"

Shulman looked over at Schind, who gave him a nod. "Very well," Shulman answered reluctantly.

With help from Ash and Walter Blount, the men were divided into separate crews for the two ships. Those for the *Beauharnois* stood to the right. Crewmen for the *Norsyd* stood to the left. When they were separated and in place, Shulman addressed them in a loud voice. "Gentlemen, look around at the men standing next to you. These are the men you will be sailing with. Over the next several months, they will become not only your coworkers but your brothers." He paused a moment as the men whispered among themselves. "Okay," he continued, "listen up. As you no doubt suspect by now, there has been a change in plans. I know we've been training for a departure still several months away, but the schedule has changed. Both ships will set sail tomorrow night."

"Tomorrow?" someone blurted.

"You gotta be kidding," another said.

"This is no joke," Shulman replied. "I am not kidding."

"I need to get home," one man spoke up. "I have to get my things. I'm not packed. I'm not ready."

"I do not think it will be possible for you to leave the ship tonight," Shulman said.

Lopez stepped forward. "I will release them this evening if they promise to return by noon tomorrow."

The crewmen nodded to each other, and Shulman said, "Okay. This is Captain Lopez. He commands the *Beauharnois*. Captain Molla," he continued, "will have the command of the *Norsyd*. They will release you this evening but you must return by noon tomorrow with whatever gear you intend to bring, ready to depart."

Schind spoke up. "Before you go, I would remind you not to tell anyone, not even your families, where you are going or when you will return."

"Where are we going?" someone in back called out.

"You will receive your final destination once both ships have cleared US territorial waters."

And with that, Schind stepped away and the crewmen moved off the ship to the dock. As they did, Schind took Lopez aside. "Listen, we're starting to get pressure from US officials about this trip, which is why we felt forced to move it up."

"I see," Lopez nodded with a concerned look.

"Once you're out of New York Harbor and beyond the international limit, the U.S. won't bother you but the British will. They regularly patrol both the Atlantic and Mediterranean."

"In my experience, Señor Schind, the British patrol the high seas everywhere."

"When you encounter them, if forced to talk, our cover story is that we are operating in the service of a UN relief agency."

"Very well," Lopez agreed. "We shall play it as you wish."

"You will relay this to Captain Molla?"

"Certainly. Will that cover story hold up under serious scrutiny?"

"To a point."

"I see." Lopez clasped his hands together and gave a thin, tight smile. "Then we shall do our best to make it work."

Much to Shulman's surprise, both crews arrived at the docks by noon the following day. When they were all aboard and in place, Schind and Shulman stepped from the ships and turned to leave. Just then, the black car that Schind noticed several days earlier appeared on the dock and rolled to a stop opposite the *Norsyd*. Two men stepped out. Both flashed government identification badges. "We're from the US Treasury Department," the driver said. "Is that your ship?" he asked, pointing.

"No," Schind replied with a straight face. "I'm just helping out."

"Looks like it's ready to depart," the second agent observed.

"Can I help you gentlemen with something?" Schind asked. "Or are you just out riding around?"

"We have reason to believe that ship is carrying contraband," the driver said in an authoritative tone.

Schind grinned. "Contraband?" he asked with a note of incredulity.

"Yes."

"What sort of contraband?"

"We aren't sure."

"Then why do you think it's carrying contraband?"

"We have sources," the second agent answered.

"And I'm sure," Schind said sarcastically, "those *sources* are somehow connected to British intelligence."

"We're not at liberty to say."

"Why not?"

"We haven't looked inside," the second agent offered.

"But you've been sitting here on the docks for weeks watching everything that happens," Schind countered, his voice taking a more cynical edge. "You've seen everything that comes and goes from this berth. Do you mean to tell me that a few merchant mariners might have slipped something past the watchful eye of two US government agents?"

"Look." The driver's tone grew even more ominous than before. "That ship cannot leave this dock until we certify that it's contraband free."

"Under what law or regulation?" Schind challenged.

"We're not lawyers in a courtroom," the second agent snorted. "We don't have to provide chapter and paragraph citations."

"You do this for all the ships in the harbor?" Schind asked. "You ride around in your shiny black cars inspecting all the ships that come and go from New York?"

"No," the driver said coldly. "Just the ones that are . . . suspicious."

"You mean the ones you associate with Jews." Schind's eyes were bright with anger. "Just like those racist sources you supposedly have."

"Mr. Schind, I don't—"

Schind wondered how they knew his name but didn't really want to ask. Instead he said with a tense smile, "Gentlemen, here's my response. We are right now in the United States of America. You work for the federal government." He gestured toward the men on the ships. "*We* are private citizens. You can't do anything to this ship without a warrant. Do you have a warrant?"

"We don't need—"

"Do you have a warrant?" Schind demanded.

"No," the second agent spoke up. "We don't have a warrant."

Schind pointed to their car. "Then I suggest you leave now, before I am forced to call your boss' best friend and complain."

The agents seemed nonplus. "Our boss is the one—"

"You don't have a warrant," Schind said, cutting them off. "You have no authority to detain this ship on mere suspicion."

"If you refuse to cooperate," the driver said, "we'll have no choice but to get a warrant. And I must warn you. If we do that, all of you could be held in custody until our investigation is complete."

"Then go get your warrant," Schind urged with a wave his hand. "Go get it."

The agents turned toward the car to leave. "We'll be back," the driver said with a smirk. "And that boat better still be here."

"It's a ship, gentlemen," Schind said tersely. "If you're going to work the docks, you should learn the nomenclature."

As the agents climbed into the car, Shulman came to Schind's side. "Do you really think they were acting on a tip from British intelligence?"

"Yes."

"What makes you think that?"

"Agents with MI6 have been following me since I arrived in the U.S."

Shulman looked worried. "The British are working with the Americans?"

"Something like that."

"And those really were federal agents?"

"Yes. Why?" Schind looked over at him. "Are you scared?"

"I'm still in the Navy Reserve," Shulman replied. "At least technically. They could make trouble for me."

"Well then, let's hope nothing comes of it."

"I could call my father," Shulman offered. "He knows people. My mother, too. She's even better connected than he. They can get this resolved."

"No," Schind snapped. "This isn't like that."

Shulman looked confused. "What do you mean?"

"This stuff they're trying is off the record. I'm sure the agency knows nothing about it."

Shulman looked even more confused than before. "What are you talking about?"

"Those two guys aren't working for someone in Washington," Schind explained. "They're acting on their own. Probably one of them knows an MI6 agent who asked them to lean on us."

Shulman shook his head in doubt. "I'm not so sure."

Schind turned to face him. "Look, you're a good man and a nice guy, but you don't know much about this sort of thing. I do. They don't have papers. If they were legitimate, they would have papers."

"But if they're legitimate," Shulman argued, "the Coast Guard will be here any moment to seize the ships."

"Then you better get them on their way," Schind replied.

"But they can't leave with a government inquiry in the works," Shulman argued. "We'll all get arrested."

"Listen to me," Schind took Shulman by the shoulders. "If you're going to help us, you have to learn the way we operate. Now, get those ships under way immediately, before those government agents return."

Shulman shrugged free of Schind's grasp and stepped onto the deck of the *Beauharnois*, then entered the wheelhouse, where he found Captain Lopez. "We need for you to get under way immediately."

Lopez glanced out the window at the dock. "Those men from that car want to make trouble?"

"They had questions," Shulman replied.

"I've seen their type before." Lopez stepped to the intercom tube and called down to the engine room. "This is the captain," he said. "Prepare to get under way."

"Aye," came the response immediately. "Preparing to get under way."

There was a rumble from down below as Lopez radioed the *Norsyd* and gave Molla the same message, then over the loudspeaker gave the order, "Now hear this. Stand by to get under way."

Shulman stepped outside to the rail and watched as the men on board both ships scrambled to make ready. He was surprised at how well they worked together. A moment later, Lopez appeared at his side. "Mr. Shulman, if you do not wish to travel with us to Europe, I suggest you step off now."

"Yes, sir," Shulman replied. "I suppose I should."

Shulman shook Lopez's hand and made his way to the main deck, then moved down the gangway to the dock. By then Schind was nowhere to be found. Shulman stood alone and watched as crewmen hauled aboard the gangplank, then freed the mooring lines. And finally, he felt a lump in his throat as first the *Norsyd* then the *Beauharnois* slipped from the dock and started across the bay.

CHAPTER 26

THE VOLUNTEERS

On the day the ships sailed, Prescott Howe, president of Howe Oceanic, a British shipping company, paid a visit to Nathan Fortas, managing partner at Fortas, Brown & Hoffman.

Howe was a tall man with salt-and-pepper hair and a neatly trimmed beard. He wore a three-piece pinstripe suit with a white pocket square perfectly folded and placed inside the breast pocket of his jacket. A watch was tucked into a pocket of his vest with a gold chain draped from it to a buttonhole where it was attached. An intelligent, accomplished man, he spoke with an aristocratic British accent and carried himself with an air of pompous dignity that befitted his position in the royal family. A minor position—twenty-sixth in line to the throne—but royalty nonetheless. His company, which he inherited from his father, was one of Fortas, Brown & Hoffman's largest clients. Fortas was surprised to see him at the office.

"I didn't realize you were coming to the city this week," Fortas said as he ushered Howe to a seat in his office. "When did you get in?"

"We flew in yesterday," Howe answered. "And to be quite honest, I didn't expect to be here this week. I have pressing business in London, but something has come up that's even more important and so I came here to take care of it personally."

"Oh," Fortas said with a look of concern as he moved to a chair behind the desk. "What's the matter?"

"To get right to it," Howe said grimly, "our company is withdrawing its business from your firm."

Fortas was stunned. "You can't be serious."

"I'm afraid I've never been more serious about anything."

The expression on Fortas' face turned from puzzlement to worry. "But why?"

"It has come to our attention that one of your attorneys is working with several organizations that are attempting to subvert our government's efforts to administer its UN mandate in Palestine. We, and the Crown, find that an affront to the dignity and sovereignty of the United Kingdom and we do not wish in any way to be associated with such . . . organizations or their supporters."

Fortas' brow was lined with deep furrows. "What on earth are you talking about?"

"You have a lawyer in your firm by the name of Palmer Collins, do you not?"

"Yes. He's one of our subordinated partners. What about him?"

"Are you aware that he recently has assisted in the formation of several corporations that are being used as fronts to facilitate a coordinated effort to undermine His Majesty's policies in Palestine?"

Fortas shook his head. "No, I was not aware of anything of this nature." He paused a moment, as if thinking, then abruptly stood. "Sit right there. I'll get to the bottom of this right now."

"No need." Howe rose from his chair. "The decision already has been made. I thought it only proper, given our long-standing relationship, that I inform you personally." He turned toward the door. "Someone from our office here in New York will send instructions on where to deliver our files." He paused at the door and turned to look back and Fortas. "I'm sorry it has come to this, Nathan. Good day."

When Howe was gone, Fortas stormed into Collins' office, his face red with anger. He slammed the door behind him, placed both hands on the desktop, and leaned close to Collins' face. "What are you doing?"

Collins was startled by the sudden outburst and instinctively leaned back in his chair. "What are you talking about?"

"I've been talking to Prescott Howe."

Collins had a puzzled frown. "Howe Oceanic?"

"Yes," Fortas growled. "Howe Oceanic." He backed away from the desk and took a seat. "Who did you think I was talking about?"

"I don't handle their files. What about them?"

"Prescott Howe informed me just now that their company is withdrawing its business from the firm."

"Why?"

"They say they have learned that one of our lawyers is engaged in activity to undermine the British government's efforts in Palestine." Collins reddened in response. Fortas leaned forward in his chair, his voice tense and low. "What are you doing?"

Collins glanced away. "I've never been to Palestine," he hedged.

"I'm not talking about you going to Palestine," Fortas snapped. "Tell me what you're doing that would make Howe pull its business from our firm. Tell me right now, or find another place to work."

Collins looked over at him. "I'm a partner."

"A junior partner," Fortas reminded. "Read your partnership agreement. It's not as permanent as it sounds. What are you doing that has them so upset?"

Collins leaned back in his chair again. He didn't want to talk about what he'd been doing, but Fortas ran the law firm, which left him little choice. "Morris Ginsberg," he began slowly, "and several others are purchasing ships to gather refugees from Europe and transport them to Palestine."

"That's illegal," Fortas retorted.

"It's not illegal here."

"It is in Palestine," Fortas argued.

"That's someone else's problem."

"What did you do for them?"

"I helped them form several corporations to own the ships and I helped them register the ships."

"Where are they registered?"

"Panama."

"Who else is involved?"

"I don't think I should tell you that," Collins replied.

Fortas didn't like the response. "Why not?" he asked with an insistent tone.

"Because it doesn't matter who else is involved," Collins replied. "Nothing they've done has been illegal. Mr. Ginsberg is a long-standing client of this firm. His word was never challenged before and I don't think we should question his integrity now."

"Morris Ginsberg is free to conduct himself in any manner he chooses," Fortas said forcefully. "But it is my responsibility to tend to the business of this firm. Howe Oceanic provides a large portion of our income." He jabbed with his finger in Collins' direction. "Income that helps pay for your lifestyle."

"The refugees are trapped in Europe," Collins responded. "The British treat them no better than the Nazis. These men just want to do something about it."

"Nazis?" Fortas said haughtily. "What do you know about Nazis?"

"They have them in camps," Collins continued, ignoring the question. "Some of the refugees are housed with their former German guards." Collins, with a sense of righteous indignation, looked Fortas in the eye as he continued. "It's a travesty and the real question isn't about why I'm helping Mr. Ginsberg do something about it. The real question is why aren't you helping them, too?"

Fortas was offended by the remark and stood. "Do you realize who you are talking to?"

"Yes, sir," Collins replied, standing as well. "And I mean no disrespect, but if I'm willing to help, I think you should be, too."

Fortas stared at him a moment, then jerked open the office door and left in a huff.

That evening after dinner, while the children were busy in their rooms, Collins found Olivia in the den and took a seat beside her on the sofa. "We need to talk a moment."

"What's wrong?" she asked in a sudden, worried tone.

"Something happened today and I . . . may have to look for a new job."

"Why?" The color drained from her face. "What happened?"

"I can't tell you the details right now."

"I'm your wife," she protested. "Why can't you tell me?"

"Because it involves a client. The things I know, I know by the confidence of our attorney-client relationship."

Olivia's worried look turned to anger. "This has got to stop," she demanded. "This right here." She pointed for emphasis with her finger. "This has to stop."

"What has to stop?"

"You come and go at all hours of the day and night. I smell alcohol on your breath. You say you're going to the office but you're not at the office. You go to . . . "

He turned on the sofa to face her. "You've been calling to check up on me?"

"Yes, I've been calling to check up on you. When you don't come home, I get worried. When I get worried I start calling around to find out if you're dead or alive or just seeing a girlfriend."

"I don't have a girlfriend," he said, defending himself.

"I don't know if I can trust what you tell me anymore."

"Don't know if you can trust me?" he railed.

"I just . . . " Olivia began to cry. "I don't . . . "

"Have you smelled perfume on my clothes?"

"No," she said between sniffs.

"Have you seen any lipstick on my collar?"

"No," she said, shaking her head.

"Have I come home drunk?"

"No."

Well, all right," he said with satisfaction. "What are we talking about, then?"

"So you're careful," she retorted. "You make sure not to leave any traces."

"Olivia!" he blurted in a scolding voice. "Stop this. I'm involved in a case with a client at work that I can't tell you about. That's all there is to it. If I could tell you, I would, but I can't. And if you knew what it was you'd be supportive."

"So . . . tell me, and I'll support you."

"Like I just said, I can't tell you."

"Why not?"

"I already told you why. It involves a client." Collins lowered his voice. "And it's dangerous."

Olivia's eyes opened wider. "Dangerous?"

"Yes."

"It's dangerous," she repeated, "you could lose your job, end up dead, and the rest of us could be out on the street, and you can't tell me what's going on?"

"No," he sighed, his voice calm again. "I can't tell you."

"But you can't tell me we won't wind up on the street, either, can you?"

"No, I can't tell you that, either."

While Collins was talking with his wife, Nathan Fortas convened a specially called meeting of the firm's senior partners and told them what Collins and Ginsberg were doing—forming corporations to buy ships to send to Europe to collect Jewish refugees and take them to Palestine—and he told them of Prescott Howe's decision to withdraw Howe Oceanic's business from the firm.

"Why does Howe care about what any of our clients might do?" someone asked.

"An even better question," another spoke up. "How does Howe know what our clients are doing and whether one of our attorneys is involved?"

"I'm sure Prescott Howe has contacts in the British government," someone commented from the far end of the table. "They must have told him. After all, he's a member of the royal family."

Felix Brown, one of the named partners, said quietly, “This business with the ships and refugees is a Haganah operation.”

“You know that for a fact?”

“Not directly. But Morris Ginsberg is friends with David Ben-Gurion and from what I hear, Danny Schind is in town. I think he’s in charge of the program.”

“You know about this?” Fortas asked. “You know for certain Schind is in town?”

“I hear things.”

“Who is Danny Schind?” someone asked.

“He’s an officer with Haganah.”

“Not just any officer,” another commented. “He’s rather high in the ranks of leadership.”

“That’s what I mean,” Fortas said. “This is the work of David Ben-Gurion. This whole thing. The ships, the refugees, Ginsberg’s involvement. It’s all David Ben-Gurion.”

“Why is that a problem?”

“It undermines British policy in the region,” Fortas explained. “Howe is a member of the royal family and doesn’t want to be associated with anyone who works against the interests of the Crown.”

“But what’s the part about Ben-Gurion? You said it like there’s a problem with him.”

“We made a commitment years ago to support Ze’ev Jabotinsky,” Fortas reminded the group. “And when he died we continued that relationship with Benzion Netanyahu and the New Zionists.”

“The Revision Zionists,” someone corrected.

“Same thing.”

“Netanyahu is coming here at the end of the week to visit with us and he’s expecting to receive a contribution from us,” Fortas said.

“Is John Patterson coming with him?” Brown asked.

“Yes,” Fortas replied. “I’m sure he will.”

“Patterson is a courageous man,” another added. “Led the Jewish League for the British during the Great War and he’s not even Jewish.”

"Can we get back to Collins?" Fortas asked sarcastically, trying to maintain control of the meeting.

"There are rumors about Netanyahu, by the way," someone sadded, ignoring Fortas' plea.

"What kind of rumors?"

"That he's actually working to raise an army."

"He'll never put together an organization like Haganah."

"Why not?"

"Because Benzion Netanyahu insists Jews should control *all* of Palestine and that all Arabs should be removed. The world will never allow that. They'll allow a Jewish state, but not total removal of the Arabs."

"An all-or-nothing proposition will only give us nothing."

Fortas stepped in again. "Regardless of the outcome in Palestine, we have made our choice and sided with Netanyahu. And I would remind you we are not alone in doing so. The outcome of all this is very much undecided. But he is coming here later this week and expecting to receive our donation."

"Which he shall receive," Brown noted.

"But tonight," Fortas continued, "we are faced with a situation in which we have Collins working with Ginsberg to further Ben-Gurion's effort to impose his views not only on Palestine, but on refugees in Europe and, ultimately, on the entire world. One of our own attorneys working with one of our major clients—a member of the royal family—on a scheme that violates British law, undermines the integrity of the British Crown, potentially places this nation in an awkward position, and puts this firm on the opposite side of its long-standing commitments."

"Jabotinsky is right, by the way," Roy Lipton added. "Partition is a bad idea. And I don't know about the rumors regarding Netanyahu and an army, but he's been doing more than just opposing Ben-Gurion. He's lobbied Congress and the Democratic Party on behalf of a Jewish state in Palestine. Activities," he informed as he glanced around the room, "which some in this firm have helped facilitate by more than donations of financial support. I'm talking about phone calls, letters, the extension of personal relationships and favors, in a concerted effort to help Netanyahu do what he's trying to do."

"We've been through that several times," Fortas said, trying again to keep the meeting on track. "Let's stick to Collins for the moment."

"Just a minute, Nathan," Bertram Cohn spoke up. "I want to take issue with what Roy just said. I don't think Netanyahu and Ben-Gurion are as opposed as might first appear. Both men want a Jewish state in Palestine, they simply have a different view on how to accomplish it." Those seated around the room nodded and murmured in approval.

"We should have the entire region," Lipton argued. "Arabs already have a state in Transjordan, courtesy of the British. And in Syria and Lebanon, courtesy of the French. The only thing left is the area that once comprised historic Israel."

"Ben-Gurion sees Netanyahu as an extremist," Brown said, joining the increasingly heated debate. "He'll never include Netanyahu in the Jewish Agency's political efforts."

"I think it's the part about moving all the Arabs out that bothers him most," Cohn sniped. "And that's the part that upsets the rest of the world, too."

Fortas was totally frustrated. "Gentlemen, please," he pleaded. "My point in bringing all this up was to say that Collins is pursuing something that is opposed to the position taken by this firm, the position of our other clients, and the position of the organizations we already support. His involvement with Ben-Gurion and with Haganah has cost us a lucrative client, and that will cost us dearly in the bottom line."

Abe Hoffman, who'd been silent throughout the meeting, finally spoke up. "Nathan, all Collins and Ginsberg are trying to do is help the refugees in Europe, right?"

"Yes," Fortas responded. "So far as I know."

"Shouldn't we be doing that?" Hoffman glanced around the room. "I think more than a few of us lost relatives at Auschwitz."

Fortas turned to face Hoffman. "Are you saying that you support Collins, even at the loss of Howe Oceanic's business?"

Hoffman's eyes went cold. His face was as emotionless as stone. "And what do you propose? Get rid of Collins?"

"Yes."

"If we do that, we'll lose Howe *and* Ginsberg."

Fortas, suddenly nervous, looked away. "Ginsberg has been a good client, but he's not Howe and he doesn't bring in as much money."

"You mean," Hoffman chided, "he's not a wealthy goy and he can't bring in wealthy goy clients."

"I resent that," Fortas snarled.

Hoffman responded loudly, "Well, I'm not happy about firing Collins, either."

"Can we fire him?" Cohn asked. "I mean, he *is* a partner."

"He's a junior partner," Fortas explained. "We used the new partnership agreement when we admitted him."

"He's still entitled to his portion of profits for the year to date."

"Yes, yes," Fortas exclaimed. "And he'll get it."

"And we should give him a month's draw extra as severance," Lipton suggested. Everyone in the room nodded in agreement.

"Well . . . " Fortas stammered. "I'm not so sure about . . . "

"Three months," Hoffman said in an authoritative tone.

"Two," Fortas snapped.

"Four," Hoffman said firmly.

The room fell silent as the two men stared at each other. Then Fortas sighed and said, "Okay. Three."

"And," Hoffman added, "you get to tell him."

"I expected as much."

"I'll be there to make sure you don't short the guy," Hoffman warned.

"You would prefer to keep him?" The tone of Fortas' voice made it sound more like an accusation than a question. "After all we've said and all you've heard, you still would prefer to keep him?"

"Collins is a good man and a good attorney." Hoffman's voice rumbled through the room. "He did precisely what we asked him to do, which was take care of the clients we assigned him and make money for the firm. Morris Ginsberg is one of those clients *we* assigned to him. Now you want to fire him for doing what we said. That's not right. And I don't like being bullied by the British." Hoffman rested his hands on the table. "And I especially don't like that it comes from Howe."

"Well . . . " Fortas said, turning away once more. "It might not be comfortable and we might not like it, but it's what we have to do. We're in the business of making money, not losing clients."

"So you think you can get Howe back?" Hoffman asked.

"He hasn't sent anyone to pick up his files yet. I think there's a good possibility we can."

Hoffman stood and turned toward the door to leave. "I think we may have just presided over the end of our firm."

CHAPTER 27

THE VOLUNTEERS

The next morning, Collins arrived at the office as usual and took a seat at his desk. A few minutes later, Fortas appeared in the doorway and slowly entered the room. He handed Collins an envelope. "The partners met last night. They voted to terminate your partnership. If you read the agreement, you know we have the power."

"Yes," Collins nodded. "I read the agreement and I know you have the power."

Fortas pointed to the envelope. "There's a notice to that effect and a check in the envelope. That's your part of the firm's profit to date plus three months' draw as a severance payment. You should leave the office today."

"Don't I need to notify the clients I have been working with?"

"We'll take care of that. Your secretary knows all your pending matters?"

"Yes."

"Then we will take care of the clients. And I would appreciate it if you would take the files for those corporations you formed for Ginsberg with you when you go. You can have those as part of your severance, too. I'm sorry it's come to this, but it couldn't be avoided."

As Fortas stepped out of the office, Hoffman appeared in the doorway. "Let me know where you end up. I have a couple of things I need to refer out. I'll send them to you."

"Yes, sir." Collins stood. "I'll do that. Thank you."

Hoffman moved to a chair and took a seat across from the desk. "What's the name of the corporation you formed for Ginsberg?"

Collins sat. "The US corporation is called Weston Trading Company."

Hoffman reached inside his jacket and took out a check, which Collins could see was already made out in the amount of $25,000. Hoffman laid it on the desk and entered Weston's name, then handed it to Collins. "Save as many refugees as possible and . . . " His voice broke and he paused a moment before adding, "I'll help you all I can."

When Fortas and Hoffman were gone from his office, Collins pushed the door closed and stared out the window at the city below. At first he replayed in his mind the conversation with Fortas, hearing again the tone of his voice and the cold, aloof manner in which he presented himself. Collins had always admired Fortas' emotional detachment and his steadfast refusal to adopt the clients' issues as his own. The firm was the singular object of his focus. His point of integration with the world. His reason for living. Collins had been headed down that path himself but that was before Rev. Thornton took an interest in him and long before Thornton introduced him to Sheldon Glaser. That changed everything and he was glad of it. He'd come to Fortas, Brown & Hoffman thinking he'd find the sense of comradery he'd missed after leaving the army. To his disappointment, there was none of that. Only fifty lawyers reflecting in one way or another the same detachment Collins had seen in Fortas and the singular devotion to the firm as well.

For Collins, the sense of belonging he'd searched for came instead from his association with Thornton, Glaser, and Ginsberg. The notes. The meetings. The notion that they were participating together in a cause much bigger than themselves—a cause that mattered, that made a difference, that was destined to shape the future not just of a region but of the world—that was what Collins had been searching for and that was what he found in his association with Ginsberg. The thought of it brought a smile to his face. A Methodist and a Jew, working together as part of the larger effort to find a place for all Jews. A place of safety and security. A place where they could achieve their historic destiny. And now he was free to pursue that goal with a sense of devotion and purpose Nathan Fortas could only dream of. Rather than quaking in fear at his uncertain financial future, Collins felt liberated.

After a few minutes, Collins turned away from the window and went in search of empty file boxes. He found two in a closet down the hall and brought them to his desk, then filled them with the plaques from the wall and personal items from his desktop, along with the files for Weston Trading Company and the associated Panamanian corporations.

When he was finished, Collins placed the boxes on the floor near his secretary's desk and left her a note indicating he would return later that day to collect them. Then he took the elevator to the lobby, stepped out to the street, and walked up to Ginsberg's office.

"What brings you here?" Ginsberg asked, surprised to see him without an appointment.

"They fired me," Collins said in a matter-of-fact tone.

Ginsberg had a questioning look. "Who fired you?"

"Nathan Fortas. Fortas, Brown & Hoffman." Collins took a seat across the desk from Ginsberg. "They let me go."

"When?"

Collins glanced at his watch. "About an hour ago."

"What for?"

"Nathan found out I was helping you with Weston Trading Company. I think Prescott Howe told him."

"British intelligence," Ginsberg said with a nod.

"That's what I figure."

Ginsberg sighed. "I should have warned you."

"About the British?"

"No." Ginsberg sat with his hands resting in his lap. "That's just part of it. I'm sure they were upset about losing the business, but there's more to it than that." He paused before continuing. "Nathan Fortas was good friends with Ze'ev Jabotinsky."

A puzzled expression wrinkled Collins' forehead. "I don't know who that is."

"He was one of the early Zionists."

"Those who wanted to return to Palestine."

"Yes," Ginsberg nodded. "But it's a little more complicated."

"Oh."

"As Jews began returning to Palestine, they met with various forms of resistance from the Arabs. Among those who returned there were various ideas of how to deal with that opposition. Over time, those factions became political parties. My father and I were part of the Zionist movement represented by David Ben-Gurion and others like him. A version of Judaism that included a practical political perspective on how to establish a Jewish state."

"Practical Judaism?"

"You would probably think of us as non-practicing Jews. The same way some might view a member of the Roman Catholic Church who doesn't attend mass."

"A Jewish identity without the religious practice."

"Something like that," Ginsberg shrugged. "From a political perspective, Ben-Gurion, my father, others of a somewhat older era, were more socialist in their views than the overtly religious Jewish sects. Settlements in Palestine were configured as communes and still are even now. When the Arabs attacked our farming settlements, the people who lived there tried to defend themselves. The mainstream of that defense eventually developed into an organization known as Haganah. This business with the ships and rescuing the refugees is part of a Haganah operation."

Collins looked surprised. "Wow! I've heard of Haganah but I never thought I'd be associated with it."

"Well, you are now," Ginsberg smiled.

"What does that have to do with Nathan Fortas?"

"I'm coming to that. As I said, people like my father and I view Judaism, and life in general, in a more practical manner. Ze'ev Jabotinsky and those who are known as Revisionist Zionists think we should remove all Arabs from Palestine—by force or coercion if necessary. Fortas was a vocal supporter of Jabotinsky and continues to support his successors."

"So, firing me wasn't just about Howe," Collins noted. "It was also about politics."

"I'm afraid so," Ginsberg said with a nod.

"Sounds . . . complicated."

Ginsberg smiled. "Sorry to get you caught up in all this."

"That's not a problem," Collins said with a gesture of his hand.

"I can speak with Nathan about this tomorrow and get your old job back."

"He seemed rather upset."

"That is Nathan," Ginsberg said indulgently. "But he'll come around. I will take my business and the ships and all the rest of it elsewhere and you can continue to work for them."

Collins thought for a moment, "I appreciate that offer, but I'd rather have an office of my own."

Ginsberg seemed not at all surprised. "You are sure of that?"

"Yeah," Collins nodded. "If you'll let me continue to represent Weston Trading."

"I shall be honored."

"Think you could help me find some office space?"

"Well," Ginsberg said with a satisfied tone. "It just so happens, I have space here on this floor. Come on. I'll show you."

As they stood to leave, Collins reached inside his jacket and brought out the check he'd received that morning. "Abe Hoffman sent this."

Ginsberg took the check from him and glanced at it. A smile broke over his face. "Abe and I have known each other since we were children. If he'd been the managing partner, you'd still be with the firm."

"You're right. But then I wouldn't be here, either." Collins turned toward the door. "Let's have a look at that office space."

While Collins was busy that day at the office and with Ginsberg, a package arrived at the apartment building. It was addressed to his wife, Olivia, and the bellman notified her it had arrived. She retrieved the package from the lobby, took it up to their apartment, and opened it. Inside she found a tape recording wound onto a single plastic reel.

Olivia didn't own a tape player but she was curious about what might be on the tape. As she considered how to find a way to play it she thought of her friend Elizabeth who lived in an apartment two floors above. Maybe she knew a way they could listen to it.

Olivia phoned Elizabeth and gave her a brief explanation. Elizabeth was hesitant at first. "Are you sure you want to play it?" she asked.

"Yes," Olivia insisted. "I have to know what's on there."

"Do you really need to listen to it to know?"

"What do you mean?"

"Olivia . . . you can't possibly be that naïve."

"I have to listen to it," Olivia insisted. "I have to. Do you know anyone with a tape recorder who could play it?"

"We know a guy who might help. His name is Donald Marshall. He has an appliance shop on Forty-Ninth Street. Electronics and all the latest gadgets. Ever been in his shop?"

"No."

"I think he could probably help you."

"I don't know him," Olivia said. "I'd feel really awkward just walking in and . . . "

"Do you want me to call and see if he'll help?"

"Yes, would you?"

"Sure. But you'll have to take the tape over there to him."

"Will you go with me?"

"Okay," Elizabeth responded. "But let me give him a call first."

Later that morning, Olivia and Elizabeth took a taxi over to Marshall's store. He greeted them at the front counter, then led them to the back where a cluttered worktable stood against the wall. A reel-to-reel tape machine sat near one end wired to separate speakers that stood on either side.

As they reached the table, Marshall turned to them with an

outstretched hand. "Let's see what you have." Olivia took the tape from her purse and handed it to him. "All right," he commented with a glance at the reel. "This should be easy enough."

Marshall placed the reel on the spindle to the left of the tape machine, unwound a length of the tape, and threaded it through the machine to an empty reel on the right side. "Okay. Let's see what it sounds like." He flipped a switch and the machine began to slowly wind the tape from the reel on the left, through the playback head, to the take-up reel.

"Hey," a woman said in a sultry voice. "I was wondering when you'd call."

"Can you meet today?" a man asked. His voice was flat with little emotion but at the sound of it, Olivia put her hand to her mouth and tears filled her eyes. Elizabeth took hold of her arm and leaned close.

"I always have time for you," the woman said, doing her best to sound seductive.

"I don't have much time," the man responded, again with a clipped, businesslike voice.

"That's okay," she giggled, "I'm just glad for anything I can get."

"Did you buy the items we discussed?" the man asked.

"Oh," she cooed. "You'll have to wait and see."

"This won't take long."

Olivia gestured for Marshall to stop. "I've heard enough. Please turn it off."

"Come here," Elizabeth soothed as she put her arms around Olivia's shoulder. "I'm sure there must be an explanation."

"I knew it," Olivia sobbed. "I knew he was seeing someone." She buried her face against Elizabeth's shoulder and cried aloud.

"Actually," Marshall said, "there's a very good explanation right there on the tape."

Olivia jerked her head up with a startled expression. "What do you mean?"

"For one thing," Marshall began, "I don't think the voices on this tape are all from the same person and they're certainly not from the same conversation."

"What do you mean?"

"I think this recording was made by splicing together bits of conversation from various people, all of whom were talking at different times and in different places."

"Why do you think that?" Elizabeth asked, still holding on to Olivia.

"You can hear it in the man's voice," Marshall said. "When you first hear the tape, the voice probably sounds the same all the way through. But if you listen closely, you can hear the noise in the background shift. It's not the same each time he speaks, or each time the woman speaks, either."

"You mean, like they were in a different location for each of those comments."

"Yes," Marshall said. "As if the snippets of different conversations from different places and different times were fitted together to make it sound like a single, new conversation."

"You can do that?"

"Sure," Marshall said. "Just splice it together."

"I didn't notice any of that," Olivia commented.

"You wouldn't, unless you listened really closely."

"Can we hear it again?" Elizabeth asked.

"Sure. And if you listen really closely, you can hear a tiny clicking sound in between each person's voice. She speaks, click, he speaks, click, she speaks again."

"What would cause that sound?"

"It's the places where they spliced the tape together. Like I said before, they edited other recordings by cutting the voices out, then putting them back as the conversation you heard."

"Literally cutting the tape?"

"Yes." Marshall pointed to an editing device farther down the table. "They used something like that. Figured out where the conversation was on the tape, cut it carefully at the beginning and end, then taped that little snippet together with others. That gave them a rough version. Then they played that rough version back through a player and recorded it from that to create a smoother version of the spliced recording."

"I'm not sure I follow you," Elizabeth replied.

"Me either," Olivia added.

Marshall pointed. "Here, put your ear near that speaker and I'll show you." Elizabeth stood near the speaker to the left. Olivia stood near the one on the right. "All right," Marshall said when they were ready. "Listen closely."

Marshall played the recording once more, and this time Olivia heard the voices more distinctly than before. "They really do sound different," she said with a smile.

"Did you hear the clicking sound?" Marshall asked.

"Not really."

"We'll do it again." Marshall rewound the tape and flipped the switch to play it again. "Listen closely."

This time, after each person in the recording spoke, Olivia heard a faint pop. "Oh," she said. "I heard it."

"I did, too," Elizabeth said with a grin. "There really is a clicking sound."

"They did a very sloppy job," Marshall said as he rewound the tape to the original reel. "A patient editor could create a version that would be very difficult to detect." He unsnapped the reel from the spindle and handed it to Olivia. "This one was easy."

On his way home that afternoon, Collins wondered how he could avoid telling Olivia about what he was doing with Ginsberg, now that he'd lost his job at the law firm. As he neared the apartment building, he realized that not telling her something would be impossible. "There's no way to dodge it completely," he mumbled to himself. "I have to tell her at least something about what happened."

As he entered the apartment, he smelled the aroma of dinner simmering in the kitchen. Collins made his way in that direction and found Olivia standing at the counter, tearing apart a head of lettuce for a salad. He leaned over her shoulder to kiss her, but Olivia moved her head away at the last moment and angrily said, "I can't take this anymore, Palmer."

"Take what?"

"First you go out at all hours of the night to who knows where. Then you tell me you might lose your job. And now this." She reached across the counter to her purse and took out the tape, then thrust it toward him. "This is the last straw."

Collins took it from her and glanced at it with a blank expression on his face. "What is this?"

"It's a tape recording," she blurted.

"I can see that. But a recording of what?"

"I don't know," Olivia railed. "And that's the worst part. The worst part of all of this. I don't know. Elizabeth and I took it to someone she knows who has a tape recorder. He played it for us. I heard the voices on it, but I still don't know what it's about."

"So, what's on the tape?"

"It sounds like a man and woman having an . . . " Olivia put her hands on her hips. Her foot patted lightly against the floor. "It sounds like a man and woman having an intimate conversation."

"And you think it's me?"

"The first voice sounds like you, but then the voices after that aren't really like yours at all. The guy who played it for us said it was a mixture of voices from different recordings."

"This is a setup. Someone wants you to think exactly what you thought when you listened to it."

"I know."

"You know?"

"Yes."

"Then why are you so upset?"

"I want to know what is going on," Olivia demanded. "I'm tired of not knowing."

Collins took her hand. "Look, I can't tell you."

"Why not?" she asked, jerking her hand away. "I'm your wife. You're supposed to talk to me about things like this."

"You know why I can't talk to you about this. I'm an attorney. The things that are happening involve a matter that relates to a client's business."

"What kind of business?"

"If I told you that, I'd be telling you all of it."

"Then how do I know—"

"Lives are at risk, Olivia. Futures are at risk."

"That's very convenient," she retorted. "You go off and do whatever you want to do, then cover it with the 'I'm an attorney. Lives are at risk.' And I'm supposed to believe you."

"They are at risk," Collins said, his voice rising in volume and intensity.

"Yes," she interjected. "*Our* lives and *our* future."

"But for us, the risk is emotional. We can handle that. For the people involved, this is a physical struggle. Some of them might actually die."

"You might lose your job. That's physical . . . sort of." Collins turned away. Olivia caught the look in his eye. "What?" she asked. He responded with a sigh. "Tell me right now," she hissed, "or I am walking out that door."

"They had a senior partners meeting last night," he said finally.

Before he could say more, Olivia started shaking her head. "No. I don't want to hear it."

"It's not as bad as it seems."

"I don't care." She continued to shake her head from side to side. "I don't want to hear it."

"You said to tell you, so—"

"I don't want to hear any more."

"They gave me a check."

"I don't care about a check." Tears streamed down her cheeks and she stared at him a moment, then leaned forward, draped her arms over his shoulders, and sobbed. "Why is this happening to us?"

"I can't tell you," he answered softly.

"Why not?" she whimpered.

"Because," he repeated lamely, the fight gone from his voice, "it has to do with a client's business."

"You just said you don't work there anymore."

"He's still my client."

Olivia jerked her head up from his shoulder. "Your client?"

"Yes."

"You're still a lawyer."

"Yes, I'm still a lawyer. They can't take that away from me. At least, not by firing me."

"And what will you do for an office?"

"I have space on the floor with Morris Ginsberg."

The look on Olivia's face turned angry again. "This is all his doing. Every bit of this, isn't it?"

"I can't answer that."

She pulled away and pushed his arms aside. "Well, you might be able to handle living like this, but I can't."

"What are you saying?"

"I'm saying, I'm thinking about taking the children to Mother's."

"What do you mean?"

"I think maybe we should not be here. If this is how it's going to be, maybe the children and I should go somewhere else until you get past this, or until you can at least tell me what it means."

Collins leaned against the counter and folded his arms across his chest. "Well," he sighed, "maybe that's best."

Olivia was startled. "You'd let me go?"

"No, but if it's like this now, it might get worse before it's over," he explained. "And maybe it's better if you and the children are somewhere safe and secure for a while." He looked over at her. "If you want to go, I won't stop you."

Olivia stared at him with quivering lips, a look of terror on her face. "What is happening to us?" she whispered. "What are we going to do?"

Collins took her in his arms. "I don't know. I really don't know."

Olivia pushed him away. "Well, I know what I'm doing." She placed her hands on her hips in a defiant pose. "I'm doing just what we said. I'm taking the kids to Mother's. You said we'd be safer there and I think you're right. When things settle down, we'll come back. But for now, I'm not taking it anymore. You can deal with whatever's happening on your own."

"We'll have to tell the children."

"Tell them if you like. I'm not trying to explain it to them. If they ask, I'll tell them we're going out there for a break."

"What about school?"

"Mother and I will take care of school." Olivia turned toward the hall. "You can take care of . . . whatever it is you take care of. I'm done with guessing what you're doing and where you're going."

CHAPTER 28

THE VOLUNTEERS

With the first ships on their way to Europe, and with Ginsberg and Stone working to acquire more, Schind turned his attention to California and Ben-Gurion's desire to acquire airplanes with which to create an air force. By then, Henry Nadelson had succeeded in scheduling a series of meetings that would take Schind from San Diego up the coast to Seattle, offering the perfect opportunity to meet with Al Schwimmer. Schind placed a call to him and confirmed Schwimmer would be available over the next several weeks, then purchased a ticket for a flight to Los Angeles, a central location from which to work the southern portion of California before proceeding north.

On the morning of his departure, Schind came downstairs to the lobby, luggage in hand, and asked the clerk to call a cab to take him to the airport. Instead of phoning the taxi company, the clerk walked out to the curb in front of the building and waved a taxi to a stop, then held it there while Schind came out.

As Schind made his way to the car, he noticed a man seated on a bench halfway up the block. Dressed in a dark suit with white shirt and muted tie, Schind was certain he was one of the MI6 agents who'd been shadowing him since his arrival from Palestine. For a moment Schind considered walking over to him and confronting him right there on the sidewalk, but the cab driver came from the car to take his luggage and interrupted Schind's concentration. When he looked back at the bench, the man was gone.

While the driver stowed his luggage in the trunk of the car, Schind took a seat in the taxi and settled in place for the ride to the airport. As they made their way in that direction, Schind glanced over the taxi driver's shoulder to the rearview mirror and saw a Ford sedan trailing behind. The sight of it put an amused smile on his face. *I've ignored them for too long,* he thought. *I should have some fun.*

At the airport, Schind dutifully checked his luggage at the ticket counter and made his way down the concourse. However, instead of walking straight to the gate for his flight, he took his time, stopping first at this gate, then that, giving the MI6 agent no opportunity to double back to the counter to learn which flight really was his. To learn Schind's destination, the agent had to tag along to see which plane he boarded.

Finally, as departure time neared, Schind worked his way past the last two gates before reaching the one with the flight for which he was ticketed. He lingered there as long as possible, then at the last minute darted through the doorway and made his way down to the tarmac. From there, he hurried to the airplane and quick-stepped up to the plane for the flight west.

The agent, Schind knew, would hurry to the ticket counter where his initial inquiries would be met with resistance, but eventually he would learn the destination of Schind's flight. By the time the airplane landed in Los Angeles, MI6 agents would be at the airport waiting for him. But Schind wasn't worried and he settled into his seat, knowing that at last he was on his way to California. And if the agents intended to tail him after he arrived, then he had a plan for that, too.

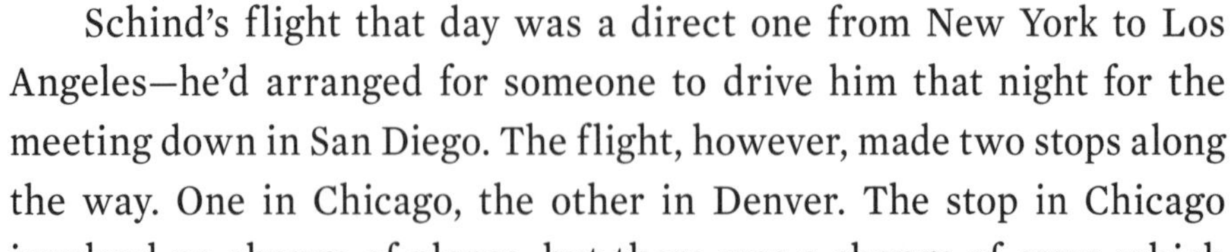

Schind's flight that day was a direct one from New York to Los Angeles—he'd arranged for someone to drive him that night for the meeting down in San Diego. The flight, however, made two stops along the way. One in Chicago, the other in Denver. The stop in Chicago involved no change of planes, but there was a change of crew, which necessitated a two-hour layover.

When the plane landed, Schind got off and went inside the terminal.

There he located a nonstop flight departing immediately for San Diego. For just a few dollars in additional fare, the ticket agent switched him to that flight. Within fifteen minutes of landing in Chicago, he was on his way.

A few hours later, Schind arrived in San Diego and glanced around the terminal as he made his way toward baggage claim. To his great satisfaction, there wasn't an MI6 agent anywhere in sight. But as he made his way up the concourse, he remembered his luggage was on its way to Los Angeles. "Hopefully," he said to himself, "I can find a few clothes to make do until I can pick up that bag."

The next morning, Schind took the train from San Diego to Los Angeles and checked in to the Ambassador Hotel on Wilshire Boulevard, located in the midst of the hustle and bustle of Hollywood. Once in his room, he placed a phone call to the airport, located his luggage, and made arrangements to have it delivered to the hotel. Then he phoned Al Schwimmer.

Schind explained that Ben-Gurion sent him and wanted them to talk. Schwimmer, who seemed to understand the confidential nature of the proposed conversation, invited Schind to his home in San Marino, a suburb east of Los Angeles. They met early that evening and sat on Schwimmer's patio.

Although Schwimmer began his career with Lockheed, he was, by then, working for TWA as a flight engineer and pilot. A slender man of forty, he had bright eyes and rounded chin. Combined with his ever-present smile, he appeared always warm and approachable, qualities which endeared him to almost everyone he met.

"I'm always glad to hear news of David Ben-Gurion and Palestine," Schwimmer said after Schind told him the most recent news of the region. "But I'm curious about what brings you to California?"

"Ben-Gurion wants to build an air force. He said you were the man to talk to about that."

"Well," Schwimmer said slowly, "that would be a big task."

"Yes," Schind nodded. "But could it be done?"

"Obtaining fighter planes from the US government would be a little more difficult. Especially if the buyer wanted to take them outside the country. I think we'd have to get approval from someone to do that. They're selling them, but not like the heavy bombers. They have thousands of those."

"Bombers?"

"Yes, the government is selling bombers to just about anyone with the money to pay for them."

"Why the difference?"

"The U.S. ended the war with thousands of them and they're slashing the size of their military across the board. They *have* to get rid of the planes. And they have other obvious applications—freight, passengers, that sort of thing. Fighter planes not so much, though a few people race them and some just want to own one."

"If we bought bombers, could we get them out of the country?"

"We could right now," Schwimmer answered. "There are rumors that the federal government wants to stop that, but so far they haven't." Schwimmer's enthusiasm seemed to grow as he talked. "You know, this could be really workable. The airplanes already are stripped of armaments, so there's less likelihood anyone would think they'd be used for military purposes."

"But could they be?"

"Oh yes," Schwimmer nodded. "If nothing else, you could open the bomb bay doors and roll the bombs out by hand," he laughed.

"But seriously," Schind said, not laughing at all. "Could the kind of airplanes they're selling be put to a military use again?"

"I don't see why not. I haven't inspected any of the planes, so I can't say for certain what condition they're in, and I doubt they have the bombsights in them—those things were top secret at one point—but the mechanics of getting the doors open in the belly of the plane and releasing the bombs from the bomb racks would take very little effort to put in working shape."

"What about armaments—machine guns, that sort of thing?"

"I think we could remount them in the turrets—if we can get the guns."

"They won't sell those?"

"Not with the airplanes. I don't know about buying them separately somewhere else. We'd have to check on that. Purchasing weapons and ammunition raises a different set of questions."

"What are other buyers doing with them?"

"With the planes or the guns?"

"Planes," Schind clarified. "What are other buyers doing with the airplanes?"

"Like I said, some companies are converting them to passenger and cargo service. A few individual collectors are restoring them to fighting trim, without the weaponry. You know, to use in air shows and that sort of thing."

"Can't get over the war?"

"Apparently not."

"Hmm," Schind said, pausing to think for a moment. "Well . . . " he said finally. "I suppose we should have a look at some of those airplanes the United States wishes to sell and see what condition they're in. Where are they now?"

"They're parked at several locations around the country. Ohio, New York, places where they already have large air force bases. The nearest location to us is in Kingman. They have a few thousand of them parked in the desert out there."

"Kingman," Schind repeated with a questioning look. "Where's that?"

"Kingman Army Air Field," Schwimmer replied. "In Kingman, Arizona."

"That's closer to us than Ohio," Schind observed. "How far away is it?"

"I don't know, exactly. West of Flagstaff. South of Las Vegas. Probably a seven-hour ride east of here."

"But you think we could buy them without any trouble?"

"I think we would have no trouble purchasing them. I'm a US

citizen. My background would show my military service, my job, my training, all of which would fit perfectly. I don't think they'd raise a single objection. If we gave them a business reason for the buy, they'd probably never ask any questions at all."

"What kind of business reason would we need?"

"I don't know," Schwimmer shrugged. "Starting an airline. Flying freight. Whatever plausible reason we can come up with."

"But if we did that, we wouldn't have any trouble, right?"

"We could buy them without any trouble. Getting them back to Palestine might be difficult."

"What if we took them to another country first? Someplace that's not a threat to the United States."

Schwimmer seemed intrigued. "That might work. We could fly them down to Argentina or Bolivia or someplace. Leave them there awhile. Then fly them to Palestine."

"We could say we were forming an airline to service business interests in that region."

"Or, rather than just saying we were doing it, as a front, we could actually do it."

"Form one?"

"Yeah," Schwimmer grinned. "Form an airline."

"Maybe. Know anyone who could help us get them to a country in South America."

Schwimmer thought for a moment. "Yes, as a matter of fact, I think I might know several. Want me to ask around?"

"That would be good. But work quickly. I think time and events are about to catch up with us."

CHAPTER 29

THE VOLUNTEERS

The following day, Schwimmer contacted Max Kohn, a friend and fellow pilot from the war who also worked for TWA. Schwimmer told him about Ben-Gurion's vision for creating an air force as part of the effort to transform Haganah into a traditional military force. "They want to create a Jewish state in Palestine," Schwimmer explained, "and I think they mean to really do it. I'm helping them. Think you'd be interested?"

"What would I be doing?" Kohn asked.

Schwimmer outlined the idea of creating an airline using surplus US bombers, flying the airplanes to South America, and ferrying them into Palestine once a Jewish war for independence began.

Kohn listened intently then sighed. "I don't know . . . " He looked at Schwimmer with a pained expression. "I'm flying as a captain. I'm in the left seat. The first Jewish captain of any American airlines. I'm not sure I'm ready to give that up."

"I know it would be a big sacrifice."

"I just don't think I can do it. My wife. The kids. They're all counting on me."

"I understand." Schwimmer gave Kohn a pat on the shoulder. "Do you know anyone who might be able to help us?"

"Well . . . If you're seriously considering locating your operation in South America, I have a friend who has contacts in that region. He might be able to help."

"Who is he?"

"Bert Miller. Do you know him?"

"No, is he . . . you know . . . one of us?"

"You mean, is he Jewish?"

"This is a sensitive thing," Schwimmer explained. "Can we trust him?"

"Yes, we can trust him."

Schwimmer was certain Kohn would keep quiet about the things he'd been told, but he was concerned about following up with a friend of a friend on a matter as clandestine as building an air force for a Jewish state in Palestine—a political state that did not yet exist. He was especially worried because Miller was not Jewish and would most likely have no understanding of the historic forces that shaped the Palestinian region. But with limited options for getting the planes out of the United States, and in light of Schind's insistence that they work quickly, he decided to talk to Miller anyway.

Using information supplied by Kohn, Schwimmer located Miller at a machine shop in Anaheim. They met during Miller's lunch break. Dressed in blue work clothes, he looked nothing like what Schwimmer had expected. "Our mutual friend, Max Kohn, suggested I talk to you."

"Oh?" Miller had a puzzled look. "What did Max think I'd want to talk about?"

"Some of us want to form an airline. Kohn thought you might be interested in participating."

"I'm not flying right now. Just working. Had to take a break from it after the war. Right now I'm back on my tools." He gestured with his hands. "Turning wrenches. But I'll be glad to talk about airplanes."

"Good, why don't we meet after work?"

"Sure, I get off around five. We could meet at the White Horse Saloon. It's just down the road," he said, pointing.

"Okay," Schwimmer nodded. "I'll see you there."

At five that afternoon, Schwimmer parked outside the White Horse Saloon, switched off the engine, and went inside. A crowd already was there, most of whom appeared to be hourly employees from the nearby aircraft companies. Schwimmer got a bottle of beer from the bartender and took a seat at a table in the corner. Not long after that, Miller entered.

"Okay," he said when he was seated at the table. "What's this all about?"

"Like I said earlier," Schwimmer began, "some of us have this idea of forming an airline that would service South America."

"Got a name for it?"

"Well," Schwimmer said sheepishly. "I was thinking we might call it Service Airline, but we haven't really discussed the name yet."

Miller grinned. "Not much of a name but the idea sounds interesting. Are you looking for pilots?"

"Yes, among other things."

"Been a while since I've flown."

"How long would it take for you to get into flying trim?"

"What kind of planes are you using?"

"We're not sure right now," Schwimmer replied. What he really wanted was someone with contacts in South America but he did his best to let the conversation unfold naturally. "We're looking at buying war surplus planes."

"Lots of people doing that. I flew B-17s in the war. Depending on the equipment you get, a review of the manual and a few check rides ought to get me back in the air. Maybe fly in the second seat for a few trips. Then I'd be in good shape."

"Great," Schwimmer said.

"Are you thinking of an airline based here in California?"

"Perhaps, but we're considering putting it somewhere in South America," Swimmer added, gently turning the conversation to the topic he wanted to discuss. "That's the region we want to target."

"How far south are you thinking about going?"

"That part's under discussion, too. Kohn mentioned you might know some people who could help with that."

Miller looked puzzled for a moment, then his eyes brightened.

"Oh," he said with a look of realization. "I'm friends with a guy who is a cousin of Enrique Jimenez, the president of Panama."

"Do you know this cousin well enough to talk to him?"

"Juan Ortiz? Yeah. He lives a couple of houses down the street from me. We went to a ball game together week before last."

"That's his name? Juan Ortiz?"

"Yeah."

Schwimmer was interested. "Would you feel comfortable approaching him about this?"

"Sure, give me a day or two and I'll see if he's willing to talk. Got a number where I can reach you?" Schwimmer scribbled his contact information on a napkin and handed it to Miller. As he did, he wondered if he'd ever hear from the guy again.

The next evening, however, Miller called to say that Ortiz could meet them the following afternoon. "I was thinking maybe we could meet at my house," Miller suggested. "Bring your family and we'll cook on the grill. Do you have kids?"

"Yes," Schwimmer answred. "Two."

"Great. Bring them and your wife and come on over."

Late in the afternoon of the following day, Schwimmer and his wife, Rena, went with their children to Miller's home. The neighbor, Juan Ortiz, was there with his family and after Miller introduced everyone, they sat around talking and eating while their children played in the backyard.

Sometime after dark, Miller looked over at Schwimmer and Ortiz and said, "Come out here to the garage for a minute. I have a car you'll like to see." He glanced over at Ortiz. "Juan's seen it before but you won't mind seeing it again."

"Not at all," Ortiz replied. "I love machines, especially ones with tires that go very fast," he laughed.

Miller led the way from the house, across the yard, to a detached garage. As they came near, he opened a side door and flipped on a light to reveal a 1931 Ford Coupe. The car had oversized tires with chrome wheels. Chrome exhausts from the engine ran along the edge of the car's running boards, but by contrast the body was painted primer gray.

"Wow!" Schwimmer exclaimed. "What a hotrod."

"It needs a paint job, but, you know, got a few other things to buy before I get to that."

"We went for a ride in it the other day," Ortiz commented. "It rides pretty good for what it is."

"Is this the car you took to the ball game?" Schwimmer asked.

"No," Miller replied. "Not this one. Too afraid it wouldn't be in the parking lot when we got back."

"Yeah," Schwimmer nodded. "I can see that."

They walked around the car, admiring it a moment, then Ortiz said to Schwimmer, "Bert said you wanted to talk to me about something."

"Yeah, a group of us are trying to start a new airline and we want to either base it in South America or at least make that region a major focus of our business plan."

"And you want me to help because Bert told you about my cousin," Ortiz said in an emotionless tone.

"Well . . . yes," Schwimmer said, suddenly feeling awkward. "If that's not a problem."

"It's no problem to listen to what you have to say. What did you have in mind?"

"We were wondering if you thought Panama would be interested in having a company like the one we're proposing to form."

"I don't know what their decision would be, but I know this. They have a magnificent airport but almost no one will fly into there. They need airline service. That's why they built the airport and I think you could probably work something out with them, but I couldn't say for certain what their official response would be."

"Well, right now all we were looking for is the name of someone to contact. We don't know who to talk to down there. Someone officially related to the government."

"The man to talk to is Vicente Varela. He is my cousin's assistant in Panama City. He will know what to do."

"Do you have any contact information for him?"

"No. But I am certain you could find it without much trouble. He is well known in Panama and I think he is listed in all the government directories."

After talking to Ortiz, Schwimmer went to work reviewing the airplanes listed for sale in government advertisements. By the time Schind returned from his fund-raising trip, Schwimmer had a list of the ones that seemed workable. "The best aircraft they have are mostly Constellations and C-46s. Large twin-engine prop planes made by Curtiss and used by the army for military transport."

"They're at Kingman?"

"No. These planes are parked at a surplus facility outside Phoenix, Arizona."

"Why not Kingman?"

"These are listed through a surplus broker."

"The army isn't selling them directly?"

"No."

Schind continued to study the list. "We're looking for bombers. Will Constellations and C-46s work for that?"

"They might," Schwimmer said. "I'm just saying, these appear to be better aircraft than the ones at Kingman and I thought we ought to take a look at them."

"Do they have anything else?"

"They have a few other kinds of planes," Schwimmer replied. "But from the information they give about them, I'd say they're in really bad shape. Most of them are listed as parts planes."

"Well," Schind said as he scanned down the list once more. "They certainly have a lot of C-46s."

"Yeah," Schwimmer nodded. "Most pilots prefer the C-47 made by Douglas. The civilian version is a DC-3. Thousands of them in service everywhere. People are familiar with them. Easy-flying airplane. But that's left a glut of 46s out there for the taking. We can get them much cheaper."

"And the Constellation?"

"Great four-engine aircraft built by Lockheed. It's a much larger plane. TWA flies these today. I'm assigned to one right now."

"Okay." Schind laid aside the sales list. "How do we get them out of the country? Make any progress on that?"

Schwimmer told Schind about his contact with Ortiz and the Panamanian opportunity. "Sounds like a brand-new airport with empty hangars. I think it would be perfect if we can reach a deal with them."

Schind was encouraged. "Have you tried to contact the person Ortiz told you about?"

"Not yet," Schwimmer replied. "I was waiting to talk to you first."

"Okay," Schind said with resolve. "We need to move forward on both—planes and Panama. Time is growing short. We need to get this operation up and running so we can move the planes to Palestine at the first opportunity."

Later that week, Schind rode with Schwimmer to Phoenix, where they looked at the airplanes. As Schwimmer suspected, many of them were in rough shape, having taken a beating during the war, but Schwimmer had a good eye for equipment and picked out three C-46s that were airworthy plus three Constellations to go with them.

Schind was satisfied with the planes—if for nothing else they could be used to ferry soldiers from one region of Palestine to another—but Ben-Gurion wanted bombers, too, and Schind didn't want to disappoint him. That evening at the hotel, he explained the situation to Schwimmer, who made a few phone calls and arranged for an opportunity to look at the planes stored at Kingman.

"They'll see us in the morning," Schwimmer reported after he'd finally arranged the visit. "But we'll have to get up early to get there on time."

The next morning, Schind and Schwimmer were on the road long before sunup and reached Kingman ahead of time. They found a small café for breakfast, then made their way to the air force base at the appointed hour.

A young lieutenant assigned to the surplus-disposal unit and an agent from a private brokerage firm gave them a tour of the surplus stockpile. Rows and rows of bombers sat in the desert just beyond the base's runway. "These things are like monuments," Schwimmer noted as they road slowly down the first row.

"When I first came out here," the lieutenant said, "I didn't like to be out here by myself. All I could think about were the men who might have died while flying in those planes."

"Or the people on the ground who died from the bombs," Schind added.

"I just think of how incredibly proud I am of the men and women who built these aircraft," the broker added. "Once they had the production lines established and running, they turned out a new plane every half hour."

"Instead of *drinking* the Germans under the table," Schwimmer chuckled, "we manufactured them under the table."

Even from the view out the window of the car, Schwimmer could see that most of the aircraft were battered beyond repair. But late that afternoon, near the back row he found a group of B-17s that were in much better shape.

"Stop the car," he said and he climbed out for a closer look.

The planes were by no means in good shape. They were in rough shape, but the fuselages on this group had only a few bullet holes. All of them still had the vertical stabilizer intact. And they all had a full complement of engines.

"What do you think?" Schind asked as they moved among them.

"They're far better than the rest," Schwimmer said. "Most of what they have here is worthless. I'm not even sure how they were able to get them in here. But these are the best of the lot."

"The bullet holes are still visible," Schind observed. "Patches on the fuselage," he added, pointing.

"Yeah," Schwimmer agreed. "But those holes are located in voids. There's nothing behind them of any importance. Bullet probably passed right through and didn't hit a thing."

Just then the broker appeared nearby. "These were selected several months ago by the Forestry Service. Thought they might be useful for flying rangers into remote areas."

Schwimmer had a doubtful look. "Smoke jumpers?"

"Yeah. Parachute out and fight forest fires."

"These planes don't have the door for that."

"That's what they found out. We got an official notice from the Service a few weeks ago releasing their hold. I think they decided to take a couple of C-46s from the ones down in Phoenix."

"Those would be perfect for them," Schwimmer opined.

"Why haven't they sold?" Schind wondered.

"No one's seen them," the broker replied. "They're parked all the way back here on the last row. No one's ever been this far back before."

Schwimmer and Schind moved down the side of one aircraft to the tail and stood alone to talk. "Can we get them out of here?" Schind asked.

Schwimmer gestured to the planes around them. "These five right here, and the two on the end of the row are in good enough shape to move—I think. We couldn't fly them very far, but we could get them up to Burbank."

"Are you sure the engines will crank?"

"No. And we wouldn't know that for sure without having a mechanic open them up and do an inspection. But I noticed fresh oil on the cowlings. None of the others have even a trace of lubricant that's not dried and crusty. These look to me like they've been operational recently."

"If we buy them now, where could we take them? We don't have the other thing ready yet."

"That's why I mentioned Burbank," Schwimmer said. "I know a place up there where we can park them."

"Okay," Schind said. "Next question. Can they can be fixed enough to make them useful?"

"Maybe. If we can get them cheap enough, they'd be worth trying."

"Got anyone to fly them?"

"We're looking at a total of thirteen airplanes. These seven and the ones we saw in Phoenix, if we get them all. I'm not sure I can find that many crews this quickly. We might not be able to get them all out of here at once. But I think we could put together four or five crews and fly them out in a couple of groups."

"Okay." Schind paused a moment and stared down at his feet. He dug the toe of his shoe in the sand as he thought, then looked up, "Let's see if we can get them."

"How many can we buy?"

"How much are we talking about?"

"Let me check the prices," Schwimmer said.

They returned to the car, found the price lists for the planes, and, with the papers lying on the hood of the automobile, began shaping an offer. Before they left Kingman to return to California, they reached an agreement to buy all thirteen planes—three Constellations, three C-46s, and seven B-17s.

CHAPTER 30

THE VOLUNTEERS

After leaving New York, the *Norsyd,* flying the Panamanian flag and traveling under the name of *Balboa,* made for Marseilles, on the southern coast of France. The *Beauharnois,* with Captain Lopez in command, sailed under the Panamanian-registered name of *Colon* and made for Italy.

As the ships steamed eastward, Hugh Clark, on board the *Beauharnois,* divided his time between boiler room and engine room, doing his best to oversee Liebman, Ritzer, and the novice crewmen assigned to help. Somewhere off the Azores, the *Beauharnois* boilers stopped producing steam. Liebman, who was in the boiler room, called for Clark.

With one look at the gauges, Clark shouted, "Kill the fire!" When no one moved, he shouted again, "Kill the fire, now!"

Liebman, who was standing nearby, turned a valve to reduce the flow of fuel oil, and the flame inside the boiler dropped. "I thought you said we weren't supposed to do that."

"You're not supposed to let it boil dry, either," Clark retorted.

"Why do you think it's dry?"

Clark jerked open a door to the firebox to let the heat escape, then pointed to a gauge. "The pressure's low on the intake side and zero on the steam line."

"Oh," Liebman replied. "I wondered what was wrong."

"Did you check the gauges?"

"Yes."

"Did you notice the difference?"

"Yes."

"Then why didn't you do something about it?"

"I didn't know what to do."

"Then why didn't you come ask me?"

"Because I didn't want to get yelled at."

"You're a novice seaman!" Clark shouted. "You're supposed to get yelled at."

"Well, what's wrong with the boilers?" someone asked.

"They've salted up."

"All of them?"

"Yes," Clark snapped. "All of them."

"How do you know?" Liebman asked.

Clark turned to the evaporator. "The pressure's too high on the seawater side," he pointed to a gauge. "And way to low on the boiler side." He tapped a second gauge with his index finger just to make sure.

"How'd that happen?"

"How do you think it happened?" Clark roared. "Didn't you clean the evaporator core?"

"Not yet."

"Why not?"

"We didn't know it was time to clean it."

"Do you know that now?"

"Yes," Liebman said meekly. "I think we know that very well."

"Don't know," Clark grumbled. "Check the evaporator output."

One of the crewmen turned to Liebman, "What's he talking about?"

Liebman turned to him. "You remember me explaining the evaporator to you?"

"Yeah, sort of. It takes in seawater, turns the water to steam, salt collects in the bottom."

"And on the evaporator coil," Liebman added. "We're supposed to clean it out of the bottom and off the core."

"We cleaned the bottom."

“Right,” Liebman nodded. “But not the core.”

“Why not the core?”

“It’s a tricky procedure, cleaning it while we’re under way.”

“That’s what you’re here for,” Clark interrupted. “I told you to keep the coil clean.”

“We did the best we could,” Liebman said, finally defending himself and the crew. “We did the best we could.”

“Well, your best has us adrift in the middle of the ocean at a dead stop.”

“So,” Liebman sighed. “What do we do?”

“We do better,” Clark answered. “If we can get the evaporator working and clean out one of the boilers, we can get under way while we clean the others.” He knelt near the evaporator access door. “Hand me a wrench. Let’s see what it looks like in here.”

A few minutes later, Captain Lopez appeared in the boiler room. “What appears to be the problem, gentlemen?”

“Salted up,” Clark replied.

“Evaporator trouble?”

“Yes, sir. Same problem they had bringing it down from Canada.”

“What’s the permanent fix?”

“It needs a new core.”

“I’ll call someone and see what we can do about that.”

“How far off course have we drifted?”

“Not too far, but don’t worry about that. Just get us back under way as quickly as possible.”

“Yes, sir.”

“Any idea when that will be?”

“We should have one boiler working in an hour or two.”

“Very well,” Lopez replied, then returned to the walkway and started back to the top.

After a few hours drifting on the ocean current, one of the boilers came back online with enough steam to put the *Beauharnois* once again under way. By then the ship had drifted south of its original course. Captain Lopez turned to his navigator. "Show me our current position."

The navigator stepped to the map table and indicated a spot on the chart. "We are here. Northeast of Bermuda and about fifteen hundred kilometers west of Flores Island."

"The Azores."

"Yes, sir."

"Let's make for the largest of them," Lopez directed. "São Miguel. We can obtain repairs for the boiler there. I know someone who will do a very good job on them. Perhaps he will fix the problem once and for all."

Using a single boiler, the ship limped westward for an hour with just enough power to maintain its course. Then a second boiler came up and the ship's speed increased dramatically, and sometime in the night the ship approached a cruising speed of twelve knots.

An hour after sunrise the next morning, one of the crewmen reported a ship sailing off the port bow. Captain Lopez stepped outside the wheelhouse with binoculars to have a look. "British," he said.

Someone standing nearby asked, "How can you tell?"

"It's far enough away I can see the ship's profile against the morning sky. It looks like a destroyer."

"Think they see us?"

"Probably."

"Will they stop us out here?"

"No one can say for certain," Lopez replied, still watching through the glasses.

"Aren't we in international waters?"

"Yes." Lopez moved the binoculars from his eyes. "But the British patrol everywhere."

The British ship drew within five miles of the *Beauharnois*, then trailed the corvette at a distance, always in sight, never close enough to be considered hostile. When they drew near the Azores coastline, the British ship faded even farther into the distance, all but disappearing from sight.

At Ponta Delgada, the primary port in the Azores, the *Beauharnois* tied up at Capella's Shipyard on the landward side of the inner harbor. A few hours later, a British ship entered the harbor and made its way to a nearby berth. Lopez watched as it moved past and read the name on the bow. "The *Wessex*. I have encountered that ship before."

Not long after that, the captain of the *Wessex* appeared on the *Beauharnois* gangway. "Mind if I come aboard?"

Lopez, standing near the rail, replied with a smile, "How may I be of service to you?"

"This is a Canadian corvette," the captain observed, still at the top of the gangway.

"And a very fine ship at that," Lopez smiled.

"Out for a pleasure trip?"

"We are sailing in the service of UN relief."

"Yes, I see," the captain replied skeptically. "Mind if I have a look around?"

"I am sorry, sir. But, yes. I'm afraid I must ask you to step ashore."

The captain stared at Lopez a moment, then tipped his hat and said, "Very well."

As the captain moved down the gangway, Clark appeared on deck. "What was that all about?"

"I'm not sure," Lopez replied.

"We should get those repairmen down here quickly."

Lopez sighed, "Yes, we should not stay here long."

From the Azores, the *Beauharnois* sailed without further incident to Savona, Italy, where the ship received final modifications—the installation of bunks, toilets, and expanded cooking facilities. As those changes neared completion, Ezer Navon, a young, eager Haganah officer, arrived to travel with the crew for the remainder of the trip. He was accompanied by five men, all of them trained Haganah operatives. Shortly after coming aboard, they gathered the crew in the wardroom.

"Final changes to the ship have been made," Navon said, "and we are bringing aboard provisions for the remainder of the trip. From here we pick up the passengers, then sail to Palestine. My men and I will accompany you for the remainder of your journey to help with . . . operational details."

Someone in the back of the room asked, "Where will we get the passengers?"

"You'll see."

"No doubt we will, but it would be nice to know ahead of time where we're going."

"I can't tell you that," Navon replied. "But it's not far."

Liebman spoke up. "Are you refusing to tell us because you think we would talk?"

"I think the lives of the passengers and of your fellow crewmen require us to act with an abundance of caution," Navon explained. "Now, when we reach the Palestinian coast, we will be met by the British Navy. They will attempt to stop us and, in all likelihood, they will be successful. Naval personnel will board the ship, take control of it, and seize all who are on board. When they board, you will hide."

"The passengers, too?" someone asked.

"No, not the passengers. Just the crew."

"Why not the passengers?"

"There will be too many of them to hide," Navon explained patiently.

"What will happen to them?"

"They'll be taken into custody. I think Danny Schind explained this to you back in New York."

"I talked to Buxenbaum."

"In any regard," Navon said, "we won't be able to do much about the passengers. At least, not at first. They will be taken into custody by the British and transferred to detention camps."

"More camps," someone groused.

"Yes, but hopefully not as miserable as the ones in Europe." Others started to speak, but Navon held up his hand for silence. "Please, gentlemen. Let me continue. We have an important task to accomplish today." He waited for noise in the room to subside. "When we're done in here, one of my men will come to each of your work areas and show you where to hide so the British won't find you. Then we will practice getting into those assigned hiding spaces so you can do it as quickly and quietly as possible. When the British board, you will stop whatever you're doing and disappear."

Someone asked, "How will we know they've boarded us?"

"For those of you working above the main deck, the boarding will be obvious. We will do our best to pass the word below."

"The ship has an intercom system."

"And we will make use of it, if possible," Navon said. "But that might not always be the best way of communicating."

"How long should we stay in place?"

"You will remain in hiding until the ship reaches port, probably at Haifa, which will take several hours."

"Then what?"

"We will get you out."

"How?"

"Don't worry about how right now. Someone will come for you. You'll know it when it happens."

There were a few more questions, then the meeting ended and for the remainder of the day, Navon and his men worked below deck showing crew members where to hide and how to reach their assigned locations by the quickest, most efficient route.

After everyone had been shown where to go and how to get there, they conducted ship-wide drills, which Navon timed with a stopwatch. When the times proved too long and crew movements too loud, they repeated the drill and continued to train throughout the afternoon in an effort to trim every possible second from the crew's response time.

CHAPTER 31

THE VOLUNTEERS

A few nights later, the *Beauharnois* slipped from its mooring and sailed quietly down the Italian coast to a wide but shallow cove. They entered it and glided gently toward a stretch of smooth sandy beach. Navon, standing in the wheelhouse with Lopez, instructed, "Get as close as possible."

"I don't like this," Lopez said.

"We have to get close," Navon replied. "We'll be bringing the passengers out in small boats and we need the trips to be as short and quick as possible."

Lopez jerked his head in Navon's location. "They are here?"

"Waiting on the beach."

"I thought we were going to a dock."

"Change in plans," Navon said with thin, tight smile. "We're ferrying them out by boat."

"This is asking for trouble."

"I know, but it wasn't my choice. Just bring us in close. We'll make the best of it."

Lopez called down to Clark to back off the engines to an idle. With the ship barely moving, and a light touch on the wheel, he guided the vessel deeper and deeper into the cove until finally the hull scrubbed the sandy bottom of the shallow bay. As he felt the ship hit ground, he signaled the engine room for a burst of speed in reverse, then dropped the anchors bow and stern to hold it in place. "That's as far as she can come and still get under way without a tow."

"We need to be closer," Navon said.

"Can't do it," Lopez replied. "This is it. This is as close as we get."

"I represent the owners of this ship," Navon argued. "I'll make that determination."

"And I am the commander of it. If we move any closer, I'm going ashore and not returning."

Forced to back down, Navon stepped from the wheelhouse, made his way to the main deck, and instructed the crewmen to lower the ship's launch. As Navon left, Lopez called down to Clark with instructions to keep the boilers fired and the ship ready to get under way at a moment's notice.

From the wheelhouse, Lopez watched as headlights appeared on the beach. For an instant, he caught the outline of a truck in the glare, then the lights went out. He left the helm and stood at the railing, hoping for a better view. Instead, he saw only the darkness of the tree line, but he heard voices echoing across the water. A moment later, the sound of an outboard motor growled in the distance, then the silvery streaks of a wake appeared on the surface, and not long after that, he saw the boat clearly as it neared the ship.

Lopez called down to the crew on the main deck and ordered the stairway lowered, then made his way to it. As the first refugees arrived at the top of the steps, he greeted them aboard, now as passengers, and urged them to hurry. "Board quickly," he ordered as they shuffled past. "Get below at once. Someone will show you to your places. Hurry. We must be prepared to sail at any moment."

On the lower decks, crewmen met the newly arrived passengers and guided them to sleeping platforms that now filled what once was the ship's cargo hold. Narrow and tightly confined, these would serve as their beds and living quarters for the duration of the trip. Already it was warm and the air was stale, but they were on their way to Palestine on the final leg of their journey. Most were upbeat. Some were altogether giddy.

Boats were arriving from shore in an almost constant stream now and before long the sleeping platforms were filled beyond capacity, yet still the refugees kept coming. To accommodate them, Lopez ordered them to sit on the main deck behind the wheelhouse. At least they would be out of the wind in the lee of the ship's superstructure. But still they kept coming and before long the deck was filled with people.

In the midst of that, a crewman came to Lopez's side and directed his attention to the seaward side of the ship. "One of the men thinks he saw something." Lopez turned to look past the wheelhouse and as he scanned in the distance where the horizon should have been, he saw the faint outline of a ship's silhouette, barely visible in the nighttime glow. "Another destroyer," he grumbled, but there was little he could do other than continue to hurry the others along. Which he did.

As the deck neared capacity, Lopez began to worry where he would put additional people but just when it seemed they could hold no more, the steady stream of boats and refugees came to an end. Onshore, headlights once more appeared and the sound of automobile engines drifted across the water. Lopez grabbed his binoculars and trained them on the lights, trying to see as best he could, but the competing of glare from multiple vehicles served only to further obscure his view. Finally he gave up and focused with naked eyes, preferring to listen and imagine rather than strain to decipher the images the lenses could give. From the shoreline, he heard the sound of voices once more, but this time they were angry and punctuated with shouts and bursts of emotion.

Half an hour later, headlights again appeared onshore, bobbing and weaving as the vehicles that arrived earlier now made their way from the beach and disappeared among the trees and shadows. In a few minutes, the sound of a boat reached the ship and not long after that it appeared near the steps. Lopez waited at the rail as a few haggard passengers clambered up to the main deck, then Navon appeared behind them. Lopez was relieved to see him but before he could say a word, Navon ordered, "Captain, get us off this sandbar at once."

Lopez turned toward the wheelhouse. "There's a ship lying just off the entrance to the cove," he said over his shoulder.

"Yes," Navon replied. "A British destroyer. Can you outflank it?"

"I doubt it."

"Well, do your best. We must leave at once."

Lopez entered the wheelhouse and called down to Clark, "Cut in steam for the anchor engine." Without waiting for a response, he turned to an aide and said, "Have them raise the anchors and do it quietly. No shouting. We need to get out of here with as little attention as possible."

When the anchors were aboard, he called down to the engine room again, "All back one-third, Mr. Clark."

Moments later, there was a rumble from below, then a shudder ran through the ship as it slid backward off the sand, reached deeper water, and slowly drew away from the beach. When they'd cleared the bottom sufficiently, Lopez called to the engine room, "Ahead, dead slow, Mr. Clark. Dead slow."

There was a momentary lull, the ship sitting still and steady in the water, then again the shuddering and shaking returned as the engines switched from reverse to forward and the propellers set to work sending the ship in the opposite direction, this time at an all but imperceptible momentum.

Lopez manned the helm himself and spun the wheel hard to the right. The ship's bow came around in a long, lumbering arc, the shoreline emerging through the window to the right, moving slowly past the window in front, then fading from view to the left. A constant stream of dark water, shadowy tree line, and faintly gray sky. He waited patiently for the moment when the starlit sky finally met the black sea, then waited a moment longer before bringing the wheel back to the left just the correct number of spins, then holding it steady. The ship settled into place, squarely aligned between the two points that formed the mouth of the cove, the bow pointed straight toward the open water.

Lopez called down to the engine room, "All ahead one third."

A bell sounded, acknowledging the order and shortly after that, the ship picked up speed. Ahead lay the inky black sea and the prospect of smooth sailing, but to the right were the lights of the British destroyer as it loitered just off the coast, less than five kilometers away. Lopez was certain a confrontation loomed, but minutes ticked by and the destroyer maintained its position. Before long, it faded in the distance and then there was only the open water of the Adriatic Sea and beyond that, the Mediterranean Sea.

When they were well clear of the cove, the ship reached cruising speed and Lopez turned to Navon. "What was that disturbance on the beach?"

"A local detachment of British and Italian authorities," Navon replied.

"Oh my. What did they want?"

"They were trying to keep us from leaving."

Lopez looked concerned. "They knew what we were doing?"

"Not exactly. They knew we had refugees who were Jewish, but they weren't able to prove they were from the displaced persons camps."

"I can't imagine the Italians cared about that."

"They didn't, but the British did," Navon chuckled. "They knew we were up to something, but they couldn't say exactly what."

"Sounds confusing."

"We did our best to keep it that way." Navon was still chuckling over the whole thing.

"How did it end?"

"I'm not sure. It was still going on when I left. But an American reporter was traveling with the refugees and when the British arrived with the Italians, he spoke up and suggested the Americans might have some interest in how we were treated."

"Did that help?"

"He sort of implied he was connected to the embassy or one of the officials and the Italians seemed unwilling to totally discount him."

"Good for him."

"They all seemed to think one of my men was in charge, so I let them. The American convinced them all to go with him back to the police station while he phoned the American Embassy to ask for direction about what they should do. My guy went with them and I took the liberty of leaving with the last of the passengers."

Lopez's eyes opened wide in a startled expression. "They let the passengers leave the beach?"

"The passengers were cold and scared and we insisted they couldn't just leave them on the beach while everyone else went off to warm offices for coffee or cocoa. The American piped up again and suggested they should board the ship with the others to await a decision. The Italians liked that idea and said they certainly didn't have the means to transport the refugees. Which meant they'd most likely have to go by ship anyway, and the British seemed interested in that idea—I think because it would give them an excuse to seize the ship."

Lopez grinned. "They were playing themselves and getting played all the way around."

"Yes," Navon laughed. "And all of it happening at the same time."

"Can't you see their faces when they realize what happened?"

"Only thing I can't figure is why that destroyer didn't try to stop us."

"Having heard all that happened, I'd say the ship's captain thought that since everyone else departed from the beach, either the men onshore had charge of the passengers, or they had reached some agreement for you to leave with them."

"Yes," Navon nodded. "Perhaps that's it."

Lopez's expression turned serious. "The British will be quite angry over our leaving, you know."

"You wanted to stay?"

"No," Lopez grinned. "After the boats stopped coming, when it seemed you were taking too long, I'd made up my mind to depart without you anyway."

Navon looked startled. "And where would you have gone?"

"To Palestine, of course," Lopez eyes twinkled. "I have a cargo to deliver. That's what I was hired to do."

Three days later, the Palestinian coastline—a thin brown strip rising above the mist and haze of the sea—appeared on the horizon. At the sight of it, passengers on deck stood and cheered. Those down below rushed topside for a glimpse and squirmed their way through the crowd to the railing. Many wept openly. Others sang. Some even danced, though space was tight and movement difficult.

Before long, as predicted, a British destroyer arrived off the *Beauharnois* port side. As the destroyer moved closer, Captain Lopez called down to the engine room, "Give me more power, Mr. Clark."

"We're running at ninety percent now," Clark responded. "Not sure the boilers can take much more."

"How hot are they?"

"Hot," Clark replied.

"Give me a hundred ten percent."

"Not sure she has it in her."

Lopez repeated, "A hundred ten percent, Mr. Clark."

Clark left his post by the engine and came around to the boiler room. Liebman was there and Clark shouted to him over the clatter of machinery, "Pinch down the check valve on both boilers."

"You told us not to touch it," Liebman replied.

"Well, I'm telling you different now," Clark snarled. "Pinch 'em down."

"How much is a pinch?"

"A quarter turn on each."

Liebman adjusted the check valves warily, and a pipe overhead near the hatchway began to hiss. Clark bumped it with his fist and the hissing stopped, then he turned to Liebman. "Make sure you don't run her dry."

Back in the engine room, Clark watched as the gauges showed the steam pressure rising. He leaned around from the far side of the engine and shouted over to Ritzer, who stood near the controls, "Move the lever past the stop."

"It won't move past the stop," Ritzer protested. "That's what the stop's for."

Clark reached overhead to a toolbox that lay atop a rack of steam pipes, snatched out a large screwdriver, and tossed it to Ritzer. "Loosen the locking screw."

Ritzer caught the screwdriver with one hand and gave him a bewildered look. "What are you talking about?"

Clark, frustrated, pointed to a large screw that held the control lever in place. "That," he snapped, jabbing the air with his index finger. "Loosen it half a turn and move the lever out so it'll slide past the stop." Clark glanced back to check the gauges, but when Ritzer still didn't move, he hollered again, "Hurry up. The pressure's getting too high."

Using both hands to grip the screwdriver, Ritzer loosened the screw and wiggled the handle farther out on the spindle. "How far do I open it?"

"Far as it'll go," Clark replied.

Ritzer pushed the handle to the left and it moved about half an inch beyond the stop. Almost at once, the engine picked up speed and the ship surged forward. Ritzer looked over at Clark with a grin. "We did that?"

"Yeah." Clark checked the gauges again, then rang the wheelhouse. "That's a hundred twelve percent," he shouted.

"Is that flat out?" Lopez asked.

"That's all she's got. Stops out. Valves are pinched. Lever's all the way down."

"Good," Lopez replied. "Keep it there. Steady as she goes."

Using all the speed the *Beauharnois* engines could produce, Lopez brought the ship around in an evasive maneuver, slicing in front of the destroyer, narrowly missing its bow and forcing it to slow to avoid a collision. With the destroyer almost dead in the water, Lopez brought the wheel back and set a course for the coastline.

Navon stepped outside the wheelhouse to check aft and returned with a grin. "Nice move. That bought us some time. They're having trouble getting under way."

"It won't help much, though," Lopez said.

"Why not?"

Lopez pointed to the right where a second destroyer was closing fast. Navon checked it through the binoculars. "That's the *Venus*. Sharp-looking ship."

"We'll never lose her," Lopez replied. "I've seen her in action. She's faster than any of the other ships we've seen on this trip."

Navon had a curious expression. "How do you know so much about the British Navy?"

"I've been sailing a long time and not all of it in a way that was friendly to the British Empire."

"Good," Navon chortled as he gave Lopez a pat on the back. "You're just the man we need. Hold your course a little longer and let's see how close we can get."

Lopez did his best, but before long the *Venus*, with its superior speed, overtook the *Beauharnois*, approaching it from astern, and drew alongside her—too close for another evasive maneuver and too fast to outrun. Lopez glanced over at Navon. "I think they mean to board us."

"I'm sure they do." Navon stared ahead, his eyes focused on the approaching coastline.

When several moments passed, Lopez said, "I don't think the crew can defend against them. If we force them to attack we'll only put the passengers in greater danger. We've come this far without serious trouble. No point in ending our voyage with a tragedy."

Navon stood silently staring out the window, then without a word stepped out to the railing and shouted down to someone on the deck below. He spoke in Hebrew, and Lopez couldn't understand what he said, but a moment later Navon returned to the doorway and said, "I've sent someone to the engine room with instructions. Do your best to keep us from colliding with the destroyer."

"I could call Mr. Clark from here," Lopez said, his face wrinkled in a troubled frown. "No need to go down there."

"It's time for the crewmen to get to their places. You remain here to man the wheel and control the ship as best you can. Our people will get you off when we reach Haifa. They will know what to do. Just do what they tell you." Then Navon gave Lopez a quick salute and disappeared from sight.

Down below, Yossi Magen, one the men who boarded the *Beauharnois* with Navon, appeared in the engine room and came to Clark's side. "Stop the engines. We're being boarded."

Having never seen him before, Clark scowled back, "Stop? I don't think so."

"Stop the engines," Magen repeated, this time in a forceful tone. "That is an order."

"I take my orders from Captain Lopez. And I haven't heard from him about this." Clark reached for the intercom to call the wheelhouse, but Magen grabbed his hand. "No," he said sharply. "This is an order. Haganah owns this ship. We are in command. Stop the engines."

Reluctantly, Clark turned to Ritzer. "Back the engine off."

"Back it off?"

"Move the control lever back," Clark shouted as he stepped to the opposite side of the engine. "And tighten that screw."

As Ritzer repositioned the lever in front of the stop, the engine slowed. The ship did, too, and once more Clark shouted through the pipe way to Liebman in the boiler room. "Reduce your power."

"You mean back off the check valve?"

"Open it all the way," Clark yelled.

"All the way?"

"Yes!" Clark shouted. "All the way."

"You said never to—"

"Well, I'm telling you something different now," Clark said angrily. "Open it all the way." As the sound of hissing steam filled the air, Clark glared over at Magen. "You better be right about this."

"I am," Magen smiled as he turned toward the hatchway. "Get to your hiding places."

A few minutes later, the *Venus* and the *Beauharnois* lay side by side, both ships dead in the water. Armed marines from the *Venus* arrived by launch and boarded. Passengers of the *Beauharnois* stood aside to make way for them, and as the soldiers took charge, someone began to sing. Before long, all the passengers joined and the sound drifted across the water.

One group of marines made their way quickly to the wheelhouse while a second group entered the superstructure and hurried downstairs toward the engine room. When the wheelhouse was secure, a British officer, standing tall, erect, and composed, entered the room. "Captain Lopez," he said with a smile. "A little off course from your usual banana deliveries, aren't you?"

"Well," Lopez shrugged. "We do the best we can."

"I am certain that a captain of your experience can find a way to steer this ship toward Haifa. Do so immediately, please, sir."

"Very well."

The navigator gave him the heading, and Lopez set the wheel in that direction, then called down to the engine room, "All ahead one-third, Mr. Clark." When there was no response, he repeated the order. A moment later, someone with a British accent replied, "There's no one down here, sir."

The British officer turned to an aide. "Call over to the *Venus* and tell them to send men for the engine room."

CHAPTER 32

THE VOLUNTEERS

In an hour or two, the *Beauharnois* once again was under way. Down below, Clark and Ritzer were crammed into their hiding place, a void behind the second engine. Squeezed between the engine, the ship's hull, and a clutter of steam pipes, the space was cramped and unbelievably hot. Before long, both men were soaked with sweat.

After what seemed like an eternity, the sound of the engines changed. Ritzer, who'd been standing with his back propped against the hull, glanced around and asked, "What was that?"

"We've slowed," Clark whispered.

"Where do you think we are?"

"Closer to the coast," Clark shrugged. "Maybe."

Ritzer grinned. "We made it?"

"Sort of."

"What do you mean?"

"I mean we still have to get off the ship and avoid being caught while doing it."

In a few minutes, a shudder ran through the ship as it bumped to a stop. Moments later, the engines whined as they slowed, then sat motionless, steam hissing from the valves and vents. Clark whispered to Ritzer, "We've docked. Can we get—"

Clark put his finger to his lips in a gesture for silence. "They're right there," he mouthed, pointing to the right. Ritzer's eyes opened wide when he looked in that direction and saw a British seaman standing just a few feet away.

In a little while, the British crewmen who'd been manning the engine room disappeared. Clark and Ritzer remained in their hiding place and waited, afraid to emerge too soon lest they be caught. The sound of footsteps, once constant from the lower decks, moved higher in the ship as the lower levels were vacated, until the only sounds they heard were that of footsteps coming from the main deck.

The noise from up above continued long enough that Clark grew drowsy from exhaustion, lost track of time, and slowly faded into a dreamless sleep. Sometime later, he opened his eyes to find he was seated on the floor, slumped against the back of the engine. Ritzer was beside him, fast asleep.

Clark felt the steel of the engine with the palm of his hand and found it barely warm. *Couple of hours have passed,* he thought. *It'll be dark outside before long.* Around him, the ship was silent—even the sounds from the main deck were gone—and after a moment he nudged Ritzer. "No one's on board."

"Can we get out?"

"Not yet, must wait a minute. They're supposed to come for us and nobody's down here yet."

"What if they came and we didn't hear them?"

"Waiting a little longer won't hurt."

"It's hurting now," Ritzer complained. "I have a cramp in my leg."

"Stand up," Clark said. "And stretch it out."

Ritzer pushed himself up from the floor to a standing position, and Clark did, too. They stood there, side by side, listening and waiting while Ritzer did his best to limber up his leg muscles.

Twenty minutes later, the sound of voices returned, along with the rumble of footsteps in the lower reaches of the ship. But this time the sound was different. "No boots," Clark explained. "The marines that boarded wore boots. Whoever's up there now isn't wearing boots."

After a while, the voices grew louder and more distinct and Clark could hear someone speaking Hebrew. He looked over at Ritzer. "Can you understand what they're saying?"

Ritzer listened a moment longer, then nodded. "He's saying, 'Anyone in here? Anyone in here?'" He squirmed past Clark, but Clark grabbed him by the arm. "What are you doing?"

"They've come for us. Haganah. They said they'd come for us. They're here."

"How do you know it's them?"

Ritzer jerked free of Clark's grasp and stepped out from behind the engine. "I'm taking that chance." Clark, sensing that with Ritzer exposed, whoever was out there would find him, too, decided to climb out of hiding also. As he staggered past the engine, he saw a man dressed in coveralls. He appeared to be a dock worker but he was dragging a large metal garbage can, which he held by the handle. Two mops and a broom stood in the can, and the man smiled over at them. "Shhh," he motioned for quiet. Then in a whisper, "Change your clothes. You look awful." He reached inside the garbage can and brought out a sack with a pair of cotton dungarees and a shirt. "Put these on," he said, tossing the clothes to Ritzer. "You, too," he said to Clark, then took more clothes from the can and handed them to him. "Quickly," the man insisted. "They're patrolling the halls."

"Who?" Clark asked.

"British MPs. They think we're up to something but they can't figure out what. Make sure you don't tip us off."

When Clark and Ritzer were changed, the man with the garbage can handed them a broom and mop. "Use these," he said. "Help us clean." He lifted the garbage can through the hatchway and waited for them to catch up, then started up the hall. "Stay close and follow my lead."

A few hours later, Clark, Ritzer, and the cleaning crew reached the main deck. As they came out into the fading afternoon sunlight, Clark glanced toward shore and saw the dusty earth-tone buildings of Haifa, a small Middle Eastern city sprawled across a tropical landscape that appeared flat, dry, and yet mysteriously beautiful.

A smile spread over his face. He was seeing Palestine for the first time and he turned his head slowly from left to right, allowing his mind to capture every image. The low buildings, the dirty unpaved streets, the palm trees rustling in the afternoon breeze. But before he could take it all in, someone nudged him in the ribs and said in a coarse whisper, "Act like you live here."

Just then a British officer appeared and moved slowly past, checking the garbage cans, glancing at the men. Clark avoided eye contact and thought of home, his wife, the smell of dinner cooking in the kitchen. He thought of how long it had been since he kissed her and how he never told her often enough that he loved her.

As the officer moved past Clark's position, Clark stole a glance across the deck once again for a glimpse of the streets and buildings of Haifa. All the way over on the ship he'd wondered what Palestine looked like but only had pictures from magazines as a reference. The pictures he'd seen did little to convey the reality of what he saw that afternoon. The contrast. The beauty. The challenge of an environment he now knew could only be understood by experiencing it. And for the first time he wondered what it would be like to live there, permanently.

When the MPs supervising the cleanup detail were satisfied with the day's work, they allowed the men to disembark. Clark fell in line with the others as they walked single file down the gangway to the pier and out to the paved loading zone beyond.

Onshore, the workers made their way to a warehouse on the far side of the facility, where they deposited their cleaning equipment. Clark did his best to appear like one of the crew. No one talked. Everyone worked with their heads down, their eyes focused on the tasks at hand. As he washed the mops he and Ritzer had been using, he caught sight of Liebman rinsing the cleaning buckets. Clark wanted to ask about where he hid and whether all the men in the boiler room got off safely, but having been warned once about his demeanor, he kept quiet and instead simply acknowledged Liebman with a nod.

As darkness descended, Clark and Ritzer found Liebman outside the warehouse. The three men sat together in the shade and waited for

Haganah's next step in getting them out of Haifa. "I just want to go to a kibbutz," Liebman said. "I'm not going back to New York."

"I'm not going back, either," Ritzer said, then he looked over at Clark. "What about you? Still set on returning to Long Island?"

"For now. I have a wife and children back there."

"Well, I don't," Liebman said. "And I'm making this my home. Free, not free, always fighting the Arabs, whatever it turns out to be. This is it."

Before the conversation went much further, a young man arrived with a car and collected them. With little or no conversation, he drove them to an apartment a few blocks away and directed them to the bathroom. "You can shower here, and I'll find something for you to wear."

When they were clean and changed, they rode together to the Jewish Agency's office located up the coast a short distance from the apartment. It was dark by then, the sun having set almost an hour earlier, but the lights were on inside the building and the staff seemed to know they were coming. Liebman and Ritzer could think of nothing but finally reaching a kibbutz. Clark hoped for an early flight home.

CHAPTER 33

THE VOLUNTEERS

As Schind had hoped, the MI6 surveillance team lost track of him as he departed La Guardia airport in New York for the trip to California, but they didn't lose him for long. A check of flight schedules told them he was bound for one of two places—Chicago, the intermediate stop on his flight, or Los Angeles, the flight's ultimate destination.

Agents in Chicago deployed to the terminal before his flight arrived for its intermediate stop and spotted him when he de-planed and changed flights. When that flight landed in San Diego, a team working the West Coast located him at the airport and followed him to the evening's fund-raiser, but that was as far as they got. Somewhere between San Diego and Los Angeles, they lost him and he was out of sight until he appeared again in New York at Ginsberg's office a few weeks later. By then, Robinson and all of MI6 knew the *Beauharnois* and *Norsyd* had sailed to Europe, picked up refugees, then continued to Palestine, where the ships were seized and the passengers taken into custody.

Through their surveillance in the United States, MI6 also learned that while Schind was in California, Ginsberg and Stone had acquired another ship. This one a bay cruiser named the *President Warfield*—which was docked at Baltimore where it was undergoing extensive repairs and refitting, presumably for another attempt at rescuing refugees from Europe.

Even more troubling, however, was news from an informant in

Arizona that Schind and Al Schwimmer had purchased surplus airplanes from the US government. Documents submitted with the transaction indicated they planned to use those aircraft as the nucleus of a new airline—which they dubbed Service Airlines. But with more than half the purchased craft consisting of bombers, no one gave the airline story much credence.

Robinson was convinced the aircraft were destined for Palestine, where they would be used by Haganah. That conclusion was reinforced when he learned that Schind, upon his return from California, met with Palmer Collins. Robinson's suspicions were confirmed by a subsequent search of public records that indicated the airline indeed had been formed as a New York corporation with documents prepared by Collins.

Faced with continuing activity by Schind, the Jewish Agency, Haganah, and influential American Jewish leaders—all of which stood in direct opposition to British policy in Palestine—and with little to show for their effort thus far, Robinson decided that more direct action was warranted against the participants—action without regard to legal boundaries or diplomatic niceties. For help with that, he phoned Geoffrey Reid and arranged to meet with him at an apartment in Philadelphia, a location midway between New York and Washington.

"As you are aware," Robinson began, "Schind has been on the West Coast, working with a guy named Al Schwimmer."

"I had the office work up a dossier on Schwimmer. He wasn't really on our radar before this. We knew about him, just hadn't kept track of him. Served honorably in the war. Seemed like a good fellow before all this."

"Well," Robinson snarled. "He's not looking so good to us now. Not after buying those airplanes with Schind."

"Yes," Reid sighed. "And bought them from the American government. Believe me," he said in an exasperated tone, "we've explained our situation to the Americans on numerous occasions, but it never seems to sink in just how critical their cooperation is to the success of our effort to enforce the mandate."

"American support or not," Robinson added, "I don't think we can let this pass unnoticed."

"Oh, it's been noticed." Reid arched an eyebrow. "Believe me. We've noticed."

"Yes, but no one ever does anything about it. We talk, and observe, and report. London reads, and files, and collates. But no one ever acts."

"Well," Reid countered, "we've done something about it. We haven't merely ignored it."

"We've harassed them," Robinson argued. "That's all. We got Collins fired and we cost his employer a client, but what did that get us? Collins is now working from an office provided by Ginsberg, and from what I hear he's doing quite well. And Schind has bought another ship and expanded into airplanes."

"What are you suggesting we do?"

"I'm suggesting we step up to the next level."

"You sound like a character in a movie," Reid grinned. "What does that mean—step up to the next level?"

"From what we know so far," Robinson explained, "Schind is the key figure in the entire operation. Everyone reports to him; almost no one reports to anyone else."

"Yes," Reid agreed. "There is very little redundancy in their system."

"Which means they are vulnerable at that one point."

"Schind."

"Yes," Robinson nodded. "Stop Schind—take him out—and the whole thing collapses."

Reid had a stony expression. "You want to kill him?"

Robinson glanced away. "Doesn't have to be that extreme. Just enough to take him out of operation." He paused a moment and turned back to Reid with a smirk. "But if it *is* that extreme, it's fine with me."

"You have people working for you who have done this sort of thing many times in the past."

"Yes," Robinson agreed. "We have several men with this sort of . . . experience."

"But understand something," Reid cautioned. "If you did this, you would be totally on your own."

"I understand," Robinson nodded.

"I'm not authorizing an operation of this nature," Reid reiterated.

"I know," Robinson nodded again.

"If you or any of your men are caught, you—and they—will be totally and completely on your own."

Robinson, barely able to contain his excitement, clasped his hands behind his back and squared his shoulders. "I understand completely. Completely and totally."

It was late when Robinson returned to New York but in spite of the hour, he met with Ian Dukes, one of his original operatives, and apprised him of the situation regarding Schind's role, first with the ships and now the airplanes. "London is unwilling to address the matter from the highest levels of government, leaving it to us to effect a solution."

Dukes, a former British Commando, seemed to know where the conversation was headed. "That's the way it always works. Top brass get the awards, we get all the work."

"This time the task has fallen to our operation and I am assigning it to you."

"Certainly. What would you like?"

"We must address the Schind issue and do it . . . in the extreme." Robinson glanced over at him. "You understand what I mean?"

"Yes, I've been in this position before."

"This must be done in a manner that does not cause a public outcry."

"Right. Something that appears to be of natural causes, perhaps."

"That would be best. And it must be handled in a way that brings absolutely no discredit upon His Majesty's government." Robinson looked him in the eye. "You and you alone must bear full and complete responsibility for it."

"Yes, I understand."

"You'll have to do this without telling the others what you are doing."

"Not a problem. I don't see much of them anyway. Except for the men on our detail."

"And you'll have to do it without getting caught by the surveillance team following Schind. I can't pull the detail off him without giving away our plan."

"Very well," Dukes replied. "I will take care of it. Be sort of a game. Me following them while they follow Schind."

"Right," Robinson nodded slowly. "But this is a game you can't afford to lose."

For the next two weeks, Dukes did just as he had suggested. He followed Schind by following the MI6 agents assigned to keep track of him. He made copious notes of Schind's regular stops—the laundry in the morning, a café for lunch, another for dinner—and after a week or two, a pattern emerged. Although Schind rarely visited any business on consecutive days, his stops were limited to a rotating list of about a dozen locations.

With that in mind, Dukes abandoned efforts to follow Schind, made a calculated guess, and obtained a job in the bar at Fuzzy's, a restaurant Schind frequented most often. If his observations were correct, Schind would visit the restaurant sometime in the next ten days and that would provide the best opportunity for him to make his move.

Dukes' hunch proved correct when less than a week later, Schind came in for dinner. He was seated at a table around the corner from the bar, but Dukes made a point of watching him long enough to note that he was seated alone and his waiter was a slender young college student named Sam.

A few minutes after Schind was seated, Sam came to the bar. "I need a Cape Cod," he said. "You know how to make it?"

"Cranberry juice and Vodka," Dukes replied with a frown. "You think I don't know what I'm doing?"

"You're new. I just wanted to be sure. That's all. This guy's a regular. And he likes it the other way around, too."

"You mean more vodka, less cranberry?" Dukes asked as he reached for a glass.

"You got it. Vodka with a hint of juice."

Dukes set the glass on the counter below the bar, out of Sam's line of sight, and filled it with ice. "Is this for that guy over by the window?" he asked as he added cranberry juice. "The guy sitting alone?"

"Yeah." Sam had a curious look. "You were watching him or something?"

"No," Dukes shrugged. He added vodka and set the bottle aside. "I just noticed him. That's all."

Dukes reached for a spoon with one hand and with the other took a small glass bottle from his pocket, then twisted off the cap. As he poured the contents into the glass, a busboy passed behind him and bumped Dukes' elbow. Some of the bottle's contents sloshed into a nearby sink. Frustrated, but with no option other than to follow through, Dukes stirred the drink and set the glass on the bar. "There you go. I hope he enjoys."

"Me too," Sam replied with a smile. "This guy tips well."

CHAPTER 34

THE VOLUNTEERS

At noon the following day, Palmer Collins came from the office and walked up the street for lunch. While he was eating, a waiter approached the table and handed him a note. "One of the guys in back asked me to give this to you."

Collins was puzzled but took the note from the waiter and unfolded it. "Come to the kitchen," was all it said. He laid aside his napkin, slid back from the table, and walked to the rear of the dining room. A hallway led to a restroom but halfway to it, a door to the right led into the kitchen. When he reached it, Collins turned aside and pushed open the door.

As he came through the doorway, a cook gestured with a nod toward the opposite side of the room. Collins made his way in that direction and found Sheldon Glaser standing behind a baker's rack near the freezer.

"Hey," Collins said with a look of surprise. "I hadn't expected to see you today."

"It couldn't be avoided," Glaser said. "They're relocating me, so I won't be able to see you much after today. But you need to know this. That memo I sent you about withdrawing from the mandate has become policy."

"What do you mean?"

"It's no longer just an idea in the Foreign Office. The prime minister is looking for an exit strategy. They're just trying to figure out how to do it without looking like failures."

"It was a difficult assignment," Collins conceded.

"Apparently, London has had enough of it. But you need to know, part of their strategy for setting up an exit is to get tough on the Jews."

Collins had a questioning frown. "Tough on the Jews? What do you mean?"

"Our military units in Palestine are set to arrest all the Jewish leadership."

Collins' eyes opened wide in a look of disbelief. "All of them?"

"All of them," Glaser repeated grimly. "Jewish Agency, Haganah, Lehi. They intend to sweep the entire country. "

"What about the Arabs?"

"This is an action directed solely at the Jews."

"Why?"

"There's been a rise in attacks and terrorist incidents. Our commanders on the ground are convinced it's all been instigated and led by the Jews. Military in the region wants them out of the way. Leadership in London sees it as an opportunity."

Collins looked puzzled. "An opportunity?"

"Apparently they've been looking for a way to shape the story toward an ending and they think this is it. Get tough. Crack down. Restore order. Claim victory and go home."

"That's crazy."

"Well, it might be crazy, but the operation is set to begin in three days, so pass the word." Glaser reached over and shook Collins' hand, then turned to leave.

"That's it?" Collins asked.

Glaser turned back to face him. "That's all I can do for you. Wish I could stay, but I have no option."

"Can you send reports from wherever you're going?"

Glaser shook his head. "Too risky. If I find a way, I'll let you know but from here on don't count on me." And with that he opened a delivery door, stepped outside, and was gone.

Rather than returning to his table to finish lunch, Collins left the restaurant and went immediately to Ginsberg's office, where he reported his discussion with Glaser. Ginsberg placed a phone call to Schind but after repeated attempts without an answer, he left the office and took a taxi to Hotel Fourteen.

When Ginsberg arrived at Schind's room, he found the door was unlocked and went inside, calling out as he entered, "Danny, are you here?" A check of the living room showed nothing out of place and he called once more as he moved toward the bedroom, but still there was no answer.

As he came through the doorway, he saw Schind lying in bed, fully clothed, with the cover pulled up around his neck. Ginsberg felt his skin and found it cool and clammy. A check of the artery in Schind's neck showed only a faint pulse and his breathing was shallow.

"You need to wake up." Ginsberg gave Schind a shake. When he didn't respond, Ginsberg stepped from the room, located the telephone, and called for an ambulance.

While he waited for someone to arrive, Ginsberg called Joe Buxenbaum and told him about Schind's condition. Buxenbaum left the office immediately and arrived at Hotel Fourteen just as an ambulance crew took Schind from his room.

Buxenbaum glanced over at Ginsberg. "How bad is it?"

"He's alive but unconscious," Ginsberg replied. "I don't know what's wrong."

Buxenbaum looked worried. "Was he sick? I mean, had he been sick before? He didn't seem sick to me."

"No, as far as I know, he was in good shape."

"Yeah," Buxenbaum said with a look of concern. "I saw him the other day and he was fine."

When the ambulance crew was gone, Ginsberg closed the apartment door and turned to Buxenbaum. "I need to get a message to Ben-Gurion. Schind has a radio connection. Do you know the operator's name?"

"Yeah. Isaac Bernstein." He pointed toward the door. "Where are they taking Danny?"

"Bellevue. Can you give Bernstein a message to send to Tel Aviv?"

"Yeah. Write out whatever you want him to tell them." Buxenbaum reached for the telephone. "I'll give him a call right now and figure out where we can meet." He glanced over his shoulder as he dialed the number. "Just keep the message short."

While Ginsberg wrote the message, Buxenbaum phoned Bernstein and arranged to meet him at the Staten Island Ferry dock at the southern tip of Manhattan. When the phone call ended, Ginsberg handed him the note. "Have him send this to Tel Aviv. For Ben-Gurion. I'm going to the hospital. Come over there after you see Bernstein."

By the time Buxenbaum got to Bellevue Hospital, Schind was in a room. Ginsberg sat in a chair near the bed. Schind, conscious but groggy, looked over at them. "Don't stop just because of me."

"We weren't going to," Ginsberg replied. "We just wanted to make sure you were taken care of."

"The two of you will have to run things until I get out of here."

"Okay." Ginsberg patted him lightly on the arm. "We'll take care of everything."

"Tell Collins to call—"

The door opened, interrupting them, and a doctor entered. "Oh, I didn't realize we were allowing visitors."

"They're okay," Schind said weakly.

"We have the results of your tests." The doctor glanced over at Buxenbaum and back to Ginsberg. "Perhaps you gentlemen should come back later."

"It's okay," Schind said. "What did you find?"

"We think you may have been poisoned with a form of cyanide."

"Cyanide!" Buxenbaum exclaimed. "Poison?"

"We found traces in your blood," the doctor said, ignoring Buxenbaum's question. "Not enough to determine the precise compound, but we're treating you while we conduct a few more tests."

"Will he recover?" Ginsberg asked.

"If no complications develop, he should be well soon." The doctor took a step back and opened the door. "But Mr. Schind needs to rest. Which means you two need to leave."

From the hospital, Ginsberg and Buxenbaum rode over to the Jewish Agency and met with Weizmann to tell him about Schind. "What does this do to our ship program?" Weizmann asked.

"Nothing," Ginsberg replied. "We must keep it moving forward, same as usual."

"That's what he told us," Buxenbaum offered. "So we gotta do it for him."

"Not to mention the hundreds of thousands of refugees trapped in Europe," Ginsberg added.

"Do we know what Schind was doing? The fund-raising trips for Nadelson, that sort of thing?"

Ginsberg realized Weizmann didn't know about the airplanes—apparently Buxenbaum didn't, either—and decided to keep quiet. "I'll go through his papers at Hotel Fourteen. But Stone and I have been operating on our own for a while now. That's the way Schind wanted it. To decentralize the operation. So we're in good shape."

"But how did this happen?" Weizmann asked. "Poisoning is a deliberate act."

"I don't know," Ginsberg answered. "And I'm not sure we want to know."

"I think the British did it," Buxenbaum chimed in. "They've been following us since he got here. They were at the airport when he came in. They've been following *me*."

"They follow us all," Weizmann offered. "It's nothing new."

"All the same, we should do something."

"No," Weizmann said emphatically. "If you respond, it will only draw the American authorities into it. They'll figure out what we're doing and that will be the end of it. They'll bring the whole thing to a stop. So do nothing."

"I agree," Ginsberg said. "We can't afford to give the authorities an opportunity to act."

Weizmann looked over at him. "Will the hospital report it?"

"I don't know. But I don't think we should discuss it with them. If we ask them not to report it, they'll only become suspicious and feel like they have to report it. So, at least for now, let's keep this to ourselves."

"Good idea," Weizmann said. "If they report it, we can deal with it then."

CHAPTER 35

THE VOLUNTEERS

A few days later Collins was busy at his office preparing documents to register the B-17s in Panama. To do that, he needed previous registration numbers for each of the planes, which he found in the transaction documents, along with a record of the total number of hours each aircraft had flown. But one of the forms asked for the model and serial numbers for each of the engines, along with the date of manufacture. That information was not included in the file Collins obtained from Schind.

In an effort to locate the information, Collins placed a call to Schind but when no one answered at the apartment, he walked over to Ginsberg's office to ask if Schind was in town. Ginsberg told him what happened. Collins was appalled. "Did anyone report this?"

"No, and we're not going to."

"Why not?"

"Think about it," Ginsberg replied. "If we report this, the police will investigate."

"Right."

"And if they investigate, they'll ask about Schind's background and why he's here."

"And that will lead to the ships."

"And the airplanes."

"I see your point," Collins conceded. "Is he going to recover?"

"The doctor thinks so."

"So I should move forward with Schwimmer and the aircraft?"

"Yes. Keep working. We can't stop just because he's been taken out for a while."

"I need some information for the aircraft registration that isn't in the file Schind gave me."

"What sort of information?"

"Serial numbers for each of the engines. Date of manufacture. That sort of thing. It's on the manufacturer's plate."

"You need this for all of the engines?"

"Yes," Collins answered. "Any idea where I could find it other than to inspect each of the engines?"

Ginsberg leaned back in his chair. "If it wasn't in the file, then someone will probably have to take a look at the engines."

"How do we do that?"

"Schind was working with a guy in California named Al Schwimmer."

"His name is mentioned in the transaction documents, but they used the New York address and phone number."

"I'm sure Schwimmer would know how to obtain the information. Aren't the airplanes out there with him?"

"Yes. Do you have a phone number for him?"

"No," Ginsberg replied. "But Schind does."

"Think he would remember it if we asked him?"

"Perhaps. You can go by the hospital and talk to Schind, if you can get past the doctors. Or you can go over to Hotel Fourteen on your own and see what you can find."

"Can I get in? I don't have a key."

"I'll call Fanny at the Jewish Agency. She'll arrange it for you."

Later that morning, Collins met Fanny Barnett in the lobby at Hotel Fourteen. They took the elevator up to Schind's apartment and Fanny unlocked the door. As they stepped inside, Fanny gasped.

"What's wrong?" Collins asked as he moved around her. Then he saw the apartment had been trashed.

"What happened?" she asked.

"Someone searched the place."

"What do we do?"

"Just stand right there" Collins made his way toward the telephone. "Don't touch a thing." He took a handkerchief from his pocket and used it to lift the phone from the cradle, then dialed a number using a pen from his pocket. A moment later, Ginsberg was on the line and Collins described the apartment. "Shall I report it?" he asked.

"No," Ginsberg replied. "I'll call Joe Buxenbaum and see if he can send someone over to straighten it up."

Collins and Fanny searched through the apartment as best they could, but Collins found nothing that mentioned Al Schwimmer. As they were about to leave, Buxenbaum arrived. He glanced around the apartment and shook his head. "British," he growled.

Fanny looked alarmed. "You think the British did this?"

Collins shot Buxenbaum a frown that told him to keep quiet and he took Fanny by the elbow. "Come on," he said. "Joe will take care of things here. We should get back to work."

She pulled her arm free of his grasp. "No, you go on. I'll stay and help Joe."

"I can handle this," Buxenbaum said. "You should get back to the office."

Collins stepped to the door and held it open. "Come on," he said to Fanny. "I'll buy lunch on the way." Reluctantly, she stepped through the doorway and walked with him up the hall toward the elevator.

After lunch, Collins took a taxi to Bellevue and went up to Schind's room. Schind was recovering, but still far from well. Collins avoided telling him about the apartment and simply asked if he had contact information for Schwimmer. "I thought it was in the papers I gave you."

"His name is there," Collins explained. "But no phone number or address."

"Right," Schind said with a nod. "We used the Hotel Fourteen address for that. I think the phone number is in my wallet. But I don't know where they put it when they brought me in here."

A small nightstand stood beside the bed and Collins opened the top drawer. "Ah," he said as he reached inside. "Here it is." He took the wallet from the drawer and handed it to Schind.

Schind opened the wallet and took a small piece of paper from the corner of the money fold, then handed it to Collins. "That should be the number." Collins unfolded it and wrote the number on the back of a business card, then gave the paper back. "If you reach him," Schind said, "he might not want to talk to you at first, but you can tell him to check with Ginsberg. Ginsberg will vouch for you."

"Should I explain what happened to you?"

"Yes. He needs to know, the stakes are rising."

"You think the British did this to you?"

"I know they did it to me. Bartender at Fuzzy's spiked my drink."

"You know that for certain?"

"I've used cyanide in other operations. It acts very quickly. I was sick before I left the restaurant. If he'd given me just a little bit more, I wouldn't be here now."

The conversation with Schind was sobering and Collins thought about it as he rode in a taxi back to the office. If the British really did this to Schind, what would they do to the others? To Ginsberg? To Stone? To him? They already knew about his involvement with the ships. That's what got him fired from Fortas, Brown & Hoffman. If they knew that much about him, they probably knew a lot more. *Maybe,* he thought, *that's the reason Glaser was transferred.*

By the time he reached the office building, Collins was worried. If the British were watching Ginsberg, they could just as easily be watching him. He glanced around as he came through the lobby and waited for the elevator, then quickly scanned the other passengers as they rode up. All the while he thought, *This really could be a life-or-death matter.*

When Collins made it upstairs to his office, he had a sense that he was being followed and kept glancing back over his shoulder with every step. As he passed the secretary's desk she said, "Your wife called." Collins jumped at the sound of her voice. "I'm sorry," she said. "I didn't mean to startle you. But she sounded upset."

"Where is she?"

"At the apartment. She wanted you to call her the minute you got back."

Collins hurried to his desk and phoned the apartment. Olivia was overwrought with emotion. "The place is destroyed," she wailed.

"Your mother's house?"

"No!" Olivia shouted. "The apartment."

"Our apartment?"

"Yes. Yes. Yes!" she screamed. "Our apartment. It's ruined."

"What do you mean?"

"It's ruined, Palmer. Ruined," she cried.

"Why are you there?"

"I came back to get some more things and when I walked in... Palmer, the place is ruined!" she sobbed. "Please come over here."

"Are the children with you?"

"No."

"Are you okay?"

"No, I'm not okay. Our home has been ransacked."

"Physically, are you okay?"

"Yes."

"Did you see anyone there?"

"No."

"They went through every room!" she wailed. "Every room, Palmer. Please come over here."

"I'm on my way. I'll be there in a few minutes."

Collins arrived to find the apartment door ajar. He slowly pushed it aside, glanced through the opening, then entered slowly. Much like what he'd seen at Schind's, the apartment had been ransacked. Furniture was turned upside down. Cushions ripped apart. Shelves emptied and the contents scattered about the room. To make matters worse, on the wall opposite the door someone had painted a swastika in red with the words *Death to the Jews* written above.

Olivia appeared in the hall doorway looking pale and in shock. "Who did this?" she demanded.

Collins looked away. "I don't know."

"Yes, you do." She crossed the room to him and took his hand. "You know who did this. Now, please, tell me what is going on."

"I don't . . . "

"Palmer, tell me."

"Okay," Collins whispered. "I'll tell you some of it, but not all." He took a deep breath. "I helped Morris Ginsberg and some other people form a company to buy ships, to go to Europe, to rescue refugees."

"What kind of refugees?"

"Jewish refugees. They wanted to pick them up from Europe and take them to Palestine."

Olivia gestured to the room. "And you think this has something to do with that?"

"The process is ongoing."

"What does that mean?"

"We're buying more ships. And there's a little more to it but I can't tell you that part right now."

"So, who would do this?"

Collins looked her in the eyes. "The British."

The corners of her mouth turned up in a skeptical, disbelieving smile. "You think the British would do this to us because you are helping Morris Ginsberg?"

"Yes."

"That is preposterous," she chided. "Why would the British do this to us because of what you did for Ginsberg?"

"Morris Ginsberg is Jewish."

"I know that."

"The people we're working with are from Palestine. Part of an underground group called Haganah."

Olivia had a puzzled expression. "Underground?"

"Paramilitary."

"What is that?"

"A unit formed to defend Jewish farming communities against attacks from Arabs."

"Because they don't want any more Jews brought to Palestine," she said with a sarcastic tone. "I read the newspapers, too. But what does that have to do with the British?"

"The British don't want any more trouble in the region and they see limiting Jewish immigration as a way of doing that."

"And these ships you and Morris Ginsberg are buying, and the people you're taking over there, are against that policy?"

"Yes," Collins nodded. "They would do anything in their power to hinder the work."

She shook her head with a dismissive smirk. "I think you've gone too far into—"

"One of the men involved with us is in the hospital," Collins said, interrupting. "He was poisoned with cyanide."

Olivia still was skeptical. "By the British."

"Yes."

"I find all of this difficult to believe."

"Perhaps, but I'm not the only one helping."

"What do you mean? Who else is there?"

"You know that day after church when I had an envelope with a note in it?"

"You're saying Reverend Thornton is involved?"

"The note he gave me was from a contact in the British Foreign Office. I met him that night in an alley in midtown."

"Oh, this is good," she said with a derisive tone. "You must have spent a lot of time dreaming this up."

"Will you listen to me?" he snapped. "I'm not making this up. Discussions were being held between US and British delegates about raising the immigration quota in Palestine. No one knew what the outcome of those talks would be, but in the end they fell apart. That night, in the alley, our contact in the British Foreign Office told me that the British were going to refuse to increase Jewish immigration and would announce that decision three days later. And three days later they announced it." He pointed to her. "You read about it in the newspaper."

"Yes, I remember that."

"I told Morris what was happening. He told David Ben-Gurion and that's how all this got started with the ships and the rescue."

"I still don't—"

"In a day or two you'll read another article in the newspaper about the widespread arrest of Jewish leadership in Palestine."

"Who will be arrested?"

"All of them. Golda Meir. Shimon Peres. All the names you would recognize."

"By the British?"

"Yes. By the British."

Olivia turned away. "I think you've lost it." She glanced over her shoulder as she started up the hall toward the bedroom. "I just came for some clothes and I'm going back to Mother's house. You do what you have to do."

"Read the newspaper," Collins called after her.

Olivia turned to face him. "Palmer, I know you were frustrated about getting sent home from the war so early, but I think with some therapy you can get past it."

"You think that's what I'm doing?" he asked in an angry tone. "Me living vicariously through Ginsberg and the others, somehow trying to atone for some supposed guilt over my shortened military service?"

"I think that's part of it."

He stepped closer. "Don't you realize there's a struggle for the soul of historic Israel?"

"Yes," she nodded. "I suppose."

"And a struggle for our soul?"

Olivia looked perplexed. "Our soul?"

"As Christians are we going to stand with the Jews or not?"

"I fail to see how one relates to the other." She turned back to the bedroom. "The children would love to see you," she called. "Think you can come out this weekend to see us?"

"Yeah." Collins turned away from the hall. "I can come out on Sunday."

She came to the bedroom doorway. "You could come on Friday and spend the night. Stay all weekend, in fact."

"I'm not sure about Saturday. I have to follow up on some business."

"What kind of business?"

"I can't tell you."

Olivia threw up her hands in frustration. "You just won't quit," she yelled.

"Just read the newspaper," he insisted. "You'll see what I'm talking about."

CHAPTER 36

THE VOLUNTEERS

Olivia found a suitcase in the closet, packed it full of clothes for herself and the children, and returned to the living room. Collins was still there. "I'll get the place cleaned up."

"Do whatever you like. Just call me when this is all over."

Collins rode with her to the lobby in the elevator and waited while the doorman hailed a taxi, then he helped the driver place the suitcase in the trunk. Olivia kissed him lightly on the lips, then he held the car door while she slid onto the backseat. When she was in place, he leaned in and kissed her again. She turned to the driver and said, "Union Station."

"You have money for the fare?"

"Yes, don't worry about us. Just take care of yourself." Collins pushed the door closed, then the taxi started from the curb and headed up the street.

As Olivia rode toward the station, she thought again of the conversation with Palmer. The things that had transpired—his mysterious meetings, cryptic comments about *other people* helping, late nights out to places he refused to disclose for reasons he wouldn't talk about. Notes passed to him at church that sent him off on one more secret rendezvous and—

Suddenly, Olivia's eyes opened wide. *Notes passed at church.* "Reverend Thornton gave him that note," she said aloud. "Palmer never actually said that when I asked him, but that's how he got the note. Reverend Thornton gave it to him. He's involved in this, too. He's one of those *other* people."

The driver glanced up at her in the rearview mirror with a questioning look. "Excuse me, ma'am. Did you say something to me?"

"No," she said with a shake of her head. "It was nothing." Then in the same instant she said, "Yes. Yes. It *is* something. Take me to St. Mark's."

"St. Mark's?"

"Yes."

"The church?"

"Yes, yes," she said insistently. "The church."

The driver turned right at the next corner, made the block, then turned left and started in the opposite direction.

When Olivia arrived at St. Mark's Church, she got out of the taxi, took her luggage from the driver, and made her way up the steps to the front entrance. She found Rev. Thornton in the sanctuary.

"Going someplace?" he asked with a nod to the suitcase.

"I've been living at my mother's," she explained. "I just came back for some extra clothes."

"Oh," he said with a note of concern. "I didn't know."

"We didn't tell anyone."

"What happened?"

"It was the cumulative effect of all that's been going on."

Rev. Thornton had a questioning look. "What's been going on?"

"You tell me."

Thornton's questioning look turned to a puzzled frown. "I haven't the faintest idea what you're talking about."

"Yes, I think you do."

"What are you talking about?"

"The notes you passed to Palmer after church. Meetings at odd times of the night with people supposedly connected to the British government."

Thornton looked away. "I'm not sure I—"

"Look," she said firmly, "I'm not interested in semantics or wordplay or whatever else you want to call it. Our apartment was broken into and the place has been trashed. It's ruined. Swastikas on the wall. Anti-Semitic slogans on the wall. Everything ripped apart. I don't have patience for a guessing game. I want to know what happened."

He spoke hesitantly. "You . . . should ask Palmer. I'm not sure I should talk about it."

"I asked him."

"And what did he tell you?"

"He told me about acquiring ships to sail to Europe to rescue refugees and take them to Palestine. And he mentioned notes from you and meetings in alleys with a British contact."

"He shouldn't have said that much."

"I want to know the rest of the story," she insisted. "I know you're involved. I saw you pass him a note after church. I know others are helping. But you're one of them." She pointed for emphasis. "So tell me what is going on."

"I'm afraid I can't do that," he sighed. "Whatever you want to know you'll have to get it from Palmer or one of the others."

"Fine, then tell me the names of these *others*. I'll be glad to talk to them."

"I can't." Thornton looked away once more. "I can't give you their names. Lives are at stake. The risk is too great."

Olivia pumped the air with her fists in a gesture of frustration. "Why can't someone tell me the truth?" she shouted. "My apartment was ransacked, my life has been turned upside down. I'm living with our children at my mother's house on Long Island because it's no longer safe in my home. I want to know what's happening!"

"Very well," Thornton sighed. "I'll tell you what I can." He glanced around nervously. "Just calm down."

She held his gaze. "Don't patronize me. I want to know the truth."

"All right. This is what I know." He paused a moment to take a deep breath, then began. "I have a friend who works for the British government. He's on the staff of the foreign secretary's office. That friend was stationed at an office in New York. One Sunday, after the morning service, he approached me as I was walking back to the sacristy. I think he heard one of my sermons about our obligation as Christians to help the Jews and because of that, he thought I might be sympathetic to the things that were on his mind. He didn't say that. That's just my hunch."

"He's a Jew?"

"No." Thornton shook his head. "Not at all. But he was worried about the condition of the Jews in Palestine and he was troubled by the things he saw happening in the British government. Policy decisions that were in conflict with his personal beliefs as a Christian. He told me he knew things. Things the Jewish leadership in Palestine might find helpful. And he asked if I knew anyone to whom he could talk. I knew Palmer had represented Morris Ginsberg and I knew that Morris was very active with the Jewish Agency for Palestine. So I told him I knew someone who might be able to help."

"And that person was Palmer."

"Yes," Thornton nodded. "I offered to introduce him to Palmer but he was uncomfortable approaching Palmer directly. Afraid he'd be too closely associated with Morris, the Jewish Agency, and all that."

"He thought someone would see him?"

"Yes."

"They can do that?"

"Oh my," Thornton replied. "I should think so. MI6, the British Foreign Intelligence Service, has offices and agents all over the world. Apparently, they even spy on their own government."

"So he got you to be the middleman."

"Yes, I agreed to be the go-between. When Sheldon—" Thornton paused to catch himself. "When my friend had news to share, he contacted me. I contacted Palmer, and the two of them got together."

Leaving the church, Olivia took a taxi to Union Station and boarded a train for Long Island. As she rode along, she thought about what she'd heard.

Rev. Thornton was not only a faithful pastor but also an intelligent man. If he was involved, then maybe Palmer wasn't so crazy after all.

Maybe he really was doing something big. Too big and too important to discuss. She never needed to know about his other clients. But the other clients never impinged on her private life, either. Still, she couldn't escape the ring of truth in what Rev. Thornton had said.

And then she thought about the apartment. "Palmer will never get it cleaned up," she told herself with a smile. "He'll come home late from the office. Tired and hungry. Find something to eat. Clear out a place to sit. Watch a few minutes of television and go to bed."

At least, that's what he would do when he wasn't lurking in some darkened alley waiting to meet someone. She had an amused smile at the thought of Palmer in an alley at night.

He was so . . . manly when they met. Muscular, athletic. Dashingly handsome. Then the war. The injury. And he was home while all his friends and classmates continued to serve. She understood the way he felt about that. They were serving and everyone was talking about them in heroic terms. Meanwhile, he was back in the United States, safe, secure, living the comfortable life . . . and stuck behind a desk. The toll on him had been painfully noticeable. Almost palpable. A neutering of a once-vibrant man.

Perhaps all this might be a way for him to regain some of that former confidence. Not just the clandestine meetings and the secret missions, but the way he was thrown from the law firm and the way he chose to stand alone rather than cower and run back to beg for his job.

A sense of pride came over her. He was her husband. Heroic in a way none of those other men could ever be. And what had she done? She'd abandoned him just when he needed her most. The overwhelming pride she'd felt just a moment earlier now gave way to shame.

"We should go back," she whispered to herself. "We should go back to the apartment." *I'll call someone to help—hire them if I have to—and we'll straighten it up, then the children and I will go back. It'll take a while to get things in order, but that's what we'll do. Straighten it up. Go back. The children will never know what happened, except that their father was a brave and courageous man. Then Palmer and I can move forward in this together, as we should have all along.*

CHAPTER 37

THE VOLUNTEERS

When Olivia was gone, Collins returned to the office and contacted Schwimmer. As Schind had suggested, Schwimmer was suspicious of the call at first and reluctant to talk, but after Ginsberg vouched for him, things went better. Collins outlined the information they needed in order to complete the registration forms, and Schwimmer noted the need to move quickly. "Our contact in the Panamanian president's office told us their officials are anxious to meet us and get this deal moving forward. We don't want to lose this opportunity."

"Get me the information, and I can complete the forms in a matter of hours. All we'll need after that is to have them delivered to the Panamanian government. Do you have someone who can fly down there and take care of that?"

"I have a better idea. Bring the forms and come out here. We can get whatever information we need from the engines, fill out the forms, and talk about what to do next."

Collins was surprised by the suggestion. "You can give me the information over the phone."

"I don't like talking business on the phone. Just come out here and we can talk face-to-face."

"I'll be glad to help you," Collins replied, "but I don't know much about this deal or your plans. All I know is what I've read in the files."

"That's about all there is to know. Look, Schind is still in the hospital, right?"

"Yes."

"So it's just you and me and the guys who fly and manage the planes."

"You already have pilots?"

Schwimmer avoided the question. "Come out here. We'll talk about it when you get here. I don't want to discuss this anymore over the phone."

Collins knew he was supposed to visit his family that weekend, but now he felt pressed to make the trip to California. He called his mother-in-law's house hoping to talk to Olivia, but she wasn't there, so he left a message telling her what happened, then made an airline reservation for a flight the following morning and went home to get ready for the trip.

The following morning, Collins took a taxi to LaGuardia and flew to California. He arrived in the afternoon and met Schwimmer at Lockheed Air Terminal in Burbank. They spent the remainder of the day obtaining the necessary information from the manufacturer's plates on each of the engines. That evening, they went to Schwimmer's house for dinner with Schwimmer's wife and children. Later that evening, Schwimmer and Collins moved outside to the patio where they could talk alone.

"We have to move the airplanes within thirty days," Schwimmer said. "That's another reason why I wanted to get to work on this."

"Someone is forcing you out?"

"We rented space for them at that airport, but it's costing us a bundle. And President Truman has announced a ban on the sale of military equipment to foreign entities and governments without prior approval."

"Effective thirty days from now," Collins noted. "I saw a notice about it the other day."

"Exactly. Which is why we need to move the planes out of the country now."

“When were you thinking of moving them?”

“If we move all of them at once, we’d have to wait a few more weeks. Several of them still need extensive work. But I’m fairly sure we could take five later this week.”

Somewhere in the conversation, the telephone rang inside the house. A moment later, Schwimmer’s wife came to the door and told him he had a call. Schwimmer went inside to take it.

The phone call that evening was from Juan Ortiz. “They talked to me again,” he said.

“When?” Schwimmer asked.

“Just a few minutes ago.”

“Is something wrong?”

“They’re really worried, man.”

“About what?”

“About whether you intend to follow through on the deal. They think I might not be telling them the truth. Like this might all be just a scam or something.”

“We’re planning to go down there later this week,” Schwimmer explained.

“I don’t know, I think you should meet with them earlier.”

“Has something changed?” Schwimmer asked. “This is the second time they’ve called about this in the last week.”

“They’re anxious to get airline service. They need to justify the expense of building the facility. Elections are coming soon. People are beginning to complain about the cost of the project and nothing to show for it.”

“Okay,” Schwimmer said, “tell them we will leave tomorrow.”

“Tomorrow?”

“Yes, we will fly down tomorrow. It’ll take two days to get there, but we’ll leave tomorrow.”

When the call ended, Schwimmer hung up the phone and went back outside and said to Collins, "The Panamanians are getting nervous. We need to meet them. Get to know each other."

"Meet them." Collins frowned. "You've never seen them?"

"No, not yet. We've communicated through intermediaries."

"So you have no way of knowing if the people you've been dealing with in Panama are actually Panamanian officials."

"Well . . . " Schwimmer hesitated. "No. I suppose not. But I know the person I use on this end. He's a friend of a friend."

"Hmm," Collins said. "Have you checked him out?"

"Yes, he's fine. But it's time to meet the Panamanians face-to-face. We need to see them and they need to see us. And," he added, "we can file the registration documents in person while we're down there. Make an event out of it. They need something to tell Panamanian reporters anyway." He smiled, "This will be perfect. Maybe we can even get a picture of it for the local papers."

"You and the Panamanian officials?"

"No." Schwimmer looked askance. "Not me." He pointed to Collins. "You."

"Me?"

"Yeah. You're our lawyer. Our New York lawyer. A picture of you filing the applications for the airplanes with the registry would be great."

"I don't know," Collins sighed, thinking of his family and the need to see them.

"It's all settled. I told them we'd come down tomorrow. We have to go."

"You don't need me to register the planes," Collins countered. "The forms are ready to go. All you have to do is file them."

"If the people we're dealing with are legitimate, they'll have documents for us to sign. I'm not signing anything until you say they're okay."

"All right," Collins said finally.

"You had somewhere else to be?"

Collins shook his head. "No, I can go. How many airplanes will you take?"

"Three."

"Just three? Not all of the ones that are ready to fly?"

"Too risky right now."

"Too risky?" Collins looked concerned. "I thought you trusted them."

"I did, but after talking to you, I'm not sure that's such a good idea," he grinned. "As you suggested, I've never even met them. If this is a setup, we could lose every plane we take down there."

"Lose them?"

"Government seizure."

"You think the Panamanians are working with the United States?"

"I think there's no limit to what the British would do to stop us."

"The British?"

"Yes, they hate us. So, yes, I'm suspicious of the Panamanians, and the British, and the Americans. We'll take the best three planes, but that's it."

"If it's a risk, you'd risk the best three?"

"We have to make it all the way to Panama, and then return home. We need aircraft that can make that trip."

"Oh. Which ones are the best?"

"The Constellations. They're cargo planes, which is what we said we were doing. Flying cargo. If we take the bombers they'll wonder why we brought military aircraft. But the Constellations will make a good show. Let them see we're doing something."

The next morning, Schwimmer and Collins rode over to the airport in Burbank. The three Constellations were parked outside a hangar, fueled and ready to go. A group of men stood near the hangar door. From the look of it, they'd been waiting for Schwimmer and Collins to arrive. As they walked up, the men came toward them.

Two of the men, Norm Moonitz and Ray Kurtz, had a worried look. Schwimmer smiled and said, "Something the matter, gentlemen?"

"It's the planes," Moonitz said.

"What about them?" Schwimmer asked.

"They might be technically airworthy," Kurtz said. "They can take off and land. But they're not in great shape."

"They took a beating in the war," Moonitz explained. "We were wondering if they would make it all the way to Central America."

"Plus, they're carrying a load," Kurtz said. "A load that's far too heavy, especially given the aircrafts' condition. We didn't know anything about taking a load on this flight."

"Yeah," Schwimmer replied. "I meant to tell you about that."

"What is it?" Kurtz asked. "What's in all those crates?"

"Equipment for the ground crew," Schwimmer replied. "Couldn't be avoided. They don't have the equipment we need down there. So we have to bring it with us."

Moonitz had a puzzled frown. "Aren't we coming back here?"

"We are, but two of the planes will remain down there. We'll need equipment and spare parts to maintain them."

They talked awhile longer, with Schwimmer answering their questions and addressing their concerns, then everyone started toward the planes. Moonitz and his flight crew took the Constellation parked farthest to the left. Kurtz and his men took the one to the right. Schwimmer started toward the one nearest the hangar and gestured for Collins to follow. Four crewmen trailed behind.

They boarded the plane and Schwimmer took the copilot's seat. Collins sat in the jump seat near the flight engineer's desk. When he was strapped into place, he leaned into the aisle, and watched as Schwimmer and the pilot, Marty Ribakoff, worked through their preflight checklist.

In a few minutes, Ribakoff reached over to the instrument panel in the center of the dash and flipped a switch. The starter motor on one of the engines began to whine. Collins turned to look out the window and saw the propeller on the outboard engine to the right slowly spinning around. After two or three revolutions, the engine caught and a plume of blue smoke billowed over the wing. The engine coughed once or twice and finally smoothed to an even idle. Moments later a propeller on an engine to the left began spinning slowly.

The process repeated until all four of the airplane's engines were running smoothly and then the plane began to move forward, rolling gently along the taxiway. When they reached the far end of the runway, the plane paused a moment. From the cockpit, Collins heard the garbled sound of radio traffic but he couldn't understand what was said. Then the plane started forward again, turned sharply left, and the engines sped up to a deafening roar.

Finally they rolled onto the runway and lumbered ahead at what seemed like the slowest pace possible. Gradually, they picked up speed and continued that way for so long Collins was sure they would roll right into the grass at the opposite end of the airfield. Then, at last, the nose lifted and the plane rose slowly into the air, engines running at full speed, straining to gain altitude as quickly as possible.

Out the window, Collins saw a mountain range to the north. The peak of it appeared close enough to touch. Slowly, they made a long, sweeping turn, crossing the mountain twice as they banked around to head south, still climbing into the beautiful blue sky.

Before long, the Pacific coast appeared beneath them and Collins noticed that cars on the coast highway seemed like tiny toys. Not long after that, the ground disappeared from view beneath wispy, fair-weather clouds and Collins settled back in his seat.

Eight hours later, the planes landed in Mexico City for the night. "We can't make it to Panama City in a day, and flying at night is a little too risky down here," Schwimmer explained. "After we inspect the facility in Panama, we might be able to finish the hop at night. But right now we don't even know if they have runway lights." Collins found that information unsettling but said nothing.

From the airport, they took a bus into the city and rented hotel rooms for the night. Collins and Schwimmer roomed together. Later that evening they went downstairs for dinner. When they were seated, a waiter took their order and when he was gone, Collins asked, "So, what are you really planning to do with these airplanes?"

Schwimmer glanced away. "We're building an airline. You've seen the files. Passengers and freight. Just as we said."

Collins gave him a skeptical smile. "You're working with Schind and Ginsberg and who knows who else. I know how they operate."

"What do you mean?"

"This is nothing like a legitimate airline."

"You did the legal work for us. We didn't violate any laws."

"No," Collins agreed. "We haven't violated any laws, but the planes don't even have seats."

"We'll get there."

"Al," Collins continued in a good-natured but pressing way, "you're flying airplanes that are only marginally airworthy. Taking them to a facility you know nothing about. From what I've seen and heard, your sole interest is in getting the planes out of US territorial control."

"Anything wrong with that?"

"Not necessarily. But you and I both know you have no intention of getting in the airline business."

Schwimmer glanced around as if checking to be certain no one was listening, "Okay, I'll tell you. But you have to keep it absolutely to yourself."

"I'm your attorney. I can't tell anyone anything."

Schwimmer leaned forward and lowered his voice. "We intend to take the airplanes to Palestine."

"The British won't like that."

"No, and neither will the Americans."

"So you're smuggling them into the country."

"Yes," Schwimmer shrugged. "I suppose we are."

"What for?"

"War is coming. When the British leave—and they will leave—we have to be ready."

"So, the airplanes won't be used to haul freight and passengers?"

"The Constellations and the C-46s will," Schwimmer answered.

"But not the B-17s."

"They're bombers," Schwimmer chuckled. "What did you think we were going to do with them? Haul oranges?"

Collins arched an eyebrow. "The FBI will be after you."

"You just said I haven't broken any laws."

"Right," Collins nodded.

"Then why would they come after me? We bought the planes fair and square. It's not illegal to take them out of the country. At least, not now. We aren't required to have a permit or to get anyone's approval."

"Right."

"So, what complaint do they have against me?"

"I don't know," Collins said with a wry smile, "but they won't like it and they'll find a way to come after you."

"By then we will be in control of Palestine. At least a portion of it, anyway. And none of this will matter."

"You don't intend to remain an American citizen?"

Schwimmer looked away again. "I don't know about all that. I don't know."

"You have a wife," Collins reminded.

"I know. She's my wife." Schwimmer grinned. "Believe me. I know she's there."

"And children."

"Look," Schwimmer said, tapping the tabletop with his finger for emphasis, "this right here—this thing we are doing—is bigger than that. Maybe not in the grand scheme of things. And certainly not always. But right now this is the biggest thing in my life. In our lives." He gestured between them. "That's why you're here. You have a wife and as many kids as I do. You're a lawyer. A New York lawyer. Yet here you are in Mexico City, on your way to Panama, helping us do this. And you aren't even a Jew." He smiled over at Collins. "Now tell me that what we're doing isn't bigger than all of us."

At sunrise the following day, Schwimmer and Collins were back inside the Constellation waiting while the other crews prepared to leave. When all the plane's engines were warmed up and ready, Schwimmer radioed Moonitz. "All right, Norm. You've got the lead."

"Roger that," Moonitz replied. "We're rolling."

Collins leaned into the aisle and watched through the front windshield as Moonitz's Constellation moved down the runway. As it neared the end, flaps on the wings lowered and the plane rose gently into the sky.

"Did you see that?" Ribakoff asked.

"Yeah," Schwimmer replied. "We should put our flaps down earlier."

"Norm probably waited that long thinking the drag would slow him down. Wanted to build as much speed as possible."

"I prefer a margin for error," Schwimmer said.

"Right."

Schwimmer looked over at him. "You getting the feel of this machine?"

"Yeah," Ribakoff said. "Thanks for letting me have the left seat."

"No problem. Good experience for you."

By then Kurtz was in the air as well, leaving only Schwimmer's plane still on the ground. "We better get moving," he said. "Don't want them to get too far ahead of us."

"Right."

"They have a tower here, but everyone takes off by visual rules." Schwimmer pointed out the window. "So check the sky and go."

The plane started forward and they slowly rolled along the taxiway. When they reached the runway, Ribakoff turned the plane and brought it to a stop on the center line. He held it there a moment and revved the engines to full throttle, then released the brake and the plane started forward, this time moving more quickly than when they took off from the airport in Burbank.

Two-thirds of the way down the runway, Collins leaned back in his seat expecting to feel a bump as the plane lifted into the air. Suddenly the plane shook violently, and Collins looked out the window to see an engine on the right side enveloped in a cloud of smoke. Flames shot from the cowling, then the propeller sheared loose from its shaft and spun toward the fuselage. It flashed against the morning sunlight as it zipped past Collins' window and struck the body of the plane near the rear door.

Instantly, the plane veered sharply to the right, then back to the left, before bouncing off the runway. A few feet farther, the landing gear on the right side collapsed and the propeller from the remaining engine on that side dug into the ground, sending dirt and dust into the air. Still the plane continued forward and slid down an embankment into a ravine, where the engines on the opposite wing caught fire.

At the bottom of the ravine, the nose plowed into the dirt, and the tail of the aircraft pitched it into the air, standing the plane on end. But when it reached the vertical point, the plane twisted slowly to the right, caught on the tip of the right wing, and fell forward, landing upside down against the opposite side of the ravine.

Over to the left, the flight engineer dangled upside down, suspended beneath his seat by the safety belts. Blood dripped from his nose and his eyes were rolled up, the pupils hidden by his eyelids. Collins was certain he was unconscious and wondered if he were dead.

For his part, Collins' shoulder throbbed and his left leg ached. He glanced up to check for the source of the pain and saw his foot over to the right, resting against the window. It was still attached to his leg but he wondered how it came to be in such an odd position.

Just then a noise came from the front of the plane, and Collins twisted to one side to see down the aisle, but before he could get into position, the seat broke free of the bolts that held it in place and Collins dropped to the bottom of the fuselage. His head banged against a bulkhead bracket, sending searing pain through his spine, and seconds later he passed out.

Sometime later Collins awakened in a hospital room. Olivia was seated in the corner, reading a newspaper. She peeked around it with a familiar smile. “Finally awake?”

“Where am I?” he asked groggily.

“Mexico City.”

Mexico, he thought, then images of the plane crash flashed through his mind and he closed his eyes trying to make the thoughts go away. “How long have I been out?” he asked finally.

“I’m not sure. I’ve been here four days. You’ve been out of it the entire time.”

“How’d you find me?”

“Morris Ginsberg told me what happened.”

“How’d he know where I was?”

“Somebody called him, I think.”

“So . . . how am I?”

“You have a broken leg,” she explained. “And some internal injuries. But the doctors think you’ll get well.”

“Where are the children?”

“At the apartment.”

Collins looked puzzled. “The apartment?”

“Mother’s with them.”

“You came back?”

“Yes.”

Collins had so much he wanted to say, but Olivia was sometimes touchy about things like that, so he looked away and asked, “Did Morris tell you why I was down here?”

“A little.”

“What about the children? Do they know?”

“I had to tell them something to explain why I was traveling to Mexico, but you can tell them the whole story when we get back home.”

“The whole story?”

"Yes, the whole story. It's affected their lives, too. It's affected all our lives and we should live it together."

Collins had an expectant look. "You're back for good?"

"Yes."

Again he was unsure whether to say more about it, so he asked, "Anyone figure out what happened to the airplane? Last I remember we were at the end of the runway and something exploded."

"It was an engine," she explained.

"An engine?"

"Someone named Joe Buxenbaum brought a crew of mechanics down to see what they could salvage. They looked at the wreckage. He thinks a bomb went off in the engine."

"How does he know that?"

"Said he found a detonator or something, I think." Newspaper in hand, Olivia rose from her chair with a knowing look. "Seems you were right," she said as she started toward the bed.

"About what?"

"The British really are trying to stop you."

"Yeah," Collins agreed. "They are."

"And," she continued, "you were right about this, too." She folded the newspaper and held it for him to see a front-page story about the arrest of Jewish leaders in Palestine.

Collins scanned the headlines. "Who did they get?"

"Just about everyone; Ben-Gurion avoided capture because he was in Paris, and Golda Meir was freed rather quickly. But Shimon Peres and almost a thousand others were sent to detention camps."

Collins looked over at her with a pained smile. "That won't be the end of it."

"I know," she nodded.

"This could get even worse," he cautioned. "We still have more to do. Maybe you and the children shouldn't be at the apartment."

She shook her head. "No, I think that's exactly where we should be." She leaned over and kissed him gently on the lips. "We should have been there all along, fighting this fight together. You. Me. The children. I'm sorry I wasn't there for you."

"It's okay," he replied as she kissed him again.

"But from now on, you have to tell me exactly what's happening."

"Okay. But if that's the way we're handling it, I have to tell you something."

She had a questioning look. "What is it?"

"I want to go with them," he whispered.

"Go with them?" She looked perplexed. "Go with whom? And where are they going?"

"They're going to Palestine. The guys who were with us are taking the planes to—"

Olivia interrupted. "Everyone in your plane except Al Schwimmer was killed."

Collins' eyes opened wide in a look of concern. "Marty Ribakoff?"

"Yes," she nodded.

"All the others?"

"Yes," she said softly. "They died in the crash."

Collins winced. "How is Al?"

"Other than a cut on his forehead, he's fine."

"Really?"

"Yes, so tell me, where were they going?"

"The plan is to take the planes to Palestine."

She seemed startled. "To Palestine?"

"Yes. Not now. We were just moving them to Panama. But later, the plan is to take them to Palestine." He paused to look her in the eyes. "I want to go with them."

Olivia's shoulders slumped but she managed a weak smile as she tucked the sheet around his shoulders. "Let's talk about that later. First we have to get you home and get you well."

CHAPTER 38

THE VOLUNTEERS

In November, UNSCOP recommended the division of Palestine into separate Jewish and Arab states, partitioning the region largely along existing ethnic lines. The United Nations General Assembly accepted that recommendation and adopted the committee's report, with a few changes, as its policy in the region. Ben-Gurion and the Jewish Agency promptly accepted the proposed division. Arab spokesmen in Jerusalem and neighboring countries adamantly rejected it. The British announced May 15, 1948, as their date of departure from the region, setting the stage for a major Middle Eastern crisis.

After clearing his plans with the Pentagon, Mickey Marcus flew to Jerusalem to see firsthand what military conditions were actually like and to review Haganah's readiness to fight. He arrived in January 1948.

At first, Marcus met with some resistance from Haganah line officers who didn't care for outside interference in their affairs, but Haganah chief, Jacob Dostrovsky, had been briefed by Ben-Gurion about what they hoped Marcus would accomplish and was glad to have knowledgeable and experienced help. He greeted Marcus with a broad grin. "At last, the Americans join the fight."

"Well," Marcus shrugged, "at least one of them has arrived."

They spent the next two days traveling around Tel Aviv and Haifa, inspecting troops and reviewing fortified positions. There was not much to see in some places. Haganah members were good at what they'd been asked to do, and they'd accomplished a lot given the close British scrutiny to which they'd been subjected, but as a modern fighting unit Marcus found their lack of formal training obvious. The absence of arms and equipment was even more so. Still, he was impressed by their esprit de corps and their can-do attitude.

From Haifa they rode to Jerusalem where Dostrovsky outlined the lay of the land. "You have a lot of hills," Marcus noted.

"This is a city of hills," Dostrovsky replied. "Mount Scopus, Temple Mound, Government House. All of them key, strategic locations."

Marcus looked to the left and pointed. "Which one is that?"

"Ammunition Hill," Dostrovsky replied. "The British had a facility there until very recently. An ammunition depot—hence the name. They've abandoned it now and local Arab militiamen have seized it."

"And the Mount of Olives?"

Dostrovsky pointed once more. "Beyond Temple Mount there are seven mountains in total. But Scopus, Temple Mount, Government House, and Ammunition are the most important."

"I agree," Marcus said with a somber tone. "Control any three of these hills and you can just about control the entire city."

"Yes," Dostrovsky nodded. "You are correct."

Marcus looked back to the west, in the direction of Tel Aviv, and scanned the horizon. After a moment he pointed in that direction and asked, "What is that hill back there in the distance?"

"Latrun. There's a British garrison there."

"They still man it?"

"They do for now," Dostrovsky replied.

Marcus studied it a moment, "That one is first on the list. We have to get control of it as soon as the British are gone. It's the key to controlling the road to Tel Aviv. If we can't control Latrun hill, we'll have a tough time stopping an Arab advance from Jerusalem before it reaches Tel Aviv."

"I've told Ben-Gurion the same thing a dozen times," Dostrovsky said with a satisfied expression.

When Marcus and Dostrovsky returned to Tel Aviv they made their way to Haganah headquarters. "Do you have a map room?" Marcus asked.

"Of sorts," Dostrovsky said. "It's back here." He led the way through the building to a room in back. A large table occupied the center of the room and on it lay several maps. Dostrovsky pointed to one on top. "This is the best we have of the region." He turned it for Marcus to see. "Our major units are positioned here and here," he said, indicating.

"I suggest we reposition some closer to Latrun, to be ready when the British leave."

"I'm not sure we can relocate the units already in the field," Dostrovsky replied. "I think they're needed where they are, but we can call up more men from the area."

Marcus frowned. "A draft?"

"No. Activate men already in Haganah but not deployed," Dostrovsky explained. "They all have jobs and work every day, but they also are Haganah members. We can bring them in for duty anytime we need them."

"That might be a good idea," Marcus noted. "Get them organized and ready to deploy. Do you have organizational charts for your units?"

"Nothing in print. But I would be happy to sketch it for you." He found a note pad and sketched a rough schematic of the units. "Few of these are standing units," he added as he wrote. "They exist only in theory."

"In theory," Marcus mused.

"We are not like the US Army," Dostrovsky noted. "We do not have a large standing military."

"What about training? Do you have a training schedule?"

"No. Not really." Dostrovsky laid aside the pen he'd been using. "Our men are good at figuring things out as they go. As I said, other than the units we've deployed, Haganah members all have regular jobs. They aren't paid to serve in the military and most of their time is spent earning a living. Any training time they might have is usually spent practicing the next operation."

Marcus scratched his head. This was even worse than he'd thought. "We need to work on organization and training. I know it sounds tedious, especially when you're used to working on a tight budget and—"

"A nonexistent budget most times," Dostrovsky interrupted.

"Right," Marcus nodded. "I understand. But even so, there is a direct correlation between training time and performance in the field. And we're not just creating a force for the coming war with the Arabs. We're laying the groundwork for a permanent military, so we need to get the basics in place from the beginning. Give it a solid footing that can sustain a defense force for years to come."

"I know we need that," Dostrovsky admitted. "We just haven't had the time to devote to that sort of thing or the money to follow through with it."

"Well," Marcus said in a sympathetic tone, "we'll get to it now. This is what I've been doing for the US Army since the day I enlisted."

CHAPTER 39

THE VOLUNTEERS

By the following February, Collins was well enough from injuries received in the plane crash to return to work at his office, albeit on a limited basis. Most days, he was at his desk by ten and gone before five. But at least he was working, which made him feel useful again after weeks in the hospital and months of lying around the apartment. And he still wanted to travel with Schwimmer when he and the others left for Palestine, though arguments with Olivia over the topic made him reluctant to discuss it further. They'd come to a truce on the matter—he didn't bring it up and she didn't yell at him—but they both knew, lingering effects of the injuries or not, he wanted to go.

A few weeks after returning to work, Schwimmer arrived in New York and came by Collins' office. The visit was unannounced and Collins was surprised to see him.

"We've moved the remaining airplanes to an airport in New Jersey," Schwimmer explained.

"We haven't talked much since the crash. What planes are left?"

"One of the Constellations is working in Panama. The other one is up here along with the seven bombers. We moved all of those out here."

"Too expensive to keep them in California?"

"Yeah," Schwimmer nodded. "And they were getting too much attention. Too many people asking about them. Made me nervous."

"Still getting them ready?"

"The bombers needed a lot more work than we planned. The C-46s were in good enough shape to make the move to Panama and we sent them on to Palestine a few weeks ago. But the bombers needed a lot of attention."

"Have any trouble ferrying them back here?"

"No." Schwimmer's face brightened. "Want to see what they look like?"

"Sure, when can we go?"

"How about now?" Schwimmer replied.

Collins and Schwimmer left the office that afternoon and rode down to an airport in Millville, New Jersey, where the planes were parked. They left the car at the hangar and walked out to the apron of the runway. Seven B-17s stood in a row, wingtip to wingtip. Collins and Schwimmer walked among them.

"They look good," Collins said.

"The outside is perfect," Schwimmer commented. "Still have some electronics to repair on two of them. Waiting on gauges for the others."

"This took a lot of work. I remember what they looked like before."

"Not exactly a restoration, but they're in pretty good shape." They were silent for a moment, then Schwimmer said, "When we were in Mexico you asked me about going to Palestine with us. Still interested?"

"Yes, I am."

"We may have to leave soon. With the British pulling out in May, the planes need to be in place and ready to go. But that crash set us back."

"I'm sorry about Ribakoff and the others."

"Yeah," Schwimmer replied. "Me too."

"When do you think you'll leave?"

"We plan to start in April. That will give us about four weeks to make the trip."

"Will it take that long?"

"I don't know, but we want to arrive there by mid-May and I don't want any more delays. We'll have to fly the planes to Panama. We can fly straight through now. Then hop our way overland into South America.

That's two days. Cross over to Africa from there and fly toward Egypt. That'll take at least two more days."

"That's the shortest route?"

"It's the safest route," Schwimmer chuckled. "You never know what will happen with these planes. They look good but they have a lot of years and a lot of flying time behind them. Most of them were shot up pretty bad from the war. So no matter how much work you do on them, you never know what's going to happen."

"Better to go down on land than to ditch into the ocean."

"Something like that." Schwimmer looked over at him. "If you want to go with us, you'll need to fly out with us when we leave. I don't think you'll be able to get into Palestine any other way. And there's one more thing."

"What's that?"

"Taking these things out of the country . . . might not be legal now."

"They're registered in Panama."

"I know, but you were right about the FBI coming after us. They've been asking questions already."

"No one told me."

"They didn't do anything. They just asked questions."

Both men stared up at the planes in silence, then Collins said, "If I went with you, what would I do?"

"Well," Schwimmer said slowly, "the Constellations will be used for hauling troops and cargo. You could work on one of them. Or you could fly in one of the bombers."

"What would I do in a bomber?"

"Somebody has to drop the bombs," Schwimmer said with a hint of ironic humor. "We don't have any experienced bombardiers. All of our guys are either pilots, engineers, or ground crew by training. You could do it as well as any of them."

"You really think I could do that?"

"Sure," Schwimmer said confidently. "The planes don't have bombsights, so we're dropping them a different way. It's not very complicated."

Collins had a questioning look. "What other way is there?"

"Manually. Sight them by eye. Press a button to drop them."

"Dead reckoning."

"Yeah," Schwimmer laughed. "See. You're already into the lingo. We have a German bombsight coming but we could only locate one and there's no way of knowing when it will arrive. And we don't know if it'll be useable with these planes. So we plan to release most of the bombs manually."

"You can drop the bombs without the sight?"

"Allies did it all the time during the war," Schwimmer explained. "In fact, they pretty much didn't use the sights after the first few sorties. Pinpoint accuracy proved ineffective from high altitude, especially for ships at sea. So they switched to dive-bombing for attacks on ships and lead bombing on land."

Collins looked puzzled. "Lead bombing?"

"First plane—the lead plane—flies in, gets close to the target. Drops the bombs. Sometimes using the sight, sometimes not. Then the other planes come behind that lead plane and bomb whatever targets the lead plane missed. Very effective." He looked over at Collins. "You could be the bombardier."

"What would I do? I mean, what kind of duties are there?"

"Arm the bombs. Press a switch to open the bomb bay doors. Press another to release the bombs from the racks."

"How would I know when to do that?"

"You could fly with me," Schwimmer grinned. "I'll tell you when to let them go."

"Okay," Collins said cautiously. "Can you walk me through the process before we actually go out to bomb something?"

"Yes," Schwimmer laughed. "I can walk you through it."

✡

During the first week in April, Schwimmer came to Collins. "We're leaving the day after tomorrow. You still going with us?"

Collins was caught off guard by the immediacy of the departure but said, "Yes. Has something happened?"

"I'm worried about time," Schwimmer explained. "We have to be in Tel Aviv, ready to go, when the British leave next month. I want to make sure we're there."

"But if we arrive too early, won't they seize the planes?"

"We can adjust the schedule along the way. Are you going with us?"

"Yes, I'm going. Should I meet you at the airport or somewhere else?"

"Meet us at the airport. Five thirty in the morning. Day after tomorrow."

Collins went home earlier than usual that day. Olivia was surprised but glad to see him. They embraced at the doorway, then he led her toward the living room. "Come on, we need to talk."

"What's the matter?" He didn't respond but tucked her arm in his and escorted her to the sofa. When they were seated she looked over at him. "Are you feeling well?"

"I'm fine."

"This is not like you. What's going on?" Her eyes were wide and she stared directly at him as if studying his face. "You're making me nervous."

Collins placed his arm across her shoulder. "Al Schwimmer came by the office today."

Olivia's countenance dropped. "Oh. I didn't realize he was in town. What did he want?"

From the tone of her voice, Collins was sure she already knew the answer to the question.

"They have to get the remaining airplanes out now."

"I see." Olivia looked worried and sad. "And you still want to go with them."

"I don't like the idea of being away from you and the children," Collins explained, "but this is something I need to do. I need to stand with Israel. With Schwimmer. With the Jews."

"Israel?" She looked perplexed. "They're calling it that now?"

"No one has said what they'll call the new state, but I don't see how they could call it anything else."

"I suppose you're right," she sighed. "How long will you be gone?"

"I don't know," he shrugged. "Maybe a year."

Her eyes were even wider. "A year?"

"I would be gone several months even if I just flew over and tried to come right back. Air service is sporadic right now and from what I hear, ocean travel is as well."

"What will you be doing for a year?"

"Flying."

In spite of the seriousness of the moment and her obvious frustration, an amused grin spread over her face. "You're going to fly an airplane?"

"No." Collins avoided the temptation to feel hurt by her derisive tone and responded in a calm manner. "I'll be part of a crew. Schwimmer thinks I could be a bombardier. Sounds rather simple. Arm the bombs. Open the doors. Press a button and drop them."

"Simple," she replied with a hint of condescension. "But people will die as a result of it."

For the first time Collins realized the consequences of what he planned to do. Most of the time he thought only of the time away from his family or worried about whether he'd be able to do a good job. Now, sitting with Olivia on the sofa, the moment seemed more real than he'd expected. He looked down at his hands and realized that one day in the very near future those fingers would press a button that dropped explosives on living humans.

After a moment, he pushed the thought from his mind. "Well," he sighed, "it has to be done. There is no other way. It's either fight or die for the Jews of Palestine, and however uncomfortable I am with that, I have to be a part of it."

She took his hand in hers. "When will you leave?"

"Day after tomorrow."

"So soon?"

"Yes. Schwimmer's worried the planes won't reach Tel Aviv on time if we don't move them now."

"You have to tell the children."

"I know."

"Tonight," she insisted.

"Yes," he agreed. "I'll tell them after dinner."

Two days later, Olivia drove Collins to the airport in Millville, New Jersey. As they approached the hangar, the Constellation and seven bombers parked on the tarmac came into view.

"Those are the planes?"

"Yes."

"They look rather large."

"They *are* rather large. The bigger one is a Constellation. Same kind of plane commercial airlines use for passenger service. The others are B-17s."

"I didn't realize you were talking about that kind of plane. I thought they'd be . . . smaller."

Olivia parked the car behind the hangar, then she and Collins said good-bye. He kissed her as he stepped out, then walked around to the driver's side, leaned through the open window, and kissed her again. "See you later," he said, forcing a smile.

"Don't be gone long," she replied as tears rolled down her cheeks.

"I'll be back," he whispered.

Collins watched as she drove away, then entered the hangar, where he found Schwimmer waiting with the crews for the other airplanes. They greeted each other and talked a moment, then Schwimmer said, "Let's get going. We have a long flight ahead of us and standing around here won't make it any shorter."

As they came from the hangar a black car rolled to a stop ahead of them near the planes. Two men dressed in gray suits got out. Schwimmer gestured for the others to continue and walked over to them while the crews moved past. Collins lingered behind with Schwimmer.

The men from the black car flashed badges identifying themselves as US Treasury agents. "Mr. Schwimmer," the first agent said, "I'm afraid those airplanes can't leave."

"Why not?"

"We have reports that they are carrying contraband."

Collins stepped forward. "Do you have a warrant of some kind?"

"Who are you?"

"I am Mr. Schwimmer's attorney."

"Then you know you can't move these airplanes without our approval," the second agent offered.

"I know these are privately owned aircraft," Collins bumped Schwimmer lightly on the hip with his fist, hoping he would take the hint to get moving. "These aircraft are registered in Panama. They're owned by a company doing business in Panama." He bumped Schwimmer once more on the hip, this time a little harder, and nodded toward the planes. "They are duly licensed and marked on the vertical stabilizer according to regulations." Finally Schwimmer took the cue and drifted away, gradually picking up his pace as he moved toward a B-17 parked nearby. "As foreign registered aircraft," Collins continued, "the Treasury Department has no authority over them."

"I think the Civil Aeronautics Board might dispute that interpretation," the second agent suggested.

"They're not subject to CAB regulations," Collins countered. "And besides, CAB and Treasury are separate agencies."

"We'll see about that," the first agent added.

"No," Collins argued. "We won't."

The second agent looked puzzled. "What do you mean?"

"I'm not sure you two are agents for anyone. Let me see your identification again."

The first agent scowled angrily. "I don't have to show you—" Suddenly his voice was drowned out by the roar of the B-17s as Schwimmer and the others started their engines. The first agent was still shouting, but Collins couldn't hear him and instead of sticking around to figure it out, he started toward the airplane Schwimmer was piloting.

Agents trailed behind him, but as Collins reached the tip of the airplane's wing, the agent stopped. Collins continued on, ducked beneath the fuselage, and hauled himself up through the access hatch in the belly. When he was inside, someone closed the hatch cover and the plane started forward.

Collins stumbled to the cockpit bulkhead and flopped down on a jump seat. Schwimmer leaned around from the pilot's seat. "Good job!" he shouted. Steve Schwartz, the copilot, added a thumbs-up gesture.

"I'm not even sure they're government agents," Collins replied.

"We'll know in a minute."

"How's that?"

"If they're actually agents," Schwimmer said, "they'll call the tower and tell them not to let us take off."

By then the Constellation was rolling down the runway. Collins watched out the window as it took off, then the other B-17s followed close behind. From the cockpit he heard the garbled sound of radio traffic, then the plane lurched forward, rolled quickly down the runway, and leapt into the sky. Moments later, New York City appeared in the distance out the left window and on the right, through the window next to Collins, Philadelphia came into view. Collins watched and wondered when he would see either of them again.

CHAPTER 40

THE VOLUNTEERS

From the airport in New Jersey, Collins and Schwimmer flew with the others to Mexico City. As they circled the airport for landing, Collins looked down at the site where they crashed on the earlier flight. The wreckage was long since removed but one side of the ravine still was charred black from the fire. Memories of that day flashed through his mind but Collins refused to dwell on them and they quickly faded away.

When they landed, ground crewmen came from a hangar with trucks and a forklift. While Collins and the others ate lunch, crewmen loaded the Constellation with crates. Even from a distance, Collins could see the crates were labeled as cornflakes and other household goods.

"We're taking food?"

"Something like that," Schwimmer answered with a knowing look.

It was the middle of the afternoon when they finished eating and Schwimmer led the way from the terminal back to the airplanes. "Sure we can find the airport in Panama at night?" Collins asked.

"It has a tower and runway lights," Schwimmer said. "Someone is there all night. We should be fine."

"And if not?"

"We need to travel as quickly as possible," Schwimmer explained. "They need us in Tel Aviv by the time the British withdraw. An extra day here will delay us by two or three farther on. We have to keep moving."

Collins, Schwimmer, and the other crewmen of the B-17 continued across the tarmac, and everyone crawled in through the airplane's belly hatch. Collins took his place on the jump seat behind the cockpit bulkhead and fastened his seat belt.

Minutes later, he watched out the window as up ahead of them the Constellation led the group down the taxiway and turned onto the runway. Without stopping, its engines revved to full throttle and the plane rolled forward. Even with an inexperienced eye, Collis could see it was heavy—too heavy—and he wondered again what really was in the crates that the ground crew loaded.

The engines worked hard to bring the Constellation up to speed and as the seconds ticked by it drew nearer and nearer the end of the runway. Collins was certain the plane would crash but at the last moment, the flaps came down and the plane rose slowly into the air.

From his seat up front in the B-17, Schwimmer glanced back and grinned. "Remember that?"

"All too well." Collins turned back to look out the window once more. "All too well."

When they arrived in Panama, Collins noticed the one remaining Constellation was at the airport. "How's that one holding up?" he asked, pointing to the airplane.

"It's doing well for what it is. Running a commercial route from Panama to Nicaragua. Half seats, half cargo."

"Are we taking it with us?"

"Not this time. Maybe later. We had no choice but to put it in regular service. We gained access to this airport on the premise that we were operating a commercial airline. To keep that cover, we had to actually offer the service."

Collins and Schwimmer planned to remain in Panama only a few days to make final preparations with the B-17s, but a problem with one of the engines required more extensive repairs than they first assumed. Rather than leave the plane behind to fly alone, the entire group remained until the mechanics finished their work. That took much longer than expected.

The group finally departed Panama early the second week of May and flew to Natal, Brazil, on the eastern tip of South America. After spending the night, they left at sunrise the following day and flew across the Atlantic to Dakar, Senegal, the nearest serviceable airport on the westernmost tip of Africa—making the flight over the ocean as short as possible. After a day's layover due to weather, they few north to Morocco, where they refueled for the final leg of their journey.

Late in the afternoon on May 15, 1948, Collins and Schwimmer arrived with the aircraft at Sde Dov Field, outside Tel Aviv. They taxied to a stop in front of the airport's lone hangar, and the ground crew came out to meet the planes.

As the engines slowed to a stop, Collins unbuckled his safety belt and waited as the crew climbed from the plane. When it was his turn, Collins crawled to the hatch and lowered himself down to the pavement. He was immediately met by a warm, balmy breeze—not unlike California but much more humid.

Collins stepped from beneath the plane and paused to turn slowly in a circle, taking in the view. The runway ran north and south, hardly a stone's throw from the beach. The Mediterranean lay just a short walk away and he could smell the salt in the air. To the east there was only the flat coastal plain of Palestine. At a distance it looked like barren desert, but the tropical climate seemed to suggest otherwise, and as he focused on the foreground Collins saw palm trees and swaths of green vegetation not far from the edge of the tarmac.

Just then Schwimmer moved past and gave him a nudge. "Come on," he said. "We still have things to do."

Across the way, forklifts arrived at the Constellation and workmen began unloading the crates. By then Collins was certain they contained munitions and once again the true nature of what they were doing was suddenly starkly real. This was a country at war, struggling for freedom, struggling to survive, and he was in the middle of it.

Collins followed Schwimmer and the flight crew toward a low

one-story building that stood next to the hangar. Inside, they found a ready room manned by Haganah officers and members. Maps of the region covered the walls, and opposite the door was a chalkboard. A list of names was written on one side. The center of the board was clean.

Other pilots already were there, including Glen King, Eddie Cohen, and Bill Gerson—all of them from the United States, most from New York, New Jersey, and California. As former US Air Force pilots, they had many hours of combat duty flying missions during World War II.

Everyone was in a festive mood and when Collins and Schwimmer asked why, they learned that David Ben-Gurion and leaders from the provisional Jewish government had issued a declaration of independence. The region no longer would be known as Palestine. From now on, areas under Jewish control would be known as the State of Israel.

Schwimmer and Collins visited with the group for a while, getting acquainted and sharing the latest news from home, then Glen King took them over to a barracks building behind the hangar. While Collins stored his gear in a footlocker, Schwimmer dropped his bags on a nearby bunk and headed off to find Yisrael Amir, a Haganah colonel with whom he'd served in the past and the commander of what was now the Israeli Air Force. Collins stayed behind to finish unpacking.

When he'd stowed his meager belongings and had things squared away, Collins lay on the cot and thought of all that had happened in the past few weeks. Before long, his mind turned to Olivia and the children and he calculated the time difference in his head. It was five in the afternoon in Tel Aviv. *With a seven-hour time difference, it must be ten in the morning back in New York.* The children would be in school. Olivia would be alone at the apartment and in his mind he saw her seated at her dressing table, combing her hair. The scent of her perfume filled his mind and he remembered the smooth feel of her neck against his lips.

"I shouldn't think of this," he whispered allowed. "This will only make me want to go home." He turned on his side and closed his eyes, then did his best to think of nothing at all and before long he was sound asleep.

A short while later, Collins was awakened by Schwimmer shaking his foot. “Come on. We should get you oriented to the plane. I’ve been talking to Amir. This thing could escalate more rapidly than any of us previously thought.”

Collins rubbed his hands over his face as he rolled to a sitting position on the edge of the bed. “I heard the fighting has already started in some places.”

“It’s started just about everywhere,” Schwimmer said with a note of urgency. “And right now our troops on the ground are having a tough time of it. Egyptian soldiers are crossing the border and we’ve been unable to do more than slow their advance.”

Collins pulled on his boots and followed Schwimmer out the door. Moments later, they reached the bomber and climbed inside. “You can sit on the jump seat when we take off,” Schwimmer said, pointing to the seat Collins used for the flight over.

“Where will I be after that?”

“Once we’re in the air, you’ll come back here.” Schwimmer pointed to the bomb racks near the center of the plane. “This is where you’ll arm the bombs.”

“How do I do that?”

“I’ll show you the bombs when we get through in here. As you can see, the plane has two racks. We’ll carry eight bombs on each rack for most of our runs.” He gestured to the space around them. “This area back here is called the bomb bay, and the bomb bay doors are beneath the rack.” He pointed to the floor. “Those doors open and the bombs fall through to the ground. Before you drop the bombs, you have to open the doors. We’ve rigged a button at your seat that does that. Not exactly standard equipment, but we’re doing the best we can.”

“Will the bombs release if the doors aren’t open?”

“No.”

Collins glanced back to the jump seat behind the bulkhead. “I didn’t see a button for any of it back there where I was sitting.”

"That's not where you'll be seated for the mission. I'll show you in a minute. For now just know, there's a green button at your seat," Schwimmer said again. "Press it and the bomb bay doors will open. If they don't open, there's a hand crank to do it manually."

"How will I know if the doors are open?"

"There's an indicator light at your seat that tells you."

"Okay," Collins said.

"So," Schwimmer continued, reviewing the procedure. "Get on the plane, strap into that seat." He pointed to the jump seat. "We take off. Once you feel the wheels come up, get out of that seat and arm the bombs. Then you come up here." Schwimmer led the way to the flight deck. When he reached the pilot's seat he stepped aside and pointed to a narrow passage beneath the flight deck. "That's your seat in there for the bombing run. The bombardier's seat."

Collins stooped to look inside and glanced around. The nose of the plane was made of clear Plexiglas that surrounded the bombardier's seat on three sides, affording a wide view of almost everything. Dials, gauges, and switches covered a panel to the left and right and there were hand controls at the ends of the armrests. Collins struggled to take it all in.

"Crawl in there and have a look," Schwimmer urged. "You have to get started sometime. Might as well be now."

With tentative steps, Collins crawled into the passage and made his way to the nose of the plane, then squeezed between the instrument panel and dropped onto the seat. Schwimmer knelt behind him and spoke through the opening from the flight deck. "Once you've armed the bombs, you'll come up here and get in that seat. We'll be airborne. It'll look creepy at first, seeing everything rush toward you, but you'll get used to the view."

Collins glanced back at him. "It looks creepy now just looking out on the runway."

"I know. Everybody has that reaction the first time." Schwimmer pointed past him and continued the explanation. "The green button on your left opens the bomb bay doors. The lights above it indicate whether the doors are open or not. Red means they're closed. Yellow, they're moving. Green, they're open." Collins nodded in response. Schwimmer continued. "On the right side there's a red button. That's the button to drop the bombs. Same lights above the switch. Red, yellow, green. Red means they're loaded and ready. Green means they're all away and the bomb racks are empty."

"And yellow?"

"That's a problem."

Collins' eyes grew wider. "What do you mean?"

"Sometimes a bomb gets hung in the rack. It doesn't happen often but sometimes it does."

"What do we do then?"

"Don't worry about that now."

Collins noticed empty brackets in front of the seat. "What's this for?" he asked, pointing.

"The bombsight would go there but as you can see, we don't have one. When we get to the drop zone I'll tell you when to drop the bombs."

"Okay," Collins said after a moment. "I think I understand the process so far. What about arming the bombs?"

"Come on, I'll show you. Nothing to it."

Collins turned to climb from the seat, then hesitated when he noticed twin machine guns at the bottom of the Plexiglas nose. "Who operates the guns?"

"Normally, the bombardier," Schwimmer answered. "Controls near the seat operate them, but for now we're going to ignore that and let the other gunners take care of things. Maybe after a few flights we'll show you what to do. Come on. I'll show you the bombs." Schwimmer backed away from the flight deck while Collins crawled out of the bombardier's seat.

Schwimmer and Collins walked from the plane to the hangar and continued to a room in back where they found rows of bombs stacked on rolling dollies, four bombs to each dolly. A thin red streamer dangled from the nose of each. Schwimmer said, "We don't have very many of these right now. More are on the way. That's one of the reasons for having the C-46s over here—and now the Constellation. They're leaving tomorrow to bring back munitions and supplies."

"We aren't going?"

"No. You and I are staying here with the others. They'll likely need us in a B-17 to support the troops in Gaza." Schwimmer stepped to a dolly and pointed to the red streamers. "These red flags are attached to a pin that runs through the end of the fuse. To arm the bomb, you simply pull the pin out and give the fuse a turn."

Collins studied the device. "Looks like a big nut."

"It is, sort of. They're screwed into the end of the bomb."

"All I have to do is pull it and tighten the nut?"

"Yes. Grab it, pull it, give it a turn."

"Sounds easy enough."

"So, after we're in the air you'll go back to the bomb rack and pull the pins out of all the bombs," Schwimmer explained. "Hold on to the pins as you pull them. Count the pins in your hand before you return to your seat. Make sure you have a pin for each bomb. Sixteen on most of the runs. If you have the pins in your hand, and tightened the fuse, the bombs will be armed. We can't afford to drop one that won't explode."

"When I pull that pin, it's armed?"

"Yes. But you need to turn the fuse to make sure it explodes properly. We'll be dropping them from a low altitude."

"And they'll explode when they hit the ground."

"Right," Schwimmer said. "The bombs fall nose first. The concussion of the nose striking the ground sets it off. The pin keeps that from happening before we're ready. Pull the pin, it'll explode when it hits. Got it?"

"Yes," Collins replied.

Schwimmer patted him on the back. "It'll be easy. You'll see. Not much to it."

Collins stared at the bombs, thinking again, as he had when he discussed his involvement with Olivia, that they would kill people. He looked down at his fingers. *His* fingers would cause it to happen. After a moment he looked over at Schwimmer and quietly asked, "Why are you doing this?"

Schwimmer seemed puzzled. "Why am I fighting?"

"No. Why are you allowing me to fly as bombardier?"

"You wanted to."

"I know," Collins said. "But why did you say yes? Don't you have more experienced people to do it?"

Schwimmer looked away. "Not really." Then he looked back at Collins. "Listen, we have pilots. And we have a few men who can handle the machine guns. A few, but not many. The pilots are just enough to fly the planes we have. And the experienced gunners give us one or two per plane. They've been showing the others how to use the guns just like I'm showing you about the bombs, but we're thin at every position. And that's our air force right now. Experienced pilots, inexperienced crewmen." He pointed through the hangar to ground crews servicing the planes. "The mechanics flew over from New Jersey a couple of weeks ago. All of them are volunteers from the U.S., just like us. Half of them aren't even Jewish, just like you. Most of them worked as mechanics of some sort back home but not many are certified airplane mechanics. They were willing. Others weren't. The willing ones came, the unwilling stayed behind. We're making do with what we have." Schwimmer grinned at Collins. "So, to answer your question, I'm letting you fly as bombardier because you're the most qualified man in our crew to do it." He grabbed Collins in a headlock and playfully pulled him forward. "Come on," he laughed. "Enough of these questions. Let's find something to eat. I'm hungry."

CHAPTER 41

THE VOLUNTEERS

Early one morning a few days later, Collins was awakened in his bunk by Schwimmer. "Come on," he said with a shake of Collins' foot. "We have to go."

"Go?" Collins rubbed his eyes. "Go where?"

"Our first mission. Let's go. We have to hurry."

Collins swung his feet to the floor and sat on the edge of the bed. "Don't we have an alarm or something for that?"

"This is your alarm." Schwimmer raised his voice. "Let's go!"

Collins, still groggy and reluctant, rose from the bed, pulled on his flight suit, shoved his feet in his boots, and stumbled from the barracks. As he moved across the tarmac toward the plane he noticed the eastern sky was just turning gray. Waves of panic swept over him and the reality of what he was about to do landed on him again, this time with even greater weight than before. He was flying a combat mission. His first. A mission to kill people. A mission that could kill him as well. *It's not even sunup,* he thought. *I could be dead before lunch. What am I doing here?*

When he reached the B-17 the props were already turning. He pulled himself up through the belly hatch and glanced around. The rest of the aircrew was in place, prepared for takeoff. Matt, the flight engineer, looked at him with an amused grin. "Sorry to interrupt your beauty rest."

"Yeah," Collins replied as he collapsed onto the jump seat. "I needed a little more of it."

A headset hung from a bulkhead bolt to the right. Collins took it down and slipped the set over his head, then adjusted it in place. As he tightened the strap, Schwimmer moved past on his way to the flight deck and paused at Collins' side. "Remember what I told you," he said. "When we're in the air, arm the bombs and move to the bombardier's seat. I'll tell you when we're near the site. Open the doors. Drop the bombs when I tell you. Two other planes are going with us. They'll follow our lead and clean up whatever we miss."

"Where are we going?"

"Those Egyptian troops we talked about are being led by a group of tanks. They're advancing north at a rapid pace. We have to stop them before they get here."

"Is that really what these planes were designed to do?"

"Not really, but we don't have any choice. The tanks have to be stopped and we're the best option at hand for the job. So strap in and get ready. We have to go."

Schwimmer climbed up to the flight deck and crawled into the left seat. After fastening his seat belt, he slipped on a headset, then glanced over at Steve Schwartz, the copilot. "Everyone on board?"

"Yes, sir, we're present and ready."

Schwimmer released the brake and the airplane rolled forward. They taxied toward the end of the field, then turned at the last crossover and moved onto the runway. Instantly, the engines roared to full throttle and moments later they were airborne. As the landing gear came up, Schwimmer called back to Collins on the intercom, "Okay, arm the bombs. Do it fast, we don't have far to go."

Collins came from his seat and climbed back to the bomb racks. Working quickly, he snatched the pins from the bombs and gave the fuses a twist. Then he counted to make sure he had the correct number of pins in his hand before making his way beneath the flight deck to the bombardier's seat.

The Plexiglas nose of the plane offered a panoramic view of the terrain below and the sky above. Off to the right, he saw the Mediterranean with its blue-green water lapping against the sandy beach. At once his mind returned to summers at Rockaway Beach, laughing and playing with his children when they were four and five. The thought of them laughing and giggling in the sun made him smile and then a sense of sadness swept over him as he remembered how far away they were now and how long it would be before he saw them again. *Maybe this isn't my place. Maybe I should have talked to Olivia more before I got into this. Maybe I should have said no.*

Schwimmer's voice on the intercom brought him back to the moment. "Open the bomb bay doors," he ordered in a clipped, official tone.

Collins pressed the green button to his left and glanced up at the indicator lights. The red light turned yellow and he heard the electric motors whine as the doors opened. Cold air rushed through the plane and the green light came on. "Bomb bay doors are open and ready," he spoke through the headset.

A check of the lights to the right showed the bombs were loaded in the racks and ready. The only thing left was to press the red button and drop the bombs. He slid his hand to that side and propped his wrist in a comfortable position, ready to go, then settled in place for the ride. Contrary to what he'd expected, the view was magnificent and although he felt nervous, he wasn't scared. *This might not be so bad after all,* he thought. *I could be back in New York telling war stories before they even realize I've been gone.*

A few minutes later, the column of tanks came into sight. Seconds later, three black objects appeared high in the southern sky. Schwimmer called over the intercom, "Bandits at twelve o'clock."

Someone asked, "How many?"

"Three."

The top gunner responded, "I see them."

Schwimmer called down to Collins, "Get ready to drop."

Machine-gun fire opened from overhead. Collins heard the burst from the muzzle and the clank of brass casings hitting the floor of the top turret. Then the plane's nose dropped and they descended into the bombing run. His chest dropped into his stomach, and every muscle in his body tensed. He hadn't expected this. Maybe he should have stayed in New York after all.

The plane whined as it picked up speed and moments later it began to shake. Behind him, Collins heard the engines increase in speed and the sound of gunfire intensified as the waste gunners opened up. Out the nose of the plane, he watched with ever-widening eyes as the ground rush toward him. A wave of nausea swept over him and he concentrated hard to keep from vomiting.

Near his feet, a dirty, well-worn pencil rolled from beneath the seat frame and as the plane continued to dive, the pencil rose on one end. Collins had never seen that before and he rubbed his eyes in disbelief. Still the plane kept falling and his back pressed against the seat. Disoriented and nauseated, he was certain he would pass out.

Then Schwimmer's voice sounded in his headset. "Now! Now! Now!" The sound of it jerked Collins back to the moment. His arm was pinned to the armrest by the force of the dive but he managed to somehow lift a finger high enough to press the red button. From behind, he heard a clattering sound as the bombs released from the racks. The indicator light glowed green and an instant later they pulled from the dive and the plane began to climb.

Down below there was a rumble and Collins glanced in that direction to see clouds of smoke rising from the ground as the bombs exploded. But seeing the ground move away as the plane climbed higher only intensified the nausea. Then they banked and that made it even worse. He closed his eyes to concentrate while machine-gun fire burst again from the top turret.

Someone shouted over the intercom, "Cohen's hit."

Collins' eyes popped open and he looked to the left. He saw nothing in that direction but as he turned to the right he saw smoke gushing from an engine on Cohen's B-17.

Schwimmer called over the intercom, "Do you see any chutes from Cohen's plane?"

"No," Collins replied. "Not a one."

More gunfire erupted and the plane shook violently, then a voice on the intercom shouted, "We're hit, too."

Collins was terrified and the thought of being in that seat, staring out the glass nose of the plane as a fighter came toward them, was more than he could bear. With a flick of the center latch he unbuckled his seat belt, climbed from the bombardier's seat, and crawled back through the passage, then scampered to the jump seat behind the bulkhead and fastened the seat belt.

When he was strapped in place, he leaned over to look out the window and saw smoke and fire coming from an engine on the right side. Memories of the crash in Mexico City flooded his mind and he had a bitter taste in his mouth from a rush of adrenalin. Now he was more nauseous than ever and vomit rose into his mouth. He clamped his lips shut and forced himself to relax, then swallowed hard. The burning sensation in his throat brought tears to his eyes but he wiped them away and continued to watch out the window.

As he did, he thought again of Olivia, his children, and home. He prayed for peace and strength to face whatever happened next, then he prayed for the engine to stop burning and for them to make it safely back to Tel Aviv. Then he prayed some more.

On the flight deck, Schwimmer and the copilot worked frantically to maintain control of the engine fire. All the while, gunfire burst from the plane's turrets. The sound of it and the rattle of empty casings joined with the engine noise in a discordant cacophony that only heightened Collins' sense of confusion and panic. He was sure they all were going to die and the thought of doing so in the scorching heat of a crash filled him with despair.

Just when their situation seemed hopeless, he glanced to the left and saw a fighter roll over, smoke trailing from it, and then plunge toward the ground. Another streaked past them, missing a wing tip by only a few feet. At the same time, the flames on the outboard engine went out and the smoke dissipated. The gunner in the top turret called over the intercom, "We got two. That's the last of them. The other one bugged out."

A sense of relief swept over the plane and Collins felt ashamed of the fear that just minutes earlier had all but overpowered him. Slowly, the noise of battle dissipated, replaced by the steady hum of the three remaining engines as they worked harder than ever to keep the plane aloft. Collins sat quietly watching out the window as the ground beneath them gradually came closer and closer. The belly gunner must have noticed it, too, and called over the intercom, "Are we gonna make it?"

"Barely," Schwimmer reported. "Get out of the turret."

A moment later, the gunner from the belly turret and took a seat across from Collins. Their eyes met and the gunner asked with a smile, "You okay, pal?"

"Yeah," Collins said. "Why?"

"You look white as a ghost."

"I'm fine."

Schwimmer glanced back at him with a playful grin. "Collins, are you sick?"

"Not now."

Everyone burst into laughter and the belly gunner slapped Collins on the back. "Welcome to the crew," he howled. "You are now officially one of us." Collins grinned. No one had ever said anything like that to him before and he liked the sound of it. The gunner reached over once more and touched Collins' shirt. "You ain't wet, though. Where'd you puke?"

"I swallowed it," Collins said meekly.

"Ha!" The gunner laughed and called to the others, "Did you hear that? He swallowed his puke." Everyone laughed again and the gunner gave Collins a nudge on the shoulder. "I tried that my first time, but I couldn't do it. After that I just left it all right there in the bottom of the turret. Let the ground crew deal with it."

Collins had a puzzled frown. "You vomited in the turret your first time?"

"First time?" the gunner said with ironic humor. "Just about every time. You sit down there you get bounced up and down like riding a seesaw. No way you can hold your cookies through that." Then just as suddenly, his face turned somber. "But I'd rather be down there than up front where you are. Takes a special kind to see what's coming, fight through the panic, and still take care of business." He gave Collins a knowing look. "Good job."

Collins' eyes filled with tears once again. This time not from the burning sensation in his throat but from the sense that he'd finally made it. The comradery, the esprit, the sense of purpose he'd been seeking all his life—he finally found it in a B-17, limping along over Palestine.

"All right," Schwimmer called as he adjusted the wing flaps. "Everyone get ready. This is gonna be close."

From beneath them Collins heard the whine of electric motors and the swish of hydraulic pumps as the landing gear came down. Out the window, he saw a row of trees pass just below the wing. A building seemed to glide by just feet beneath the plane's wheels, followed by another, and another. Power lines reached up to grab them, just missing by inches. Then the power on the engines dropped and before Collins could figure out why, they settled onto the end of the runway. Everyone shouted and cheered.

A few minutes later, the plane taxied to a stop in front of the hangar. Collins climbed from his seat, pushed open the hatch, and dropped down to the tarmac. As he staggered from beneath the plane, he opened the front of his flight suit and felt the cool air against his damp skin.

Halfway across the airport apron, Schwimmer appeared at his side. Collins looked over at him. "Do you think Cohen and the others got out?"

"I don't know, but I wouldn't think about it too much. We have many more missions to fly and you can't be worrying about what might happen. You have to concentrate on the job. Speaking of which," Schwimmer said as he draped an arm over Collins' shoulder. "You did a good job out there today."

"Thanks."

"Got any more bombardier lawyer friends in New York? We can use all we can get."

Suddenly tears filled Collins' eyes and this time he did nothing to stop them. "I've never done anything like this in my life."

"Did it feel like you were doing something?"

"Yes, and not just something that mattered, but like maybe I mattered."

"Good." Schwimmer gave him a pat on the back. "Now come on, let's check the reports and see if we stopped that column of tanks. I know we hit the first two. They were on fire as we turned away."

In the ready room, Schwimmer and Collins read the initial reports from the battlefield. "The column of tanks you were sent to hit was decimated," Colonel Amir said, "but we have another problem."

"What's that?" Schwimmer asked.

"Some of our units are pinned down at Latrun, west of Jerusalem."

"What are they doing there?"

"They're trying to take the hill. It's a strategic location. We need it to control the road."

"Who's in charge up there?"

"An American named Mickey Marcus."

Schwimmer seemed surprised. "An American?"

"Yes."

"Commanding Haganah troops?"

"We're not Haganah now." Amir showed them an order signed by Ben-Gurion. "We're now officially the Israel Defense Forces."

Schwimmer scanned the document, handed it to Collins, and glanced back at Amir. "What do we do about Latrun?"

"Someone at headquarters thinks we might be able to dislodge Arab positions. They haven't made a final decision yet, but I suspect we'll have to get into it. So relax. Get a bite to eat and then be ready to go at a moment's notice."

Collins was exhausted from the tension of the flight and found a seat at the nearest table. He folded his arms for a pillow, rested his head on them, and closed his eyes. Schwimmer took a seat beside him and leaned close. “Five minutes,” he said calmly.

Collins opened his eyes and looked over at him. “What are you talking about?”

“That’s all you get. Five minutes to rest, then back to work.”

“Do we have bombs?”

“There’s enough in the storeroom for one more run, but the cargo planes will be back in a day or two with more.”

“What do we do if we run out before they get back?”

Schwimmer grinned. “Don’t worry about that. Just focus on the next mission and before you know it, New York will be the furthest thing from your mind.”

“Who said I was thinking about New York?”

“I could see it in your eyes.”

“When?”

“This morning, when you were walking out to the plane.”

“This morning seems like a lifetime ago.”

“Yes, it does, doesn’t it? But just think about this. Before you know it, this war will be over, Israel will be free and truly independent, and you’ll be calling your wife and asking her to bring the family to Tel Aviv.”

“Why would I want them over here?”

“Because by then, this will be more your home than the home you used to know.”

Collins smiled over at him. “You may be right. You just may be right.”

A NOTE ABOUT THE BOOK

THE VOLUNTEERS

At the end of World War II, Jews who survived the Holocaust were not permitted to return to their former residences. Instead, they were forced to remain under armed guard at facilities known as displaced persons camps, most of which were the former death camps where the supposedly liberated Jews had been held by the Nazis. In many instances, they were required to live, eat, and sleep in camps populated by their former Nazi captors—men and women whom they'd watched murder and annihilate six million of their friends and family members.

Most Jews held in European camps wanted to immigrate to Palestine, but the British government, which controlled the region under a United Nations mandate, refused to permit more than one thousand Jewish émigrés per month, a quota that was filled even before it was announced. With the Allies unwilling or unable to address the refugee situation, Jewish leadership in Palestine and abroad sought a remedy of their own. Using surplus warships, many of which were purchased in the United States and manned with US volunteers, they began a boatlift to rescue Jews from the European camps and bring them to Palestine.

At the same time, diplomatic forces began to pressure the British government to alter its Palestinian policy. By 1946, that effort seemed to propel events toward a decision to end British control of the area and to divide it into separate Jewish and Arab states. David Ben-Gurion, head of the Jewish Agency for Palestine's office in Tel Aviv, foresaw the day when a Jewish state would be authorized by the UN and undertook to create a military force capable of defending that state.

To do that, Ben-Gurion sent agents throughout the world in search of arms, ammunition, and war materiel. Some of those agents came to the United States where, with the help of prominent businessmen, they acquired US surplus airplanes and munitions, which were exported to Palestine. They also acquired surplus industrial equipment used to help create an indigenous arms industry in the newly independent State of Israel.

The story you've just read is loosely based on a compilation of events that occurred between 1945 and 1948 as part of both those efforts—the operation to rescue Jewish refugees from European displaced persons camps and the work to arm and equip a military force to fight for the independence of a Jewish state. Events in this book have been portrayed as realistically as possible but with an eye toward creating an entertaining and engaging story.

Characters, events, and locations in this book are the work of fiction and have been arranged and complied in conjunction with the story of Palmer Collins, a likewise fictional character, to give a poignant glimpse of the broad and far-reaching effort by many Americans to support what became Israel's 1948 War of Independence—support that not only included gifts of time, money, and influence, but in some cases the loss of life as well. Our hope is that in seeing events in this manner you will be inspired to read further on the subject and come to a better understanding of the history of the modern State of Israel and the influence that history has on the nature of the Israeli-Palestinian conflict today.

ACKNOWLEDGEMENTS

My deepest gratitude and sincere thanks to my writing partner, Joe Hilley, and to my executive assistant, Lanelle Shaw-Young, both of whom work diligently to turn my story ideas into great books. And to Arlen Young, and Peter Glöege for making the finished product look and read its best. And always, to my wife, Carolyn, whose presence makes everything better.

MICHAEL DAVID EVANS, the #1 *New York Times* bestselling author, is an award-winning journalist/Middle East analyst. Dr. Evans has appeared on hundreds of network television and radio shows including *Good Morning America, Crossfire* and *Nightline*, and *The Rush Limbaugh Show*, and on Fox Network, *CNN World News*, NBC, ABC, and CBS. His articles have been published in the *Wall Street Journal, USA Today, Washington Times, Jerusalem Post* and newspapers worldwide. More than twenty-five million copies of his books are in print, and he is the award-winning producer of nine documentaries based on his books.

Dr. Evans is considered one of the world's leading experts on Israel and the Middle East, and is one of the most sought-after speakers on that subject. He is the chairman of the board of the Ten Boom Holocaust Museum in Haarlem, Holland, and is the founder of Israel's first Christian museum—Friends of Zion: Heroes and History—in Jerusalem.

Dr. Evans has authored a number of books including: *History of Christian Zionism, Showdown with Nuclear Iran, Atomic Iran, The Next Move Beyond Iraq, The Final Move Beyond Iraq,* and *Countdown*. His body of work also includes the novels *Seven Days, GameChanger, The Samson Option, The Four Horsemen, The Locket, Born Again: 1967,* and coming soon, *The Columbus Code*.

Michael David Evans is available to speak or for interviews.
Contact: EVENTS@drmichaeldevans.com.

BOOKS BY: MIKE EVANS

Israel: America's Key to Survival

Save Jerusalem

The Return

Jerusalem D.C.

Purity and Peace of Mind

Who Cries for the Hurting?

Living Fear Free

I Shall Not Want

Let My People Go

Jerusalem Betrayed

Seven Years of Shaking: A Vision

The Nuclear Bomb of Islam

Jerusalem Prophecies

Pray For Peace of Jerusalem

America's War: The Beginning of the End

The Jerusalem Scroll

The Prayer of David

The Unanswered Prayers of Jesus

God Wrestling

The American Prophecies

Beyond Iraq: The Next Move

The Final Move beyond Iraq

Showdown with Nuclear Iran

Jimmy Carter: The Liberal Left and World Chaos

Atomic Iran

Cursed

Betrayed

The Light

Corrie's Reflections & Meditations

GAMECHANGER SERIES:

GameChanger
Samson Option
The Four Horsemen

THE PROTOCOLS SERIES:

The Protocols
The Candidate

The Revolution

The Final Generation

Seven Days

The Locket

Living in the F.O.G.

Persia: The Final Jihad

Jerusalem

The History of Christian Zionism

Countdown

Ten Boom: Betsie, Promise of God

Commanded Blessing

Born Again: 1948

Born Again: 1967

Presidents in Prophecy

Stand with Israel

Prayer, Power and Purpose

Turning Your Pain Into Gain

Christopher Columbus, Secret Jew

Finding Favor with God

The Jewish State: The Volunteers

COMING SOON:

The Columbus Code

See You in New York

Finding Favor with Man